PENGU[I]

The Ic[

Caroline Mitchell is a *New Yo[rk]*
*Post* and international No. 1 bes[
2 million books. She originates from Ireland and now lives in a
woodland village outside the city of Lincoln. A former police detective, she has worked in CID and specialised in roles dealing with
vulnerable victims, high-risk victims of domestic abuse and serious
sexual offences. She now writes full time.

Her books have won first place as 'Best Psychological Thriller' in
the US Readers' Favourite Award Contest, been shortlisted for the
International Thriller Writer Awards in New York and been short-
listed for 'Best Procedural' in the Killer Nashville awards and the
Audie awards. Her crime thriller *Truth And Lies* is a No.1 *New York
Times* bestseller and has been optioned for TV.

*Praise for Caroline Mitchell*

'The very definition of a page-turner.'
John Marrs

'The tension built up and up . . . I devoured every page.'
Mel Sherratt

'Fast-paced, twisty, and chilled me to the
bone . . . I loved every minute of it!'
Robert Bryndza

'For me, this book had everything . . . there was
nothing more I could have asked for.'
Angela Marsons

*Also by Caroline Mitchell*

Witness

Silent Victim

The Perfect Mother

The Village

The Islanders

The Last Guest House

The Survivors

The Family at Number 1

Series

*DC Knight*

Don't Turn Around

Time to Die

The Silent Twin

*Detective Ruby Preston Crime Thriller*

Love You to Death

Sleep Tight

Murder Game

*Detective Amy Winter*

Truth and Lies

The Secret Child

Left For Dead

Flesh and Blood

In Cold Blood

*Slayton Thriller*

The Midnight Man

The Night Whispers

The Bone House

# The Ice Angels

*An Elea Baker Novel*

## Caroline Mitchell

PENGUIN BOOKS

# PENGUIN BOOKS

UK | USA | Canada | Ireland | Australia
India | New Zealand | South Africa

Penguin Books is part of the Penguin Random House group of companies
whose addresses can be found at global.penguinrandomhouse.com

Penguin Random House UK,
One Embassy Gardens, 8 Viaduct Gardens, London SW11 7BW

penguin.co.uk

Penguin
Random House
UK

First published 2026
002

Set in 10.4/15pt Palatino
Typeset by Falcon Oast Graphic Art Ltd

Printed and bound in Great Britain by Clays Ltd, Elcograf S.p.A.

The authorised representative in the EEA is Penguin Random House Ireland,
Morrison Chambers, 32 Nassau Street, Dublin D02 YH68

A CIP catalogue record for this book is available from the British Library

ISBN: 978-1-804-95528-4

Penguin Random House is committed to a sustainable future
for our business, our readers and our planet. This book is made
from Forest Stewardship Council® certified paper.

MIX
Paper | Supporting
responsible forestry
FSC® C018179

*To Maddy,*
*who made my publishing dreams come true.*
*This book is here because of you.*

*'Dark are the days of wintertide.'*
William Morris

# Chapter One

## Liisa

### *Porvoo, Finland, 2016*

A comet of pain shoots up my back as we are jolted by a bump in the road. My face is pressed so hard against the car door that my neck feels like it's going to snap. Gagging, I try to breathe, but I'm overcome by the stink of fish embedded in the blanket thrown over my head. I try to focus on the memory of my school bag lying in the snow. Someone will find it, right? They'll call the police and . . .

'Stop crying!' The man leans on my back, stealing whatever breath I have left. He's not big, but he has a weapon. I choke back my tears, scared he'll electrify me again. The blanket is wrapped so tightly around me. My tights are damp from where I've wet myself and pain erupts from the gash on my knee from when I hit the icy road. The bindings on my wrists force my hands against my back. But all that fades into panic because now he's pressing so hard on my back that I can't breathe.

'Give her some air.' The woman's voice rises from the front of the car. 'Just keep her head down.'

I shouldn't have stopped to talk to her on my way home from school. Mother has always warned me to be sensible, and we've been told about stranger danger in school. But she looked so much like my grandmother that I thought it would be OK. Grandmothers aren't meant to hurt children. They take you to the petting zoo or bring you Fazer chocolate on candy day. They don't force you into the back of a little yellow car with daisy stickers on the windows. She even looks like Grandmother Hilma, with her fur-lined navy parka and grey hair wound into a bun. She doesn't have evil eyes or a scary voice. How was I to know? I twist my head, desperate for a sliver of air.

'Stop struggling!' The man shakes the scruff of my neck as you would a dog when it's misbehaved.

At last some relief, when he finally shifts position. I wheeze and splutter for breath. He tugs the blanket off my head, but I'm too scared to move. I hear the crackle of the stun gun in his hand. When he first jabbed it into my back, my body turned to jelly and flopped to the ground. It felt like a thousand bees were attacking my skin.

'That's better,' he says, as my breathing steadies. 'Don't make me use it again. You might shit yourself next time.'

'*Hei*, mind your language.' The woman driving issues a warning.

The man beside me sighs.

The car shudders as we hit another bump in the road. I stare at the footwell, still pinning my hopes on my school bag being found. His laces are undone. The snow crusting his boots is melting in the weak heat of the car. Soon it will be dark. I flinch as his thin fingers clamp down on my head and he begins to stroke my hair.

2

'Would you like me to loosen your bindings? I will, if you behave.' His voice is soft now, coaxing. I nod. I'm lying on my side, the thin blue washing-line cord cutting into my wrists.

'Best not to,' the woman driving replies sternly. 'For her own safety.'

'But the doors are locked,' he whines, still stroking my hair.

My shoulders rise towards my ears. I'm trying not to react. What do they want with me? Fear grows a lump in my throat and I try to swallow it down.

'What if she jumps into the front?' The woman's voice takes on a hard tone. 'What if we crash the car and she gets hurt? We can't take her to hospital. What will you do then?'

'Sorry, Mamu,' the man replies, his voice full of remorse. I open my mouth to speak, but he responds with a sharp tug on my hair. 'Shush! Quiet time.'

The wind whistles through the car as it takes a sharp bend. I can feel every bump on the ice-caked road. It's so unlike my mother's car, with its comfy seats and happy tunes playing on the radio. I think of my family and silent tears stream down my cheeks, dripping off the tip of my nose. Snow pelts the windscreen and the wipers swish back and forth. If my bag hasn't been found yet, then it will soon be covered up.

The man's breath is liquorice-sweet as he leans over and whispers to me not to cry. But I'm so very scared. I peep up at his face. He seems almost as old as my mother. Tinted glasses mask his eyes, and a fat brown moustache covers the whole of his thin top lip. His hair looks strange as it skims his shoulders, and I wonder if he's wearing a wig. He looks out the window before pulling me towards him and forces my head to rest on his lap. 'Shhh,' he says, as I wriggle. 'Don't

3

be a brat.' There's a growl to his voice, and the warning of the stun gun in his other hand is enough to make me give in. The tick-tock of the car indicator means we're pulling off this road. 'Go to sleep.' The man clamps his hand over my head, and he starts stroking me like I'm his pet. 'When you wake up, we'll be there. Then you'll see your new room.'

'Everything OK?' The woman gazes over her shoulder in my direction, but she's speaking to him. She turns up the car heater, although it provides little comfort against the cold.

'Oh yes, we've got a good one,' the man replies. 'A real angel. I can feel it.'

'I hope so,' the woman sighs wearily. 'Because this is the last time.'

I want to ask what's happening, but my tongue feels glued to the roof of my mouth. Mother will be so cross. She's told me so many times not to talk to people I don't know. I close my eyes tight, wishing I could block out my kidnappers.

'Isn't she pretty?' He makes my skin crawl as he lifts a strand of my hair. 'It's like the sun.'

I want to inch away, but there is nowhere to go and I am conscious of the small metal object in his other hand. Instinctively I know that being calm is my best chance of staying alive. I listen as they talk between themselves. It seems she is his mother and we are going to her home. He laughs, buzzing with excitement.

But his mother is more cautious. 'I meant what I said. This is the last time.' Silence passes for a few seconds before she continues, 'I'm doing this for you.'

'I know,' he says. 'I love you, Mamu.' There's no response. 'Say it,' he demands; that edge is back in his voice and it's as sharp as a blade.

'To the moon and back.'

The words sound forced, but I feel him relax. I swallow, quietly sniffling on the man's lap. No good can come from this, because people who tie you up mean to do you harm. I'm twelve and a half years old, almost a teenager. I know a lot of things, which is why I shouldn't have walked the rest of the way home alone after the school bus dropped me off. Grandmother must have forgotten to pick me up. Mother will come looking, but not until she finishes work. For every minute that passes I'm being driven further away from her. I remind myself that I'm not like other children. I'm strong. I'm Liisa the brave. I love horses, snowboarding and climbing trees. I'm clever, too. One day I'm going to be a judge and lock all the bad people up. I spend the rest of the journey imagining the police searching for me. Someone could have seen what happened. They would have picked up my school bag and dialled 112. The police will have set up roadblocks. There's a helicopter overhead following the yellow car, and any second now . . .

The car slows, then grounds to a halt. 'We're here!' the woman cheerily announces.

'Welcome home.' The man watches me intently as he allows me to sit up.

As the car door opens, the nothingness outside crushes me. It's almost completely dark and the moon illuminates a lone cabin embedded in deep snow, bordered by miles of thick woodlands. I don't know where I am. The sky is clear, and the air is crisp and silent. There is no sound of chopper blades. No police sirens in the distance. No flashing lights. Nothing but my kidnappers' boots crushing the snow as they tell me to get out of the car. Hot tears of hopelessness sting my eyes, because I was wrong. I'm alone in the wilderness, toes numb, fingers tingling, and a pain blooms in my chest as panic takes hold. Nobody's looking for me yet. My kidnappers have got too big a head-start. Then I see it in my mind's eye and all hope dies – my school bag still at the side of the road, buried in snow.

# Chapter Two

*Lincoln, present day*

Swann rested his car keys on the hook in the hall. They'd only lived in Orchard Cottage for three months, but the peaceful Nettleham location suited them better than his previous apartment on the Brayford Wharf. The silence that greeted him confirmed that the twins were down for the night. Alice had given up trying to keep them awake for when he came home. Most men his age had grandchildren, but his eighteen-month-old sons made him feel young. At least that's what he told Alice. His job tainted his perception of the world, leaving him forever terrified that something awful would happen to his boys. Love gifted fear when you sampled evil in the world at first hand.

He did his best to leave the job at the door, but Operation Turnstile was proving all-consuming. The three girls who went missing in Lincoln rarely left his thoughts. Twelve-year-old Jenny Flynn's body was discovered partially covered in snow on West Common, three weeks after she disappeared in January 2021. It had been a brutal winter, and his team worked to the point of exhaustion investigating the case. There were no obvious injuries, and nothing to suggest family members had been involved.

Chelsea Hobbs got off the school bus in January 2023, but she never made it home. Chelsea did not have the happy home life afforded to Jenny, and when her belongings were found in an ice patch in Burton Waters Marina, her stepfather was suspected of foul play. However, it was impossible to charge him for her murder when her body was never found. It was presumed that the current had dragged her downriver. But the CPS had argued that the girl could just as easily have abandoned her school bag and run away. Now twelve-year-old Sophie Miller had been found barefoot and shaking in the doorway of Lincoln Cathedral after being picked up by operatives on CCTV. Another winter snatching, it had gained media attention worldwide. She had been missing for twenty days, which was an eternity to her young parents, who had basically camped out in Lincoln police station, waiting for news. They were now by her hospital bed as she recovered from her ordeal. An officer had been posted in the paediatric ward for when she was well enough to talk. Nobody was more surprised than Swann when she was found. Especially when he'd discovered what Sophie was holding in her hand. This new piece of evidence connected the investigation to a case from his past that he would now have to face.

He hung his coat on the hook in the hall and kicked off his shoes, his mood lifting as the smell of garlic bread enticed him inside. Entering the kitchen, he cast an eye across the pan warming on the stove.

'Spaghetti bolognese,' Alice said, as Swann watched her prepare the food. Alice made everything from scratch.

'Spag bol? My favourite. You must be after something.'

'It's a celebratory meal,' she said, blowing her long fringe from her eyes. Her brunette hair was piled into a messy ponytail, and splodges of baby food decorated her shirt, but to Swann it made her even more endearing. How she managed to raise the twins and cook proper food every day was beyond him.

He turned to take a bottle of Merlot from the wine rack before looking for the corkscrew in the drawer. 'What are we celebrating?' he asked, as Alice handed it to him. He watched her pull a knife from the block.

'Sophie Miller turning up, of course. It's amazing news. You must be so relieved.' She began to top-and-tail onions on the wooden chopping board.

'I'd be happier if we were the ones who'd found her. Her kidnapper should be behind bars.' The cork of the wine bottle gave a satisfying pop. 'But she's alive, and that's a start. God knows what she's been through, but we'll keep pressing on.' He sat the bottle of Merlot on the kitchen counter to breathe. Not many families ate such heavy meals at midnight, but Alice was used to shift work and scheduled their meals around them. She didn't eat a lot, but she enjoyed the adult company after a long day with the twins.

'Hasn't she spoken to anyone yet?' Alice resumed her chopping.

Swann nestled his chin in the dip of her shoulder as he hugged her from behind. The rising stench of onions didn't quite mask the faint scent of baby lotion on her skin. Alice lived by routines and always gave the twins a bath before bed. He would check in on them later, if they didn't wake in the meantime. His urge to keep them safe from the world was growing day by day.

9

'Not a word. I've just come from the hospital. She's dehydrated, so they're keeping her in overnight.' The sight of Sophie's frail body attached to a drip had filled him with guilt. Her abductor must have been right under their nose all along. He wanted to ask Alice about the twins, and how her day had been. But he knew where the conversation was leading, and he allowed it to take its course.

'Does this mean you won't be hiring Elea now?' Alice's voice became strained. Swann watched his partner chop the onions with a little more force than necessary.

He poured two glasses of wine. A large one for Alice. 'No, she's due to start tomorrow. We still need to find Sophie's kidnapper. And there are other elements of the case that she can help us with.' These were elements he couldn't share with anyone, not yet.

'Yes, Elea *is* very helpful, isn't she? An all-round *helpful* kind of gal.' She was taking her frustration out on the onions, hacking them into minute pieces.

Swan gently rested his hand on Alice's, before taking the knife and exchanging it for her glass of wine. 'Why don't you bring this up to the bath and have a soak? I can take over from here.'

Sighing, Alice sipped the wine before resting her glass on the counter. 'I shared a bath with the twins.' Her annoyance evaporated as she turned to face him. 'I'm fine. And you look beat. Let's enjoy our meal, because I have a feeling I won't be seeing a lot of you over the next few days.' She turned back to the onions and plopped them into a sizzling frying pan, along with some garlic and other ingredients she had to hand. Alice was usually understanding, being an ex-police officer herself. But it wasn't his long hours that was bothering her; it was Elea.

He was about to speak when his mobile phone rang. *Saved by the bell*. He saw his former boss's name on the screen and answered quickly. 'Commissioner Heikkinen,' Swann said, being careful not to call him 'Heineken', as Alice had nick-named him. 'I'm at home if you want to ring my landline. It's cheaper than a mobile call.'

'No need,' Heikkinen replied. 'This won't take long. I just wanted to congratulate you. I hear your missing child has turned up safe and well.'

Swann was pleased that his old boss kept in touch. He still addressed him formally, but considered him to be a friend.

'I'd like to take the credit, but I'm afraid I can't. She managed to escape all by herself.'

'But she's all right?'

'Physically, she appears unharmed, apart from some flesh wounds. Mentally, she's traumatised. She hasn't spoken a word.'

'Hence why you need Elea?' he said, with a smile in his voice.

'She might be able to get through to Sophie.' Swann cast a cautious eye over to Alice. She might have her back turned, but he knew she was listening to every word. 'And I'd like her to profile the kidnapper. Strike while the iron is hot.' But the iron wasn't hot. Sophie Miller had disappeared almost three weeks ago. Whoever took her had covered their tracks well.

'Indeed,' Heikkinen replied, a clink of a bottle against glass. 'Lincoln won't know what's hit it. Are you sure *you're* ready for this?'

11

The comment elicited a smile. 'Is anyone ever ready for Elea?' Swann said, noticing that Alice had stopped stirring, her wooden spoon held in mid-air.

'Seriously, though,' Heikkinen replied, his Finnish accent shaping his words. 'She's been on a destructive path since you left. If she wasn't such a gifted detective . . . Well, I'm hoping the distance will help her to see sense.'

'I see. I didn't realise things had got that bad.' He knew his boss would not offer specifics, as he was not interested in gossip or small talk.

'While I have every respect for her, I urge caution when it comes to allowing Elea to take a lead role in the investigation. Keep her under supervision. Don't leave her alone.'

'Thanks for the heads-up,' Swann replied.

'I thought it only fair to warn you, although I'd appreciate it if you keep this call to yourself.'

'What call?' Swann said good-naturedly.

'Excellent. In that case I will say farewell. Have a nice evening, Swann.'

'And you.' Heikkinen never thought to ask about family because he had always lived alone. Not for the first time, Swann wondered how he'd cope after his retirement, which was due soon. He paused to digest his former boss's words. He hadn't spoken to Elea in months. Had he done the right thing in hiring her to consult on his case?

# Chapter Three

Elea groaned as her alarm drilled into her brain. Squinting in the darkness of her hotel room, she groped on her bedside dresser for her phone. A soft snore rose beside her. *Dammit,* she thought, *he's still here.* She had fallen into such a deep sleep. She could blame being exhausted from the travelling, but the trip from Finland had only taken a few hours. It was more likely the fault of the numerous cocktails she and her new friend had consumed before bed. But now her ringing phone was like a wasp in her ear. Clutching her duvet against her naked body, she sat up in bed and turned off her alarm. She groaned a second time as she read the display. It was 4 a.m. Three hours' sleep. Not bad.

She picked up her bra from the floor, her gaze on her sleeping companion. What was his name again? Jake? Or was it Mike? He was facing away from her, his tousled brown hair soft against her pillow, his muscled shoulders facing the wall. It had been reckless, going to bed with a virtual stranger, but she had seen it as one last treat before she knuckled down to work. She finger-combed her cropped blonde hair, wondering what it would take to wake the man up.

'Hei,' she shook his shoulder. 'Rise and shine. Time to go.' She needed to find her trainers so that she could start the day with a run.

'What . . . what time is it?' the man asked, rubbing his eyes.

'Just gone four. And I must get ready for work, so I need you gone.'

'What are you? A milkman?'

Elea smiled at the thought. 'Yes, that's right, so get a move on or all the kids will be going to school without their Weetabix, and we can't have that.'

He stretched his arms as he yawned. In the light of sobriety, he appeared an awful lot younger than her. *God!* she thought. *He must be in his early thirties.* Not far from a ten-year age gap. She did not allow the thought to slow her as she darted into the bathroom and brushed her teeth.

He was still there when she came out. She arched an eyebrow when he spoke.

'Can we do this again?'

A smile curled on Elea's lips as she stood, assured in her nakedness. 'Sorry, no. But it was fun.' Realising how callous that sounded, she approached and kissed him on the cheek. 'It was more than fun. But I start a new job today and I can't afford to get distracted. You understand, don't you?'

'Ah yes, the milk round. You've got my number if you change your mind.' He smiled, pulling on his trousers.

She stood at her window watching him walk along the Brayford, head down, collar pulled up against the January chill. Not that it was cold for Elea. Compared to where she came from, English winters were positively balmy. She turned her gaze to the inland harbour, appreciating the frost-glistened view. The DoubleTree hotel was ideally located, accommodating her need to be close to nature with the convenience of bars and restaurants. It was certainly convenient last night, given that she'd met her new bedfellow in The Electric cocktail bar on the hotel's fifth floor.

Elea slipped two paracetamols into her mouth and swigged from a bottle of water. The last thing she felt like was a run, but if she didn't get out and move, she'd be agitated all day. Besides, she had a bet to win. Swann had told her she'd never make it up Lincoln's precipitous cobbled Steep Hill without getting out of breath. She tingled at the thought of seeing him again. *That man.* He drove her crazy, and yet she'd dropped everything to help him. His call had come during a turbulent period of her life and had been a welcome one. She needed to straighten herself out and couldn't wait to get her teeth into the case. Swann had spoken of similarities between this set of kidnappings and the case in her home town more than a decade ago. She'd dealt with many investigations since then, throwing herself into solving the most violent of crimes. But she'd never forgotten Liisa. Time stood still as she rested one hand on the windowpane, watching a quiet flurry of snow line the ground outside. She wondered what Liisa was doing now, just as she'd wondered every day since she had disappeared on her way home from school. According to her senior officers, the case was closed and Liisa was most likely dead. But one day Elea would prove them wrong. She would not rest until she brought her daughter home.

# Chapter Four

By the time 7 a.m. came, Elea was suited and in the hotel lift, ready for work. Her phone signalled a text. *Have you left yet?* Swann knew her well. She had already declined his offer to pick her up from the airport yesterday. Knowing he'd come anyway, she had refused to tell him what time her flight was getting in. But today he'd most likely worked out that she'd showered after her run and was ready to walk out of the door.

*On my way. I'll get a taxi*, she replied. She'd already tried Uber, but Lincoln was a small city and there were none to hand. She would get to grips with the area over the next couple of weeks, learning the most challenging routes to run, the nicest pubs and the best restaurants. Because there was something she hadn't mentioned to Swann. While this investigation was under way, she had no intention of going home, even if it meant her working the case for free. Her thoughts went to Anu and Venla, both fair-haired, blue-eyed and twelve years old. Liisa was two when Anu disappeared in 2006. She was four when Venla was snatched. Ten years after Anu, it was Liisa's turn. Elea's friendship with Anu's mother, Maria, had grown over the years. United in their grief, Elea had promised to bring their children home. She'd also made a silent vow to Venla, who, as an orphan, had no parents to fight her corner. Elea thought about the cards that had come in quick succession in the wake of each kidnapping. The letters from strangers offering support. Accusations from others, saying the children had been neglected. And then there were the singular white feathers posted to each of the families. One to Maria, one to Elea and one to the children's home where Venla had lived. It was hardly any wonder the Finnish media dubbed the three the 'Ice Angels'. The same discarded school bags, the same lone journey on their way home. Then the feathers – Elea had spent long hours trying to work out their significance.

She slid her arms through her coat, her thoughts anchored in the past. Anu's case was the first child abduction that Elea had investigated as a detective, and it haunted her that she'd been unable to resolve the case. Had she caught Anu's kidnapper, would Liisa and Venla be alive today? She pressed the ground-floor button in the hotel lift. This wasn't a holiday. She had a daunting task ahead and not a moment to waste. Her boots crunched on the salted pavement as she left the hotel. She could have asked reception to call her a cab, but she hated small talk and would pick one up from the road to avoid it. *Which way into the city centre, right or left?* She was about to search her phone for directions when a rich, deep voice rose from behind.

'Your taxi is waiting, ma'am.'

She looked up at Swann, a giant of a man, commanding in his suit and tie. Still smiling, still possessing the power to make her heart lurch. It was amazing how this man in his fifties, who had high blood pressure and an expanding waistline, could still make her feel that way.

'You couldn't have texted me to say you were here in the

first place, could you?' Her words were delivered with a smile, and she sighed as she relaxed into his embrace. Most Finnish people weren't tactile by nature, and Elea reserved physical contact for the very few. But Swann's quiet strength and comforting presence made her feel at ease. They had history. And as much as they would try to go in opposite directions, fate brought them together again. It was why she was struggling to accept his request for a divorce. A small part of her hoped that they would reunite.

'I'm parked over here.' This part of the Brayford seemed to be mainly pedestrianised. He guided her to his Mercedes parked nearby. 'I'll fill you in on the way to HQ. It's a ten-minute drive away.'

'Looks like it's time to earn my pay,' she remarked, her mood lifting in his company. 'Congratulations on the promotion. How does it feel to be a DCI?'

'Oh, you know . . . same job, just more pressure for results.'

They sat in comfortable silence as Swann negotiated the morning traffic. He braked as they waited at the traffic lights on Lucy Tower Street.

'Had a good run this morning, did you?'

'Please don't tell me you were watching.' Elea groaned at the thought. She couldn't risk running too fast because of the night frost.

'Certainly not; it's hard enough to leave the house on time these days. Did you try Steep Hill? That will give your calves a good workout.'

'I already have.' Elea had the stiff muscles to prove it. 'Tell me about the case.' She didn't have time for chatter, even with people she loved.

Swann's face grew serious as he negotiated the streets of Lincoln. Traffic was busy coming in at the roundabout, but mercifully quicker driving out. The windscreen wipers came on automatically as another snow shower blotted their view. 'Three girls this bastard has taken. Always in winter. Always in broad daylight.'

Elea was familiar with the guts of the story, having avidly followed the news reports on TV. Jenny Flynn, Chelsea Hobbs and Sophie Miller. Three blonde girls of the same age who disappeared on their way home from school. The gaps between each case were wide enough for the public to forget. For parents to relax. For children to grow complacent. Until it happened again. Winter was the kidnapper's friend, and Elea's blood had run cold when Swann told her about the feathers that had been sent to the families. The link was enough for her to say yes when he asked her to consult on the case.

Elea's silky white feather had arrived in a small black envelope. Exactly as with Maria, Elea's home address had been printed, the postmark from Helsinki. There was no other correspondence inside. Elea tracked down staff who had been working in the children's home the week that Venla disappeared. They remembered receiving a white feather, but hadn't informed the police. Three missing children. Three feathers. Investigators had not spent too long working on that lead, convinced it was a wild goose chase. But now it was happening in the UK. Each family of a missing child had received a white feather, each black envelope carrying an English postmark.

As Swann turned off at another roundabout, Elea asked him if there had been any other connections.

'I'm still not one hundred per cent positive that Liisa's kidnapper is in the UK . . . despite the evidence.' His brow creased in a familiar way as he threw Elea a look of concern. When they had first formed a relationship she'd been so broken, and he'd helped put the pieces back together again. But their marriage had been cursed from the start. How could anything good emerge from so much pain? Had he not been investigating Liisa's case, they never would have met.

'What are you saying, then?' Elea's words were clipped.

'There *is* something,' he confirmed. 'But whoever's behind it could be a copycat. You know Liisa, Venla and Anu's cases inside out. I had a choice: I could spend weeks reacquainting myself with the paperwork or I could fly you over here. Granted, boxes of files wouldn't be as much of a pain in my backside . . .'

Elea stared out at the pretty tree-lined country road. 'You know what they say – in need, you know a friend.'

Swann didn't disagree as he turned onto Deepdale Lane, following the sign for the police and fire services HQ. There were several car parks, each one occupied by vehicles caked in a light dusting of snow. A couple of uniformed officers passed them on foot, each one giving Swann a nod of respect. He continued to his parking spot, finally bringing his Mercedes to a halt. The building ahead of them loomed over the landscape. The façade was punctuated by countless rows of uniform windows. As the sun rose higher in the sky it created a display of light and shadow, offering a glimpse of the world within. But it was lost on Elea, who was anxiously waiting for Swann to speak. Her stomach clenched as she met his eyes. He'd looked at her with the same fixed expression on the day he informed her that they'd found Liisa's school bag in the snow. She clasped her fingers together and squeezed tightly.

'It's because you're a friend that I brought you here,' he said, his eyes still bright with concern. 'When I called you, we were looking for Sophie. But now that she's turned up, I know I've done the right thing. She might even lead us to Chelsea, when we can persuade Sophie to speak. But before we go inside I need to tell you what we've found.'

He glanced up at the vast building, then back to Elea, as if the presence of the police headquarters would give him the strength to carry on.

'Out with it then!' Elea barked, unable to wait a second more.

'Sophie was holding a small wooden doll.'

Elea's heart jolted in her chest.

Swann sighed, his discomfort evident as his face creased in concern. 'Don't get carried away. Anyone could have sent those feathers, and the doll – it might not be the same one.'

'What sort of doll?' She dug her fingers into his arm, ready to shake the truth out of him. 'Tell me.'

'A Martta doll. It's being tested for forensics, but I've got a picture . . .' He rooted for his iPhone.

Elea's hand trembled as she rested it lightly over her mouth. To think that they'd been laughing and chatting just moments before. Why had he waited until now to share the news? The pretty wooden Martta dolls were a rare commodity from Finnish company Kupittaan Savi, designed by Okki Laine in the sixties. There were whole families of them, all hand-painted. At just nineteen centimetres tall, the dolls were stamped for authenticity with 'made in Finland' on the base. Liisa's had been a gift from her grandmother, and she'd treated it with the respect it deserved.

'Do you think . . .' Elea paused for breath as the temperature dipped in the car. 'Could it be Liisa's?' Because while her captors might have disposed of her school bag, her daughter had kept the little doll in her coat pocket and carried it everywhere she went.

'I honestly don't know. It could be a weird coincidence. Or, on the other hand, someone could be fucking with us.'

'But how – why?'

'I've pissed off a lot of people. Anyone could look into the high-profile cases I've worked on over the years.'

But the words felt like a lie. Swann wasn't living in Lincoln when the first child, Jenny, was taken. He came to the UK to consult on the case. Elea cleared her throat, pushing her emotions down. She wouldn't cry. Not today.

'Well, then,' she said, picking her bag up from the footwell, 'we'd better get to work.'

# Chapter Five

Elea strode into the serious-crime-team office, her head held high. She'd been in many since she first became a detective at the age of twenty-three. They all had the same sense of urgency amid the chaos of phones ringing, printers humming and stained cups littering each desk. They all carried the same aroma of coffee and takeaway food.

Uniformed officers mixed with detectives as updates were brought in. It was a high-pressure environment, with officers so immersed in their work that they didn't notice the two of them arrive straight away. The office was open-plan, well lit from the wall of windows accommodating the rays of feeble January sun. Elea cast her gaze in turn over the whiteboards outlining each missing girl's case, all under the heading of 'Operation Turnstile'. The name held no relevance, but this was a turning point for her. She watched the officers interact, appreciating the sense of camaraderie within the team. A few heads glanced upwards, but Elea didn't have time for introductions.

'Is this fish bowl your office?' she said to Swann, before walking ahead of him. It was an office within an office, and she didn't like it all that much. 'What is it with you English and your need for transparency?' She glanced around Swann's workspace. 'How can you bang your head against your desk if you're constantly in view?'

Swann smiled. 'Some of us don't need to resort to self-harm.'

'Bully for you.' Elea picked up a framed family photo from Swann's desk, taking in the image of domestic bliss before putting it down again. Alice had given up begging her to grant Swann a divorce.

'I was about to introduce you to the team,' he said, as Elea dropped her bag on his desk.

'Why?' She frowned. 'I know all I need to know about them.'

'But you've only just walked in.' Swann shrugged off his coat, his face creased in confusion. It seemed he'd forgotten about their old late-night phone calls as he'd discussed each member of his team. That was back in the days before Alice voiced her disapproval. Elea could hardly blame her, given that Swann spent most of his time at work.

She stood at the window blinds. 'That bearded guy with the grumpy face. That's your sergeant, Ray Davies, and he hates his job. He's coasting, doing what it takes to get through each day.' She pointed at the young black man standing at a printer. He was wearing a similar shirt and tie to Swann, details not lost on Elea. 'That's Jamal Jones. He looks up to you, sees you as a father figure. Possibly bullied as a kid.'

Her glance fell on a curvy middle-aged woman who blew in through the door, glasses steamed, with bags in her hands and snow on the shoulders of her bright-red coat. Flapping the snow from her mac, she heartily apologised for being late.

'Ah,' Elea stated. 'That's Ness. A good soul. The mother hen. You excuse her tardiness because she keeps the team in line better than your sergeant ever could. How am I doing?'

'Not bad.' Swann watched as he took in Elea's assessment of her team.

'Where's your DI? Ralph Banbridge, isn't it?'

'He left, three weeks ago.'

'Hmm, well, given that you haven't phoned me lately, I wouldn't know.' Elea didn't wait for a response as she pointed at a dark-haired woman in the corner of the room. 'That must be DC Kelly Maxwell. Bit of a chip on her shoulder.' Elea tilted her head to one side. 'And I'm guessing she fancies that fella over there . . .' She paused to think. 'What's his name now? Evans. That's it. DC Ollie Evans. But she'll never date him. She's way out of his league.' But there was one member of the team she hadn't counted on. She didn't see him until he knocked at the door, paperwork in hand. Her eyes widened as he walked in. *Shit!*

'Boss, I took a phone call from—' His words fell away as he stared at Elea. 'Um . . .' He closed his eyes, took a breath. 'Jade from social care. She was returning your call. She said she's on the road today, but she gave me her mobile number. I'll . . .' His eyes flicked upwards towards Elea and a rush of blood rose to his cheeks. 'I'll leave it here.' He turned on his heels and left without delay.

Swann gave Elea a measured stare. 'Why don't you finish your assessment, while you're pulling my team apart. What about our new DI, Mitch Harding? Seems you've had quite the effect.'

'Huh?' Backing away from the window, Elea cleared her throat. 'I need a log-in. For the computer. You said you sorted it?'

But Swann wasn't about to let the subject drop. 'It didn't take you long.'

Elea couldn't bear to hear the disappointment in his voice.

'I don't know what you're talking about.' She immediately regretted bringing up the subject of his staff. She couldn't help but read the room. She'd been working too long in the police to be any other way. But Swann was good at reading people, too. Elea closed each blind in turn.

'Did you set it up beforehand?' he continued. 'Do it to piss me off? Because I've told you, Elea, I don't play those games any more.'

There was no point in lying. 'I met him in the hotel bar. He said he worked in security. I didn't know who he was.'

'And what does he think you do? Because he looked pretty shocked to see you here.'

'Milkman.' Elea's mouth twitched at the memory. 'Or should it be milk person?'

But Swann's face was a picture of annoyance. If Elea needed proof that he cared, she had it in spades.

'Come on now,' she coaxed. 'Finnish women have control of everything. Our bodies, our minds and our sexuality. It's not as if we're together. It's been five years.' She glanced at the family photo on his desk. 'How busy you've been. Twins and now marriage on the cards. And you're pissed at me for having a one-night stand?'

'What you do in your own time is your business,' Swann grumbled. 'But not with members of my team.'

'Fine,' Elea agreed. Anything to move things on. 'When's the briefing? I've got a kidnapper to bring in.'

# Chapter Six

## Liisa

### *2016*

I sit stiffly in the back seat of the little yellow car, refusing to bend my knees. 'I can't . . .' The man grunts. 'Help me, Mama, I can't get her out.'

The woman makes a low growling noise before shoving her son out of the way. The stillness of this place is crushing me and my blood swishes in my ears. I don't want to leave the car, but the snow isn't stopping and I'm so cold. There's a promise of heat as a thin string of smoke rises from the chimney of the log cabin at the end of the cleared path.

'*Hei*. Listen to me,' the woman snaps. She's not smiling, but nor does she seem angry. She's a broad, thickset woman with strong shoulders and stale breath. She leans in close enough for me to see all the tiny broken red veins on her face. 'Don't be scared. We won't hurt you, as long as you behave. There's no point in running because we're miles from civilisation.' She points behind her. 'In an hour, that snow will be waist-deep. You'll die from hypothermia long before you reach the road.' She raises a gloved finger to the weapon in the man's hand. 'Know what this is? It's a Taser. It can give you a shock strong enough to stop your heart. That's the last thing either of us wants, isn't it?'

I nod furiously. She's lying. It's not a Taser, it's a home-made stun gun. I clench my freezing hands into fists. I want to scream that my mother is a detective. That they'd better let me go, or else. Then I hear her voice in the back of my mind. *Wait it out*, she warns. *We'll find you.* The last thing I need is for these creepy people to panic right now.

The woman's strength frightens me as she scoops me up and out of the car. She lifts me like I'm made of air and talks softly into my ear. 'My son just wants to be your friend. It gets lonely out here. He needs someone young to talk to.' But her words make no sense, as he is far from my age. She signals for him to join her as she drops me onto my feet. 'Walk. You could do with the exercise.' She looks me up and down. 'What has your mother been feeding you?'

My teeth click and chatter as I look up at them both. I'm too scared to stay still and too frightened to move. Will I ever see outside again if I go in? I inhale the forest air as my kidnappers stand on either side of me. They push me towards their cabin. My arms ache from being pulled across my back. A path has been made, but the snow is so deep, and the trees in the distance stretch on for miles. There's no sign of anyone. No twinkling lights far away, no sound of cars. How much time has passed since I was taken? Where am I? Crumbs of snow work their way into my boots. I can tell, by the man's heavy breathing, that his heart is beating as hard as mine. He keeps checking behind us, then staring up at the empty sky. Fresh tears brim my eyelids as my feet move, one in front of the other.

The cabin's getting closer, and it's giving me the creeps.

There's a window on either side of the front door, but the shutters on one are nailed shut. It's like the cabin is winking at me, and not in a friendly way. There's a sudden soft thud of snow falling from trees. Wind burns my cheeks, my damp tights freezing against my skin. Thoughts of my mother are making me cry all over again.

'Stop that!' the man snaps. 'This is a happy day. I won't have you spoiling it.' His nose is red from the cold and his moustache is coming away. He peels it off completely and shoves it in the pocket of his coat. I notice the scar leading from his lip to his ear and I avert my eyes as he catches my stare. The chill snaps and bites at my skin and the woman's warning about hypothermia is in the front of my mind. Last year a hiker froze to death after camping in the Haltiala forest. Mama warned me about the dangers of the cold. I hesitate as we step on the creaky porch. Nails are battered into the wood in such a mishmash way, it feels like it's going to give. They stamp the snow from their boots before raking them against a thick grate.

I'm pushed roughly forward and instructed to do the same. Panic rises up my throat. The woman opens a screen door before pushing me inside, and the sudden warm air makes my cheeks and the tips of my fingers sting. I'm told to kick off my boots, but I almost lose my balance, as my hands are still bound. The woman exhales a loud huff before roughly yanking off each one. The hall is dark and musty, and I blink when a light is switched on. 'Go on, that way.' She pokes me in the back as she pushes me into a big open space. There is a small kitchen at one end, with a thick wooden dining table and chairs. The living-room section is bigger and there's an open fire at the end. It is filled with mismatched furniture, books and old junk. A layer of dust covers every surface, and a smoky smell rises from the sofa that I am pushed onto. I scoot backwards as she produces a knife, and her son's weird laughter fills the room. His moods are like a see-saw, and I don't know how to react.

The woman smacks my legs sharply. 'Look at me. I'm going to cut your restraints. You misbehave, you get another smack. You hear me?'

I nod.

'Quit nodding. Speak!' she says sharply. 'Say: yes, Johanna.'

Johanna. I draw in a cold breath. Is that her real name? Then I remember something my mother told me: it's bad for the victim if they find out who their kidnappers are. A thought enters my head. 'Are you my father?' I look to the man hopefully. It seems a safer option than them being complete strangers.

'No, sweetness.' He removes his glasses, then gives me a creepy smile as he peels off his wig to reveal cropped brown hair beneath. 'But you can call me Daddy, if you like.'

The pair of them chuckle like it's some kind of private joke. Johanna slices the blue binding as if she's cutting through butter, and I rub my stinging wrists. I should have known he wasn't my father. There is no way my mother would spend time with someone like him.

'You will call him Mikael,' Johanna squeezes my chin. 'And you will be his friend.'

Now he's staring at me with his cold eyes and it makes me uncomfortable all over again. I hug myself as the world grows blurry from tears. Everything hurts, I want my mother and I don't know what's going to happen next.

# Chapter Seven

Elea rolled her eyes as her mobile phone rang in her pocket. After checking she was on the right street, she walked towards the address and answered the call. 'Yes?' she said, shouldering her way through a group of Lincoln College students chatting on the pavement.

'Where are you?' Swann's words were laced with urgency.

'Why? Has a lead come in?' Elea waited for a number-fifty bus to trundle past before crossing onto Monk's Road.

'Not yet,' Swann replied. 'But we've a lot to get through.'

'And I'm making headway, but instead of staring at a screen I'm immersing myself in the evidence.'

'What's that supposed to mean?'

'I'm on a reconnaissance mission,' Elea grinned, checking the address. She'd sweet-talked a police officer she'd met in the station toilets into giving her a lift back into the city.

'Elea, stop playing games and tell me where you are.'

'I'll be back in an hour. Don't call again unless you have an update.'

'Back from where? Where are you?'

She hung up, then set her phone to silent. Swann would find out where she was soon enough.

According to his Facebook profile, Phil Hobbs had just returned from the bookies. He was probably sitting down right now with a few cans of beer, barking orders at his punchbag of a wife. But Elea had someone else to see first. She entered Monks Road Café and ordered herself a black coffee from a cheerful-looking woman behind the counter. The small, brightly lit café was a cosy haven, the air thick with the aroma of sizzling bacon, fried eggs and buttered toast. The faint echo of a radio playing a nostalgic pop song added to the charm. Gary Reynolds was already sitting in the corner, mug of tea in hand. She recognised him from the staff photo on the website of The Birdcage pub. 'Thanks for agreeing to meet.'

Elea sidled in across from him, resting her coffee on the table and her bag on the rung of the chair. The café was relatively busy, but its customers appeared too wrapped up in their own conversations to notice her. Gary dressed like a man in denial of his age, wearing a baseball cap that was no doubt covering a bald patch, with skinny jeans and a navy puffer jacket that had seen better days. Judging by the way his gaze kept flicking to the door, Elea guessed this was the last place he wanted to be.

'As long as it's off the record.' Gary cradled his tea, mouth downturned.

'I told you. I'm not a cop. Just a mum looking for her little girl.'

'Hmm.' Gary eyed her suspiciously. He wasn't buying it.

Elea heaved a sigh. 'All right. I'm a detective, but in Finland, not here. And I wasn't lying about my daughter.' She paused to check her watch. She didn't have long. 'You served Phil Hobbs the day his stepdaughter went missing, didn't you?'

'It's all in my statement. I don't know what you want from me.'

'It's what's *not* in your statement that I need to hear. You know something, otherwise you wouldn't have agreed to meet.'

Gary snorted. 'You said you'd stalk me if I didn't. I don't need the grief.'

Elea didn't have time to play games. 'What was Phil like that day? Was The Birdcage his local?' She was referring to the pub where Gary used to work. It seemed like a welcoming place, with themed nights and a pub garden, according to its website.

Gary shrugged. 'He's in all the time, at least he was when I worked there. He hangs out with some right dodgy blokes.' A thought seemed to occur as he paused. 'You're not recording this, are you? Cos . . .'

Elea uttered a laugh. 'This is Phil Hobbs we're talking about, not some Mafia kingpin. I said it would be off the record and it is.'

Gary's shoulders dropped a little. 'The guy's a tosser, right enough. But I still don't want this getting back to him.'

'What, exactly?' Elea tapped her nails against her cup. 'Off the record.'

Gary leaned in towards Elea. 'He was acting odd that day, that's all. He was sweating, too, like he was going cold turkey. Twitchy. It was January. The pub wasn't that warm.'

Elea nodded, waiting for him to continue.

'When you spend all day serving pints in a boozer you notice this kind of stuff, y'know? I've dealt with all sorts of folk over the years.'

'Right,' Elea uttered, disappointment threading her words. Was that it? Hobbs was twitchy? She'd need more than that. The bell over the café door jingled as a group of people left.

'I overheard him on the phone,' Gary's voice interrupted her thoughts. 'He was arguing about some debt, too pissed to realise how loud he was being. There was one other fella at the bar . . .' He rubbed his chin. 'I can't remember what he looked like, apart from having this ruddy great moustache that looked too big for his face. I kept my head down, served him his pint. Phil was still on the phone, then he started banging on about his stepdaughter, saying something about it being "a waste", as she was being taken into social care.'

'Go on.' Elea leaned forward. He had her attention now.

Gary sighed, mouth downturned. 'I might have misheard him. I mean, it could have been the beer talking. He might not have meant it . . .'

'Meant what?' Elea's voice grew firm.

But Gary stared straight ahead, lips pressed into a thin white line.

Elea read the emotions playing out on his face. 'It's been keeping you awake at night, hasn't it? Your conscience. Maybe you've been wondering if you should have said something at the time.' She caught his gaze and saw the flicker of guilt hiding there. 'Then you justify it, telling yourself that whatever happened, happened. That there's not much anyone can do about it now.' Her heart fluttered in her chest as Gary delivered a slow nod. 'Let it go, Gary. Whatever it is. I'll take it from here.'

Seconds passed as Gary seemed to consider his options. At last he took a breath to speak. 'Phil was hunched over his pint, phone in hand. His voice was slurred, but I could still make him out when he asked what his stepdaughter was worth. I couldn't believe my ears.' He delivered a small shake of the head as he stared into his cup of tea. 'Then he rambled on about which school she was in and how she walked home alone – as if it was some kind of asset. He said they'd have to move soon, before the social took her into care.'

'Christ,' Elea muttered softly. People never failed to surprise her in the worst kinds of ways. 'And you didn't think to report this at the time?'

'There was nothing to report.' Gary shrugged. 'Whoever he was talking to had a right go at him. I could hear them effing and blinding down the phone. Phil turned as white as a sheet. Then he started stuttering and said he was at home. I had my back turned to him, but I heard enough to know that his dodgy friends weren't too impressed.'

*Weren't too impressed with what?* Elea wondered. *That he was suggesting such a thing or doing it in public where anyone could hear?* 'What happened after that?'

'Nothing. He ended the call, had a shot of whisky and left shortly after that.'

'Which was . . .'

'Half three. A week to the day before that girl disappeared.'

'Chelsea.' Elea uttered. 'Her name is Chelsea. And she'd probably still be here if you'd had the balls to report that call.'

Gary delivered a haunted stare. 'I told ya. I've seen the type of people Phil hangs out with. They're dangerous.' He checked over his shoulder. 'I've said too much as it is.'

'Too little too late.' Elea's tone was cold. She would not ease his conscience just yet. After finishing their conversation, she let Gary go. She'd had her suspicions about Chelsea's stepfather, whose history with the police was as long as her arm. Taking her phone from her bag, she found her Facebook app. It was time to make Phil Hobbs an offer he couldn't refuse.

# Chapter Eight

Elea knocked on the door of the two-bedroomed ground-floor flat. She waited as soft shuffling footsteps approached on the other side. A chain was pulled across and a latch clicked open. Then she was face-to-face with Karen Hobbs, mother of three children: one missing, two taken into care. Her hair hung limply around her thin face, and a faint yellow bruise dappled her cheekbone. But the most striking thing was how small the woman was. She had the build of a twelve-year-old child. Elea had seen the map of injuries on her body from past domestic-incident reports. Her husband must have towered over her.

Phil Hobbs was a known domestic abuser with a history of offences under his belt. Such was his violence that the police were convinced his stepdaughter Chelsea died at his hands.

'Karen?' Elea flashed a perfect smile as she faked a British accent. 'Phillipa Laine. *Rio* magazine. I spoke to your husband online.' She glanced over Karen's shoulder into the narrow hall. Her message to Phil Hobbs had been delivered from a fake Facebook profile that had come in handy in the past.

Karen stared ahead, her eyes lifeless, her expression flat. After checking with her husband, she eventually allowed Elea inside. Elea found the offer of money nearly always

37

opened doors. She was led into a poky sitting room and her predictions proved to be correct. Can of Stella in one hand and remote control in the other, Phil Hobbs sat on his throne, which in his case was a grubby leather recliner that had seen better days. His T-shirt was speckled with crisp crumbs, his tracksuit bottoms stained from wear. The ceiling was yellowed from nicotine, and the stink of cigarette smoke hung heavy in the air. Elea cast her gaze over the litany of empty beer cans and crisp packets littering the floor.

She took a seat on the edge of the leather sofa as Phil muted the TV, finally acknowledging her presence. She wasn't leaving this flat without answers. 'Thanks for seeing me at such short notice.' She forced herself to be pleasant to the man before her. 'As I said, I'd like to write a piece for *Rio* magazine on your missing daughter. It's part of a bigger story about the missing girls.'

'You've got 'alf an hour,' Phil replied, punctuating his sentence with a loud belch.

Elea wrinkled her nose as the stench of Stella came her way. 'We'd better get started, then.' She switched on her mobile-phone recording app. 'I think it's best we start from the beginning. Tell me about your relationship with Chelsea.'

'Hang on a minute.' Phil adjusted his recliner to an upright position as he asserted himself. 'We want cash up front. This is a big story. I'm saying nothing without money in my pocket first.'

Elea gazed at the man intensely, making no effort to hide her disgust. 'It's not a big story – that's the problem. Your daughter disappeared in 2023 . . .'

'Stepdaughter,' Phil corrected.

'Fine, stepdaughter,' Elea continued. 'There's nothing about her in the media. People have forgotten who she is.'

'She's dead,' Phil blurted, swigging from his can. 'Got to be.' A thin drool of beer streaked down his unshaven face. 'And even if she's found, she ain't coming back here.'

'Let me clarify,' Elea responded. 'You're saying that you're not bothered about Chelsea being found, as long as you profit from it?'

She turned to Karen. 'Do you feel the same?'

Elea expected Karen to back him up. She'd given up her children to be with Phil, after all. But instead her face crumpled and she sobbed into her hand. 'Please. I don't care about the money if you help me find my little girl.'

Phil snorted. 'She ain't so little now. That's presuming she's still alive.'

Elea ignored the man before her as her fake accent fell away. She was surprised that she'd managed to keep the act going this long. 'I can help, Karen. But you need to help yourself too, yes? Because Chelsea won't be allowed back here. It doesn't need to be anything fancy, just not with him. The women's refuge will help you start again.'

'What the fuck are you on about?' Phil slammed his can on the coffee table as Elea snatched up her phone. 'You're no reporter. You're a cop. Get out!'

'Why?' Elea stood. 'What are you hiding?' Her temper rose as Phil tried to intimidate them both.

'Fuck off out of my house. The cheek of it, coming into my gaff pretending to be a reporter.'

Karen flinched as he threw a hand in the air.

'Go,' Elea said to her. 'Pack a bag, make it quick. I'll find you somewhere to stay.'

Karen looked at her uncertainly.

'Go!' Elea exclaimed. 'I'll take care of him.'

As Karen turned to leave, Phil reached out a meaty hand to grab her hoodie and Elea kicked him firmly on the shin. It felt like kicking a wall, but judging by Phil's shocked expression, she'd left her mark. Karen stared, disbelieving, before running off to her room.

'What the fuck!' Phil roared indignantly. He wobbled slightly as the effects of too many cans of Stella, combined with the pain of the kick, took hold. 'I'll 'ave your badge for this! You can't hurt me! Coming into my home under false . . . false—'

'I think the word you're grappling for is "pretences",' Elea said drily. 'And I'm not leaving until you tell me about your involvement in Chelsea's disappearance.' She was following a hunch, bluffing her way through their conversation after her chat with Gary. But Elea had read the case file inside out. Phil mixed with the underbelly of society. People who would sell their own grandmothers for a quick payout.

'If I say you're leaving, you're fucking leaving.' Phil swiped a meaty paw to grab for Elea, but she was quicker as she stamped the heel of her boot on his foot, then pulled his arm behind his back.

'Not so nice when you're on the other side of it, eh?' A smile crept onto her face as she pushed his fingers backwards. 'You think you're a hard man, beating up women half your size . . . Looks like that crumpled old chicken has come home to roost.' With a sudden leg sweep, she twisted his body and sent him crashing to the floor. She straddled his back and restrained his wrists using her own belt.

'Police brutality!' Phil screamed. 'Karen! Get back in here and call the old Bill. This tart's fucking nuts!'

But there was no response, only silence.

'You're going down for this,' he grunted. 'You'll never work in the police again.'

Elea pressed her face close enough to smell the beer on his breath. 'There you go again, making assumptions, you stupid piece of shit. I'm not a police constable in this country of yours. If you want to keep your fingers intact, then tell me. Who took Chelsea the day she disappeared?' It wasn't really a lie. Elea's base was in Finland, after all.

The more she read about Chelsea's case, the more certain she was that Phil had to be involved. He hadn't been with Karen long before they tied the knot, and when Chelsea disappeared she was due to be taken into care. Her younger siblings were already settled in foster homes. 'You thought that if Chelsea was going anyway, you might as well make some cash from her by offering her up to the highest bidder. You were heavily on the gear and in a shitload of debt, which is why you went to the pub for an alibi instead of picking her up from school.' Elea yanked Phil's arm an inch until he roared in pain. 'Don't think I won't break it. It wouldn't be the first time. And at least it will give some poor cow a rest from your punches for a while.'

She checked over her shoulder as she sensed movement behind her. Karen was standing there, holding a pair of socks. 'Did you mean it? Can the refuge help me find somewhere to live?'

41

'Yes.' Elea kept a firm grip on the man beneath her. 'And I'll keep you updated on Chelsea. One way or another, we'll find her.' Big promises were needed to remove Karen from the dangerous situation she was in.

'Here.' Karen handed her the rolled-up socks. 'Stuff these in his gob until he's ready to confess.'

Elea was beginning to like Karen more and more. Gritting her teeth, she forced the socks into his mouth to earn them a little more time. She didn't need his wails attracting attention. 'Right,' she said, 'you're not taking me seriously, so let me prove this isn't an empty threat.' She reached for his index finger. It took surprisingly little effort to pull it back until it snapped. Sweat beaded the man's brow as he screamed into his gag. Elea wrinkled her nose as the smell of his body odour rose. 'Now are you going to tell the truth or will it be finger number two?'

Karen ran round the room, packing bits into a big brown holdall. She seemed brighter than before. Elea pulled the sock from Phil's mouth and he yelled a string of obscenities. 'I'll kill you. Both of you bitches!'

'Uh-uh,' she mimicked the sound of a game-show buzzer. 'Wrong answer.' She forced the socks back into his mouth and stretched another finger back until it released with a snap. Another muffled scream was returned. The man's shoulders shuddered as pain kicked in. 'Oh dear,' Elea spoke without sympathy. 'You're crying already? What will you do when I break your arm?' She leaned over, whispering in his ear. 'Or I could use my gun. Right between the balls.'

He was sweating profusely now, blood trickling from his mouth from where he had bitten down hard. A part of her was enjoying the experience. She didn't have a gun, at least not here. But people like Phil thought they could do what they liked to girls like Chelsea. Girls like Liisa, too. 'Last chance,' she whispered darkly, removing the sock.

'You're crazy,' he whined.

'You've no idea,' Elea retorted. At least the screaming had stopped. She moved to reinsert the sock, wondering if she had got things wrong. If Swann found out about this, he'd place her under arrest.

'Wait!' Phil's nostrils flared as he inhaled a few strong breaths. 'I might have said something when I was pissed. I didn't mean nothing by it.'

'To who, Phil?' Elea reached for his third finger as he failed to respond.

'W-wait!' Phil stuttered. 'One of my old dealers. I owed him money and he was hassling me down the phone . . . I can't remember which one.' He gulped for breath, a trickle of sweat rolling down his face. 'I said Chelsea was being taken into care. That we had a lot on our plate. A waste, he called it.'

'I'm going to need more.' Elea gave up on his finger and wrenched back his arm.

'He asked what school she went to. What time she got home. I was so pissed I didn't know what he was getting at, so I told him. That's it. I didn't agree to nothing!'

'Yet soon after she was gone.' Elea felt resistance as she pushed his arm higher behind his back. 'You set the whole thing up to pay off a drugs debt, didn't you? I know what you've been up to, you cowardly shit!'

'Go ahead, break it,' Phil cried miserably. 'Because it's

43

better than what they'll do to me if they find out I've blabbed to the cops.'

'I told you, I'm not police.'

'I don't care if you're Mrs fucking Claus. It'll get back to them.' His words were interrupted by a swift kick between the legs.

'You little bastard,' Karen screamed. 'I'll kill you!'

Suddenly Elea had a situation on her hands. Broken fingers she could manage. But she couldn't afford for Phil to be murdered on her watch.

'Stop!' she shouted to Karen, panting from her exertions. 'Trust me. This isn't the way.' Karen had most likely dreamed about this moment for years.

'Where is she, you bastard? Who has her?' Spittle flew from Karen's lips.

'I swear,' he replied miserably. 'I don't know.' Tears and snot drizzled down his face. 'Oh God, it hurts so bad.' But he wasn't crying for Chelsea, he was crying for himself.

'Hang on,' Karen said. 'I have a list of all his dealers. It's in his notebook.'

'No!' Phil shouted. 'Don't!'

Elea decided that she'd got enough out of him and shoved the sock back in his mouth. 'You brought this upon yourself. If you'd been honest with the police, they might have been able to get her back.' She leaned down, pushing her knee between his shoulder blades. 'Now you listen to me. I wasn't here; this didn't happen. I won't rat you out if you don't rat me out.' It was a phrase she liked to use, having picked it up from a black-and-white gangster movie when she a kid dreaming of being a detective. She stepped

44

off Phil's hulking body and turned to Karen. 'Ready?'

'God, yes.' Karen wiped her tears with the back of her tracksuit sleeve.

Curled up in a foetal position, Phil was recovering from the battering he deserved. Elea only hoped that the ferocity of her questioning wouldn't get back to Swann.

# Chapter Nine

The dying fluorescent light blinked overhead as DCI Swann paced down the corridor. How could Elea have disappeared already? She only went out for a leak. He glowered as he recalled their telephone conversation. *Reconnaissance mission, indeed.* He'd just come out of another briefing and hated having to cover for her. She hadn't been here a day and already everything was turned on its head. A hard knot formed in his stomach at the thought of her sleeping with Mitch Harding. His own DI, for God's sake. After being fast-tracked into the role, Mitch was only weeks in. It wasn't the best of starts. Swann's frown deepened. He had no right to be jealous, but it raged within him all the same. Ever since he'd left Finland, Elea's presence had felt like a phantom limb, aching with a frightening reality. God knows, he'd tried to move on, and now Alice was pushing for marriage. He'd hoped that by seeing Elea one more time, he'd be able to put his feelings for her to bed. But her dalliance with Mitch had made things a hundred times worse.

'*Voi helvetti*,' he uttered the swearword. The years he'd spent living and working in Finland had granted him a plethora of them. His move was meant to be temporary – respite after a particularly harrowing case. But a holiday turned into a sabbatical before he committed to the move. He'd enjoyed his time in Finland, but a messy break-up with Elea had left him wanting to return to the UK. So many times he wondered how his life would have panned out had he stayed. The case they were working on was treacherous enough, without the added weight of their complicated past. But it seemed that he and Elea were destined to be intertwined. He couldn't believe that he'd lost sight of her already.

The burst of cold air was sobering as he pushed through the rear exit door. He glanced around the back yard, grateful for the trees that dotted the outside space. It used to be a smoker's gathering space, but the smoking ban had turned it into a refuge from the pressures of work. He pulled his phone from his pocket and called Elea's number. As he found privacy beneath a sycamore tree, he was met with the cold, impersonal tone of her voicemail. 'I don't know what you're playing at,' he lowered his head, pressing his phone to his ear, 'but if you're not back here in the next thirty minutes you're off the case.' He jabbed at his iPhone to end the recording, knowing it was a waste of time. Elea would come back when she was good and ready, but it was *his* reputation on the line. His future promotions hung in the balance. His plan of retiring as a superintendent wasn't solely about the bigger pension on offer. The role would pave his way for better consultancy jobs after retirement, too. But one small misstep . . . He exhaled a long breath. It didn't bear thinking about.

His phone buzzed in his hand, but his initial relief at receiving a message that he hoped was from Elea turned to guilt. It was Alice. Elea's return had unsettled her. Her jealousy was palpable, even from afar.

*Everything OK?* she'd texted, most likely hoping for a conversation.

He responded with a thumbs-up emoji. He didn't want her to detect the worry in his voice or to hear her say 'I told you so.'

Had he made a mistake by bringing Elea here? She was too close to the case, too consumed with finding her daughter to make rational judgements now. The pull of work tugged. He needed to get back. His desk phone was probably ringing, the tannoy echoing in the corridor as it called out his name. The barren branches above him creaked as they swayed in the breeze. The darkening skies did little to ease his discontent. Where had Elea gone? He'd never met Liisa, only knew her from the old photographs that Elea had given them to work from. She'd barely known Swann until he got involved in Liisa's case. God, she'd been so broken back then. He recalled the first time he'd met her, anguish streaked across her face. 'Don't worry about me,' she'd uttered, her words sharpened by fear. 'Put your energy into finding my daughter.' The rawness of Elea's pain still clawed at his chest. She'd tried to stay strong, but identifying Liisa's school bag almost finished her off. Yet she wouldn't leave the police station until their commander forced her into the car one evening and drove her home himself. Heikkinen had stayed with her for hours that day, afraid to leave Elea alone.

Swann thrust his hands into his pockets. Was he being too hard on her? Having children of his own afforded him a deeper understanding of what she was going through. The Ice Angels would forever haunt them both.

'Boss?' Ness's quietly respectful voice broke through

Swann's troubled thoughts. She stood before him, her colourful clothes contrasting sharply with his tailored suit. He'd always liked Ness and encouraged her to go for promotion, but she preferred doing the groundwork, and given the number of times that she was late, it was probably for the best.

'What's wrong?' It had to be important for her to come looking.

'We had a call from a Ms Baker. She said to tell you that she's on her way back.' She gave him an apologetic smile. 'I wouldn't have bothered you, but she was very insistent.'

'That's all right,' Swann rubbed a hand over his weary face. He hadn't had time to introduce Elea to the rest of the team. Why hadn't she rung his mobile? What had she done now?

He accompanied Ness back to the main office, his thoughts fixated on the case. 'Any joy getting through to Sophie Miller?' Officers had frequently tried to speak to twelve-year-old Sophie since she had been discovered on the steps of Lincoln Cathedral clutching a small wooden Martta doll. The trauma of her kidnapping had numbed her, stealing her words as she retreated into herself. But she was a precious witness, and they needed her to catch the monster who had snatched her off the streets. They had to keep pushing.

Ness pressed her security tag against the panel next to their office door. 'I've spoken to the FLO. No progress yet, I'm afraid.'

This was not the news that he'd been hoping for. Sophie's parents wanted nothing to do with the family liaison officer.

'Keep putting the pressure on,' Swann replied. 'If anyone can get through, it's you.'

Ness smiled at the sentiment. Sophie's family had built a wall around her and who could blame them? Their mistrust of the police ran deep. Right now, all they wanted to do was protect their little girl. Swann cast an eye over Sergeant Davies, who had just picked up the phone. He wondered if the call was real or a ploy not to speak to him. The office was busy with activity, with printers spewing out paperwork and phone calls in progress. The atmosphere in the room was tense, each officer focused on catching the monster responsible for snatching three young girls off the streets. They had managed to recruit assistance from other specialist teams, but the budget for this operation would only stretch so far – especially with Elea on the payroll.

Swann retreated to his office, the door shutting behind him with a resounding click. Surrounded by the familiar scent of stale coffee and old editions of *Blackstone's* manuals, he sank into his chair. His desk phone flashed with messages and his email notifications were now running into the hundreds. He had a million things to do, but yet again he was distracted by Elea as she finally returned. She walked with confidence, giving her new colleagues a nod of acknowledgement. Swann watched her intently, his fingers drumming against the smooth surface of his desk.

# Chapter Ten

Elea entered the SCT office, a smile tugging at her lips. She had done the serious crime team a favour, proving her worth less than twenty-four hours in. The old feeling was back, that delicious sense of exhilaration from a job well done. The Finnish author Maria Jotuni's quote had always resonated with her: 'A few moments of distress teach a person more wisdom than decades of stable circumstances.' Phil Hobbs now knew all about that.

It was still there, the faint flicker of hope that refused to dim, because surely finding Chelsea would lead her to Liisa. The image of her daughter was like a faded Polaroid in her mind. What did she look like now? She was out there, somewhere. She had to be. Otherwise what was the point in carrying on?

Now it was time for Elea to clear things with Swann. She wanted him to be as pleased as she was about the new lead. But Liisa was not his daughter. Swann had only been acquainted with the ghost of her presence and with the remains of her sodden school bag after it was found the morning after she went missing, in the snow. How could Elea expect him to feel the same? She envied his relationship with his children. She only hoped that now he had them, it would make him more understanding of her cause. But judging by the look on his face as she joined him, fatherhood was not having the desired effect.

'Where the hell have you been?' He rose abruptly from his chair.

Elea refused to be deterred. 'When's the last time you had your blood pressure checked? You're looking a little red around the gills.'

'Elea . . .' Swann began. 'What have you done?'

'I have intel on Chelsea Hobbs. Her mother's in a refuge, all thanks to me, and her father – actually, stepfather,' Elea mumbled, 'he made *that* quite clear – he was helpful . . . in the end.' Another wry smile. She couldn't help herself. She didn't mention her chat with Gary Reynolds from The Birdcage. That was off the record, after all.

'Oh God,' Swann groaned. 'What have you done? Is he still in one piece?'

*Pieces*, Elea almost corrected him. She could still hear the satisfying snap of his bones in the back of her mind. But Swann looked upset enough as it was. 'Of course he's all right.' She spoke with an off-kilter cheeriness. 'He just needed a little gentle persuasion to see the error of his ways.'

Swann picked up his desk-phone receiver. 'Gentle persuasion to you is a force-five hurricane to everyone else.'

'What are you doing?' Elea asked.

'What am *I* doing?' Swann snorted. 'I'm requesting a unit to do a welfare check on him.'

Elea tilted her head to one side. 'Shouldn't your priority be his wife? Because judging by her bruises, *she* hasn't had any welfare checks in a while.'

'She wouldn't give a statement. You know the drill. There's nothing we can do if she won't go to court.'

'You could've launched a victimless prosecution.'

'Don't you think we tried?'

'Well, I tried harder.' Elea slipped the worn blue address book from her bag. 'Put down the phone, so I can show you what I've got.'

Swann glowered in response.

'Sit,' Elea instructed, as she pulled over a swivel chair. She pushed the address book across the desk. 'This will lead us to Chelsea. Phil was in over his head with his dealers around the time that she disappeared. I reckon that they agreed to wipe his debt if he forgot to pick her up from school. I haven't bagged it up because I need to photocopy it first.'

'What has that cost me?' Swann eyed the battered notebook cautiously. 'If you've put me in the shit, I need to know how deep.'

Elea shifted in her seat. There was no getting out of this. 'Just a couple of broken fingers. It was self-defence.'

'And . . .' Swan stared, unblinking, as he waited for more.

Elea chuckled. 'I might have threatened to shoot him in the balls.'

'Jesus!' Swann muttered. 'We need to update this on the system.'

'Relax, it's all under control.' She stared at the address book, willing Swann to pick it up. 'If he wanted to make an official complaint, he would have done it by now.'

'And what if we get a result and this goes to court? It won't stand up as evidence.'

But Elea had already thought of that. 'His wife is giving

a statement as we speak. It was self-defence, like I said. She gave me the address book – no duress. She's behind us all the way. Look,' she tapped the cover. 'We've got all these lovely names to chase up. Think of the intel. What if they didn't only deal drugs? They might have trafficked people, too.'

'And what about the white feathers? Traffickers treat people as commodities. They're hardly the sentimental type.'

'I don't know!' Elea snapped. 'But you can be sure as hell I'll find out.'

Swann seemed unimpressed. 'We're not in Finland any more. If you're hoping to find Liisa, well, it's unlikely, you know that, don't you?'

Elea couldn't believe the words coming out of his mouth. She wasn't expecting fanfares, but she'd reeled in a lead within hours of getting here. 'This isn't just about what *I* want. Chelsea is someone's daughter, too. Don't give up on her, like you gave up on Liisa.' She pinned him with a glare until he looked away.

'I never gave up on her.' His words became hushed, his anger diminishing.

Elea folded her arms, unconvinced. Outside, police car sirens blared, but she was focused on the past. 'You gave up the day you left Finland. It was quite the defining moment in our relationship.'

The sudden ring of the desk phone interrupted her flow.

'I know what you're doing.' Swann leaned forward and silenced the phone. 'But here's the rub. Your police powers hold no weight here. You're a consultant. You're expected to toe the line.'

Elea didn't like where this was going. Her muscles tensed as her frustration grew. 'You've changed. We used to be the perfect team.' In the years following Liisa's disappearance Elea had thrown herself into work. She and Swann had progressed to leading a team of detectives and their success rate was second to none. But there was one case they could not crack. The Ice Angels.

'The world has moved on.' Swann's voice rose once more. 'If you don't follow the rules, then where will it end?'

Elea pushed back her swivel chair as she got to her feet. 'It will end with my daughter walking in the door!' She took a sudden breath. She hadn't meant to blurt it out. But Swann had a way of getting under her skin.

Heads swivelled in the outer office, but their observation was momentary, as work soon resumed.

'Then I have no choice.' Swann stood. He had taken risks in the past, but those days were over.

'Answer me one thing. Why did you employ me to consult on this case? Did you think I had stopped caring? That I'd mellowed over the years?'

'Of course not.' Swann spoke in stiff, measured tones. 'The feathers were one thing. But the Martta doll . . . I saw the look on your face when you found out. It's too close to the bone. I'm scared of what you might do.'

'Well, I'm scared of what you *won't* do!' she countered. She grabbed the notebook from his desk and waved it in the air. 'Why are we wasting time when I have the evidence in the palm of my hand?' A heavy silence filled the space between them as Swann seemed to contemplate his next move. Elea watched as he logged off his computer.

'Photocopy the notebook, upload it onto the system and book it into property. We'll take it from here.'

'What in the smoking hell? Where are you going?' Elea's annoyance flared as she watched Swann make his way to the door.

'To speak to the super. Go back to your hotel and pack. We won't be needing your services any more.'

# Chapter Eleven

Swann rapped on his superintendent's door, fumbling with his emotions. Superintendent Jessica Collins (Jess to her friends) had been a steadfast presence in his career. She and Swann were in the same intake in the Met Police when they'd joined as youthful probationers in 1990. Jess had been instrumental in bringing him to Lincolnshire Police force when he returned from Finland. Despite this long friendship, he was hesitant to seek her out. He was known for his unwavering certainty, but today he conceded that his judgement had been off. Elea didn't belong on his team, not even as a consultant. She was an unpredictable firecracker. The woman needed therapy, not another case to remind her that her daughter was still missing. On top of that, her presence was making Alice nervous. The electricity between him and Elea, however unwanted, was undeniable. He couldn't blame Alice for feeling insecure. He hated himself for thinking it, but she had every right to be.

He entered Jess's office, unable to ignore the multitude of trophies that dominated the back wall. A devotee of ju-jitsu, his superintendent was proud of her achievements. Now she was climbing the ranks of the police force and was effecting some real change. But he knew a part of her yearned for the gritty action of the streets, and that his weekly updates were something she looked forward to. But today he was here to deliver disappointing news. She sat behind her wide desk, watching him intently, the low chatter of her police radio playing as a backdrop to their meeting. She was only five feet four, but her muscular build and assertive nature left people under no illusion as to who was in control.

'Take the weight off.' She gestured towards the swivel chair. Jess's highlighted brown hair was pulled into a bun. Her skin was tanned from a recent trip to Thailand, and she smelled faintly of Tiger Balm.

'It's Elea,' Swann began, sinking into the offered seat. 'Her consultancy isn't panning out . . . ma'am.'

'Is that so?' Jess arched an eyebrow, a familiar mannerism. 'What's with the "ma'am" crap? You only pull that out when you're in deep water.'

She had him there. Elea, with only one day on the team, had left him compromised. Swann tried to form a coherent explanation that wouldn't land her in cuffs. 'She's too personally involved with the case. I should never have brought her here.'

Jess studied his expression. 'She's passionate, which is exactly what I expect of my team. Unlike your bloody sergeant, who walks around in a daze.' She scratched her arm and Swann caught sight of a bruise dappling her skin. 'Sparring injury,' she winked, following his gaze. 'You look tired, Swann. Are you getting any sleep? Must be knackering managing the twins . . . at your age.' She delivered a teasing smile. 'How's Alice? I still think it's a shame she left the force when she did.'

Jess was only being courteous. Alice was never suited for the hustle of police work. She was Elea's polar opposite: risk-averse and strictly by-the-book. She completed her work, no more, no less, and her detection rate reflected it. 'She's fine. Home front's stable,' he answered curtly, veering the conversation back to Elea. 'Now, as I was saying—'

'I'm aware of Elea's call-on,' Jess cut him off. 'She's cracked a lead on her first day here.'

Swann stiffened. She'd cracked more than a lead. 'But Hobbs—' He stalled, preparing his words.

Jess pointed at her computer screen. 'Haven't you read the statements? Hobbs turned on his missus for letting Elea in. Elea acted in self-defence as she came between them, and now that we've got his wife's statement covering years of domestic abuse, he's going to be nicked.'

'She broke his fingers.'

'Self-defence isn't a crime. She did a good job. Proper old-fashioned police work.'

Swan was dumbstruck. It seemed that Elea had beaten him to it, presenting her own version of events. No wonder she was smiling when she came into his office. But next time she might not be so lucky.

'She has guts,' Jess added. 'And her track record is impressive, although I'm surprised at you, leaving her in the lurch after everything she's been through.'

'What?' Swann stiffened as he was caught off-guard. 'What else did she tell you?"

'We had quite a chat. She's loyal, your ex-wife. I'm not sure you've earned it, mind, considering that you came in here to throw her under the bus.'

Swann's laughter was devoid of humour. 'Is that what she said?' He clasped his hands together, hating thoughts of Elea sharing details of their private life.

Jess inhaled a deep breath as she rested her elbows on her desk. 'I want Elea on our team long-term. She's ready for a change, and you're going to provide your unwavering support.'

'Seriously? Even if she's breaking the law?' Swan retorted.

'She's worth the risk.' Jess stared at him, resolute. 'And you're responsible for making sure she doesn't. Any law-breaking is on you.'

Swann bristled as he got to his feet. 'I can't watch her twenty-four/seven!'

'Which is why you'll pair her with DI Harding. Give her time. She'll get us results.'

Swann ran a hand through his hair. Elea couldn't have told Jess about their one-night stand. Either that or his boss didn't care. This was turning into a nightmare. 'Why Mitch? Granted, he's a DI, but he's wet behind the ears. Shouldn't we pair her with one of our veterans, like Ness?' To Swann, experience wasn't judged by rank, but by results. Mitch had yet to prove himself.

'Mitch needs some mentoring in his new role, and the responsibility won't hurt. This isn't up for debate. The pressure's on, Swann. We need results, and Elea's dug up some promising leads.' Jess checked her watch before flapping a hand in his direction. 'Go on then. Off you fuck.'

Swann sighed. In what universe was Elea a suitable mentor for someone new to their role? But there was no point in arguing. Once you got the 'Off you fuck' from Jess, there was no going back.

# Chapter Twelve

## Liisa

### 2016

My grandmother always told me to treat my elders with respect. I was taught about stranger danger in school. But I wish my teacher had told me that ordinary people do bad things, too. Because the people who took me aren't monsters, at least not the kind I imagined during our talks in class. The woman and her son in the cabin in the woods seem more like the people that my mummu told me to respect. I'm not like other girls my age. I know that I'm in trouble. When your mum investigates murders, you learn things. Things you can't share with your friends. I heard Mikael whispering, something about me being 'the right fit'. I sit, legs crossed, as he watches me from the other side of room. The open fire is blazing now and I'm grateful for the heat.

'There are three bedrooms in this cabin.' Johanna stands before me, blocking my view of Mikael. 'One belongs to me, the other is Mikael's and one will belong to you.' Her voice lowers as if she's telling a scary story. She leans so close that I can see the tiny red veins in her bloodshot eyes. 'Then there's the hole. That's underground. It's dark and cold and has big hairy spiders that bite.' She makes a gnashing motion with her teeth that makes me jump on the spot. 'You don't want to stay there, do you?'

I shake my head so much that it hurts. My eyes are puffy and I want to answer properly, but my throat feels like it has closed up. Everything comes out: the pain, the emotion, the fear that has been building in my chest as I sob. I sit here, my shoulders jerking, hoping she'll feel sorry for me and take me home. I don't see her open palm coming until it's too late. It makes a sharp slapping sound as it hits the side of my cheek. Mummu never once hit me, not even when I misbehaved. The sudden stinging sensation hurts so much. Shocked, I cup my cheek with my hand.

'I've already told you – stop crying!' Her voice booms like thunder now, as she leans over me once more. Her face is red, a film of sweat breaking out on her upper lip. 'This life isn't for the weak, do you hear? Pull yourself together and do as you're told!' Flecks of her spit land on my face, but I'm too scared to wipe them away.

'S-s-sorry,' I manage to say, gulping back the tears that won't stop. I part my lips and force myself to smile. That's when I notice Mikael touching the scar creeping up from his mouth. It's almost like a lopsided grin.

# Chapter Thirteen

They say that the depth of love is measured by the pain of loss. But what about the refusal to give up hope? When Liisa disappeared, Elea was thrown into a world of uncertainty. There was no firm indication that her daughter was dead, but neither was there anything to suggest that she was still alive. Elea could see it on people's faces when the subject was raised. She didn't want their pity. She wanted them to have witnessed what happened that day. Her last moments with Liisa were forever locked into Elea's memory to be played on a loop. Elea had got annoyed over the most minor of things, sullying their last precious minutes together. Because even if Liisa was found alive, she would never be that little girl again.

Lost in thought, Elea sat in Swann's office, sipping from the cup of coffee that Ness had kindly made. She wasn't going anywhere, despite his earlier orders to return to her hotel. She knew how he'd react and had pre-empted him. She cradled the mug in her hands, relaxing in the comfort of Swann's leather chair.

The kitchen sink had been dripping the morning that Liisa disappeared. A dripping tap was the sole reason for Elea's annoyance. No, Elea corrected herself, it went back further than that. She had woken up late. There was a power cut in the night, and her alarm hadn't gone off. She'd been disorientated after a nightmare that she could no longer remember, but felt. Then she'd checked her watch, cursed, stumbled out of bed and stubbed her toe. She'd been working late every night and had barely seen her daughter all week. Oh, those precious days. She'd missed so many, working for a world that did not deserve her loyalty as she tried to keep the streets of Helsinki safe.

By the time she reached their small kitchen, her daughter was dressed and eating some porridge that she'd made. Liisa wasn't only gifted academically, she was blessed with common sense, too. Yet Elea didn't praise her daughter for her independence, or remark on how pretty her hair looked that day. Instead she'd grumbled because they had run out of coffee and asked why Liisa hadn't woken her up. Elea often relived that morning in her mind and fantasised about turning back time. If only she could go back to how it should have been. She would have got up early that morning, called in sick to work, then given her daughter a day off school. She imagined Liisa's surprise as she told her that she was taking her somewhere nice. 'But we can't,' Liisa would say, then list some school project she had to complete. Liisa didn't skip school. Elea's vivacious, intelligent daughter planned to be a judge one day. That girl was born middle-aged. Elea swallowed back her regret as she forced her dream to conclude. She couldn't leave her imaginary daughter hanging there. 'Where would you like to go?' she would say, already knowing the answer. 'To the horse farm!' Liisa would reply, because she adored all animals, but horses were her absolute favourites. The 600-acre farm in Sipoo was only half an hour away.

Elea would agree, urging Liisa to wear something

appropriate. 'I'll call the school, tell them you have a dental appointment.' But this is where the daydream turned, because Liisa would frown, worried about her mother's sudden change of character. 'What's going on?' she'd ask. 'What's wrong?' Then Elea's dream would fade away. Because she wasn't the type of person to allow her daughter to skip school, not even for one day. She rubbed her chest with the heel of her palm to ease the physical pain. Why must she put herself through this time and time again?

Her police colleagues knew the depressing stats. After forty-eight hours of being missing, the chances of someone like Liisa being found alive dropped dramatically. Ten long years had passed. She would be a woman now, celebrating her twenty-second birthday this year. After all this time it was unlikely Liisa was alive. If she'd managed to escape, then why hadn't she been in touch? As usual, when revisiting the case in her mind, Elea's thoughts turned to the other Ice Angels. Their school bags were also discovered in the snow, but their remains had never been found. Why were there so many years between each disappearance? Elea thought of Anu's mother. Maria was heading into her seventies. Like Elea, she refused to give up hope. Like Elea, she had kept her child's bedroom exactly how it was on the day she disappeared. How many more ghostly museums to missing children existed in the world? She dragged herself back into present day as Swann returned.

By the look on his face, Swann's meeting with her new friend the superintendent had gone as she had hoped. It seemed that Elea would not be packing her bags for Helsinki just yet.

'Up.' He gesticulated, approaching his chair.

Elea conceded, cradling her coffee mug as she walked to the other side of the desk. Swann's office was organised and clean, his shelves filled with well-thumbed law books. But the office was too open for her liking. In Helsinki she had total privacy.

'You think you have it all figured out, don't you?' Swan sat heavily in his chair.

Elea suppressed her smile. This was not a game to her, and she refused to be treated like a child. She was a determined crime inspector – the Finnish equivalent of a DI – who aimed to achieve results where others had failed. 'I take it I'm staying, then?'

'Clever move, speaking to the super and getting her onside. But I'd prefer it if you didn't go over my head next time.'

'*Pata kattilaa soimaa, musta kylki kummallakin.*' Elea drily spoke the words. Swann would know enough Finnish to understand 'The pot bad-mouths the kettle.' Before he left his job in Finland, *she* was *his* boss, which was why she would not allow him to treat her as an insubordinate now. 'When is the briefing?'

Swann let her comment go. 'We're waiting on DIU. But speak to the team before you go galloping off somewhere else.' He had a point. The Divisional Intelligence Unit was a valuable resource, but Elea had little time to play with. Getting the rest of Swann's team on board would do no harm in the long run.

'All right, if it makes you happy. We all want the same thing here, but remember – I'm best positioned to get it. You're lucky to have me.'

Swann failed to keep the emotion out of his voice. 'You'll risk your job for this, but would you risk going to prison? Because that is where you're heading if you pull another of your stunts. And what if we find Liisa then? You're no good to her inside.'

He had a point. Elea couldn't help her daughter from behind bars. But if she did nothing, then nothing was what she was going to get. She drained her mug and placed it on his desk. 'Well, if that's all.'

'Not quite.' Swan gestured through his office window and waved at someone to come in. 'There's one condition of you staying on this team, and it's non-negotiable. And before you go running to the super, this comes from her.'

Conditions usually tied Elea's hands, but judging by the colour rising in Swann's face, this was not up for discussion.

Mitch Harding entered the room, more composed than the last time he had made an appearance. His shirt sleeves were folded to his elbows and, unlike Swann, he wasn't wearing a tie. But the cut of his clothes suggested that they weren't bought from some cheap clothing outlet.

Swann stood, looking at Elea, his brows lowering in discontent. 'You're being partnered with Mitch. Wherever you go, he goes. Pull one more disappearing act and he'll be giving you a ride to the airport.'

Elea blinked twice as she absorbed the news. 'You're kidding me, right?' Her voice was tinged with irritation. She didn't want, or need, a chaperone.

'Not at all,' Swann looked at them both. 'Mitch has been briefed, and I suggest you take the situation as graciously as he did.' Swann slid up his shirt sleeve and checked his watch. 'I've got to be somewhere. Whatever's happened before, draw a line under it, so you can get on with your jobs.'

Elea wanted to ask him who the hell he thought he was talking to, but Swann did not hang around for a reply. This would cut deep on both sides. She knew it would pain him to pair her up with someone she'd slept with less than twenty-four hours before.

'I don't believe this.' She rounded on Mitch as the situation sank in. 'Well? Say something!'

'If it helps, I know this case inside out. I've been studying it in my spare time.'

'Police detectives don't have spare time,' Elea snorted. 'And I'm not having this.' She shook her head. 'Talking to me like I'm some sort of probationer. I was his boss in Helsinki, did you know that? No, I bet you didn't . . .' Her voice descended into muttering as she uttered some Finnish swearwords. It was just as well Mitch didn't understand.

An amused smile rested on Mitch's face. 'Is the prospect of working with me that bad? I've not been long on the team, but I was an experienced uniformed officer and have more intel sources than anyone else in here. I'm respected on the street.' He gave her a sideways glance. 'Hell, I lived on them once.'

'You were homeless?' Now that Elea hadn't expected. She sighed, releasing her anger to ground herself once more.

'Yeah, that and everything that went along with it. It's made me a better officer. I won't do anything to jeopardise my job.'

*Great*, Elea thought, resting a hand on her hip. *He's not only green, but a stickler for the rules, too.*

'About last night,' he began. 'I don't want things to be awkward.'

'Awkward?' Elea stared. 'Why would it be awkward? It was just sex. As long as you don't go blabbing, then I don't see a problem with it.'

'No problem.' Mitch cleared his throat, but seemed unable to meet her gaze. 'Well, um . . . I'd better get back to work. Do you want to join me?'

'Where's your office? I hope it has more privacy than this fish bowl.'

'This *is* my office. Swann's office is down the corridor.'

'Then why?'

'He's not quite been able to let it go.' Mitch shrugged. 'I'm fine working with the team for now.'

Elea shook her head in disbelief. It was exactly like Swann to want his cake and eat it.

'There's a spare desk next to mine. We can set up there. It's good to be in the thick of everything. That OK with you?'

The situation was far from ideal, but what choice did Elea have? She was tired of all the drama. 'Three girls,' she replied. 'Your team has failed three girls so far. So, yes, I want to join you, because we need to solve this shitting case before anyone else gets hurt.'

# Chapter Fourteen

The SCT office comprised a dozen desks cluttered with computers, desk phones and stacks of paperwork. Warm air pumped from the radiators, wrapping Elea in a blanket of heat. She rested her suit jacket on the back of a swivel chair. She couldn't help but compare it to her own office in Helsinki, where the chill lingered despite the old equipment's best efforts, and the coffee machine was in constant use. She stood in the middle of the room and cleared her throat. Mitch had offered to introduce her, but she preferred to do it herself.

'Good morning.' Elea addressed her new colleagues with an air of confidence. 'You're probably already aware, but my name is Elea Baker. I'm a detective inspector with Helsinki Police, but will be working with you in a consultancy role.' As she spoke, she noticed curious eyes studying her, their gazes ranging from respectful to speculative. She continued, 'I'm also the mother of Liisa Baker, the twelve-year-old girl who disappeared on her way home from school in Porvoo in 2016. I have intimate knowledge of Liisa's case and the two that proceeded it, involving the twelve-year-old children Anu and Venla, who are still missing to this day. The cases were dubbed the "Ice Angels" by the press.'

A murmur rippled through the office, their curiosity

piqued by Elea's words. The team exchanged glances, which Elea interpreted as intrigue.

'I'll be partnering up with Mitch and updating Op Turnstile regularly, but if any of you need anything, then don't hesitate to ask,' Elea added, hoping to encourage them to open up.

'Welcome, DI Baker, I'm Jamal,' DC Jones replied, his tone sincere. 'It works both ways. If you need anything, just let us know.'

'Thank you,' Elea said, appreciating the genuine offer of support. She could have told them to call her Miss Baker, but the formal title felt more respectful, even if her Helsinki police powers as a *rikoskomisario* held little weight over here. 'I'll need an extra board,' she continued, pointing to the mobile briefing boards that contained details of the Op Turnstile case. Soon her daughter's face would be added, as well as those of the children who had disappeared before her. Elea's voice remained steady but determined. 'We'll be working on the assumption that the Ice Angels are connected to your case. I have no doubt that the Finnish Martta doll found in Sophie Miller's hands belonged to my daughter.'

'Kelly Maxwell.' The young DC leaned against her desk. Her eyes were sharp, her glossy dark hair skimming past her shoulders. 'We've been trained never to assume. How can you be sure?' The ABC approach was practised nationwide: *Assume nothing. Believe nobody. Check everything.*

Elea bristled at the challenge in the young woman's voice. She kept her composure as she turned to face her. 'The doll is extremely rare. Either it belonged to Liisa or someone has gone to a lot of effort to source a replica. Either way, it's enough to link the cases.'

71

DI Mitch Harding watched the exchange from his desk, observant but quiet.

'Is this official? Will the media be made aware?' Jamal turned to Mitch for a response.

But the voice that replied was that of Swann, who had just entered the room. He was holding a wad of paperwork, no doubt accumulated from the meeting he had recently left. He shook his head, his expression guarded. 'Not yet. If the press gets hold of this, it could spook the killer and send him underground. This is in an unofficial capacity.'

Elea nodded in agreement, happy with Swann's sensible approach. She turned back to the team. 'I can give you whatever you need from our end. The case could benefit from fresh eyes.' Although there was a conflict of interest, she had been cleared by her commander to share details. She wasn't allowed to investigate her daughter's disappearance when she lived in Finland, but while he was there Swann had kept her in the loop. Elea's heart beat a little bit faster, because somewhere in the shadows the truth was waiting.

The room fell silent for a moment as Elea's words settled. For once the phones had stopped ringing and email notifications were paused. It was as if the world was acknowledging that something important was taking place. The merging of two forces to find one perpetrator. Swann took advantage of the quiet to address the team. 'Elea has obtained a list of names from Chelsea Hobbs's stepfather; they've been uploaded to the system.'

Kelly raised her perfectly formed eyebrows, clearly surprised. 'Really? I tried speaking to him a few times. He was a bloody nightmare. I couldn't get anything out of him.'

'Couldn't you?' Elea gave a slow nod. 'Interesting.'

Mitch shot Elea a smile, acknowledging her ingenuity at getting so much so soon. Swann caught their interaction and frowned. He quickly continued, 'The list contains potential drug dealers who might have been involved in Chelsea's abduction.' He shared Phil Hobbs's explanation of events.

'Damn,' murmured Ollie Evans. 'Sounds like a good morning's work.' Ollie was leaning against his desk, wearing his usual jeans, shirt and boots. Elea remembered Swann complaining about his casual attire in the past.

Swann grudgingly agreed, his deep voice resonating through the room. 'DIU is sourcing as much information as it can, focusing on suspects with links overseas.' As he spoke, he looked into the eyes of each team member, ensuring they understood the gravity of the task ahead. 'Hobbs could be bullshitting us. Or we could be dealing with human traffickers. There's no telling where this will lead.'

Elea listened as he prioritised jobs and discussed potential scenarios with his team. The temptation to take over briefings was strong, but she didn't want to piss Swann off any more than necessary today.

As the meeting concluded, Ness cleared her throat. 'I've spoken to Jade from social services. Sophie Miller's going home in the morning and her parents have agreed to let us speak to her.'

'Good. Very good.' Swann nodded towards Elea. 'Pair up with Mitch for the interview. Just remember, don't put words in the child's mouth.'

Elea bristled at the implication, her eyes narrowing as she responded coolly, 'I am a highly trained interviewer, Richard.

You need not worry about that.' She emphasised the word 'highly', reminding him of her expertise. The use of his first name would also remind him that she was far more than a team member. Like it or not, she was still family.

As they settled into their respective workstations, Elea allowed herself a brief moment to absorb the atmosphere of the serious-crime team office. The hum of computers, the steady rhythm of fingers tapping on keyboards and the quiet murmur of voices created an orchestration unique to this space. *Different, but the same*, she thought to herself. She only hoped this team would be able to do what she and her Finnish colleagues couldn't. She had plans for their perpetrator and would find a way of making him talk. Darkness bled into her thoughts, exactly as they had a thousand times before. If her daughter wasn't alive, then the lowlife who took her would not survive her rage. That revenge *would* be worth going to prison for.

# Chapter Fifteen

There were times when Elea rejected phone calls. Like when Swann was chasing up her whereabouts, or when her mother rang to see if she was getting enough sleep. But a call from Maria Korhonen was not to be ignored. Swann had once called Elea and Maria 'tragedy buddies' during a heated row many years ago. But their relationship n far deeper than that. They kept each other afloat, even after all these years. Anu's mother was an artist who had grown successful in the last decade. She poured her grief for her child into her snowy landscape creations, each one a portrait of desolation and beauty. But it hadn't always been like that. Maria was a heavy drinker when Anu was snatched. She would never forgive herself for neglecting her child, but she had remained teetotal ever since. At sixty-seven years old, she was one of the bravest people Elea knew. She had moved forward with her life, yet never gave up hope of seeing her child again.

'*Moi*,' Maria said, her warm voice reminding Elea of home.

'*Moi*,' Elea replied to the woman she wished she had never had reason to meet, but whom she now considered a friend. She sat on the office chair, watching Kelly talking to Ollie, who was standing at the printer.

Elea slipped easily into Finnish, appreciating the privacy it offered, as Maria asked how she was. 'I'm good. Very good.

We're making real headway on the case.' Her tone was calm and carried a hint of satisfaction.

'You know,' Maria started, her voice thoughtful, 'I was standing here at my easel and this feeling came over me. I can't quite explain it. But now I've spoken to you, I think that's what it was. I felt your excitement. Well done.'

Elea smiled. So that was why she had rung. Maria was very in tune with her feelings. 'I can't share the details yet, but—'

'I trust you,' Maria interrupted gently. 'I know you're doing everything you can. Take care of yourself, OK?'

Elea chuckled softly. 'Have you been speaking to my mother?'

Maria laughed, a sound that put Elea at ease. 'I'm old enough to *be* your mother. Listen to her – her concern comes from a place of love. There's nothing quite like the mother-and-daughter bond.' She continued to talk about the importance of family, and Elea checked her watch. She needed to get back to work.

Kelly glanced in her direction before returning to her desk. She had been tasked with liaising with outside forces to identify any cases that shared similarities with Operation Turnstile. Long-winded and tedious work. There were so many incidents of missing children in England, it was a huge task to tap into them all. In the UK more than 100,000 children were reported missing every year. But the numbers were mercifully fewer for children who went missing long-term, under 2,000 each year. But Elea sensed that Kelly was looking in the wrong direction. It was near-misses with strangers that she should be researching; they needed to find the lucky ones who could provide details about their suspect. Elea made a

76

mental note to have a word with Kelly later on. She pulled at the collar of her shirt. The air was too stale. She got up and opened the window and was met with a collective groan.

'I'll let you go,' Maria said, picking up on the shift in Elea's attention. 'I know when I've lost my audience.'

'Sorry,' Elea apologised. 'I'm listening. I'll have news soon.'

'I'm teasing, dear. Get back to work, but take care of yourself, too, yes?'

'And you,' Elea said, before ending the call. Her head turned as the window was slammed shut. Kelly. Elea ground her back teeth. She strode over to Kelly's desk. 'Come with me, please.'

Kelly rolled her eyes. 'What is it? I'm busy.'

What was wrong with this woman? Elea had always been respected by her team. She was not used to having to ask twice. She spoke on the inhale, forcing a patient smile. 'It's important.'

Kelly's expression relayed her annoyance as she followed Elea into an empty office used to assist witnesses in identifying offenders on the police database. It was a small but private space and Elea closed the door behind them.

'What's with the attitude?'

'There's nothing wrong with *my* attitude, thank you. I'm busy. Why have you called me in here?'

'We're supposed to be working together as a team. So I'll ask you again: what's the problem? Spit it out.'

A pink flush spread up from the base of Kelly's neck. Her lips thinned.

'It's OK to speak your mind, Kelly. If you have a problem with me, say so, instead of acting like a child.'

'I don't like your little digs,' Kelly replied, resting one hand on her hip. 'Acting like you've swept in here to save the day. I work hard, and you're not my boss.'

'I never said I was.'

'You bloody well act like it!' Kelly's voice rose a notch. She stopped herself. Took a breath.

Elea bit back a smile. 'Are you finished?'

Kelly nodded, perhaps worried that she had overstepped the mark. Word had clearly got out. People knew Elea was married to their boss.

'I'll take on board what you said. You've got real *sisu*, you know that?'

'*Sisu*?'

'It's hard to explain, but it's in you. Grit. Determination. If you put your fighting spirit into the case instead of resenting me, there's no reason we can't work well together. You know I have a vested interest, right?'

Kelly nodded, her eyes downcast. 'The hours we've worked to get those girls home . . . I've not seen my mum in a month.'

'You're paving the way. It takes time to build a case. Your work won't go to waste. We OK?'

'We're OK,' Kelly confirmed.

Elea opened the office door. She needed every member of the team onside. 'And, Kelly?' Elea said, as she walked past, 'go and see your mum.'

Elea sank into the passenger seat of the car as tiredness swept over her. Her limbs felt heavy, and a dull ache pulsed behind her eyes. She'd turned down Swann's offer to drop her to her hotel. Mitch could drive her back. If Swann insisted on pairing them up, then that's exactly what he would get. She was still pissed with Swann for the way he'd treated her today, but she knew how to play him and would assert herself in time. At least the office dynamics had improved, and Mitch seemed content to allow her to take a leading role – in and out of bed.

She massaged her temple as she inhaled the new-car smell. 'Have you had it long?' She glanced across at Mitch, who was reversing out of the space. 'The car,' she added. Elea hated small talk, but it was better than sitting in awkward silence for the drive home. The words 'small talk' weren't part of the Finnish language. The concept of chatting for the sake of filling silences was a bit of a cultural oddity. But Elea recalled enough of her father's English ways to understand the differences between the cultures.

'I bought it yesterday.' Mitch glanced her way. 'But you're not interested in cars . . . remember?'

A splinter of a memory returned: Elea, slightly drunk at the time, bluntly informing Mitch that he was boring her when he mentioned that he'd bought a car.

'Mmm.' Elea nodded, letting down the window a touch. The cool evening air and change of scenery offered a welcome break from the office. It was odd how police HQ was nestled in the Lincolnshire countryside, a few miles away from the hustle and bustle of urban life. Soon they were heading out of Nettleham and towards the city of Lincoln. They drove in silence, passing under orange street lights as tiredness washed over them both.

'Long day, huh?' Mitch stifled a yawn as he waited for the traffic lights to change from red to green.

'Yes, you look tired.' A smile tugged at the corner of Elea's mouth. 'Someone keep you up late last night?'

His lips formed a grin. 'Yeah, and they kicked me out of bed in the early hours to do their milk round.'

'Milk ladies lead such busy lives.' Elea exhaled a tired laugh. 'You won't be seeing her again.'

'That's a crying shame,' Mitch said wistfully, as the traffic lights changed. 'I'm missing her already.'

Silence fell between them once more, but it was becoming a comfortable one. Elea gazed out of the window at the darkened streets. Was her daughter's kidnapper holed up here somewhere? Tomorrow would be a big day, which is why they'd all been sent home to get some sleep. In the morning Elea and Mitch would speak to Sophie and hopefully glean some information about her kidnapper. Then, if needed, they'd turn their attention to the suspects named on Hobbs's list. The Divisional Intelligence Unit had already confirmed that some of them were known for using the Dark Web, with dealings both nationally and internationally. Elea had no doubt that it was a strong lead.

Mitch's car rolled to a stop outside a row of terraced houses. 'This is Yarborough Crescent.' He leaned forward and pointed out of the window. 'Over there. That's Sophie Miller's home.'

Elea studied the red-brick detached building, which looked like any other house on the street. 'She's just an ordinary child,' she said softly.

'That's what makes it so frightening for the people around here.' Mitch pulled slowly away from the kerb. 'There's no telling who could be next.'

Elea couldn't think about it any more. 'We should head back.' Her stomach grumbled. She had barely eaten all day.

'Right you are.'

Her phone buzzed in her pocket. She glanced at Alice's text, blinking to ensure that she'd read it correctly. Sighing, she typed a quick response.

'Everything all right?' As he headed towards the Brayford, Mitch threw her a curious glance.

'Just an offer I can refuse.' She slipped her phone back into her pocket and gazed out at the darkened streets.

# Chapter Sixteen

Elea was sweltering in the office heat. She'd noticed a pattern: the radiators blasted out warmth in the early hours, despite ongoing budget cuts. By morning the air had thickened with the stench of congealed takeaway that was lingering in the bins shoved into the corners of the room. Scents had always stood out to her. The sharp tang of a fine wine, the lingering spice of expensive aftershave, the crisp, resinous scent of pine needles during her walks in the Finnish forests. But this? This was an assault on the senses. She resisted the urge to throw open every window. She glanced at Mitch, who was signing out a job car. They would be leaving soon. This morning's briefing had been short and perfunctory as they were each allocated their jobs.

'We've gone from a stinking office to a smelly car.' Elea wrinkled her nose in disgust at the grease-lined takeaway wrapper in the passenger footwell as she got in. 'What is it with you Brits and your takeaways?' She was partial to a pizza on occasion, but not every single day.

'It's just come in from a night shift,' Mitch informed her. 'I've driven worse job cars. At least it's got a full tank.' He navigated the frost-kissed roads of Lincoln, slowing as a group of schoolchildren crossed the road. 'Blimey, it's Baltic today.' He turned up the heating in the marked police car.

'You call this cold?' Elea snorted. 'This isn't cold. Where I'm from, the chill seeps through you like ghosts passing through walls.'

'That's very . . . um . . . poetic.' Mitch threw her a grin.

Elea should have known that the words would be lost on him. They were something her daughter once wrote in a poem. She carried bits of Liisa around with her, unpacking them from her memory whenever the opportunity arose. She could not bear the thought of losing even the smallest piece of her.

'What's it like?' Mitch interrupted her thoughts. 'Living in Helsinki, I mean.'

'I'm not from Helsinki, I'm from Porvoo.'

'Oh, I thought—'

'I work in Helsinki. It's almost an hour's commute. Porvoo is . . .' Elea sighed, trying to find the right words. 'It's a small town. Pretty.'

It was much more than that. Porvoo held everything and nothing for Elea. Her heart swelled at the thought of the expansive forests and lakes. Then there were the people who went quietly about their business, with no fanfare. How spoiled she had been, in her beautiful little town, with the sea on her doorstep and sunsets so beautiful they mesmerised you. It was as if mother nature had thrown everything she had to offer into one place. But Liisa's absence had placed a shadow over everything Elea once considered beautiful.

She gazed out of the window to the bare branches of the trees lining Yarborough Road. In the thick of the dark Finnish winters, even the branches of the trees were cloaked in a layer of ice. 'It's a place of contrasts,' Elea spoke wistfully. 'Summer days stretch on for ever, winters can feel like one endless night. There's a silence, deep in the forests and across the lakes. It can fill your soul, if you let it.'

'And the worst part?'

'The isolation.' Her response was immediate. 'It can be your best friend or your worst enemy.' It had been both to her.

There was a pause before Mitch ventured another question. 'Why did Swann leave Finland? He never talks about it.'

Elea's blue eyes hardened momentarily. 'The same reason he went there in the first place – he was running away.' The shift in her tone suggested that Mitch should let the matter rest. He took the hint and they continued to their destination in silence, heavy traffic making the journey to Sophie's home take twice as long as it should have done.

The red-brick house appeared quiet and respectable, a three-bedroom testament to conventional family life. Elea had researched the property on Zoopla. Sophie's parents, Fiona and David, had bought it five years ago. While they weren't under suspicion when it came to their daughter's disappearance, Elea had wanted to get the feel of their home.

She climbed out of the car and smoothed down her clothes. She'd taken care to dress appropriately for this meeting. A suit was too formal, a jumper too laid-back, so she'd paired her black blazer and shirt with designer jeans. She couldn't blame Fiona and David for being critical of Swann's team so far. She bent to retrieve her leather bag from the car footwell. Gaining the trust of Sophie Miller's parents wouldn't come easily. She recalled her own fraught past and how her disbelief had morphed into anger, until finally hatred had set in. *If I ever get hold of that bastard . . .* Elea's jaw hardened at the thought, *he'll be begging for a quick death*. This was more than a job to her. This was as personal as it got.

She followed Mitch down the front garden. Terracotta pots dotted the path, their withered contents killed off by the frost. An old Volvo estate car sat on the driveway, its bumper sticker advising drivers not to get too close. *If only it was that easy to keep danger at bay*, Elea thought, steeling herself as she approached the front door. She'd already seen photos of Sophie, and her resemblance to Liisa could not be denied. Is that why Sophie had been targeted? But why now? And why here? Elea forced her emotions down. Today's visit was about gaining valuable leads in order, hopefully, to mend what was broken.

A blurry figure came into view behind the glass door panel. Elea watched Mitch straighten his posture and it occurred to her how little she knew him. Was he a good detective or merely winging it? What drove him? What was he like on the inside? They might have shared a bed, but she struggled to second-guess him. She only hoped that he wouldn't mess this up.

The door moved silently on its hinges, and Fiona Miller's bloodshot eyes briefly met Elea's before fixing on Mitch. Elea noted the weariness etched into her features, the brunette ponytail not quite containing all her hair. Fiona's Lincoln University sweatshirt, crumpled joggers and stained slippers signalled a domestic life interrupted by a nightmare.

'Come in.' Fiona's tone was flat as she ushered them inside. Mitch had already made her acquaintance, and it was obvious that Fiona wasn't impressed.

'Would you like us to remove our shoes?' Elea asked out of courtesy.

'No need. We're getting the carpets cleaned next week.'

Another memory chimed with Elea: cleaning every inch of her house to stop herself from going mad.

Fiona's living room was a homely space, with nice but worn furniture and family photos lining the walls. Sophie's father stood, watching over his daughter as she sat curled up on the couch. David had just turned twenty-nine, which meant he was only seventeen when he became a dad for the first time. According to intel, he had put himself through college, becoming an electrician's apprentice before branching out on his own. Elea's heart clenched at the sight – a child, safe at home – a reflection of the void in her life. The presence of this little girl who looked so much like Liisa was enough to steal the breath from her lungs. She quickly regained her composure. Getting emotionally involved was dangerous territory right now.

Sophie glanced up at her momentarily, her small hands wrapped tightly around the edges of an iPad.

'So?' Fiona stood, arms folded. 'Have you found him yet?'

'There are several lines of enquiry under way.' Mitch's words sounded practised as he ran through the usual spiel. Elea groaned inwardly. This didn't help their cause.

'That basically means you haven't got a clue.' Disgust seeped into Fiona's words. 'Your team is so bloody useless that my twelve-year-old daughter had to rescue herself.'

David rested a protective arm over his wife's shoulders. Fiona was several inches shorter than him, but Elea got the feeling that she often spoke for them both.

Sophie's gaze shifted between the adults, observing anxiously. Elea crouched down to her level. 'Is that your high score?' she pointed to the iPad screen. 'Wow! You're good. I can't even get half that.' Sophie remained silent, her little fingers stilling on the screen. Elea could sense the level of fear fencing the child in. Her blonde hair cloaked her face as she dipped her head to continue her game.

'Fiona . . .' Elea stood, her voice soft as the woman continued to vocalise her discontent, 'you're right.'

Mitch stiffened, seeming slightly affronted as Elea pressed on.

'The police have let you, your family and, more importantly, Sophie down. They should have done better. They should have done more.'

'Save your apologies,' Fiona replied. 'The damage has been done.'

'I know how you feel.' Elea uttered the words that were guaranteed to get a reaction.

Fiona's eyes blazed with indignation. 'How? How could you possibly know what we've gone through?'

Elea dipped her hand into her bag and produced a Polaroid photo of another blonde girl. Wrapped up in her pink winter coat, Liisa sat astride a stout Icelandic pony, a broad grin spread across her face. Fiona and her husband stared at the image before glancing back at their own little girl.

'My daughter.' The weight of Elea's loss was evident in her tone. 'She disappeared ten years ago.'

Surprise registered on the parents' faces. Here was shared ground.

'I haven't given up on her,' Elea continued. 'And I won't stop looking for the monster who took Sophie.'

A new understanding rose between them as their eyes met.

'You don't think . . .' Fiona's brow furrowed. 'They're not connected – are they? That's not why you're here, is it?'

Mitch shot Elea a warning glance. She wanted to tell Fiona that the small wooden doll her daughter had been found clutching might have belonged first to Liisa. But Swann had warned her not to connect the cases publicly yet.

'We won't know anything until we speak to your daughter.' It was the most Elea could say. 'She's our only witness, so she's very precious indeed.'

Fiona gestured towards Sophie, inviting Elea to sit with her. As she settled beside the girl, Mitch looked on, his presence superfluous. The sudden ring of his phone shattered the new-found peace and Elea seized her chance.

'Take it outside. I'll be there shortly,' she said curtly, her eyes never leaving Sophie.

David escorted Mitch out. As the front door clicked shut, the room fell still and quiet, as if respectful of the traumatised child.

'Sweetheart,' Elea began, her voice a gentle whisper, 'I know things have been scary and you've been *such* a brave girl.' She tried to lock eyes with the child, who was avoiding her gaze. 'But there's someone who needs your help.' She slid two photos before Sophie's iPad and pointed to the first. 'Her name is Liisa. She disappeared in 2016, so she'd be all grown-up now. She pointed to the second, fresher photograph. The blonde-haired girl carried the smallest of smiles in her school photograph. 'Her name is Chelsea. This was taken a few months before she disappeared. Have you seen either of these girls? Can you tell us anything about the person who took you?'

She watched Sophie's eyes, seeking a glimmer of understanding. But the girl shook her head, her lips pressed into a thin line. Elea withdrew the photos. Caution was needed when dealing with vulnerable victims and she had to be careful not to put words in her mouth. She asked the same question in different ways, her heart beating a little faster at the thought of being so close to the truth. But each time Sophie shook her head.

'Do you remember that little doll you were holding? Where did you get it from?' Elea bit the inside of her bottom lip as she recalled Swann's warning not to overshare details of the case. 'Nothing?' she prompted softly, her heart sinking. She glanced at Fiona and David, their hopeful expressions fading with Sophie's persistent silence. 'We'll take things slowly,' Elea assured them. Her eyes returned to Sophie. 'Did you see their face?'

Sophie stared at her iPad, refusing to engage.

'The person who took you – did they say they'd hurt your family if you talked?'

Sophie's eyes widened for just a second. *There it is*, Elea thought. 'That's OK. We won't let anything happen. But I tell you what,' she continued. 'What if a police artist comes? They can help to draw a picture instead. That way you won't have spoken a word.'

Sophie seemed to think it over as she sat, staring into nothingness.

'Sophie?'

The girl delivered a cautious nod before laying her iPad aside and walking out of the room.

'That's enough for now,' Fiona insisted, before following her little girl out.

Elea straightened, massaging the knot that had formed between her brows. If only she could tap into Sophie's memories. She picked up her handbag and handed David her card. 'We'll arrange for a sketch artist. This is my personal number. Call me, day or night, if she says anything at all.'

Elea hadn't expected Sophie to be waiting at the front door.

'She's been rooting in my wardrobe upstairs.' Fiona was holding a white plastic bag. 'She wants me to give this to you.' In Fiona's hand was a bag containing a pair of brown Velcro-strap shoes. 'I bought them as a joke,' she shrugged. 'For a hen-do. We dressed up as old ladies for a laugh.' She glanced at her daughter. 'I don't know what Sophie wants with them, though.'

'Is this for me?' Elea asked, double-checking.

Sophie advanced from behind her mother as she nodded.

'Did *they* wear these?' Not 'he'. Not 'she'. Not her 'kidnapper' or 'abuser'. It was as close as Elea could get without leading Sophie. She had seen cases fail in court because of errors like these. *They'll go after the police procedure*, her boss Heikkinen had once warned. *When they're up against the wall, they'll pick it apart.* Phil Hobbs was quite a different story. But Sophie needed to be handled with finesse. Elea's blood turned cold as Sophie delivered another nod.

Gingerly the girl took the shoes from Elea's hands and placed them back inside the bag. Elea watched, mystified, as she tied the handles in a knot before handing them back. 'Sophie?' Elea called after her as the girl sprinted back upstairs.

David stood in Elea's way, finally breaking his silence. 'Leave her alone. She's had enough.'

'Can you talk to her?' Elea turned to Fiona. 'Because I need to know what the significance of these shoes is. Please.'

'I'll try.' Fiona sighed, unlatching the front door. She wasted no time in ushering Elea out and locking the door securely behind her. The sounds of chains and bolts being drawn was another facet of how their lives had changed.

Mitch was waiting in the car. Elea stepped backwards, shielding her eyes as the morning sunshine pierced her vision. Staring down from the upstairs bedroom was Sophie, her pale face framed by her blonde hair. Elea wanted to reach out to her, to ease her obvious pain. The world was too much for her right now. But as her father closed the bedroom blinds, Elea realised something. Sophie hadn't been gazing at her, she'd been staring at the street, her anxious face a portrait of fear. So that was why she'd hidden the shoes in a bag – so that nobody would know what was inside. Sophie's kidnapper was nearby.

# Chapter Seventeen

## Liisa

### 2016

Johanna's heavy hand presses down on my head and glides across my hair. 'There, there. It's not so bad, is it? Now how about we get you out of these horrible clothes?'

I grip the cup of warm milk that she has given me, squirming as Mikael catches my eye. 'I'll take her.' His thin lips pull back from his teeth as he smiles.

When Mama bought me a new doll, the first thing I did was to change its clothes. Now *I* am the new doll, and I don't want Mikael anywhere near me. I stare imploringly at Johanna before finishing my milk. As much as I hate this woman, I need her.

'Why don't we both go?' She's looking at Mikael the way I look at a dog that I want to pet, but don't trust. Johanna takes my empty cup. Her hand is warm and weirdly comforting as she wraps it around mine. She's frightening, but I'm glad that she's here because I don't want to be left alone with Mikael.

Like a good girl, I follow her out into the corridor, watching my step around the empty Leijona vodka bottles lying on the floor. I try to take in the layout of the cabin. I could pull out strands of my hair and leave traces of myself in the dark corners that nobody cleans. You learn about things like forensics when your mama chases murderers around.

The floorboards creak beneath Mikael's slow footsteps. I hunch my shoulders, because I can almost feel his breath on my neck. Johanna stands next to a door, looking pleased with herself, and I fix my face to match hers. 'This is your room. We've worked hard to get it right, haven't we, Mikael?'

He doesn't answer, just stares as he slowly licks his lips. Now he's swaying from one foot to the other, and I wonder how I ever found these people normal enough to stop and talk to. Why didn't I run across the road? Grandmother was on her way. Then I think about the blue coat that Johanna was wearing, so similar to my grandmother's, and I wonder if she is OK. It's becoming hard to breathe, but I force it. I need to stay strong. Mother is coming. She'll bring police backup and . . .

The bedroom door creaks open. The place they're going to force me to stay in. My stomach lurches, like I've eaten something rotten. I feel like throwing up. This is my prison. Johanna's fist thumps hard against my back and I stumble forward a couple of steps, where I'm hit with the smell of fresh paint and damp. I try to take it all in, because they're both watching me. The space is bigger than my room at home, and it has a toilet and a sink in the corner. Splinters of bluish light from the night sky slice through a boarded-up window, falling onto a double bed. My spirits sink as I take in the metal bath in front of the blocked-up fireplace.

'This is my old room,' Johanna informs me as she takes me

inside. 'I used to light the fire and have a bath here, didn't I, Mikael?'

My stomach churns once more as they look at each other over the top of my head.

'Perhaps when we can trust you, we'll light the fire again.' Johanna lets go of my hand and tells me to sit on the bed. At least the bedspread is clean.

My legs feel like jelly, so it's a relief to sink into the mattress. I look around the room. The single light hanging over my bed is in a small square cage, and I wonder how they change the bulb. The wooden ceiling has been painted blue to look like the sky, with small daubs of fluorescent white paint, which I guess are meant to be stars. I fix a smile on my face because that's what Johanna needs to see.

'That took Mikael hours, didn't it?' Johanna speaks of her son with pride in her voice. 'We went to a lot of trouble for you, young lady.'

'It's lovely.' I find my voice long enough to lie. 'Nicer than my room at home.' I could scream for them to let me go, or cry until my eyes swell shut, but neither of those things is going to keep me safe. All I have to do is to hang on. Mama will be here soon. I blink as Johanna fiddles with a dimmer switch on the wall. The light is stronger now, and it's all too much to take in.

'This is your home now.' Johanna nods to Mikael. 'Get the dress.'

Only now do I notice a big, dark wardrobe looming in the corner of the room. There's a faded panel where a mirror has been removed. My eyes flick to the chair next to it, so that I see it's been bolted down. Only now do I realise why there's a cage over the light. Suicide is something Mum's talked to me about, too. In a country with such long winter nights, we are all familiar with it.

Now Mikael is smoothing down a navy-blue full-length smock-dress with a white lace neckline and buttons that serve no purpose, other than to be ugly.

Johanna points to the drawers in the bottom of the wardrobe. 'You'll find fresh underwear in there.'

The fake smile drops from my face. I don't want to get changed in front of these people.

'Don't be shy.' Johanna's fingers bite into my shoulder as she gives me a little shake. 'We're your family now. You'll get used to being around us.'

I notice her other hand sliding over the home-made stun gun in her pocket. I take the dress from Mikael, rest it on the bed and turn around as I quietly remove my clothes. I can feel his eyes on my skin, but I tell myself to be brave as I unbutton my blouse. I hold it to my chest as I pick up the dress with one hand, then pull it over my head. I'm used to getting changed in front of people. I swim in the lake with my friends all the time. But nobody has ever looked at me the way Mikael is looking at me now. My cheeks burn as I drag the ugly garment over my shoulders and shove my arms inside the long sleeves. I pull my skirt off underneath the dress. I'm not changing my knickers in front of them both. No way.

'Aw . . . Look at this one, all shy.' Johanna chuckles as I turn to face her.

Mikael's eyes bore into me. I glance at the door. Even if I could get past them both, I wouldn't survive the night in the cold.

'*Hei.*' Johanna shakes my shoulder. 'You can keep your

95

modesty tonight, but you'll have to fit in with the rest of us if you want to stay in this nice room.'

I nod, folding my arms tightly against the scratchy material of the hateful dress.

She picks up my old clothes from the bed. My bottom lip trembles. I know I won't see them again.

# Chapter Eighteen

Swann studied the images of the five individuals spread out on his desk. The Divisional Intelligence Unit had narrowed down Phil Hobbs's contacts list to a few potential leads. Each came with its own unique set of circumstances. Elea would be desperate to hunt them down. He gathered up the images and added them to his briefing pack. Everything was online, but he was old-school and printed everything out. *Paperless office, my backside*, he thought. He'd seen a lot of change during his time working for the police, and not all of it was welcome. Standing at the door, he glanced at his team as he prepared to delve into the underbelly of the criminal world.

Elea sat hunched over her desk, too engrossed in the investigation to notice him observing her. She had written up her statement covering the seizure of the Velcro-strap shoes and had organised a police sketch artist to visit Sophie's home. She rarely came back empty-handed when she was on a mission, but the shoes would remain a mystery until Sophie was willing to say more. They'd searched intel for the keywords 'Velcro shoes', but nothing had come up. That wouldn't slow his team down. The tension in the room was palpable, its weight settling on Swann's shoulders as he clutched the intel pack.

'All right, everyone.' Swann's deep voice cut through

the low hum of chatter. 'We've got a lot of work ahead of us.' Mugs clinked on Ness's tray as she handed out coffees and teas. Swann caught Elea's frown as she watched Ness bustle around the room, making sure everyone had a drink. He knew what Elea was thinking: that Ness was a detective, not a teas maid. But such acts of kindness helped keep team morale going, and the team sergeant made sure they took turns. Long hours and cancelled rest days took their toll. A mug of coffee or tea at the right time went a long way.

Swann began his briefing, attaching the mugshots to the board. He gave a stack of printed pages to Mitch to share out. It pained him to delegate, but Mitch was the DI now. Swann had enough high-level strategic work to keep him occupied. However, Elea wasn't the only person with demons. She had no idea how much Liisa's case still haunted Swann. But he was looking for a body, while Elea was searching for the living. He took a deep breath as a burning sensation rose in his chest. Years of eating at odd hours had given him the gift of acid reflux. Or was it the stress of having Elea on his radar again?

She sat, fully attentive as he shared the intel that he had received. He nodded to Mitch, instructing him to take over. He couldn't bear to see the hope etched on Elea's face. If this led to her daughter's kidnapper, it would not end well. Was it easier to live in hope than to know that the person you loved most in the world was dead? Yes, it brought closure, but looking for Liisa was what got Elea out of bed in the morning. The woman was relentless.

'Fergus McCarthy.' Mitch pointed at a mugshot of a bearded man with deep-set eyes. 'He was banged up six months ago for a string of violent assaults. Once a major player in the drugs scene until a rival gang took over his patch.'

Swann was well aware of McCarthy, having been instrumental in sending him down.

Mitch's hand hovered over a picture of a gaunt pock-faced male. 'Malcolm "Monzo" Tanner. He dropped out of sight over a year ago. Rumour has it he's still in the drugs trade, but no one knows where he is or what he's doing.'

'Our third lead, Danny Blackwood.' Mitch referred to the image of a bald man with a thick neck. 'He kicked the bucket three months ago – suspected overdose. He organised teenage dealers and recruited his own kids before the social got involved.'

*The social.* Swann groaned inwardly. *Not 'social services', but 'the social'.* Mitch had grown up on the streets and lacked professional finesse. He could see why Elea was attracted to him. She had a soft spot for forbidden fruit. He focused his thoughts on Mitch's words, pushing his personal feelings aside.

'Sienna Thompson.' Mitch pointed to the only female among the leads. A petite redhead, the young woman had deceptively soft features. 'She's married to our fifth lead, Anthony "Ant" Thompson. Both known for violence offences and are still active in the drugs scene, though they haven't been nicked in a while.'

Swann folded his arms across his chest. 'Handle these suspects with care. There are ongoing operations involving Tanner and McCarthy and we can't compromise them.'

'It's a shame your handlers didn't have eyes on them when Chelsea Hobbs was taken,' Elea muttered.

Swann wouldn't justify the comment with a response.

'Jimmy Kemp is still inside,' Ness chimed in. 'We could arrange for an interview, speak to him about his connections, but he'll probably tell us where to go.'

'Not if there's something in it for him,' Elea murmured under her breath. Swann knew of her tactics and wasn't having any part of it.

'Malcolm Tanner will be harder to find,' Kelly spoke. She was perched on the edge of her table, mug in hand. 'We could do a deep dive with our informants. See if anyone's heard anything.'

'Speak to the CHIS handlers for that area first,' Mitch advised. 'We don't want to step on anyone's toes.' The covert human intelligence sources often provided valuable information.

'Sienna and Ant Thompson are our best bet,' Elea said.

'All right,' Swann continued decisively. 'We'll start with the Thompsons and gather more intel about the others in the meantime. Keep me informed of any developments.' He reminded his sergeant to oversee the taskings and to delegate if anyone was falling behind.

'Yes, boss,' Ray said, rubbing his unshaven face. He shouldn't have needed the reminder, but his heart didn't seem to be in the role.

Swann had seen it many times before. It was called the 'golden handcuffs' by people in his team. Officers who hated their jobs, but couldn't afford to lose the pension if they left. So they stayed, working half-heartedly through each day, counting the hours until retirement came. Mitch would bring it up in his next performance review.

'I'd like to pay the Thompsons a visit.' Elea's Finnish accent subtly coloured her words. 'Today. There's no point in surveillance. Too much time has passed.'

'I doubt surveillance would be on the table, to begin with,' Swann intervened.

'It should be. Chelsea's still missing,' Elea reminded him.

'Leave it with me. It's all in hand.' Swann rubbed the knot forming between his brows.

'You think Liisa's dead, don't you?' Elea stood.

Swann prickled as her words filled the room. This wasn't just about his missing girls. She resented his past handling of Liisa's case. He leaned towards his estranged wife, speaking softly into her ear. 'This isn't the time or the place.'

He waited until Mitch had finished before calling Elea into his office. He'd had enough of her negativity when his team was doing their best. Theoretically she shouldn't be working on this case – not when she was so heavily involved. But there was no official link between her daughter's disappearance and Swann's victims. They'd managed to keep it under the radar so far and she'd been given the all-clear.

'What is it?' she asked, pulling on her coat. 'Because if you've brought me in here to tell me off, then make it quick.'

Swann sighed, wishing he could reach out and give her a soothing hug. He'd whisper in her ear and tell her to breathe, before saying that everything would be all right. 'It's about the doll,' he said gently. 'The forensic results have come back.'

# Chapter Nineteen

There were moments in Elea's life when darkness dropped in on her unexpectedly. The first time was when her mother called saying that her daughter was nowhere to be found. It came again when she learned that her mum's tyres had been slashed. The next heart-stopping moment was when her daughter was officially declared missing. The visits had become less frequent, but even now, when darkness stopped by, it had the power to suck the breath from her lungs. She squeezed her fists, her fingernails pressing crescent-moon shapes into her palms. She had made it this far and would cope with whatever news Swann was about to impart. She recognised the look on his face, as she'd seen it many times before. The 'I hate to hurt you, but you need to know' pitying expression that made her want to turn and walk away.

'What is it?' she blurted, wishing he'd get on with it. *Pull the damned plaster off*, she thought.

Swann crossed his legs, calm as always when delivering bad news. 'We rushed the tests through on the Martta doll that Sophie was holding when she was found.'

Elea raised an eyebrow. 'I thought you didn't have the budget.'

'So did I,' Swann admitted. 'But I requested it anyway and, to my surprise, the powers-that-be accepted it. A lot of money is being thrown at this operation because of the pressure for results.'

'Or maybe you don't want to see me suffer any more than I already am,' Elea said knowingly.

Swann's brown eyes were deep with understanding. 'Either way, the tests came back inconclusive. We don't know if it was Liisa's doll.'

'Of course it was hers,' Elea insisted. 'Where is it now?'

'Property department.' Swann watched her closely. 'But it has to stay there for the duration of the case.'

'Obviously,' Elea smirked. 'What do you take me for? A rookie?' She glanced out of the window at his team and felt a surge of determination. 'Just because Sophie has been found doesn't mean this case is any less urgent. There's still Chelsea Hobbs to consider.'

Swann sighed, the weight of his worries deepening his frown.

Once, several years ago, Elea had held the power to make him smile. 'You never answered me before. You think she's dead, don't you?' She couldn't hide the tremor in her voice.

'If I'm honest, yes,' Swann replied. 'Why else would her kidnapper take another child?'

'Because Chelsea isn't twelve years old any more.' Elea stared into the distance, as if searching for an answer that would bring her daughter back. 'That age is significant to him. But it doesn't mean he's murdered any of them.'

'He's not the child-catcher from *Chitty-Chitty Bang Bang*, Elea. It's hard enough keeping one child hidden, never mind a whole clutch of them.' They exchanged a glance. 'Is that what you really think? That Liisa is part of some band of kids being moved from pillar to post? Because he murdered Jenny Flynn – strangled the life out of her. We . . .' his tone saddened, carrying more than a hint of regret, 'we've just not found the rest.'

'Liisa's alive. A young woman now. And I know that sounds ridiculous,' Elea conceded. 'But all I'm asking is that you keep an open mind.' She stood up then, her eyes glistening with unshed tears. 'I won't be long.'

'Want company?'

Elea shook her head, steeling herself for what lay ahead. She left Swann's office without looking back. Her footsteps echoed in the sterile hallway as she made her way to the property department. Voices echoed from further down the corridor as officers went on with their work. For them, it was another ordinary day.

She approached the uniformed officer behind the property counter, flashing her temporary pass. 'I need to see an item from the Sophie Miller case.' She reeled off the exhibit number. By the look of recognition on the young officer's face, it was evident that Swann had called ahead.

The officer scanned the logbook and handed her a pen. 'Sign in here.'

As Elea signed her name, she glanced at the clock on the wall. She handed the pen back to the officer, who disappeared into the depths of the evidence room. When he returned, he brought a clear sealed exhibit bag that contained the small Finnish Martta doll. Darkness dropped in again. Elea forced her hand to remain steady as she took the bag.

'*Kiitos*,' she said in a low voice, because in that moment

she'd forgotten where she was. The man acknowledged her thanks regardless, and she straightened her spine as she turned, shoulders back, head held high.

Elea made it to an empty side-room before opening the sealed bag. It was all right to handle it, now that it had been tested. She would keep up the chain of continuity and sign, seal and bag it upon her return. Her chest constricted as she stared at the seven-inch wooden doll nestled on her palm. She barely made it to the plastic bucket chair before her legs almost gave way. An anguished cry escaped her lips as she cradled the doll against her chest.

'No. It can't be,' she whispered to herself. She blinked beneath the fluorescent light, turning over the doll in her hand. The small peg-like toy was made from one piece of wood, painted and marked with MARTTA on the bottom. But there was an extra feature on the doll, one she had overlooked: eyelashes. This doll had lashes. A long-buried memory bloomed, suddenly vivid in her mind. Liisa had drawn them on with permanent marker – delicate lashes on this small family heirloom, making her one of a kind. How could she have forgotten? '*Herranjumala.*' Elea whispered to a God she had given up on. Despite everything she had said to Swann, part of her had wondered if there really was a connection or whether the presence of the doll was merely a weird coincidence. The feather she'd received had been one thing, but this . . . This was physical proof.

She stared at the lashes that Liisa had taken great pains to create. 'See? I've made her pretty!' her daughter had said with pride.

'So you have.' Elea had stroked Liisa's fine blonde hair,

unable to be angry at the unexpected defacement. 'Take care of her now. She's a very special gift.'

The doll had been crafted in the fifties and handed down from Liisa's grandmother. And so Liisa had taken care, until now, when it had crossed time and many miles to reach her. Elea closed her eyes, tightening her fingers around the doll. She swiped away her tears, planting a kiss on the doll's small wooden head before returning it to the bag. There would be no more tears. She needed to share this development with the team.

She stood, smoothing down her clothes as she regained her composure. She had a job to do.

# Chapter Twenty

## Liisa

### 2016

I scratch at the yucky stuff on my teeth. Johanna has taken my toothbrush as punishment, and I haven't brushed my teeth in three days. I've been here for a week. At least I think it's a week. I don't own a watch or a calendar, so all the days feel the same. Apart from slaps from Johanna, I've not been hurt under this roof. In the morning we eat porridge with defrosted bilberries, and lunch is leftovers from the day before. For dinner we have fish or some kind of stew from whatever Mikael has hunted in the forest that day. Then he comes into my room and stares at me, like I'm a strange animal that he trapped in the woods and brought home. He's not as excited as he was when he first brought me here. He's a lot, lot quieter these days. No, not quiet. Dark and moody. Like when Christmas is over and you've unwrapped all your presents. Like when you're bored of your Barbie and want to pull off its head. In the deadness of night when everything turns quiet, I stare at the white blobs of paint on the ceiling and think of where I went wrong.

\*

I was walking home from school when it happened. My grandma was supposed to pick me up from the bus stop to take me the rest of the way home, but she was late. I hate waiting in the cold, so I started walking home. My coat wasn't warm enough – I was supposed to get a new one for my birthday. Mum is careful with money, so presents are always things I need rather than want. I was distracted, thinking about my friends and the project we were working on in class. We were making a family tree and I only had half the branches. I looked at my friends' trees, with their parents, brothers and sisters. Some of their branches were really full.

The road was quiet, like usual. That's why the yellow car seemed so weird. Johanna was looking at the front tyre, but I didn't know who she was then. Someone was sitting in the passenger side, and I realised it was a man – Mikael. I checked my watch and walked a little faster, hoping Grandmother would turn up soon. From the corner of my eye I watched Johanna staring at the tyre before she fixed her gaze on me. Mikael got out and looked up and down the road. He seemed nervous about something, but it was too late for me to cross over to the other side. The woman looked nice enough, and I told myself that they *had* probably just broken down. But the tyre she was kicking wasn't flat. I shoved my hands into my pockets and kept my head down as I walked. My nose was throbbing from the cold, and I remember wishing that I hadn't forgotten my scarf.

It all happened so fast.

Johanna was about the same age as my grandmother, but sturdier. She wore the same blue coat, and her hair was tied back in the same style. But her smile was so strange, as if someone had fixed it onto her like a Mr Potato Head. Her eyes were cold and narrow. Nothing on her face matched. 'I thought we had a flat tyre,' she said, in an accent that I couldn't figure out. 'Looks like I was wrong.' She rested her hands on her hips, staring me up and down. 'Would you like a lift home? You shouldn't be walking these roads at your age.'

Mikael was staring at me like he'd never seen another living person before. Sweat glistened on his forehead, despite the frost. He trudged towards me, the sound of his boots in the snow cutting through the quiet winter air. His hand was tucked in his pocket and he moved in a strange way. I didn't like Mikael at all.

'No, thank you.' I spoke politely but firmly as I walked past.

Then Johanna nodded her head. But not at me, at Mikael. Next thing, he was on me and something sharp and painful was jabbed into my back. My teeth clenched from the pain, which felt like fire under my skin. My legs stopped working and my backpack hit the snow. I remember my books spilling out, and Johanna shouting at Mikael to make it quick. I wasn't able to scream, because I couldn't breathe. My legs felt like rubber bands as I was dragged into the back of the car. Then the doors thudded shut and the car started perfectly fine. We were moving, being spun round in a circle before turning the other way.

And now I'm here, stuck in this strange room with no way out. The air smells musty and I can hear water dripping somewhere. It's cold and the darkness is scary. But not as scary as the people who took me. I heard Johanna talking today. She thought I was asleep. Mikael was complaining and I heard her say that I've had enough time to settle in. 'Tomorrow,' she told Mikael. 'Tomorrow we'll tell her why she's here.' Now I'm scared to go to sleep because I don't want to know.

# Chapter Twenty-One

Elea sat in the unmarked police car, Swann's words still ringing in her ears. 'No contact today, only light surveillance. Tomorrow make a softly-softly approach.'

There was no 'softly-softly' in Elea's eyes. When it came to criminals like Sienna and Ant Thompson, you went in hard or not at all. This evening it was not at all. It had taken two hours to get the necessary permission to sit outside the Thompsons' address. To sit. Not to listen or take photos. Just to sit on her backside from the vantage point of a car that smelled like a pizza delivery van. This wasn't surveillance, in Elea's eyes. At the very least they should be camped out in an upstairs room of a nearby building with wide-lens cameras and officers ready to move at each end of the street. Actually, no, that should have happened after Phil Hobbs handed over his stepdaughter on a plate.

Swann had mapped out his reasoning. Sienna and Ant Thompson would be a lot more cautious once they knew the police had eyes on them. But although the couple's car was on the drive, Elea had yet to catch sight of them. She tutted in disgust. This was the pits.

'You all right?' Mitch's eyes creased in amusement from beneath his baseball cap.

'This is a total waste of time. We should go in there and—'

'And nothing,' Mitch interrupted. 'Unless you want me to get the sack?'

'I'm only saying . . .' Elea stared across at the window of the two-bedroom mid-terraced house. 'We've been sitting here for hours. What's the likelihood of something happening tonight, given how long ago Hobbs spoke to them?'

'All the same, we stay put. Due diligence.'

Elea rolled her eyes. Silence fell as the temperature in the car dropped. She willed Ant and Sienna to come out. What did she expect to occur? For Chelsea Hobbs to make an appearance, ready to tell all? Such things happened only in the many fantasies she'd created in her mind. She had dealt with enough crimes over the years to know the lie of the land. Perps weren't clever or calculating. They were of low intelligence and short-sighted. It always came down to the same things: money, sex, drugs, stupidity. But sometimes, just sometimes, Elea met her match. A thought rose in her mind, pushing all others aside. Half an hour, that's all she required. There was no need for violence. She simply needed to talk to them before they called it a night.

'Why don't you go home?' She threw Mitch her most persuasive smile. 'It doesn't take two of us to sit here.'

'And leave you to go full Bruce Willis? I don't think so.'

Elea's smile faded. 'Who?'

'Bruce Willis,' Mitch stared at her, mystified. '*Die Hard*? The greatest movie ever made?'

'Never heard of him,' Elea lied. She wasn't in the mood for banter when she was so close to discovering the truth.

Mitch snorted. 'As if!' An empty beer can rattled down the

road, which was littered with parked cars on either side. They had been lucky to find a space.

Elea groaned as an upstairs bedroom light came on. They weren't seriously going to bed. At this hour? It was only 8 p.m.

'There she is.' Mitch straightened in his seat as he watched Sienna close the curtains. Elea could just about make out that she was clutching a book in one hand.

'And there she goes,' Elea grumbled. 'Off to bed early, to dream about kidnapping more little kiddies.' She turned to Mitch in earnest. 'Let me go. I'll get the truth out of them, like I did with—'

'Not on your nelly.' He grabbed her arm as her other hand crept to the door handle. 'You're not authorised. You were lucky with Hobbs because his missus backed you up, but *she* won't.' He pointed to the upstairs window. The main light flickered off and a softer light bloomed, most likely a bedside lamp. 'She may be small, but she's got serious form, and if it all kicks off, it'll be you who gets arrested, not them.' He paused, studying Elea's face. 'I know it's frustrating, but procedure is there to protect us. We'll speak to them tomorrow, yeah?'

'Seriously?' Elea spoke sharply. 'I didn't win this job in a raffle, you know.' Her voice lowered to a mumble. 'Condescending little prick.'

The blue flashing light of a television screen flickered through the downstairs window of the Thompson abode.

'Sorry. You're right.' Mitch shifted in his seat. 'I'm actually . . . a little in awe of you. I've just got this promotion and I don't want to lose my job.' He stared out at the streets that had not been kind to him once. 'I don't know what I'd do without it. I'm not much good at anything else.'

'I wouldn't say that,' Elea stated reluctantly, lightening the mood. 'But all right. If I must wait, then so be it.'

She stared at the house, imagining Ant settling down before his Xbox or PlayStation for the night. Her gaze lingered over their surroundings, but there were no clues to be had. The couple's black refuse bin sat on the kerb, waiting to be emptied by the council in the morning. The compact front garden was paved over, with a red-brick wall and metal gate protecting their privacy. The car on their drive was nothing flashy. They seemed like any other couple on any other street. But Ant and Sienna had history. Apart from the numerous drug-dealing offences, they had both served time in prison for grievous bodily harm. Then there were the string of suspended sentences, which were becoming more commonplace now that the prisons were full.

The team had worked hard, uncovering a solid link between the Thompsons and Phil Hobbs. It wasn't simply the address book tying them together. Mitch had tapped into his street informant, who claimed that Phil wasn't merely acquainted with the couple; he was deep in debt with them. Word on the street was that the Thompsons had their hands in something darker. Human trafficking.

Elea blinked as droplets of rain splashed their car windscreen, quickly obscuring her view. Mitch cast his eyes beyond the street lights at the dark clouds blotting the moon, their bellies full of rain. That would put an end to their surveillance. It wasn't as if he could start the car to activate the wipers; that would only draw attention to them. There was no point sitting here freezing. She would speak to them tomorrow – all above board.

'Looks like it's down for the night. Let's go.' Mitch didn't wait for a response as he started the car engine and slowly pulled away from the kerb.

Elea's phone beeped with a text. It was another offer from Alice. Maybe it was time for this war to end.

# Chapter Twenty-Two

Swann parked his car in the narrow driveway of his country-side cottage. He sat for a moment, staring up at the blackening sky, a heaviness settling on his chest. It had killed him to pair Elea with Mitch, and he imagined them bonding while they watched the Thompsons' address. Elea didn't do small talk, but Mitch was good at reading people and wouldn't wind her up. You had to be, Swann supposed, when you spent five of your teenage years living rough. Mitch was a decent person – and right now Swann hated him for it. With a sigh, he dragged himself from the driver's seat, turning his thoughts to the family waiting for him.

Everything had happened so quickly with Alice. They'd been dating for six months when he'd ended their relation-ship. Work was demanding too much of his time. Alice had always wanted more than he'd been able to give. She gave him an ultimatum: his job or her. He chose his job. Then she came round to see him one night, armed with his favourite blended Scotch. Work had been tough, and he'd found him-self letting her in. He *had* always wanted children, but his relationship with Alice had run its course. That was the night that she'd conceived the twins.

Swann opened the front door. The familiar scents of home greeted him as he entered the hallway. He'd tried to finish early tonight and had texted Alice at half seven to say that he'd be home within the hour. The savoury aroma of garlic and herbs wafted from the kitchen, but as he rested his coat on the hook in the hall, he picked up on two sets of voices. Who else was in his house?

Jazz music was playing low in the background. It was from the Spotify playlist entitled 'Dinner Party Music' that Alice used to play for guests. That was back before they had the twins. She was at her happiest when entertaining high-ranking colleagues and their wives. She was rarely praised for her policing, but her cooking was something else. He pushed open the door, the smile fading from his face at the sight of their dinner guest. Alice was sitting at the table with Elea, a bottle of red wine between them as if they were old friends.

Alice joined Swann's side with the grace of a panther laying claim to her mate. She rested a hand on his chest and planted a kiss on his cheek with wine-stained lips. She was wearing make-up and had straightened her hair. Gone was the shirt decorated with splurges of puréed carrot; this evening she was wearing a figure-hugging dress that he'd never seen before. She flashed him a dazzling smile, but her eyes were disturbingly cold. 'I invited Elea over for dinner. I hope you don't mind.'

The awkward laugh that left his mouth came all on its own. 'Of course I don't mind. You could have told me, though. I would have bought some wine on the way home.' He almost said, 'You could have warned me', but stopped himself in time. It wasn't Elea he was worried about – it was Alice, who, by the looks of it, didn't need any more booze.

'All taken care of.' She raised the empty bottle from the

table. 'Oops, gone already? Never mind, I've got another one here somewhere.' A tinkly laugh escaped her as she turned to get some more. He didn't believe her cheerful tone for a second. She was up to something, but what? He raised his eyebrows at Elea, who really shouldn't have come. This was no *Fatal Attraction* moment. Her body language suggested that she was just as uncomfortable as he was with the situation. Elea delivered a slight, almost imperceptible shake of her head, a small acknowledgement of his surprise, and that he was right: she shouldn't have accepted whatever invitation Alice had sent. No doubt it wasn't the first. She was probably trying to get Elea here from the moment she touched down in the UK. His stomach knotted as the tension in the room grew. This was going to be a long night.

'How are my boys?' he uttered as Alice handed him a glass of wine.

'Asleep.' She looked at him over the rim of her glass as she took another sip.

Swann sat at the table, avoiding Elea's gaze. Alice wobbled on her heels before muttering something beneath her breath and kicking them off. She filled his plate with osso buco, tortellini and sautéed asparagus, the rich aroma intensifying the uneasy churning in his stomach.

Elea thanked Alice for preparing the meal, her tone polite yet strained. 'You shouldn't have gone to so much trouble.'

'My pleasure,' Alice countered. 'Now eat it all up!'

Swan caught the triumph in her eyes as she rested the veal on her plate. Elea used to be a vegetarian. Now she ate some meat, but certainly not veal. 'I don't eat babies,' she'd said to him once when he'd tried to persuade her to order some lamb. But could Alice have known that? They never ate veal. He stared at the bone sitting in a marrow sauce.

After topping up all their glasses, Alice took her place next to Swann, while Elea sat across from them. For Richard, this obvious show of unity was stiflingly hard to bear.

Alice's smile turned brittle as she filled the silence. 'I always cook for Richard, don't I, darling? Family time is important, after all.'

Swann watched as Elea's jaw tightened, but as she picked at her vegetables, she kept her tone light. 'It must be exhausting, managing the household and the twins. I don't know how you do it.'

'I make it work.' Alice picked up her wine glass. She took a large swallow, a plume of colour rising in her cheeks.

An awkward silence fell over the table as they chewed their food. Swann racked his brain for a neutral topic of conversation, but came up blank. He watched as Elea chased her vegetables around her plate.

'So, Elea.' A hint of a slur tainted Alice's voice. 'There must be more to your life than work, work, work. What do you do for fun?'

Elea's fork paused mid-air, a piece of buttered asparagus hanging off the end. 'There's not much to tell. I keep busy.'

'Of course,' Alice leaned forward. 'Because you have no life of your own, right? That's why you want mine.'

'Hey, that's enough.' Swann squeezed Alice's arm, his voice low. He'd known that this was coming, but the outburst arrived sooner than he'd thought. When Alice got like this, alcohol accelerated her words.

119

She shook him off, eyes blazing. 'What's the plan, eh? Aren't you going to share?'

'Alice,' Elea spoke calmly. 'You'll wake the twins.'

'Why are you worried about them?' Alice snorted. 'You already have my partner. You want my kids, too? After all, you couldn't hang onto your own.'

'Alice!' Swann stared in disbelief. But the damage was already done.

Elea slowly lowered her fork to the table. But Swann saw the flicker of pain in her eyes as she was reminded of her grief. She pushed back her chair and stood. 'I'll see you tomorrow, Richard,' she said softly. 'Goodnight.'

She took her bag from the back of her chair before turning and leaving the room. Swann got to his feet, torn between going after Elea and dealing with the mess Alice had made. The twins' cries drifted from the baby monitor, their sleep disturbed.

'What is wrong with you tonight?' He wanted to shake some sense into Alice as she stared down at her plate, her chest heaving with angry sobs.

'What's wrong with . . .. *me*?' Her words came in stops and starts. 'She's the one who won't give you a divorce!'

But there was no sympathy from Swann as he leaned over her. '*She*'s lost everything.' He snatched the bottle of wine from the table. 'And you've had enough.' He marched over to the sink and allowed the bottle to release its contents down the plughole.

He caught Elea at the front door, pulling on her boots. 'I'm sorry . . .' he muttered, palms outwards in apology.

'I should never have come,' Elea mumbled, barely able to meet his eye.

'Then why did you?' Swann's voice lowered to a whisper.

'Because she kept shitting well texting me.' Elea pulled her phone from her pocket and drew up Alice's recent texts on the screen.

'Even so . . .' Swan sighed.

'The funny thing is, I was actually starting to feel sorry for her. She'd made such an effort – it was pitiful really. But then that comment . . . She couldn't help but stick the knife in.' She gave him a half-smile, the anger evaporating from her words. 'Go. Hug your babies and put them back to bed.'

Her exit was silent as she slipped out through the front door. Sadness carried in her words, because Elea loved children. Alice's remarks would have cut her to the bone. A floorboard creaked in the kitchen. Alice had been listening in. The babies' cries grew louder. Swann loosened his tie and popped open the top button of his shirt. He was getting too old for this. He climbed up the stairs to settle his children, wondering if things could ever be made right.

# Chapter Twenty-Three

'Keep the change.' Elea pressed a twenty-pound note into the hand of the taxi driver before getting out of the car. It was a generous tip, given that she'd only gone a few miles, but he had a look of her father, and the memory of his presence had been enough to calm her down.

'Cheers,' he said, glancing up at police headquarters. 'Stay out of trouble!'

'I *am* trouble,' Elea winked, before closing the car door. She'd have to enquire about hiring a car of her own soon, and perhaps rent a place in Lincoln for the near future, too. If anything, Alice's attitude had made her all the more determined to stay. Tonight it had taken all of her self-control not to launch herself across the table and pull out a chunk of her hair. Alice had not only pushed the knife deep into her chest, but she'd taken pleasure in twisting it. She checked her watch: 10.30 p.m. A lot had happened in the short time that she'd been in Richard's home. Whoever had said, 'Sticks and stones may break my bones, but words cannot hurt me', well, they'd never experienced the loss of a child. *Not loss*, Elea shook the words away. Liisa wasn't dead, and she hadn't lost her, either. She'd been taken, and she would get her back. She stared up at the looming police building, clenching and unclenching her fists.

Dark clouds blotted the moon, casting the car park in a gloomy monochrome. She approached the building, head low, her security pass in hand. Tonight had escalated so quickly. But then again, Alice had already downed half a bottle of red wine by the time she got there. The 2020 bottle of Châteauneuf-du-Pape was one that Richard had kept for a special occasion, according to the mother of his children. There was no inhaling the bouquet for Alice, or swishing it on her tongue – she'd knocked it back as if it was a bottle of cheap plonk. She'd seemed almost pleased to see Elea when she had first let her in.

Richard's presence had changed everything. Elea couldn't deny their chemistry. The knowing looks across the table. The familiarity that only their history could bring. There was love there. Always would be. Alice had felt it, too.

She fumbled with her pass, pressing it against the black electronic pad at the thick metal back door. With a final turn, the door clicked open and she pushed her weight against it to step inside. Had she gone straight back to her hotel, she knew how it would end up – with a drink or three in her hand and a stranger in her bed. She wasn't getting on that merry-go-round tonight. Work would soothe her frayed nerves and stop her endless analysis of Alice's hurtful words.

It was a relief to see that the team had all gone home. She stood among their desks, basking in the smell of stale air, uneaten food and coffee that had turned cold. She clicked on a small desk lamp. Yes, she was exactly where she needed to be. Her footsteps moved quietly as she glanced at each work surface, cluttered with the remnants of a long day. Kelly's desk was neat and tidy, her pens laid parallel next to a thick A4 pad. Her cup had been washed, her computer powered down.

Elea would have known Ness's desk even if she hadn't seen her sitting there. It was just like her personality: disorganised, but comforting. A half-empty plastic tray of cupcakes was perched on one side, an empty Gregg's wrapper next to it, and a chipped but clean mug that read 'World's best nanna' on the other side. The photos on Ness's desk displayed her grandchildren, two boys with bright-pink faces as they posed proudly next to their sandcastles on a sun-washed beach. Elea passed the other desks, each one reflecting the personality of the officer who used it. She thought of her desk in Helsinki, which displayed a photo of Liisa – a constant reminder of her failures as a mum.

She arrived at the office that Swann had yet to hand over, its door slightly ajar. His monitor hadn't been turned off, and the Windows logo bounced softly around on the screen. He was just the same in Finland. She recalled something that she'd told a victim of domestic abuse once: *The people who promise change are the ones who repeat the same patterns over and over again.* Swann had sworn he was moving on, yet now that they were back in each other's company, she was certain this wasn't the case. Were they destined to be in each other's lives for ever?

'Where else would you be?' Swann's voice startled her. He stood, his tall frame filling the doorway, brown eyes locked onto hers.

Elea felt a familiar warmth spread through her and she quickly corrected her posture, relaxing the hand she'd clasped to her chest. 'Are you trying to give me a heart attack? Come to finish me off?'

Swann's smile faded and she immediately regretted the joke.

'Sorry again about Alice's behaviour. We've had words.'

'Unnecessary apology,' Elea replied, a little amused at the thought of Alice getting a scolding from Swann. 'Alice is marking her territory. She wasn't getting a reaction, so she pressed my buttons. She's lucky I didn't take the bait.' She leaned against the desk, her eyes never leaving his. 'I saw your children, by the way. Alice insisted that I visit the nursery while they were sleeping. They're beautiful.'

A mixture of pride and vulnerability flickered across his face, but no words came.

Elea drew in a pensive breath. She was tired of playing games. Everything Alice had said tonight had come from a place of hurt.

'They've got their own language.' Swann smiled. 'I mean, I've heard about twins being close, but Jake and Josh . . . they're so in tune with each other. If Jake hurts himself, Josh will cry, too. I've seen it happen when they're in different rooms.' Elea was going to speak, but Swann continued talking. 'Jake is ahead in everything, walking, talking – he encourages Josh to follow him around.' He chuckled to himself. 'I hope they'll always be like that.'

Elea waited until he was finished. She could feel his pride. There was happiness in his voice when he spoke about them. It helped her to make up her mind. 'Your boys deserve a father, which is why I'm going to do something I should have done a long time ago.'

Swann took a step towards her. Elea swallowed hard, her throat suddenly dry.

'I'll give you your divorce.' A police siren rose in the distance. A reminder that life went on.

She expected relief, gratitude even, but instead an unreadable expression settled on Swann's face. He hesitated for a moment, and her pulse quickened as he leaned towards her. She tried not to get lost in the familiar musky smell of his aftershave.

'Don't sign those divorce papers yet.' He laid a warm hand on her arm.

'Swann,' Elea started, a warning in her voice.

'I'm not sure I want to marry Alice. And it's not just about tonight.'

'She was drunk—' Elea began, trying to brush off his concerns.

'It's deeper than that,' Swann interrupted her once more. 'I'm having . . . doubts.' His eyes searched hers for understanding. An ounce of encouragement.

'Why are you doing this? You left me. Move on with your life.'

'You told me to!' Swann's words stabbed the air.

'I didn't think you'd actually do it!'

Elea closed her eyes. *Dammit*. She hadn't meant to say that. Her words came from that space from which no good could come. From the times when she'd cut a boat free from its mooring and sat like a ghost in her nightdress, floating in the midnight lake. From when Swann had brought her home and whispered into her hair that he would make everything all right. From the times when she'd hugged Liisa's pillow to the hollow of her chest, bereft because she couldn't smell her daughter any more. Each year she grieved for the loss of Liisa's childhood. It had almost broken her.

'I . . .' Swann's voice wavered. 'I should never have left. I'm sorry.'

'Don't apologise. You have your children. I couldn't give you that.' Having another child would feel like a betrayal to her daughter, so Elea had always refused to consider it.

'They weren't planned,' Swann admitted softly, his gaze never leaving hers.

'I can't . . .' Elea spoke in measured tones. She didn't have the bandwidth for anyone else right now. 'Once we find Liisa, once all this is over, I'm going back to Finland.' The words carved a hollowness in her chest. Because at that moment, more than anything, she wanted her husband back.

Swann opened his mouth to speak, but seemed to think better of it. He reached into his pocket and pulled out a set of keys, placing them in Elea's hand. 'My old flat on the Brayford,' he said quietly. 'You need a place to stay while you're here.'

Elea nodded, curling her fingers over the keys. It felt natural somehow.

Swann shifted his weight. 'There's not a day that I don't regret leaving. I should have weathered the storm.'

Elea looked at him for a long moment, studying the lines that had deepened on his face since they'd last been together. The storm was still brewing, but she wouldn't let him know. Hearing him acknowledge his abandonment made something inside her shift. 'I don't blame you,' she lied. 'But I appreciate the sentiment. Now go home, get some sleep.'

'*Hyvää yötä.*' The Finnish words rolled softly off his tongue as he wished her goodnight.

Elea exhaled the breath she had been holding as he left the room. All this time, when she'd presumed Swann was desperate for a divorce, it was Alice pushing the narrative. Alice, who fought like a tiger to keep her family together. Swann said his children weren't planned. She wasn't so sure about that. *Not my circus, not my monkeys,* she reminded herself. She stared at the keys to his Brayford flat. What was she setting herself up for?

# Chapter Twenty-Four

## Liisa

### 2016

Last night I cried so hard that my stomach muscles ached. I haven't cried this much since my dog, Onni, died last July. But then Mother was there to comfort me. She took a day off work for his funeral and that morning we picked tufts of blue vetch and ox-eye daisies to lay on his grave. It was hot that day, the stems of the plants sticky in my hands. Mother bought ice cream and we had waffles for dinner with chocolate sauce. She wasn't a good cook, but she was always there when I needed her the most. I remember the warmth of her body that night, as she spooned me in my narrow single bed. Her chin resting on my shoulder, she whispered that Onni was old, and we'd been lucky to have him for so long. Dearest Onni. Now my heart hurts and my eyelids are swollen, but this time I'm on my own. I close my eyes tightly, trying to imagine what she'd say.

The dripping hasn't stopped. *Drip . . . drip . . . drip . . .* It's been going on all night as I try to plan my escape. Mother would tell me to think bigger. *Tyvestä puuhun noustaan*: you climb a tree from the base; start from the roots. My nights are dark and scary, but at least Johanna and Mikael leave me alone, giving me time to think. Now where was I? My thoughts have wandered. Oh yes, start at the base. I'll begin with my room. Is there anything here that can help me to escape? Because I can't do this on my own. I'm not strong, but I *am* fast. If only I had run that day. *Stop it. Back to the base: my room.*

I do this all the time: start thinking about getting away, but then I feel scared and it's easier to imagine all the things I should have done. I need my mother. I need her to take my hand and tell me what to do. *Start at the base*, she says, once more. But there's nothing in this room to help me. Everything is nailed down or caged. The windows are shuttered, thick nails battered from every direction. I imagine Johanna: with her hammer, her strong arm lashing out at the wood. It is splintered in places, but not going anywhere. Like me.

So what next? *Drip . . . drip . . . drip.* The weather. I stare at the ceiling, each splatter of melting ice bringing hope. The snow is thawing. Good things come slowly. If the weather warms up, maybe I could survive outside. But it's January. I know how to forage, but there's little at this time of year. Unless I try to store away some food? Johanna: I think of the nails flattened into the wood – she'd give me a beating, or worse. There's a darkness about her that frightens me speech-less. As for Mikael, his face is a mask I can't see through.

I hug myself and count my breaths to calm down. In, out – no time for tears today. Morning will be here soon. Mama will come. That's all there is to it. So I don't need to start from the beginning and work my way out of here. Still, my thoughts creep to the door. There's a small chink of light underneath. Johanna always leaves a light on in the hall at night. There's a bolt on the other side. Sometimes Mikael grunts when he has to pull it across, but Johanna slides it like a knife through butter. There is always someone in the cabin. Johanna might go to the outhouse for wood when Mikael is hunting in the forest, but she's never far away.

I jerk at the sounds of movement coming from the hall. I must have fallen asleep. Johanna's heavy footsteps make the floorboards creak in protest. I am grateful for the rickety cabin that warns me when she is near. I sit back on my elbows, tiredness making my body heavy. She slides the lock across and I get ready to do as I'm told. Johanna does not like to wait. She is not patient, like my grandmother. Nor is she kind. My heart flip-flops, as it always does when my prison door is open. The smell of meat cooking reaches my nostrils and my stomach growls loudly.

Johanna is smiling. Her face is expectant, like it's her birthday and she's waiting for me to give her a cake. It's not her birthday, is it? I try to remember everything she's said since I've come here.

'Good morning.' Her voice is strangely upbeat. 'Get dressed. Today is the day.'

My mouth falls open as I try to understand.

Another smile. It unnerves me. I don't trust it.

'Don't you want to know why we brought you here?'

# Chapter Twenty-Five

Elea closed her eyes against the cascading water of her rain-fall shower. She'd had to drag herself outside for her morning run, but she felt better for it now. A short sleep had left her with scattered nightmares and a lingering sense of unease. Her daughter's yellow school bag was part of a recurring narrative that wouldn't let go. Every night in vivid colour she was presented with the image of that damned yellow rucksack rotting in the heavy snow. If only someone had seen it that day. Too much time had been wasted searching in the wrong places and knocking on neighbouring doors. Because it was Porvoo, right? A place where a neighbour would let you use their phone or even give a child a lift home. The town had convinced itself that what had happened to Anu and Venla could never happen again. Yet it had, years later, on the same date.

With her thick towelling robe wrapped around her, Elea stood at her hotel window, staring at the silvery-grey clouds that seemed to be a permanent fixture in the Lincoln skies. She clutched her mug of coffee, tendrils of steam carrying the scent of instant granules that tasted like tar. Her thoughts firmly in Porvoo, she pictured the small wooden sauna at the side of her home. She missed the ritual of heating the sauna stones, the hiss of steam as she ladled water and the comfort of being enveloped in a soothing cloud of warmth. She missed sitting in quiet reflection, the firmness of the wooden bench beneath her body as she relaxed. And oh, how she missed the invigorating shock of stepping into the cold, crisp air. Her sauna had been her sweaty sanctuary from the world.

Nestled along the Porvoonjoki river, her house sat amongst a mosaic of pretty pastel-coloured wooden houses with cobblestone streets full of storybook charm. Her buttermilk-coloured two-storey abode came with cute trimmed window boxes that hosted a variety of flowers soaking up the summer sun. Being a single parent, she didn't have a lot of money, but her life had been idyllic. She just didn't realise it at the time. But now she was deep in the belly of grief, after being plucked from her happy existence and swallowed whole. She sipped her coffee, grimacing at its bitterness. Swann was right: she really needed a place of her own. Somewhere she could make a decent brew, at the very least. She turned away from the window. This room was too small, too restrictive. She tipped her coffee down the porcelain bathroom sink, watching the dark-brown liquid circle the drain. Soon. She would move into his flat. That's if Alice didn't find out and set the place alight first.

The ring of her phone snapped her out of her reverie. Only her mother would call at 6 a.m. '*Hei.*' Elea gave a half-smile as she answered. Her mother proceeded to speak in Finnish, although her English was perfectly acceptable. Pete, her dad, had been a taxi driver before he moved to Finland for a change of scene. The hippy and the British taxi driver. It had been quite the love story, back in the day. It was why Elea had got on so well with Swann, she supposed, as she had recognised his need for a respite from his normal life.

'I didn't wake you, did I?' her mother asked. 'You sound tired.'

'I'm fine. Been up since five.' Elea walked to her bedroom and stood before the wardrobe. 'How are you? Still beating Otso at chess?'

Her mother exhaled a chuckle. 'He gets so cross. I let him win sometimes.'

'Men and their pride.' Hilma and Otso had been lifelong friends. Otso, with his kind face, oversized glasses and shiny white dentures. It comforted Elea that her mother wasn't alone while she herself was busy chasing answers thousands of miles away. Silence passed between them. This was the space Hilma always gave her before bringing up Liisa. Her mother's devotion to Buddhism had got her through the toughest of times. Elea envied her calm ability to accept whatever life threw at her, even when it hurt like hell.

'How's it going?' Hilma probed gently. 'Any more leads?'

'I don't want to jinx it.' Elea stood before the wardrobe, working out what she was going to wear. 'But we're close.' She pulled out a Filippa K tailored blazer, matching it with a white shirt and slim-fitting black trousers.

'Meditate,' her mother advised. 'It's food for the soul.' Hilma's words were soft, but focused. She was the kind of person that it felt good to be around. She had cried for three days solid after Liisa disappeared, blaming herself for not being able to pick her up on time. It took her another two weeks to pull herself from the mire of despair. Elea knew her mother would never get over what happened, far less forgive herself for not being there. Elea didn't have the capability to help her at the time. Otso had been her rock.

'You're Buddhist. You don't believe in souls.' Elea slipped off her robe.

Hilma exhaled the type of patient sighs usually reserved for four-year-olds. 'You know what I mean. How's Richard?' She had a soft spot for Swann.

'You know very well how he is.' Hilma had met Swann's mother when she first visited Helsinki and they had kept in touch ever since. Elea cradled the phone on her shoulder as she stepped into her underwear. Her clothes were carefully orchestrated, but her bras and knickers rarely matched. She didn't have *that much* free time on her hands.

'Any . . . sparks between you?'

'Not a flicker,' Elea lied. 'Mum, I've got to get ready for work.'

'Have a beautiful day, my darling. Be kind to yourself.' The compassion in her voice made Elea bite her bottom lip hard. *Hold it together*, she warned herself.

'Will do. Love you.' Elea ended the call. She rested her phone on the hotel bed. Was she as close to finding Liisa as she'd hinted to her mum? She wasn't sure which was the most frightening prospect: still looking for her daughter when she reached her mother's age or finding her remains before then. Because common sense – dreadful, brutal common sense – told her that Liisa couldn't still be alive. Too much time had passed. If the killer had come to England, there was no chance in hell that Liisa was in tow.

She fiddled with the buttons of her crisp white shirt. One question nagged like a painful hangnail that she couldn't stop playing with. How the hell had he lured Liisa into his car? And there had been a car or a van, or transport of some sort.

A witness had reported seeing Liisa walking home on the day she disappeared. Fifteen minutes later another passer-by saw nobody on the lonely stretch of road. Elea didn't want to think about the level of force someone would have used to make her daughter comply.

She sat at the dressing table and unzipped her make-up bag. She couldn't imagine her life outside this existence of grief and hope and work. She both loved and hated the police. Loved it for being something she could cling on to; hated it for not being there when she needed it most.

She stared into the mirror, remembering her mother's advice, 'Don't give up.' She spoke the words that Elea needed to hear. 'You'll find her. She's still out there.' That was as close to being kind to herself as Elea could get.

# Chapter Twenty-Six

Elea followed Mitch from the police-station car park to the unmarked vehicle he'd booked out for the job. The sky was iron-clad, the sun yet to make an appearance. She was comfortable in her hoodie and tracksuit bottoms, while jeans and a puffer jacket seemed to suit Mitch. They had dressed to pass for a couple on the hunt for a fix. The couple they were visiting would be twitchy about visitors, and paranoid about being watched. She smiled to herself as Mitch shoved his hands deep into his coat pockets. In Finland winter wasn't just a season, it was a force. It wrapped itself around you, quiet and unforgiving as it hung on your every breath. English weather was a little kinder. January brought a creeping discomfort, the chill more of a wet slap than a Finnish icy cut.

'Are you cold?' she spoke with a smile. 'Would you like me to buy you some gloves? A scarf, too, perhaps?' She trod carefully on the road, which was coated with a fine sheen of ice. 'Or some cosy socks for your chilly little feet?'

'There's nothing little about my feet.' Mitch pressed the central locking button on the key and the car lights flashed into life. 'As well you know.'

Elea bit back her smile as she opened the car door. There were times like these – brief glimmers of amusement – when she felt like a normal person going about her work. She was happy to let them in. She couldn't be angry twenty-four/ seven. She had been there, done that and set herself on a path of self-destruction that could have cost her more than her job. Heikkinen had been supportive, but even her usually placid boss had lost his patience in the end. It wasn't her raging hangovers that bothered him, or the strangers she slept with at weekends. It was how she'd constantly crossed the line at work. An angry detective with a loaded gun made for a dangerous cocktail, especially when dealing with crimes involving children. Those suspects invoked an anger that she could not control. She would have ended up killing someone eventually. Heikkinen had forced her to take a holiday. Swann's call couldn't have come at a better time. As he kept reminding her, she was no good to her daughter in jail.

She clicked her seatbelt into place as Mitch turned the heating on to full. It was an early start for both of them, to make up for their fruitless stakeout the night before. Everything was arranged. Two colleagues would meet them at Ant and Sienna Thompson's address. The warm air infused with the Magic Tree car freshener dangling from the mirror was making Elea feel nauseous. She jabbed at the button to turn down the heat. For the last twenty-four hours she had immersed herself in the case files, reading statement after statement from those who had come into contact with the abducted girls: teachers, football coaches, Girl Guide leaders. But the people they were visiting today had never been linked to the case – until now.

'I don't know why we can't arrest them,' Elea complained. Mitch was driving too slowly for her liking, cautiously negotiating the frosty Lincoln roads.

'Why *I* can't arrest them, you mean. I'd be taking responsibility, not you.' Mitch turned back onto the street they'd left the night before. He slowed the car next to the pavement, expertly reversing it into a parking space two doors down from Ant and Sienna's terraced home.

'There's no need to be so pedantic.' Elea sniffed, undoing her seatbelt. 'You only need suspicion to make the arrests. Bring them both in.'

'And send the rest of their cronies underground? Nah. Not today.'

Mitch had a point. He stared out onto the streets as a pensioner walked past, his terrier wrapped up in a tartan coat. Had Chelsea gone missing a week or even a month ago, then suspects would be apprehended today. But too much time had passed. Whatever they had going on now needed to be handled with care. Secret undercover operations were already ongoing with regards to Ant and his associates. The team hadn't been aware of it until now. A warning had been issued by senior officers. Elea and Mitch could speak to the couple, but that was it. A gentle, patient approach was the best thing right now. But it didn't mean Elea felt any better about it.

'I'll do the talking,' Mitch eyed her sternly as he pressed the rusting buzzer on the door. Police backup had been brought in, in case things took a turn for the worse. An officer had been posted near the back, in case Ant or Sienna tried to do a runner, and DC Ollie Evans sat in an unmarked police car up the road. Mitch updated them both via the police airwaves, his radio discreetly placed inside his coat. Elea had been given a radio too and she turned the volume down.

139

It didn't take long for the door to open, and both Elea and Mitch were met with dismay.

'Whatever you want, the answer's no,' Ant Thompson said, looking them up and down. He was wearing striped pyjama bottoms, looking slim but toned in a sleeveless white vest. His auburn beard was neatly trimmed, his deep-set blue eyes filled with suspicion.

'Who is it, babe?' The voice of Sienna Thompson trailed from the hall.

Mitch was about to speak when Elea butted in, giving a very discreet flash of her Finnish warrant card. It was quick enough for them not to realise what country it had been issued in. 'Here's the choice. Let us in or we'll make this public, and you won't want that.'

'Oh, for fuck's sake.' Ant rolled his eyes. 'What do you lot want now?'

'A few minutes of your time, that's all. And it's in both of our interests if we do this inside.'

'Let them in,' Sienna said flatly, joining Ant in the hall. She was in her dressing gown, her blonde hair trailing over her shoulders. 'We've done nuthin' wrong.' She peered out onto the hostile streets before allowing them both inside. It would not do their reputations any good if the police were seen hanging around their home. Criminals sometimes turned informant for a few extra quid. Sienna and Ant Thompson couldn't afford such rumours getting out about them.

The house was cleaner than Elea expected. The carpets were thin but spotless, the walls decorated with photos of far-flung places. Images of the cobbled streets of Lincoln were positioned near A4-sized photos of Thailand, Vietnam

140

and Singapore. Elea recognised them all. The walls were a burnt-orange colour, and as they were led into the living room Elea took in every facet of it. The smell of cannabis tainted the air. No surprise there. A purple bong sat on a coffee table next to an old bookcase. Its shelves contained a mixture of novels, from Colleen Hoover to Stephen King. Elea's eyes wandered over the Xbox in the corner, accompanied by a variety of war games. But no family photos and, thankfully, no children present.

'Don't make yourselves comfortable.' Ant glared at them both. 'What do you want?'

Mitch cautioned them both before Elea had time to speak. 'You're not under arrest,' he reiterated as he explained that the interview was voluntary. 'Does the name Chelsea Hobbs mean anything to you?'

'No. Why should it?'

But it was too late for denial. Elea had already caught the glimmer of recognition in Sienna's eyes.

# Chapter Twenty-Seven

There was no greater challenge than bringing a murderer to justice. Unsaid promises were made to the victim's families from the moment the news broke. A vow had been made to Elea, too. The burden of these promises never weighed as heavily on Swann's shoulders as they did now. He sat at his desk, watching the grim crime-scene video for what felt like the hundredth time. It had been filmed as dawn broke, with the rising sun colouring Lincoln's West Common in an eerie sepia hue. Each small sound was amplified in the stillness of the new day – a day that would bring pain to so many people, its aftershock wide-reaching.

The girl had been discovered next to a walking trail, her body positioned on its side beside a wooden fence. The 250 acres of grassland were enjoyed by locals seeking peace from the noise of the city, and it was an early-morning jogger who had found Jenny Flynn semi-buried in the falling snow. Every aspect of the discovery had been filmed. Linda, their crime-scene manager, had been meticulous with her recording, taking her time as she scoped every aspect of the scene.

Swann was familiar with every sound and sight. Every breath that Linda had inhaled. The pressure of her boots driving the stepping plates deeper into the snow. He closed his eyes, placing himself back there. The whinny of horses in the distance. The rare kee-yaa call of a buzzard as it circled the skies above. The icy breeze flapping the crime-scene tape – the air cold enough to numb the tips of your fingers and toes and to make your eyes and nose run. He opened his eyes because he knew what was coming next. The sight of twelve-year-old Jenny lying on her side, her face half buried in the snow. The image was burned into the back of Swann's mind. The blueness of her lips. Her pale, mottled skin. He rubbed his chin, missing the beard that Alice had forced him to shave off months ago. It made him look old, apparently. But in reality it just made him look his age.

Swann watched the video pan slowly across the garland of fake flowers placed on the girl's soft blonde hair. According to forensics, she had been initially laid on her back, then later moved onto her side, her face placed downwards into a pillow of snow. Had her killer returned to the scene? Been unable to stand the accusation in her open eyes? Or had somebody else interfered? They might never know. The camera moved slowly, capturing the white dress with its delicate ribbon and lace. Hundreds of man-hours had gone into investigating the clothes Jenny had been found in. The dress was home-made. It was old, and they hadn't been able to source the material or the design. It was too tight for her body, the zip at the back a little undone. The screen showed Jenny's slim ankles and her white patent shoes. Shoes that weren't scuffed or worn until that day, by the look of them. Swabs had been taken from Jenny's face and clothing, and tape used to pick up any fibres or DNA. But there was nothing – apart from the bleach that the killer had washed her body in. There were traces of

143

plastic, too, most likely what she'd been wrapped in while they made the journey there. Whoever put her down was forensically aware.

Hundreds of officers had worked on this case, as well as resources from other forces brought in to supplement staff. Leads could come from any number of places, and Swann's team had worked themselves into the ground to chase them all. He had never immersed himself so deeply in a case, apart from when Liisa disappeared. Ever since then, Swann had been careful when describing victims within his team. It was something he'd learned from Elea – something that might not have occurred to him before. Usually, in a briefing, words such as 'corpse', 'cadaver', 'remains' and 'body' were bandied around. Now he avoided such terms when he could. Personalising the victims made them more real.

There were times when officers needed to distance themselves. Their mental health was important, too. But when it came to Jenny Flynn and the other kidnapped girls, Swann continually personalised the case. He told officers about her hopes and dreams. Showed them videos the girls had uploaded online. Made them as real as somebody they knew: a daughter, a sister, a niece. He worked with their media team to keep them alive in the press. He had even been interviewed on Sky News and *Good Morning Britain*. But now he couldn't publicly reveal the biggest lead they've ever had – that it appeared as if the case of the Ice Angels and Operation Turnstile were linked. It was too early for such a big presumption, and linking the case would get Elea kicked off the team. *Would it be such a bad thing?* He dismissed the thought. As unpredictable as Elea was, she got results. Besides, he knew how much this meant to her. She'd camp out, if she had to. She'd never leave this case now. Swann stopped the playback. She would be here soon. Had someone dressed Liisa like that? Placed her deep in the snow? Somewhere she would never be found?

Swann had spoken to Heikkinen again. He'd needed to know more. The Ice Angel case had turned cold years ago. It was hardly surprising, given how old it was. Elea kept pushing for reinvestigation, becoming more insistent, more violent, until she was forced to take a break. Swann had unknowingly thrown Elea a lifeline by inviting her to consult on this case. And now she was returning to the station, having got nothing from Ant and Sienna. She had left their address without fanfare as the couple refused to help. But Swann knew Elea. She would never have given up on them so easily. What was she up to now? He braced himself as she entered the office. He would find out soon enough.

# Chapter Twenty-Eight

## Liisa

### 2016

I try not to stare at Johanna's crooked brown teeth as she stands over me, clothing hanging limply over her arm. Each night she spends an hour on her sewing machine. She dresses me up like a doll. But the material is always rough on my skin, the dresses ugly and ill-fitting. The welcoming smell of freshly cooked pastries and coffee wafts in from the kitchen.

'Get up. Breakfast is ready.'

She hands me the thick, flowery material. It's a dressing gown, with a frayed blue waistband. The floor chills the soles of my feet as I quickly step out of bed. She waits as I go to the toilet in the corner of my room. I wash my hands with a sliver of soap and water from the pail before shrugging the dressing gown on. Today is different. She usually makes me get dressed first thing. There are no days off in this horrible place. Each morning she puts me to work – scrubbing, cleaning, cooking, washing, which has given me callouses on my palms. She's said she'll teach me sewing and knitting, too. If only that's all I was here for. The thought of what could be waiting for me keeps me awake at night. My fingers peep out from the end of the wide sleeves.

Johanna's smile turns small and pinched as she tugs on the ends, folding them over until she can see my hands. 'That's better.' Then there's the horrible sudden thump of her fist on my back that I've come to hate. I'm pushed forward a couple of steps, my eyes still sticky with sleep. 'Move it. I haven't got all day.' She goes to push me again, but I'm ready this time and briskly make it to the door. You don't question Johanna. You do as you are told.

Mikael is waiting at the table, which holds quite the feast: boiled eggs, rye bread, cheese and Karelian pastries that Johanna seems to have made herself. The imprint of her thick fingers is pressed into the pastry, which holds a generous portion of rice porridge, served with egg-butter mix. But I don't want any of it, because my stomach is rolling over. This is the moment when Johanna and Mikael tell me why I'm here.

She pushes a cup of coffee in my direction and watches as I sip. I try not to grimace as the bitter liquid scalds the back of my throat. 'Thank you,' I say, because in Johanna's home, manners are everything.

Johanna nods, seeming pleased that my house-training is going well. 'Today is a special occasion.' She looks to her son. 'Isn't it?'

'Yes, Mama,' he nods obediently, but his eyes are dark as they creep in my direction.

Johanna rests a pastry on my plate. 'I'll show you how to make them,' she says proudly. 'You'll need to know, now that you're . . .'

I wait for her to finish, but she reaches for a boiled egg

147

and slices through the shell with her knife. Turns out that the eggs are soft-boiled, as orange liquid oozes from the over-sized blade. She carries it in a sheath that is buckled around her waist. It's the same knife she uses to gut fish, or what-ever creature Mikael hunts down in the woods. Goosebumps prickle my skin as Mikael and I exchange a glance. The air thickens between us as I study his face. The scar on his cheek. Those wide, haunted eyes. He is so quiet these days. Who should I be most scared of here? The pastry turns to sand in my mouth. I sip the strong coffee, forcing it down. At home, I used to drink milk. How I miss it now. We work our way through the rest of the food. I don't know when I'll eat again. That usually depends on Johanna's mood.

She brushes the crumbs from her woollen jumper and sits back, satisfied. It will be my job to clean up the mess, but I can't move, not yet. I count each second of silence. Eleven . . . twelve . . . thirteen. The cup of coffee shakes as I bring it to my mouth. I hold it firmly with both hands. I don't want to hear this. I want to run. *Tick, tick, tick* – the clock on the wall counts the time with me.

'We brought you here for a reason.' Johanna's voice breaks the quietness of the room.

My cup clinks as I rest it on its saucer. I can't swallow any more. The air feels so thin, I can barely catch my breath.

'We know who you are . . . were.' Johanna rests her eyes on me. 'You come from good stock. Your grandmother was a university lecturer in Helsinki. Your mother a police detec-tive. You are a clever girl. Good blood.' She nods to herself.

What does she mean by 'were'? I stare, unblinking as I wait for answers.

'But you're not that girl any more. You live with us now. We will call you Lia.'

I squirm in my chair as every cell in my body screams at me to run. She clamps a firm hand down onto my forearm, pushing it hard into the table. I press my lips together as her dirty nails dig into my arm.

'Tell her, Mikael. Tell her why she's here.'

Mikael's Adam's apple bobs as he clears his throat. His mouth spreads in a slow smile. The sound of his fingers drumming on the table gets under my skin. I can't read him, and that's what scares me the most. Mother is good at figuring people out. She's taught me little bits. Like how to take in what she calls 'non-verbals': how to study traits like blink rates (a normal blink rate is eight times a minute) and how people appear when they're angry or uncomfortable. Someone's appearance – such as bloodshot eyes or unwashed hair – can tell you a lot. But I think a place can tell you a lot too, and this creepy old cabin has spoken to me many times. I see the selection of knives that Mikael keeps in the kitchen and how comfortable he is handling them. I see the mounted deer heads on either side of the fireplace and know that they weren't bought in a store. I see how dirty the place is, and how fine Johanna is with that. It tells me that she came from a home that wasn't well cared for. I see the bolts on the doors. Mikael's high-powered binoculars and the sharp-edged teeth of the traps that he sets. The gun cabinet. The home-made stun gun.

Sometimes Mikael can be cruel. Other times he looks like he wants to die. His moods are like a rusty old see-saw. Today it feels like he wants to crawl under my skin. My heart is rising up into my throat and a chill sweeps beneath my oversized dressing gown. He's enjoying making me sweat. I am a little girl playing grown-up, not ready to hear whatever he is waiting to say. The fire in the living room delivers quiet flames. I'm getting used to the smoke that is blown back down the chimney when it's storming outside. It used to sting my eyes and make them water, but now I'm grateful for the heat when I'm allowed out of my room.

I wish that I'd been able to get dressed. I feel naked, even though Johanna's old home-made dressing gown is covering me, right down to my ankles. It's giving off this sickly smell like cheap, flowery perfume, and the collar is edged with a crust of black dirt. Who puts perfume on a dressing gown? Still, I want to shrink inside it, like a tortoise hiding in their shell. The silence is deafening. Mikael was different when he first took me, like a toy wound up too hard. Then I think of the sepia bottles of tablets piled up in Johanna's bathroom and it makes me wonder. Had he taken something that day? She won't let me clean there alone. I watch Mikael's tongue dart from his mouth and slide across his lips. It's a weird habit that makes me feel like I'm his next meal. The drumming stops. I clutch a handful of dressing gown as he takes a breath to speak. From the way he is looking at me, no good will come from what he has to say.

'Mother . . .' he starts, his eyes flicking to Johanna's. 'She's not well.' His jaw tenses, then he looks at me once more. 'She doesn't have long left, do you, Mother?'

I inhale a sudden breath. Touch my collarbone and pinch my skin to stay in this moment. I do this a lot now, because I can't afford to react. I had not expected this.

'That is correct,' she replies, with the calmness of someone checking homework, instead of saying they're dying. She leans forward, her eyes turning dark as she looms over me. Her voice is as low as a growl. 'But do not mistake illness for weakness. I am still as strong as ever.'

Mikael laughs. A low, dry sound. It's so out of place in this moment. The cabin creaks around us. Watching. Listening.

I nod at Johanna because I don't know what to say. *Why are you doing this? What has you dying got to do with me?* I want to ask, but can't. I force myself to look sad. She seems satisfied by my reaction.

Mikael sits back in the hard wooden chair as Johanna takes over explaining why I'm here. 'This thing inside me – this cancer – it's taking me quickly. But I can't leave my darling alone.' She gives her son an encouraging smile.

His face turns serious as his pale, mistrustful eyes land on me. 'We are to be together. You will cook and clean, and I will mend the house and get food. We will live here, as a family. Understand?'

I frown. What does he mean, 'as a family'? Is he related to me after all? I realise that I am rocking slightly, back and forth on the chair, and I stop.

Mikael picks up a small, sharp knife from the table and uses the point to pick his nails. 'You are to be my wife.' He stares at his nails as he speaks. 'We will have children.'

And then my world begins to shift, like it does when you're in a nightmare. You want out, but you are trapped. Forced to watch it play out. I look to Johanna, because surely he is wrong. This is a joke . . . isn't it? A silly cruel joke. Any minute now they will both laugh. Because how can I be his

151

wife? I am twelve years old. Children – he wants children. I grip my throat with my hand because I can't swallow now. I am a child. How can that be? I can't do this. Johanna is watching me, but her expression is far away.

'I . . . I don't understand,' I finally say, because they're waiting for a reply. Another gust of wind drives its way down the chimney with a howl and the sudden influx of smoke makes me cough.

'You don't need to understand.' Johanna fixes me with a stare. 'You just need to get used to the idea. You are going to own this lovely cabin with Mikael. You will live off the land, and once a month you will go shopping and buy supplies. You will be a family. You will use your new name, and you will look after my boy when I am dead.' She nods to herself, giving a crooked smile to Mikael. There are cold sores on either side of her mouth and her lips are so badly chapped that she makes my stomach churn.

I can't look at Mikael. I want to plead with Johanna instead. She's a woman. She must understand how wrong this is. 'But I'm only twelve.' Fresh tears find their way into my eyes.

Johanna tuts. 'You're not getting married today, silly girl. Not until you are a woman. After your first bleed.'

Mikael's knife glints as he scrapes the dirt from beneath his fingernails. I don't know what to say. Time passes. Johanna stares at me so hard and I push down the scream rising up into my throat.

# Chapter Twenty-Nine

'When are you moving out?' Elea picked up a marble paperweight from Swann's desk and laid it back down again. She was dressed in her suit, the casual clothes discarded for now. The briefing had been conducted and she had shared details of her fruitless visit to Sienna and Ant's home. 'Your new office is down the hall, isn't it?' she teased as she stood by his desk. 'Having trouble letting go?'

'You're one to talk about letting go.' Swann sat back in his chair, watching her every move. He seemed to regret the comment as the smile slipped off her face. 'Sorry. I meant . . .'

'No apology needed. You're right.' Elea felt strangely upbeat as she wandered around his office, taking everything in. 'But it's a strength, not a weakness. If your boys went missing, who would you want on the case?'

'We both know the answer to that.' Swann folded his arms during the rare moment of respite. He was always on the go, attending strategy meetings and press conferences, trying to make the allocated budget stretch, managing the number of people needed to keep the investigation moving forward. 'But it's your inability to let go that makes me wonder,' he continued. 'Why did you walk away from Ant and Sienna so easily?'

'Ah. So that's why you sent backup. You thought I'd kick off, didn't you?'

Swann didn't deny it. Elea saw herself as a competent officer with many years of experience under her belt. She could read a situation. Knew when to use force and when to wait it out. Must she always be babysat by those below her rank? It was insulting to be seen as some deranged, grief-stricken woman. Had she been a man, things would have been different.

'I'm playing the long game with those two,' Elea admitted. 'Or rather, with Sienna. She knows something about Chelsea Hobbs. I could see it in her eyes.' She straightened a certificate on the wall – one of the many commendations that Swann had received.

'That may be so, but she won't talk to you while Ant's around. Her loyalty is to her husband.'

'I wouldn't be so sure about that.' Elea had met lots of people like Sienna in the course of her career. Respectable young women who fell in love with 'bad boys'. Addicted to the initial excitement, they gave up everything they knew – friends, family, their jobs; decisions they would come to regret. They spiralled into violence, mistaking their partner's intense possessiveness for love. Elea had looked into Sienna's history and the intelligence pack provided by DIU. Sienna's past episodes of violence could also be viewed as self-defence. None of the so-called victims were innocents, but you can't use a sledgehammer to crack a nut, in the eyes of the law. Her use of a knife had gained her time inside. Prison would have changed her. Made her feel like there was no way back. Even her accent had altered to reflect her surroundings. She was born in a village in Kent; now she spoke with a ghetto twang. Sienna was a chameleon. Elea articulated all of this to Swann as she tried to explain. 'I bet she's tooled up every time she goes out,' she continued. 'She has to be. Ant has pissed a lot of dealers off, encroaching on their patch. No wonder they were so jumpy when we stopped by.'

'They won't improve things by dobbing in their mates,' Swann replied. 'Unless we bring them in for another offence.'

Deals could be made, but Elea wasn't sure this was the way forward. Not for Sienna anyway. She had seen the look on her face. She didn't want to criminalise Sienna any more. There was a chink of good in there somewhere, buried beneath all that mistrust. Elea would never admit it, but her maternal streak was strong. 'I have a plan. Leave it with me.'

'Why do I not like the sound of that?' Swann asked.

'*Ei se pelaa, joka pelkää,*' Elea said softly. *The one who is afraid won't play.*

'At least let me in on your games. This isn't only about you, Elea. Any cock-ups and it's my neck on the line.'

'And Mitch, don't forget him. Or don't you care whether or not he gets fired?'

'Elea . . .'

'I'm kidding. *Hei.* If I was going to kick off, I would have done it at the house when Ant Thompson told us to eff off.' She looked pointedly at the clock on the wall. 'Haven't you somewhere to be?'

Swann frowned. Checked the time. Realised that she was right. 'Shit. How did you—'

'I memorised your calendar. The devil is in the detail. Enjoy your meeting!'

Then he was gone, leaving her to sink into his warm leather chair. It was a luxury that most officers weren't granted and she wondered if he'd bought it himself. She input his password into his computer and it opened up for her. Swann had been sloppy, allowing her to watch as he typed it in. And he called himself a detective. She took in the video he'd been watching, brought it back to the start and allowed it to play again. Jenny Flynn. West Common. Her case clearly still haunted Swann. Elea felt a pang of guilt as she remembered the awful accusations she'd made about his lack of commitment to Liisa's case.

She'd accused him of giving up. Of focusing solely on the worst possible outcome. But she was wrong. She knew Swann. He never stopped hoping. He was just more pragmatic than her. But he was wrong, too. She wasn't a loose cannon. Not every action needed to be tempered with violence. She was being honest about playing the long game. Some things needed a slower approach. Which is why she'd slipped a note into the pages of Sienna's Colleen Hoover book. There was no way Ant would see it. His sort preferred to play war games and blow stuff up online. Elea had seen the bruises on Sienna's wrists. The look of desperation in her eyes. She'd pre-empted what she'd needed to hear and had written it down. A promise of Elea's support. Of a way out of the life Sienna had found herself in. Then she'd left her mobile number, telling Sienna to ring – day or night. Would she search her name online, find out who she was? Deem her trustworthy as she wasn't a member of the English police force? Elea could only hope so. Because if she didn't hear back in the next twenty-four hours, she was going back – without Mitch in tow.

# Chapter Thirty

## Liisa

### *2016*

'I want to go home,' I say quietly. 'I don't want to get married. I want my mother.'

We've been sitting at the table for so long that the food has gone cold. It feels like a test. As if they're waiting for me to run. Mikael watches me cooly, the same way I imagine him quietly watching the forest animals before they step into one of his traps. I jump as Johanna brings her meaty fist down onto the table.

'I am your mother now!' Her brown teeth flash. 'Smile, because this is a good day. You *will* get married – isn't that something all little girls dream about? This isn't easy for me, you know!' She begins to cough. It's this horrible hacking sound. Mikael goes to jump up from the table, but she shakes her head. I've heard her cough many times, but not like this. She presses a tissue to her mouth and droplets of bright-red blood bloom. It's more than the smoke from the chimney causing this. It's her illness. What makes you cough up blood? I push aside my panic to work it out. Lungs? Lung cancer? I glance at Mikael for some silent reassurance, but he looks away, unconcerned.

We sit and wait for the awful hacking sound to pass. At last it stops. Johanna shudders, red-faced and sweating as she regains her breath. She pulls her cardigan around her, a brown, smelly home-made thing with holes in the elbows. I think about what she's said as the fire crackles and spits in the fireplace. I've seen her making garlands, working fake off-white flowers into some kind of crown. During her last shop she bought all sorts of things: ribbons, flowers, wire. Then there are the nights when I've heard her messing about on her sewing machine. Now it makes sense. She's planning everything out. Why is she so weird? How did she even have a child of her own? I've wondered about Mikael's father, but have never been brave enough to ask.

Johanna pours herself another cup of coffee and slowly sips. Mikael mirrors her movements and I do the same. She dabs her eyes and normal colour slowly returns to her face. 'I will make your wedding dress, and you will be beautiful. Everything will be as it should be.' She pauses to take another sip. 'I will teach you how to cook properly. How to look after the house, and you will love my boy.'

My mind races ahead. Johanna has always been dangerous – too dangerous for me to escape. If I wait until she dies and then it is just Mikael, I might be able to get away. I wonder how much longer she has left. Her eyes narrow. I have to say something, otherwise I will feel her rough palm against my cheek. 'Sorry that you are sick.' It's the best I can come up with. Mother told me that sometimes in life you have to tell people what they want to hear, even if it's not the truth. I doubt she meant a moment like this.

'Yes, well. God has plans for us all.' Johanna's large bosom heaves up and down as she takes a deep breath. There are crucifixes in this house, nailed to the walls and hung around her neck. But she is not a good person. Nothing makes any sense. She nods towards the window. 'That world out there is wicked and evil. You're better off here with us.'

I want to scream. I want to shout, but instead I dry my tears and focus on what I can take from this. Johanna is dying. She controls us all. Without her – well, without her I might have a chance of getting away. I'm not getting 'married' yet. Not until I get my period and . . . well, that's never going to happen, as I won't tell her when I do. I breathe. This might work. This could be worse. I hope she dies soon. But then I look at Mikael and I don't know if I can trust him. I've always been scared of us being left alone. So far, Johanna keeps a watchful eye.

'Well, that's that out of the way.' Her coarse voice breaks the silence, making me jump. 'You can wash up, change into your clothes. I'll show you how to make the lovely food that you've had today. But first . . .'

She stands behind us and my shoulders rise an inch. I watch in horror as she picks up Mikael's hand from across the table and lays it on mine. I almost snatch my hand away. The feeling of his cold skin is repulsive. But Johanna seizes my wrist, her dirty, stubby nails pinching me.

'Don't be shy,' she chuckles darkly. 'There must be a court-ship before the wedding. You can start by holding hands.'

Mikael squeezes my fingers and I want to throw up every scrap of food. But Johanna is standing behind me and I know

159

for sure now that this is a test. At the back of my mind, I remember something they said in the car. That I wasn't the first. That it had to work out this time or . . .

I freeze, head down, hair shadowing my face. Johanna laughs, saying something about me being shy. I don't want to see Mikael's expression. I just want to come out of this alive.

# Chapter Thirty-One

'Congratulations,' Elea said to Ness as she negotiated the Nettleham road roundabout. 'You must be honoured, being my babysitter.' They were in an unmarked job car, an old Ford Fiesta that had seen better days. Elea was on a mission – to get to know Chelsea Hobbs. A visit to her old football coach might provide insights that police reports couldn't. Ness brightened up the space with her usual colourful clothing – a cheerful floral shirt teamed with navy trousers and an orange cardigan. Her perfume carried a citrus tang.

'I'm happy to get out of the office,' Ness replied with a smile. 'I don't mind ferrying you around.' She glanced in Elea's direction, a twinkle in her eye. 'Although I'd love to know what you've done to get such a reputation. I've enjoyed watching them running around after you.'

'Them?' Elea raised an eyebrow, already knowing the answer.

'Swann and Mitch. They've been watching you like a hawk since you got here. What did you do? Murder a suspect? Plant evidence?'

It seemed Ness was a woman who wasn't afraid to speak her mind. 'Nothing like that. I'm perfectly harmless.'

Ness's mouth twitched in a smile. 'Perfectly harmless people don't get chaperones every time they leave the room.'

Elea decided that the safest thing to do was stare out of the window. She was comfortable with silence – it couldn't get her into trouble. Ness contented herself with humming a David Gray song out of tune. The police car radio filled the rest of the space, as the controller requested officers for incidents ranging from domestic abuse to shoplifters on the high street. It was never too early or late for crime. Elea admired Ness's generosity of spirit. She helped with outstanding tasks when they weren't part of her workload. Picked up CCTV for her colleagues when she was in town, and assisted in interviews when she had work of her own to be getting on with. As Elea's father would have said, she was a 'good egg'. Swann had built up a strong team, and Elea was enjoying immersing herself in their dynamics. It felt good to be needed again.

'You'll be all right waiting here, won't you?' Elea asked Ness as she parked the car outside the school. She didn't want to turn up mob-handed, and how much trouble could she get into, interviewing Chelsea Hobbs's old football coach? They were meeting for an off-the-record chat, nothing more.

'Sure. As long as you've no plans for taking hostages or demanding ransom?'

'Shoot, I forgot my balaclava. You're safe leaving me today.'

'Take your time,' Ness smiled, slipping her phone from the pocket of her cardigan.

Elea surveyed the school football pitch as the game came to an end. There was no mistaking Chelsea's football coach, who was cheering the team from the sidelines. Pauline appeared to be aged in her mid-fifties, of short, stocky build with cropped grey hair. Her sweatshirt was slightly too small for her frame, her stomach edging over her baggy jeans, which were grass-stained at the knees. She cheered and clapped her team loudly, obviously passionate about the game. Elea observed at a distance, watching Pauline interact with her team. 'Next time, yeah?' she said, patting one of the girls on the back. 'You did great. Don't beat yourself up,' she said to another. The freckle-faced teenager had narrowly missed scoring a goal during the last thirty seconds of the game. Despite her team losing, every comment Pauline made was an encouraging one. Elea waited until every girl and spectator had left before she approached.

'Good game,' Elea said, 'although I only caught the tail end.'

Pauline shielded her eyes from the sun as it lowered in the sky. 'Yeah, they've been doing well this year, but they've got to take their failures on the chin. Anyway,' she turned her back on the sunset, 'you didn't come here to talk about football. You're the lady who called earlier. Sorry, I'm terrible with names.'

'Elea . . . Elea Baker. I wanted to talk about Chelsea Hobbs.'

'Yeah, sure.' She gestured to a nearby bench for them to sit on. 'Oof!' She rubbed the base of her spine. 'My bloody sciatica is giving me hell today.' Pauline walked with a limp towards the bench, groaning once more as she sat. She dragged a tissue from her coat and loudly blew her nose. Elea joined her, pushing her shoulder bag aside before crossing her legs.

Pauline shoved her tissue back into her jeans pocket and pulled out a pack of cigarettes. 'Do you mind?' She looked over her shoulder. 'I'm not meant to on school grounds, but it's been flaming hours since my last.' The football pitch was empty, the tail-end of the sun casting it in ribbons of orange and gold.

'Not at all,' Elea said, politely declining the offer of a Marlboro from the pack.

'I've already spoken to the cops. Told them everything I know.'

'You have, and I've read Chelsea's file. I just want to get to know her a little better.'

'Chelsea was . . .' Pauline paused, shielding her cigarette from the breeze as she lit it. She puffed twice before returning the lighter to her pocket, and the smell of tobacco drifted over them both. She quickly flapped it away. 'Chelsea was a good kid,' she continued. 'A great footballer, too. Had the potential to go far, if it wasn't for her shitty home life, but you'll know all about that.'

Elea nodded.

'Her parents didn't come to watch one game. I went home with her once, but Jesus – that stepdad of hers.' She shook her head. 'What a prick!'

'I second that. I've met him.' Elea would have liked to disclose her adventures with Phil Hobbs, but she couldn't afford for it to get around the school and back to the wrong person at the station.

'Then you'll know that Chelsea didn't have it easy.' Pauline exhaled a thin stream of smoke from the corner of her mouth. 'She was only on the junior team, but she lived for her time on the field. Wanted to be a Lioness one day.' She was referring to playing for the England team. Did girls like Chelsea stand a chance when it came to such high aspirations? Elea hoped so. 'Yeah, she was a good kid.' She sighed. 'She was gutted when social services took her siblings away. Proper broke her heart, that did.'

'Why are you talking about her in the past tense?'

Pauline shrugged. 'Cos there's no way she would have left of her own accord. She loved her mum too much. God knows the woman didn't deserve it.'

'You think Chelsea's dead?'

'You don't?' Pauline turned the question back on her. 'Remember Jenny Flynn? Long blonde hair, twelve years old – wouldn't surprise me if it was the same bloke.'

Elea monitored Pauline's body language, listened to the cadence of her voice. She hadn't flinched when she was challenged. Sadness emanated from every word. 'We haven't given up on her yet,' Elea said. 'Sophie Miller came home alive.'

'No thanks to the cops,' Pauline uttered, taking a deep drag. 'Sorry. I'm not having a pop, it's just . . .' She exhaled another plume of smoke. 'Chelsea, that poor kid has been through enough. Trying to keep her family together, defending her mum when her stepdad waded in. Nobody should have to deal with that. And now . . .' She flicked a crumb of ash from her cigarette and it blew away in the wind. 'Well, we've warned our girls to be careful. You don't know when it could happen again. Are you any closer to finding them?'

'I won't stop until we do,' Elea assured her. Their talk had made her more determined than ever to bring Chelsea home. Her mother, Karen, was making slow progress, with the support of social services and her IDVA. The independent domestic violence adviser was making good headway.

A divorce had been requested. Phil had been arrested and bailed, with strict conditions. At least now Karen had the flat to herself. Elea only hoped that mother and daughter would get the chance to start again.

# Chapter Thirty-Two

Sienna Thompson's call didn't come until Elea was back at her hotel. She was packing her belongings, ready to move into Swann's flat. She hadn't visited it yet, but Swann liked nice things: soft furnishings, deep carpets, a cosy home. It was why he had struggled to give the flat up, despite Alice's wish to put it on the market. He'd confided in Elea earlier in the evening when he drove her to hire a car. It had been almost like old times – except that Alice was now pulling his strings. Elea's face soured at the thought of her as she folded a cashmere jumper and placed it gently in the suitcase. It was obvious that her 'surprise pregnancy' had been planned all along. Like you wouldn't realise you were expecting twins. 'It was me who asked if she could be pregnant,' Swann had confided, before he dropped Elea back to the hotel. 'She'd got so big, and she was sick all the time, so I bought her a test.' He'd shaken his head at the memory, hands lightly on the steering wheel of his car. 'She couldn't believe it when she found out. And twins – we were shocked.'

Elea tutted. How gullible Swann had been. She thought of those beautiful boys, so peaceful in their cots when Alice had taken her upstairs to see them. She was being manipulated, too, but it had worked. As much as she loved Swann, she couldn't break up their family. He was having cold feet, that's all, and she couldn't blame Alice for defending her brood. If only the woman wasn't so bloody defensive, they might all have got along. It would have been nice to spend time with Swann's sons. She'd missed so much of Liisa growing up.

Elea's phone rang. She frowned, as she didn't recognise the number. She stepped away from the wardrobe as she remembered. Of course, Sienna. A bolt of excitement rippled through her. Was this the lead she was waiting for?

'Hello?' Sienna's voice was a whisper. 'Is that Elea?'

'It is, am I talking to Sienna?' Elea held her breath.

'You are. I . . . I can't talk for long.' In the background, a door was closed. 'He'll kill me if he finds out.'

'Nobody's killing anyone. Do you want to meet? Can you get away? I can send a taxi—' Elea stopped herself. She was sounding desperate.

'Give it half an hour. Ant's heading out for the night.'

Elea tapped the address on her Waze app, grateful for the rental car.

'Don't park outside the house,' Sienna warned. 'I'll meet you at the top of the road. Come alone.'

Elea stood at the hotel window, staring out at the twinkling lights of the Brayford. The skies were clear tonight, another frost was due. *Hold on*, she sent a silent message to her daughter, *I'm coming for you.* But was it too little, too late? She had appeared in every newspaper after Liisa disappeared, and as many media outlets as she could make time for. She'd had her long blonde hair cropped short, then forced herself to brush her teeth, and Swann had helped her choose some clothes. It had gone against her nature to beg with her daughter's kidnapper, but beg she did. She'd tried to keep the interest going, balancing work with the desperate need to keep her daughter's memory alive. After just two weeks off, Heikkinen had urged Elea not to return. But she'd needed to have her finger on the pulse. Some days it was too much. Some days she crashed and burned. When it came to the missing children, the public's attention wavered as time went on. She thought about Chelsea and her fractured life. She'd barely received any coverage on TV. Other more 'newsworthy' stories about war and terrorism had overtaken her. Elea would speak to Swann tomorrow. Push the police media team to drum up something new.

Caution muscled its way into Elea's thoughts as she made her way to the street where Sienna had arranged to meet. This could have been a set-up. A way of getting Elea on her own. A warning to back off. But when it came to finding fresh leads, Elea was willing to take that chance. She pulled the rental car over to the kerb and turned off the headlights. It was an old BMW 3 Series, not so new that it would stand out. Sienna was waiting. She wore a black hoodie and blue jeans, and a pair of Doc Martens graced her feet. She opened the passenger door and slid in beside Elea.

'Did anyone follow you?' Sienna checked over her shoulder, her warm breath fogging the window.

'I'm not being tailed,' Elea reassured her. 'Relax, I promise you're safe.'

'Like I'd take your word for it,' Sienna snorted, peering at a car as it drove past.

'This isn't a drugs deal, Sienna. I'm not even a police officer – at least not here.' It pained her to say the words. Policing was in her blood. She was never off-duty. But tonight she would say anything to find out the truth. 'Tell me, then: what do you know?' She needed to get to the point.

'Behave!' Sienna's laugh came in sudden, sharp bursts. 'As if I'm going to tell you that!'

'So you do know something.'

'I know *everything*.' The look on her face left Elea in little doubt that she was telling the truth. She was seeing a sharper side to Sienna and she didn't like it one bit.

'Then why come here?' Elea asked through gritted teeth.

'Everything has a price, babe.' The words came with a cold smile.

'How much?'

'One hundred K.'

Seconds passed as Elea pretended to mull it over. Was Sienna merely on the take? 'For that kind of information, I'd expect my own missing daughter to walk in the door.'

'Who says that Liisa won't?'

Elea eyed the woman cautiously. The sound of her daughter's name delivered hope that she was too scared to feel. 'You know about her?'

'I told ya. I know stuff. But I'm not giving it away.'

'Or you researched my name online. I know when I'm being played.' Elea sat, in the quiet stillness of the night, wishing that the world would give her a break.

'I ain't. So how much is she worth?' Sienna hunched down in her seat as the glare of passing headlights glided over her face.

'Why now? You could have come to me before this.'

'I have . . . reasons. I need to get away.' Sienna crossed her slim arms over her waist.

'From who?'

Sienna exhaled a bitter laugh, clearly unwilling to go into any more detail.

'Sienna, you can't expect me to play the game with half a deck of cards. Woman-to-woman: what are you running away from? Is it Ant? Drugs debts? Are you in trouble? Has someone threatened you?'

But Sienna stared straight ahead. A fox crossed the road, glancing at them momentarily before dipping out of sight behind a parked car.

'You're asking me for one hundred K. I need to know why. It's not purely for the money, is it? Are you going on the run?'

A flicker of emotion crossed Sienna's face. *There it was.*

'Both of you?'

Sienna sat in weighted silence.

'Is Ant hurting you?'

Another shake. Sienna's chin wobbled. Her mouth became small and tight.

'I saw the bruises on your wrist.' Elea gave her a level stare, making small dents in the armour that Sienna had layered on over the years. 'I can help. But you need to be straight with me. Because I'm getting my daughter back. If you're with me, that's good. But if you're not – I'll take down anyone who stands in my way.'

'I need to keep her safe,' Sienna eventually said. 'And I can only do that on my own.'

'Who?'

'*My* little girl . . . at least, it feels like I'm having a girl.' She rested her hand on her stomach. 'God, I've been so ill these last couple of weeks. My pregnancy has wiped me out. He doesn't even know.'

*Clang!* Elea could almost hear the sound of the huge penny dropping in her mind. 'You're pregnant.'

Sienna nodded. 'I love Ant. But he can't keep us safe. We've had so many arguments over it.' She rubbed her right wrist, caught Elea looking. 'He doesn't hit me, all right? Our rows just . . . get out of control. He's off his head half the time.'

'And you need the money to start again?'

Another nod. 'A new life.' She sighed. 'I'm clean. No drugs. No booze. No smokes. But I need to get away. Start fresh: me and my girl. I'd sell my soul for that.'

'Then tell me what you know and I'll see what I can do.'

Sienna tilted her chin upwards, giving Elea a defiant stare. 'As long as it doesn't end up with me getting nicked, because I'm not having my baby on the inside.'

'You have my word.' Elea meant it. Because Sienna's reasoning was something she could understand.

Sienna's nostrils flared as she took a deep breath and met Elea's gaze. 'I know who took Chelsea Hobbs and . . .' she paused for another nervous breath, 'I can tell you where she's being kept.'

Elea tried to remain steady as she was hit with a dizzying wave of hope. 'Is she alive?'

'Maybe.' Sienna blinked her long, enhanced lashes.

'And Liisa?'

'Money first.'

'Will this lead me to Liisa?' Elea demanded. 'Tell me that much. Is my daughter still alive?' She barely dared to utter the words.

Closing her eyes, Sienna delivered a slow nod of the head.

# Chapter Thirty-Three

Swann crossed the floor of his flat, relaxed in his sweater and jeans. His suit and tie were the uniform that he shed the moment he got home. Changing into comfortable clothes was his way of leaving his job at the door. But lately that was impossible. The case haunted his thoughts night and day.

'What do you think?' He turned to Elea, hoping she was suitably impressed with his old Brayford abode. If she set down roots in Lincoln, would it be so bad? Op Turnstile was concluding. He could never quite explain it, but he always sensed when they were closing in on a case. A stillness in the air when he first awoke. The way his racing thoughts finally calmed. An assurance in his movements. The case coming full circle as the answers lined up. A feeling of anticipation. Of hope.

But he didn't want Elea to face the truth alone. The intelligence team had shared information on the gang listed in Phil Hobbs's address book and it was blowing Swann's previous theories apart. All this time his team had been hunting for an individual, but new intel on the gang revealed a darker truth: human trafficking.

The information was on a need-to-know basis and was part of an ongoing police operation. Could the Ice Angels abductions have been orchestrated by the group? There were connections that couldn't be denied any longer. But deny them he would, if it meant keeping Elea on the case. Free from the ties of bureaucracy, Elea had done more in a day than his team had been able to do in months. God knows they had worked hard, watching hours upon hours of CCTV, scouting for witnesses, taking statements, chasing up countless dead-ends.

Hobbs had betrayed his stepdaughter to some extremely dangerous individuals. Had Swann realised what they were capable of, he might not have allowed Elea to visit Ant and Sienna's home. Ant Thompson was connected to a gang of armed individuals who were immersed in the Dark Web and capable of anything. Three separate sources now confirmed that the gang had been abducting homeless people, forcing them to work in drugs farms. They needed cheap, disposable labour to water cannabis plants and maintain the hydroponic set-ups. But had the gang gone further? Were they snatching children to order, too? Undercover officers were involved, due to cases of human slavery, and now it seemed that children weren't off the cards. Those people were the lowest of the low. Swann and his team had been warned to step back. They couldn't risk compromising an investigation that had been ongoing for months. The police weren't privy to everything. Swann had known nothing about it until Elea seized the address book.

He switched on a lamp, observing her taking in the living room. One whole wall was thick tinted glass, which looked out onto the Brayford.

'This is amazing.' Elea seemed in awe. 'I knew it would be nice, but this . . . Why on earth did you move out?'

'It wasn't practical.' Swann spoke with more than a hint of regret. 'Alice wanted a house for the children, and Nettleham is handy for work.' He was glad of the opportunity to speak to Elea in private without any interruptions. 'About Alice . . .' he began. 'What I said—'

'Water under the bridge,' Elea replied, taking everything in. His pictures of Finnish landscapes were still on the walls, because Alice preferred modern art in their house. His bookcase was still half full of books about forensics, poisons, famous murder cases and everything in between. Elea would love them all. Her blue eyes were alight. She seemed happier today.

'Emotions were running high. It's been an adjustment having you here. It all feels a bit,' he paused, 'surreal.'

'It doesn't to me. England is my home, too.' She was remembering all the times she'd visited her English father and stayed with his family in the past.

'Funny how we both have a foot in both countries,' Swann mused. He looked out onto the Brayford, at the slightly murky waters and the swans that settled on the small islands, which were wildlife-protected. 'It's not as clean as Finnish lakes, but there's a good canoe club if you'd like to join.' They exchanged a glance. 'I tried it once, but I couldn't keep up.'

Elea smiled. 'Yes, you've put on weight. Alice has been feeding you well.'

'Too well.' Swann patted his belly.

'Do you want your divorce?' Elea blurted out. 'Because I can sign the papers. Just get them to me and—'

The smile faded from Swann's face. 'Can we leave it for now? There's no immediate hurry.' He shoved his hands into his pockets. It was better to wait. Because Alice would have him down the registry office before the ink was dry on the divorce paperwork. He couldn't divorce and remarry in such quick succession. He needed time to come to terms with everything.

'Then what will you tell Alice?'

'That you refused.'

'You want me to lie?'

He turned to face Elea. 'I need more time to process everything. Alice . . .' he sighed. 'Don't be surprised if you get a call. She's planning on asking you out for a coffee, so she can apologise.'

Elea grimaced in response.

Swann appreciated her efforts to be diplomatic, but she would never be besties with Alice. He didn't blame her in the least. Had he been in her position, he would probably have felt the same.

'I was planning on letting this place out, but I couldn't bear to let it go to people I didn't know.' He walked around the room. 'It's too nice to spoil with strangers.' He didn't tell Elea that it also eased his conscience to help her out. 'Oh, there's one more thing I want to show you.'

Elea arched an eyebrow. 'Oh yes? What have you up your sleeve?'

Swann forced himself to focus as she delivered a heart-stopping smile. 'Come with me.'

Elea followed him down the corridor, past the bathroom. She watched as he opened another door. 'It's a sauna.'

She gasped in delight. 'Oh my goodness, this is perfect!'

Swan's grin broadened. 'I missed it so much that I had one

fitted. It's the only one in this entire block. On the whole of the Brayford, probably. There's a communal swimming pool in the basement, too. I think you'll be happy here.'

Elea pressed her hands together and touched her lips. 'I think so too. I'll pay rent. The going rate.'

'Let's not talk money now.'

'Oh, let's,' Elea said. 'You don't want people thinking I'm a kept woman, do you? Have a tenancy agreement drawn up on a month-by-month rolling basis. That way everything will be above board.'

'Whatever makes you happy.'

Elea wasn't finished. 'We need ground rules. You can't just walk in here whenever you like. And I'm allowed guests . . . After all, what's good for the goose is good for the gander.' Elea had a whole plethora of English sayings that she had picked up from her father.

'Yes, of course,' Swann agreed, not wanting to think about Elea with anyone else. 'Anyway, I'm glad you like the sauna. The place is yours for as long as you need it.'

Elea arched an eyebrow. 'No matter what? You won't kick me out if I put a foot wrong? Because I can't have that hanging over my head.'

'It's yours. No matter how many times you piss me off.'

'Good.' A slow smile spread across her face. 'Because I've made a deal with Sienna Thompson. She's going to tell us everything.'

'You what?' Swann couldn't believe what he was hearing. 'After everything I said in the briefing. The warnings not to interfere . . . Jesus, Elea, are you desperate to get me the sack?'

177

'Did you not hear me? She knows where Chelsea is.' She laid her hand on his arm. Drew him so close that he could smell her perfume. She was intoxicating. 'Liisa's alive. Sienna knows where she is.'

Swann looked away. He couldn't bear to see the hope in her eyes. Because he knew people like Sienna Thompson. They did favours for no one. 'How much?' he asked, stepping around her emotions, which were still so raw.

'For what?' But Elea's eyes betrayed her. She knew exactly what he meant.

'How much money does she want?' He waited for her answer. Watched a shadow of doubt cross her face. He folded his arms.

Elea sighed. 'One hundred thousand pounds.'

# Chapter Thirty-Four

The day had been so perfect. Another breakthrough. Real progress. The old camaraderie between her and Swann that she would never get enough of. His Brayford flat had immediately felt like home. She'd inhaled the scent of fir cones and pine needles, her eyes alighting on the Scandinavian reed diffusers that he'd bought for her. She melted a little inside at his subtle welcome to his old home. The place came fully furnished and was exactly her style – Scandi comfort with a modern twist. The books on Swann's bookshelf were just what she wanted to read. Then there were the pictures of Lincoln Cathedral that immediately drew her in. It was the blend of England and Finland that she didn't know she'd needed until now. She even gave it a name: 'Finglish'.

Then, in the midst of all that happy perfection, she'd dropped her bombshell. She had to. 'Donating' £100,000 to a criminal could end up with her being prosecuted and Elea would find herself on the wrong side of the thin blue line. There was also the small matter of getting her hands on so much money. She'd accumulated savings over the years – enough to help Liisa piece her life back together again. But she had to find her daughter first. She could remortgage her house in Finland, but Sienna had demanded untraceable cash. Not an easy task these days. She needed Swann's help. Of course she'd had doubts, but her maternal instinct was a force in itself. It spoke with the regularity of a heartbeat, repeating the same three words: 'Get Liisa back'.

'There's no way . . .' Swann's muscles were taut as he disengaged himself from her grip. 'No way in hell that you're giving that woman a penny.' Now he was looking at Elea as if she'd lost her mind. 'Do you know what they've done? They've been supplying people to order. Homeless people promised a job and ending up as modern-day slaves. Runaway kids taken off the streets. They're sold to people, Elea. *Sold*. Left to live in a cupboard under the stairs. But this isn't a fucking Harry Potter fairytale. The house is stuffed to the rafters with cannabis plants, and God help them if they let one die.'

Elea rolled her eyes as he ranted, gesticulating one hand in the air. When Swann got like this, she had two choices: have a blazing row or wait until he ran out of steam. In the olden days, such rows usually ended up with them having sex. But there were no consolation prizes today. Judging by how the atmosphere was crackling between them, it was safer to wait it out. She would defend her decision when he was done. She stood barefoot on the deep-pile living-room carpet, trying to find the words she needed to get him onside.

'Sienna's in over her head.' She looked up at him. 'I know she's no angel. But now she wants out.' Elea told him about their meeting, and the potential pregnancy – because she wasn't gullible enough to believe every word that Sienna said.

'So Sienna gives you Liisa, then walks off into the sunset with one hundred grand?' Swann tutted as if she were four years old. 'I thought you had more sense than that.'

'Sense?' Elea retorted, hating the words leaving his mouth. 'What sense would you have, if it were your boys' lives on the line?'

'Elea.' Swann sighed. 'I'd give Sienna the money myself if I thought it would bring Liisa back. But she's scamming you. They both are.' He swore beneath his breath, low rumblings of discontent.

'Don't say that. Don't say any of it.' Her shoulders slumped. Because she didn't want to hear what she already knew in her heart. Nothing in life was that easy, and the Sienna Thompsons of the world could not be trusted to help. She turned away from the window. Away from the sight of other people without a care.

'I'm not saying that we can't do *something*. We'll explore other avenues.'

Elea's throat constricted as the small doorway to finding her daughter slammed shut. It had been a fairytale to think that she could buy her return. 'I need more time with Sienna. I know I can get her to talk.'

'We've had this conversation. How many times must I say it? You're no good to Liisa in jail.'

Elea shook her head. Swann only discussed the potential of Liisa being alive as a tool of manipulation. 'OK,' she continued. 'Not me, then. There are other people. People who are good at finding things out.'

Swann gave her a pitiful look. 'You know my answer to that.' He closed the gap between them. He smelled good. Familiar. Like home. She could feel his warm breath on her hair. 'We're close. Just a few more days. We can't do anything to compromise the ongoing investigation.'

Elea turned to face him. 'You think so?'

'I know so.' He placed his hands on her forearms. 'Can you handle it? Because whatever happens, I'll always be here for you. You know that, don't you?'

She nodded tightly, unable to speak. Because she had felt it, too – and as much as she wanted the truth, she was scared of what was coming her way.

# Chapter Thirty-Five

## Liisa

### 2016

I'm not tired, but I'm lying in bed because there's nothing else to do this afternoon. I'm actually enjoying learning how to knit, but Johanna won't let me take the needles into my room. I shift my weight on the lumpy mattress, which feels like it's a hundred years old. I'm on my back instead of my side, so I don't have to breathe in the stinky pillowcase. Johanna doesn't do laundry much, but when she does, it doesn't make things fresh. She eats a lot of fish and the stink gets everywhere. The wide kitchen sink is marked by their stringy guts, their shiny scales dotted on the kitchen sides. Sometimes I find them on the soles of my socks. Little bits of the rainbow trout that end up in Johanna's rotten belly – a woman who takes more than she gives to the world. I think of my soft, feathery pillow at home, which sometimes smells of Mama's sweet perfume. Of my bed, which feels like lying on a cloud. The small double that is big enough for her to cuddle up next to me. I've always preferred her stories about work to bedtime fairytales. Sometimes she says it's not good for me, but I pester her until she tells me more. Once I was at my friend Sofia's house and told her about a case that Mum was working on.

The week after, her mother came round, all red in the face and annoyed. I hadn't meant to get Mama in trouble. Sofia's mother said I'd given Sofia nightmares, then she looked at Mama like she was weird. I told her that people like Mama keep her safe in her bed at night. Mama reprimanded me for shouting, but I knew that secretly she was pleased. I wouldn't mind, but I only told Sofia about a burglary where the man hid under the bed. I couldn't see what the fuss was about. I wasn't invited round to Sofia's house again. I'm glad Mum told me all that stuff. If they had kidnapped Sofia instead of me, I don't think she'd be here any more.

I've been watching Johanna's routine. Mother said that people are usually easy to work out. She talked about the hours she'd spent, watching and waiting for them to slip up. She said sometimes the police know exactly who's done bad things, but they don't have the evidence to lock them up. I hadn't thought of it like that before. We are creatures of habit because it makes life easier. Our brains are kind of lazy – they don't waste energy thinking about every little move we make. It's why we do stuff without thinking, like blinking, brushing our teeth or even making breakfast. Once we get used to it, we do it on autopilot. That's how habits are made. Mum said that bad people have habits, too, even when they're covering stuff up or on the run. They end up stuck back in the same old routines, or returning to places they know. Mum said that when you watch and wait long enough, you can work out their next moves.

That's what I've been doing, stuck in this room. I've been

here for four weeks now. I know the date from the calendar that Johanna marks off in the hall. I've done everything that Johanna has asked. Cooking. Cleaning. Holding creepy Mikael's hand. Sometimes Johanna is moody. She slaps me for no reason, but I try really hard to keep her happy and do the right thing. She doesn't hear me cry when I'm alone in my bed, curled up against a spare blanket because I need to hug something, even if it's prickly against my skin.

Mama isn't perfect. She often gets things wrong. She forgets to order milk, and we're always running out of food. Sometimes she sets her alarm clock wrong and wakes up grumpy and late for work. She doesn't look after herself, but she *does* look after me. At least she did, because it's all in the past now. Where is she? I can't believe she hasn't found me yet. Is she OK? What if my kidnappers hurt her? They won't tell me anything. I'm not allowed to talk about my life before I came here. I miss my old clothes. I miss my little wooden doll that was hidden in the small inside pocket of my jacket. How I wish I had it now. I sit up straight on the bed as the floorboards in the hall creak. Small shafts of light peek through the crooked wooden slats nailed over my windowpane. The outside world is calling. The melting snow still drips. I think we are in mid-February. Every day we have the same routine.

I'm allowed out of my room in the morning to light the fire and make breakfast for everyone. Then I clean the cabin while Johanna sits in her armchair, watching me over her knitting. Mikael goes into the forest. Sometimes for walks, sometimes to hunt and catch fish. He always says that he only catches what we need to eat. He doesn't hunt for fun. When he gets back, Johanna tells me to go to my room. She says it takes 'too much energy' to watch me all the time. That's when I hear the drilling sound of her electric sewing machine. Once a week she goes into town to do a food shop.

Sometimes Mikael lets me out when she's not there. He knows he shouldn't. That it's against the rules. He likes me to sit next to him on the sofa, so he can stroke my hair. It makes me feel icky inside. He tells me about the wildlife in the forest and knows the names of all the trees. I think he is lonely. Sometimes he opens his mouth to speak, but then changes his mind. Johanna isn't easy to live with. I hear them arguing all the time. Sometimes I catch Mikael staring at her with hate in his eyes. I can't imagine what it must be like, having her as a mother, because I've never looked at Mama like that. Did he go to school? Have any friends? I think Johanna likes to keep him to herself. Today I wait at the door, wondering if he will let me out. Because it's that time of the week again. Johanna has left the cabin. Habits.

I stand, hugging myself, waiting for the bolt to be pulled across. I'm wearing an ugly brown dress with wide flappy sleeves, a lace collar and three black buttons that hang on loose threads. Thick black tights usually keep my legs warm, but today it's so cold that I'm wearing two pairs. I smell like I haven't washed in a while. But I'd rather be dirty than have Johanna watch me in the bath. Mikael unlocks my door. It is rusty on its hinges, making a squeaking noise as he pushes it open. He doesn't say anything, just looks me up and down before walking into the sitting room. The tips of my fingers and toes are cold. I wipe my nose with the back of my wizard-like sleeve, seeking out the heat. I follow him and sit in the wide armchair next to the fire. The material is frayed, the cushion hard, but at least this spot is warm. It's good to get out of the room. I catch a glimpse of his rifle, which is leaning against the sofa. It's not loaded. Johanna won't allow loaded guns in the house. Another one of her rules.

Mikael pats the sofa cushion for me to join him. I pretend that I haven't heard.

'*Hei*,' he says, because they rarely use my name anymore. When they do, they call me 'Lia.'

'*Hei*,' he says, louder his time. His light-brown hair is greasy, he hasn't shaved and there's dried egg yolk on his face. He chews on liquorice. I can't ignore the insistence in his voice as he calls me one more time. I think of the way he holds his hand over mine. How he touches my hair. And I can't. I just . . . can't. It all happens so fast. I stand. His lips jerk upwards in a weird half-smile that turns the rest of my body cold. I look behind him and gasp. It's something Mama taught me: the distraction trick. Then I'm moving, faster than I have ever moved before. Darting towards the gun leaning against the sofa.

Now his rifle is in my hand, and its weight takes me by surprise. I grab it by the barrel and swing it towards his head. The metal is ice-cold. I swing with all my strength, connecting with his face as Mikael turns back round. In that second I see the flash of surprise in his eyes. It's too late for him to do anything. There's a crack as the gun connects with his jaw. His head wobbles to the side and he flops face-down on the wooden floorboards with a thud.

I pant, disbelieving. I can't believe that he's down. I throw the gun onto the floor, taking a second to catch my breath. I'm shaking. I want to cry. I grab one of Mikael's coats and pull on his waterproof boots next to the door. They are far too big for me, but should protect my feet from the snow. If only I had more time, better clothes, smaller boots. But a moan rises from the living room and I know that I have to run. My hands are shaking as I release the heavy bolt from the front door.

The air hits me like a slap in the face, cold but welcome. It's so fresh in comparison to my smoky, fishy hell. I'm out, my eyes stinging against the brightness of the snow. Legs pumping, I force myself out into the wilderness, but the boots are clunky and feel like lead. I want to ditch them, but I can't. Wading through the knee-deep snow, I head towards the forest, making a perfect trail for Mikael to follow me down. I think of the steely traps that he has set for the animals. I've seen the damage they do. The imprints of the pointed metal teeth as they capture their prey and break bone.

I glance over my shoulder, my breath coming in jerky gasps. I'll take my chances in the woods. Maybe I'll be able to find help. One person. It only takes one other person to be able to help. A cabin. A phone. I hold the image in my mind. My lungs burn as I gather speed. It can't be just us living out here.

# Chapter Thirty-Six

Alice had laid out an array of toys, most of them new. Joshua and Jake gurgled with delight as they chewed on the purchases, which were surely bought to give their parents some quality time to speak. As always, the children were clean, fed and dry. They were happy. Swann knew that he took Alice for granted. She did everything for their children while he worked. He was blessed in so many ways. So why wasn't he satisfied? He thought he loved Alice, until Elea had got here, then all the old feelings for his wife had hit him like a tsunami. He couldn't help but feel guilty as he took a seat.

Alice's brunette hair cascaded over her shoulders. She was wearing jeans and a jumper that hung loose on her frame. She seemed tired, a little harassed, and was eyeing him with the intention of someone who needed to get something off their chest. Swann kicked off his shoes. It was meant to be his day off work, but he'd ended up going in for a meeting with the Corporate Communications Team. Then he'd met the superintendent to discuss the situation with Sienna Thompson and her request for money in exchange for information. That couldn't wait, rest day or not. Elea was settling into the Brayford flat, and he'd told her to catch up on some sleep. If anything came in with regards to the case, officers would let him know.

'Earth to Richard,' Alice's voice brought him back to ground. She was one of the few people he knew who called him by his first name.

'Sorry.' He gave her an apologetic smile.

Alice quickly picked up his shoes and put them aside so that the children wouldn't stick them in their mouths. 'Sit down, love.'

He took the shoes from her hands and rested them in the cupboard in the hall. 'Would you like me to run you a bath?' he asked as he returned. 'I'll take the twins tonight.'

Alice heaved a weary sigh, her shoulders slumped. 'I won't say no.' She cupped her mouth as she yawned. 'I can't remember the last time I had a full night's sleep.'

She looked so small in that moment, so ragged with exhaustion, that Swann pulled her in for a hug. 'Sorry. I'll try harder.' It dawned upon him how thin she had become. He was filled with the need to find other people's children when he should be helping out with his own.

She drew away from his embrace. 'Why don't you start by pushing Elea for a divorce?'

'You haven't exactly helped the situation there.' Swan smiled.

'What are you getting at?' An edge grew in Alice's voice as she turned to face him.

'You went behind my back and invited her into our home. You must have known you couldn't keep your feelings in check.' It hadn't meant to sound like an accusation, but it did.

The twins continued to chat and babble in their own special language. Alice stretched to give Jake a soft, crinkly toy flower. She turned back to face Swann. 'I thought I could sweet-talk her – show her the kids. They deserve a full-time father.'

'I *am* full-time,' Swan replied. 'As much as I can be. But you planned a pregnancy without consulting me.' He tried to keep his voice low as Jake wobbled towards the sofa.

Alice blinked, her cheeks flushing as she was confronted with everything that had gone unsaid. She did not deny the accusation, just stared rigidly ahead.

'That's not how relationships work.' He pressed his point home. 'Especially when it comes to something as big as starting a family.' He smiled at Jake, smoothed over his soft wispy hair before handing Josh a toy to distract him. It felt distasteful, arguing about his children, whom he loved with all his heart. But it needed to be said.

Alice picked up the remote control and played an old recording of *Peppa Pig*. Jake clapped his hands. Squealing in delight, the boys crawled towards the big TV screen.

'So you don't want them.' Alice's voice was tempered with quiet fury as she watched them both. 'You don't love your children.'

'That's a horrible thing to say,' Swann reprimanded as her words hit home. 'Really? Is that what you think?' No answer came. 'Alice, the boys are the best thing that's ever happened to me. But my point is . . .' He grasped for the words. 'You can't railroad people into doing what you want, then wonder why things aren't perfect afterwards. It goes for Elea and it goes for our relationship, too.'

Josh emitted a giggle as Peppa Pig played out. As always, Jake followed suit.

'What about me?' Alice whispered, her voice choked with emotion. 'Don't you love me?'

Swann took in the crumpled look on her face. 'Of course I love you . . .' He swallowed. 'You gave me perspective on life, and I know I'm struggling to find a balance – that's all on me.' He gazed lovingly at his children. 'Family is everything. But we have a lot to sort out. I think we should get counselling.' Given how much he struggled to share his feelings, it pained him to say the words.

'Are we in that much trouble?' She sniffed, her eyes wet with tears.

'It can't do any harm.' He turned to face her. 'This has nothing to do with Elea, you know that, don't you?' It was meant to be reassuring, but his words lacked conviction. Elea's presence had sent him into a tailspin.

Alice's expression was one of mistrust.

'I can't drop her now,' Swann reasoned. 'Not with everything going on.'

'Oh, please.' Alice rolled her eyes as her mood took another turn. 'Elea brings drama everywhere she goes. She feeds off it. But there comes a cut-off point. It's been years.' She swiped away an errant tear before crouching to give Joshua and Jake some toys. Uninterrupted time to talk was a luxury for them both.

Swann slipped a clean tissue from his pocket and handed it to Alice. He hated to see her like this. He tried to empathise as he watched his boys play. His father hadn't been there for him growing up. He would not do the same. But he couldn't carry on pretending everything was fine. 'We're close to finding Liisa – or at least what happened to her. I'm not abandoning Elea now.'

Alice stared miserably at the floor, blotting her tears. 'I've been living in her shadow for so long.' The happy jingle of another *Peppa Pig* episode played in the background – a laughable juxtaposition to the gravity of their conversation.

'We'll have a result soon – one way or another. Just give Elea some slack. Then, I promise, we'll book a holiday. Get away from everything.' He was about to say more when his mobile phone rang from its resting place on the coffee table. It was work. He and Alice exchanged a glance.

'Answer it,' she said, before getting up and joining the twins on the floor.

'Swann,' he said, with little hesitation.

'Sorry, mate, I know it's your day off, but something's come in.' It was Jess. Superintendents didn't ring on rest days unless something serious came up.

'Everything all right?' Swann's pulse was already picking up speed.

'It's more than all right,' Jess said cheerfully. 'It's Sophie Miller. She's ready to talk, but only to Elea. I thought that you should know.'

'I'm on my way.' Swann rose from the sofa. Their only witness had found her voice.

'There's no need – we can handle it from here.'

But Jess's words didn't register. If they were closing in on Sophie's kidnapper, then he was going to be there. 'I'll be with you in fifteen.'

# Chapter Thirty-Seven

Elea waited patiently for the officers to filter out of the briefing room. Their chatter was low as they talked between themselves. Heads down, Kelly and Ollie were comparing their workloads, while Ness, who had arrived late, was sorting out her paperwork, which she had dropped on the carpeted floor. Elea glanced at Mitch, who had agreed to her request for five minutes alone. Today Swann had left him to take the helm. Swann had booked the rest day the week before, but Elea had it on good authority that he had popped back in to see the Corporate Communications Team. Helsinki Police had a similar team, which handled press enquiries. Their jobs involved disseminating information between journalists and investigating officers and, most of all, protecting the department's public image. Over the years, Elea had got to know the staff by their first names.

Her mind drifted back to a day that she often revisited. Niall was the longest-standing member of the Helsinki communications unit, an ageing Irish man with a penchant for cigars. She recalled the last time she saw him, before she left for the UK. He was leaving work, a cloud of smoke in his wake. The evening was crisp and clear, and their bodies were illuminated beneath the street lights as she caught up with him. The lines on his face deepened into a smile.

'I hear you're off soon,' he'd said, puffing on his cigar. He was dressed for the weather, his woollen hat pulled down over his silver hair. The potent, earthy smell of cigar smoke wrapped itself around Elea as they briefly chatted about her trip to England and her consultation on the case. 'Liisa's story . . .' The tip of his cigar glowed orange as he puffed. 'Don't keep me waiting any longer, eh? You promised I'd be the one to handle it.' There was no pity in his voice, just the quiet, unshakeable kindness that kept him steady through every tragic story that the department had shared.

Elea gave him a look that said more than words could. 'Of course.'

'And if it's good news, you'll buy me that cigar?'

She'd nodded then, remembering her vow to gift him a Romeo y Julieta from the Havanna-Aitta cigar shop in Helsinki. Determined to keep her spirits buoyant, she'd bought one before she left for the UK. It sat in her suitcase, in an addressed envelope, ready to make the journey back. She hadn't stopped hoping that Niall would get to share the story that he'd been waiting to handle for a decade.

She stared at the briefing-room whiteboard, its surface littered with images, maps and case notes, bringing herself back to the present moment with a deep sigh. Today DC Jamal Jones had discussed geographic links and provided maps to identify hotspots where their victims were seen or evidence was found. Timeframes had come into question, and the patterns between disappearances. Then Ness discussed the known predators who had been interviewed. But none of the information that the team shared brought Elea one step closer to her daughter. She needed fresh action, tangible leads.

She thought she'd found them with Sienna, but today they were going over old ground. She hugged the paperwork to her chest as she waited for everyone to leave. The team had been cooperative, including her in every aspect of the investigation, but they danced around her feelings when it came to discussing the Ice Angels, glancing her way as if she was one big open wound. Still, she could not fault them. They had made her feel welcome. But there was one big obstacle to overcome. She cleared her throat as Mitch pushed the door shut. The soft click of the latch finding its home signalled privacy.

'Everything OK?' He gathered up the discarded pieces of paperwork that had been left behind. Soon iPads would take over from paper printouts and Post-it notes.

Elea wasn't in the mood for pointless questions. 'Who's the head honcho at the EMROCU? I need to speak to them.' She was talking about the specialist police unit tackling serious and organised crime across the East Midlands.

Mitch's eyebrows rose at the request. 'Why?'

'Because I'm buying a new bra and I need lingerie advice.' Sarcasm came naturally to Elea and she couldn't stop the words. 'Why do you think I want to talk to them?'

Mitch tried, but failed, to hide his smile. 'It's a big organisation. They cover the five East Midlands police forces, not just Lincolnshire.' He turned his attention back to tidying up the space.

'You haven't answered my question.' Elea's fingers dug into the paperwork, which had done little to advance the case.

'They're working with the NCA . . .' He paused to find the words to explain. 'The National Crime Agency. Those names you found – they're at the bottom of the food chain. You stumbled onto something big. It goes way higher than we first thought. We're talking organised crime across multiple counties.' He left the pile of paperwork on the table and began to tidy up the chairs.

'And this takes precedence over young girls' lives? If these people are low-level, then why am I being told to back off?' She ground her molars. 'For God's sake, will you stop with the bloody chairs and look at me!'

'OK, OK.' Mitch raised his hands in mock-surrender. As a DI, he had better things to do. But he was also considerate, trying to leave the room as he found it after everyone had left. He sighed, resting his backside on the edge of the briefing table. 'We don't want to spook off the main players. We're talking drugs, weapons, human trafficking; the laundering of millions of pounds through shell companies and cryptocurrency. Any contact from us could put undercover officers at risk.'

Elea knew of the challenges that undercover officers faced. She'd been one herself, many years ago. Backstories would have been invented and memorised as false identities were taken on. Fake ID would have been created as officers embedded themselves within the group. Distance from family and friends was necessary at such times. Every interaction would have been logged and backed up with intercepted communications. In the background, specialist officers would have provided monitoring and tracing of suspicious financial transactions. When it came to such big sums of money, the risks were immense. One wrong step could unravel months, or even years, of work. But still, frustration burned like a branding iron in her chest. 'There must be someone I can talk to. Sienna knows something. If I could just reason with them.'

'They know that you're here, Elea, and they know about Sienna, too. It . . .' He stepped towards her. 'It changes nothing.' Mitch's words were heavy with compassion. It wasn't what she wanted to hear.

'Don't look at me like that.' She spoke with tight conviction. 'Like I'm something pitiful. Someone to be fobbed off.'

'Seriously? You couldn't be further from the truth. I've tried making headway with the EMROCU.' Their stare remained unbroken. 'I didn't want to get your hopes up. They told me to back the fuck off. It's delicate, Elea, but try to look at it this way: you've got some serious workforce behind this. So let them get on with it, and we'll investigate the other avenues. Because there's still a chance that we're chasing a false lead.'

Elea nodded. He was right. Every decision was crucial. But which one would return to haunt them all?

# Chapter Thirty-Eight

The blue sofa cushions seemed to swallow Sophie as she sat beside her mother. Her hands moved restlessly, twisting and untwisting the frayed strings of her oversized pink hoodie. She pulled them taut, then let them go slack, over and over again. The suite was there for vulnerable victims, the cameras discreetly tucked away in each corner of the generously sized room. Toys lay invitingly about the floor, and a vase of artificial flowers added a splash of colour to the space.

'Hello, Sophie.' Elea lowered herself to speak to the girl. 'It's really nice to see you again.'

'Hi,' Sophie whispered, her wide blue eyes never leaving Elea's face. The sound of the girl's voice was the most beautiful thing she'd heard all year. Everything was ready. Ness was monitoring the interview and making notes from a separate room. A social worker was present and had agreed to sit in the monitoring room, so as not to overwhelm Sophie. It was important to have her there, to limit the need for Sophie to be asked the same questions time and time again. The small earpiece in Elea's ear granted communication with Ness, in case she had any questions to raise.

Elea settled into a chair across from Sophie, waiting until the girl was at ease. The first part of an ABE interview was about establishing a rapport. It was in everyone's interest to achieve the best evidence and get it right the first time round. Elea talked about Sophie's iPad and the games she played. She mentioned her own daughter, forever twelve in her mind. She talked about Liisa's love of ponies, and Sophie spoke of her own riding lessons. Finally, when Sophie's shoulders relaxed, Elea leaned towards her. 'I'm going to ask you some questions, OK? You're safe. There's nothing to worry about any more.'

Sophie glanced at her mother, who nodded encouragingly. She had come a long way since their first meeting.

'What happened the day you disappeared, Sophie?' Elea asked gently. She followed up with the time and date, more for the benefit of the recording than anything else. This was the section of the interview in which Sophie would be encouraged to give a free recall of events. The finer details would come later. When interviewing a child, interruptions were kept to a minimum.

Sophie continued to work the ends of her hoodie strings between her fingers. 'I was walking home from school. There was this man. I . . . I knew him – from before.'

Sophie's young mother, Fiona, frowned. She was about to speak when Elea delivered a small shake of the head. She'd been briefed before the interview. She was there to provide comfort only.

'I . . . I don't know his name,' Sophie continued, 'but he had a dog. Just like the one I wanted.' Sophie glanced up at Fiona. 'A Yorkie.' She told Elea about the furry Yorkie keyring that her friend had bought her, and how she'd attached it to her school bag. Elea's breath quickened. This was a premeditated kidnapping, exactly as Liisa's had been, when her mother's car tyres had been slashed. But was the kidnapper a human trafficker or working alone?

'His dog was nice,' Sophie continued. 'Her name was Trixie. She had a pink collar. He said it belonged to his daughter. He used to let me stroke her.' Sophie glanced at Elea, who gave her an encouraging smile.

Elea thought of Ness, who was probably multitasking, quickly sending an email to the team as well as monitoring each word that was said.

'That day,' Sophie carried on, 'he said Trixie had run away. He asked if I'd help him look. We walked down the road. He said he needed to get her lead from his van.' She swallowed, her fingers wrapping tightly around the strings.

'It's OK,' Elea reminded her. 'You're safe now.'

'He . . . he grabbed me. Then – he put something over my mouth. It smelled weird. Everything went dark.'

A wave of anger surged through Elea, but she kept her expression composed, focusing on extracting the crucial details from the young girl, who was struggling to give a free account.

'Can you tell me what he looked like? Start from the top of his head and work your way down to his feet. Can you do that for me?'

Slowly, and without faltering, Sophie spoke of an ordinary-looking white man with a beard and shoulder-length brown hair. Such simplified descriptions often came from children. Elea drilled into the detail, comparing his height with her father, as well as asking about his skin colour, gait, smell, accent and more.

'He smelled of liquorice. He spoke like you.'

Elea faltered, her heart seeming to stop mid-beat. She wanted to go into details about every word he spoke, but this was about getting Sophie's first account. She blinked as her body seemed to right itself.

'He had a scar on his face.' Sophie's voice turned quiet.

Each response was a gift landing in Elea's outstretched hands. Her chest tightening with emotion, she eyed the glass of water on the table. Swann would surely be watching. If he detected a shake in her hand, then he'd have her out of there. She was too invested, too emotionally involved, but she was making progress. She coughed to clear her throat and left the water where it was.

'You OK?' Ness's voice filtered through her earpiece. Elea delivered a tiny nod.

With each question, Sophie's mother grew more tense. Elea sensed her need to intervene. 'Where was the scar exactly?' she quickly asked, her thoughts half in the room and half with Liisa: dare she dream that, after all this time, she'd finally got a substantial lead?

Sophie nodded, touching the right side of her mouth. 'Here. Behind the beard.'

Elea wanted to hug the young girl, to tell her that she was doing great. But she kept her features even. Sophie had paled and she hadn't got to the worse bit yet. 'And when you say he spoke like me – in what way? Do you mean he was serious, or was it his tone or his—'

'His accent. He sounded like you.'

*Oh my God*, Elea thought. *It's him. We're so close.*

'What happened next?' she ventured, after exhausting the list of descriptives. But Sophie was turning inwards, tightly interlocking her fingers. 'You had a doll when we found you: where did that come from?' Changing the subject sometimes helped to move things along.

'He gave it to me.' Sophie's voice was barely above a whisper. She looked to her mother. 'I want to go home.'

'And you will, sweetheart,' Elea said, giving her mum a pleading look. 'Soon.' She would have to quicken her questioning, get to the guts of the matter while looking after the little girl in her care. Deeper probing could come later on. 'But we really need to know what happened next, if you can.' Elea hadn't forgotten about the social worker in the other room.

Sophie scratched her head and pushed her fringe off her face. 'He was carrying me into the house when I came to . . . My room was cold, always dark. He took my shoes. Sometimes,' she whispered, her eyes brimming with unshed tears, 'he would shout at me to be good; and once, when I tried to run away, he slapped me across the face.'

Fiona's lips formed into a thin white line as her daughter shared the details of her ordeal.

'Thank you for being so brave, Sophie.' A small smile of encouragement rested on Elea's face. 'Every detail is so important. Is there anything else you can remember about the house? Any sounds? Were you in the city or the country, do you think? Could you hear sounds outside?' Given that she'd been found at the cathedral doors, they'd presumed Sophie had been kept nearby, but that might have not been the case.

'He . . . he said if I shouted, he'd know. Sometimes I could hear the bells.' She stared down at her hands and unlocked her fingers. 'There was a woman,' she said finally, her eyes meeting Elea's. 'I heard her voice.'

Elea's heart jolted, as if someone had clamped down with a defibrillator and suddenly brought it to life. The part that died the day she lost Liisa. She took a breath to speak and nodded slightly as Ness checked in over her earpiece. 'Can you tell me anything about the woman? What you saw or heard?'

But Sophie shook her head. 'I didn't see her. They were in another room.' She stared into the middle distance, caught in the past. 'Once, I heard crying. That's when he'd turn up the TV.'

Elea's mind was racing. He turned up the TV to drown out the sounds of another person crying. Surely that meant that they were captive, too?

'Did you hear any names? Was she a grown-up like me and your mum? Or younger, like you?'

Sophie shrugged, retreating into silence. The strain of recounting her ordeal was beginning to take its toll.

'Listen, Sophie, you've been incredibly brave today. Let's move on to something else, OK?' Elea suggested, trying to ease the tension in the room.

'OK,' Sophie agreed, wiping her eyes with the back of her hand.

'Can you tell me how you escaped?'

'I was in a van,' Sophie began, her voice steadier now. 'It was white. Small. Smelly. He was moving me somewhere else. But he left to get something.'

'Is that when you escaped?'

Sophie nodded. 'Yeah. He didn't close the door properly. I pushed it open and ran away. I was in my bare feet, but I just kept running. Down past the school. Through the car park. To the cathedral. Mummy said that if I was lost, to go to a public place. But everywhere was closed, so I hid in the doorway.'

'Clever girl.' Elea was grateful that she'd had somewhere to run to. If only Liisa had been able to do the same thing.

'I want to go home now. I'm tired.'

'OK,' Elea said. She couldn't make Sophie stay. More would come, piece-by-piece, when she was well enough to give it. A thought occurred. 'The shoes. I was wondering why you gave them to me.'

'He wore Velcro shoes. It was weird, cos he was a man.'

'I think she's had enough,' Fiona said.

'Please. One more question,' she pleaded with Fiona, who responded with a sigh. At least it wasn't a no.

Elea returned her attention to Sophie, who covered her mouth as she yawned. 'We're going to look for that man, and the place where you were kept.' She paused. Just one more small push. She weighed up her words. 'Do you remember where it is? You said he carried you into the house. If we take you in the police car, can you show us where that is?'

Sophie looked from her mother to Elea. 'He won't see me, right? Because he said . . .' She bit her bottom lip. 'He said he'd come get me if I told.'

'Nobody's coming to get you,' Elea reassured the girl. 'The police: it's like a gang. The biggest gang in England. And everyone in this gang is there to keep you safe. He's just one person. We,' she circled a finger around the room, 'all of us, we outnumber him. We'll use a car with tinted windows. You can see out, but nobody can see in. Is that OK with you?'

The silence was agonising, but Elea allowed it to lay claim.

# Chapter Thirty-Nine

## Liisa

### 2016

My breath leaves my mouth in tiny clouds and the cold creeps deep into my bones. I've lost all track of time. I don't know how long I've been in the forest. There is less snow in the sheltered spaces, but the sun doesn't reach them and the air feels colder here. The ground glistens like a carpet of ice. Twigs become fragile shards and snap beneath my oversized boots. The sun has dipped and Johanna's words return to my mind. I won't survive out here on my own. My body shudders with the cold. Teeth chattering, I stare up at the pine trees that make me feel oh-so-small. The wind stirs, carrying an earthy smell as it shifts the fine powdery snow. In the distance the ravens call as they settle down and I wonder how they can stand the cold. I put one foot in front of the other. I've been walking for so long. The trees seem to merge. I cannot find a way out. I cry. I run until I can barely feel my feet. My heart thumps a-lub-dub in my chest at the sound of an engine in the distance. A car, maybe?

'Mama!' I cry miserably. But she is not here.

I don't hear Johanna creep up behind me until it is too late. Her cold hand clamps hard over my mouth and nose. I kick, I lash out, the stink of Johanna's glove making me gag. Fish and smoke. Then I feel the fiery sting of the home-made stun gun as it hits me in the base of my spine.

I awake with a start, groping in the blackness. I can't . . . I can't see. My tongue is swollen. I taste blood in my mouth. Hands shaking, I touch my face. My lashes tickle my fingers as I open and close my eyes. Have I gone blind? I stare around me, looking for something to latch onto. Then I see it. A silver thread of light far above my head. I try to stand, but a mattress wobbles beneath me. I reach beyond it. It's on the ground, not a bed frame. My legs are weak and everything hurts. Where am I? Warm tears trickle down my face as I remember what happened. The forest: Johanna. I pat down my body. No cuts. No blood – I think. But I'm so sore. My toes are pins and needles freezing. There are thick, loose tights on my legs and I pull them up. My hand brushes against the rough material of another of Johanna's home-made dresses. There's a rip in the hem. She has changed my clothes.

Heavy blankets layer the thin foam mattress. I spread out my fingers and find something small and metal. There's a grid. I flick a switch on the side and two orange bars of light beam in the darkness. Heat. It's a heater. I pull it to me, being careful not to burn my fingers, and drag the blankets over my shoulders. She wasn't being kind. I was freezing in the forest. Cold can kill. I whimper as I try to see through the darkness. The glow from the heater is dim. There's a lead – the electric cable is plugged into an extension lead, which stretches . . . I stare, blinking as I wait for my eyes to adjust. It snakes up the wall, then disappears through the roof of this place.

I want my mum. Because I know where I am. I'm in the hole. I push my face into the damp blanket, because I can't let Johanna hear me cry. I don't want it getting any worse than this. I feel something move in my hair, so light that it's barely there. I can't keep in my scream as I grasp something with legs and fling it away from me. I don't want to know what it is.

'Please!' I call, getting to my feet and feeling my way around. I touch a cold wooden structure as I walk outside the glow of the heater. My fingers run carefully over splintered timber. Firm wooden posts are holding this space up. The walls feel like hardened dirt. What else is down here, besides me? I feel like I'm being watched. I remember Johanna's comment about the big hairy spiders that live in the hole. I stare up at the roof. 'I'm sorry!' I cry. 'Please, let me out! I'm so sorry!' My breath is coming faster. I can't control it. I'm buried underground. I can't reach the light above my head. This place is taller than my mother. Six, maybe seven feet high? 'Please, Mama Johanna!' I beg, hoping that by calling her she will feel sorry for me. I swipe at my hair, brush imaginary spiders from my body. It feels as if an army of insects is closing in on me. I can't stop screaming. My whole body is shaking now.

Time passes and I run out of screams. My throat is scratchy and raw. I think of the last time I saw Mikael. Is he even alive? What if they have left me down here to die? What if this really is my burial place? I think of Mama finding me, far too late. My body nothing but bones, somewhere the spiders have made a home. The cries that leave my mouth sound like the animals in the woods.

There is noise. Footsteps on the wooden floor above. I try to stop, but my breath is jerky as my sobs rise up my throat. There is dirt under my fingernails. My tears are salty as they reach my mouth. There's a sudden burst of light. I recognise the outline of Mikael's face. His left eye is puffy and there's a bruise rising on his face. 'Please, let me out,' I whisper as he gestures at me to be quiet. 'I'm sorry,' I add, and I mean it, because as much as I hate it here, I don't want to hurt anyone. He throws down a bag. It lands with a soft plop on my blanket beneath. I don't stop to look at it, because there is something else in his hand.

'Take it,' he says.

'But . . .'

'Take it.'

I reach up, squinting. He drops it into my hand. He checks over his shoulder. Johanna doesn't know about this. I accept the secret gift. I peer in the dim light, my spirits lifting as I recognise its shape. My small wooden doll, the one Grandmother gave me. It was in the pocket of the jacket that Johanna took away. I hold it close to my chest. My last link to home.

'Hide it,' he whispers, before pulling the trapdoor shut.

I want to call out, but I know there is no point. I feel on the ground for the bag. The plastic rustles under my fingers. I wrap my hands around a small torch. I switch it on, relief flooding through me as the space lights up a little more. I search each corner, seeing the dead spider that I pulled from my hair before. I am here for the night, but at least I have light, heat and a reminder of home. I peek inside the bag. Food is wrapped in foil. A drinking flask. I look around my space, which is just as I had imagined. I am in a small hole of dirt and blankets, the roof held up by beams of wood. I clutch the doll tightly in my hand. It tells me so many things. That it is our secret. That Mikael is not evil. That he took it to give me comfort. That he is afraid of Johanna, too. For the first time since I got here I don't feel so alone.

# Chapter Forty

In normal circumstances Elea would not expect a twelve-year-old child to be able to give adults very good directions. But trauma had profound and long-lasting effects. Sophie's information-processing would have been different from that of any other child. Her trauma wasn't caused by one single life-changing event, but by several. Neurochemicals would have rushed to her brain, taking a snapshot of each and every defining moment. Exactly like the snapshots that Elea still saw from the day her daughter disappeared. These memories would haunt Sophie for years to come. It was a fine balance, taking care with a traumatised victim while extracting the information necessary to hunt their abductor down.

'That way.' Sophie's voice rose from the back of Swann's car, fragile but determined as they drove down Yarborough Road. She was sitting in the back seat with her mother, pale-faced and cautious, holding her hand. Elea was next to Swann in the front, staring through the rain-speckled window, barely daring to imagine what lay ahead.

'Up there. That's it. Over there.'

Swann looked left and right, indicating to turn. Carline Road was innocuous, with pleasant red-brick homes each side, flanked by brick walls bordering small front gardens. Double-yellow lines striped down the street, with a selection of trees shading an array of parked cars.

'That's it. That yellow house, behind those trees . . .' Sophie pointed ahead to the right. But there was a tremble in her hand. A catch in her throat when she spoke.

'I don't like this,' her mother said. 'Don't get too close.'

'We won't compromise you.' Elea turned back to them both as Swann slowly drove past. 'You have my word. He'll most likely be long gone.' But there was hope. The tiniest spark of hope that her kidnapper was still there. And maybe, just maybe, he wasn't alone. The air was thick with anticipation. Elea felt a magnetic pull, and it took all her restraint not to jump out of the car. Swann continued down the road, eventually bringing the car to a halt.

Elea glanced around. There was no sign of CCTV cameras anywhere on this road. 'Are you sure, sweetheart? Really sure?' It was a well-populated road, with houses on either side.

Fiona began to sob. 'All that time, you were no distance from us.'

Sophie nodded. 'My friend, Priti, she lives a few houses up.'

That was enough for Elea. Sophie's memory would be sharp. She had no reason to lie.

'Can I go home?'

'We're leaving right now,' Fiona said firmly, looking to Elea for confirmation. 'Aren't we?'

'Right away,' Elea replied.

'Good.' Fiona settled back into her seat. 'You've got what you wanted. Now leave my daughter in peace.'

Elea wished it was that easy. But for today Sophie had done good. Swann spoke into his police airwave radio, updating the system with their results and tagging Mitch to be made aware, so he could get events under way. Warrants would be authorised. A search of the building would be made. Hopefully, there would be arrests. But right now they had to get Sophie home.

Swann turned back to Sophie. 'You've been a very brave girl.' He looked to her mother. 'I know that wasn't easy for either of you. We'll keep you updated.'

'Just get him off the streets,' Fiona said, her arm wrapped protectively around her daughter.

'Sophie,' Swann continued, 'we're going to get you home now, OK? Ness is waiting around the corner. You remember Ness? From the interview?'

Sophie nodded, her eyes large with an understanding of the darker side of the world.

'She's going to take you and your mum home. Don't you worry now. We'll handle it from here.' His voice was smooth and reassuring. They had rehearsed for this moment and knew exactly what to do.

'Can't we just go down there?' Elea's hand rested on the door handle of the car. Her body was moving of its own accord, itching to get going now that Sophie and her mother were safely in Ness's care. The clunk of the internal locking system made her stiffen. She glared at Swann.

'You know the score.' He stared steadily ahead. And she did. Strict procedures were in place. But it didn't stop her emotions running away with her. 'I'll drive back round. We'll keep eyeballs on the place until surveillance get here.'

But Elea's voice rose as Swann pulled away from the kerb.

'Let me out, will you? She could be in there. He could be hurting her right now. We've got to go in.'

'And Sophie could be wrong. She's twelve years old, Elea. Go thundering in there and mess everything up, and you'll be sent home . . . or worse.' He shrugged as she threw him a death-stare. 'I'm no fan of red tape, either, but it's there to protect us.'

Elea tilted her head defiantly as Swann manoeuvred his car around. 'We have suspicion. You can make an arrest.'

'And what if he legs it out the back? What if he has a gun? What if your sudden appearance forces his hand? We're always playing with variables. Surveillance will be here soon.'

Elea's heart ached with the need to find her daughter or, at the very least, the man who took her. But she knew what would happen next. This was a high-risk, high-profile case. A team of plain-clothes officers would be posted to observe while the main operation was under way. Elea was torn. Should she stay and observe or be part of the strategic planning? She turned down the car heater as she began to perspire. The traffic passed by in a blur. Her heart began to race as she wondered how long Sophie had been kept there. Was it for the whole time that she was missing? What about Chelsea, and Liisa: were they there, too? Questions raced in her mind. All she knew was that she needed to get inside that house because it was torture sitting here when she was so close to the truth. The minutes that passed felt like hours while Swann sorted everything out. Common sense dictated that Sophie's abductor had long since fled. But common sense was for rational people. Murderers and kidnappers – they were a law unto themselves.

# Chapter Forty-One

Swann sat with his team, breathing in recycled air in the back of the police van. This was where he loved to be, on the cusp of a discovery. This was what he'd joined the job for. His phone was on silent, his senses heightened. They were parked in the nearest car park to the suspect's location. He was the head of this operation and he would not put a foot wrong. He'd seen what happened when cases were botched. The ones that made it to court didn't go any further, as the perpetrator's defence lawyers pulled apart the police procedure. Frustration didn't come close to describing it. But there was a balance to be met. Time was of the essence and, given the nature of the case, they had to move fast.

He had already performed a quick tactical briefing and now they were waiting for the go-ahead. Adrenaline rushed through his bloodstream. Whatever happened next would fall on his shoulders. It had taken some persuading to get Elea to leave the suspect's address. Now she sat in the van with the rest of them, staring into space, fists clenched on her lap. She was too professional to sulk, but beneath the surface there was a dark, brooding resentment at having to take a step back. Had Swann thought children were inside the house, he would have smashed the door in himself. But according to Sophie, her kidnapper was leaving the area when she escaped from his van. The property was a rental, paid up to the end of the month. But there was no vehicle on the drive, no signs of life, according to the officer who had discreetly posed as a delivery driver. Firearms officers had been called down. The tactical team had been briefed. It was highly unlikely anyone was still inside. The question was: what awaited them? What had the suspect left behind?

Surveillance officers were still in place, discreetly dotted around the area, keeping an eye on all comings and goings relating to the address. The last thing they wanted was the suspect being tipped off. A search warrant had been obtained by Mitch in record time. He had presented his findings to a local magistrate, explaining the urgency of the situation and the potential valuable evidence that could be disposed of. Nearby uniformed officers were on alert, ready to act as backup if needed.

Swann went through the dynamic risk assessment one more time with his team. They had already assessed the threat level and planned the safest approach. The tactical support group was in position. The time was almost upon them. This was a dangerous offender. If the suspect *were* inside, he wasn't getting away. Swann listened to raised voices outside as people complained about the cost of the car park. They had no awareness of what was going on within the confines of the police van.

'Bloody daylight robbery!' a woman exclaimed.

'It's cheaper after six,' the man in her company concluded.

They seemed to linger for a moment. Swann listened as a cigarette lighter flicked, then they moved on at a steady pace. In his job he had always felt separate from ordinary life. If he wasn't investigating crime, it was playing on his mind. He went over a mental checklist one more time.

A negotiation strategy had also been considered, included the likelihood of a hostage situation. Had Elea been thinking clearly, these were all things that she would have considered, too. They had planned a soft approach in order to preserve as much forensic evidence as possible. Elea was allowed to tail along, but only on the periphery. Swann's muscles tensed as the call came in on his airwaves. He nodded to his team. It was time to go.

# Chapter Forty-Two

Elea stood at the double entrance gates situated at the side of the property. The building stood out from the others. Cheerful bright-yellow painted walls with white gloss timber windows and hanging baskets on either side of a red door. The contents of the baskets were dead, the brown, thready stems of whatever flower lay within now shrivelled and hanging to one side. Unlike the other properties on the street, this house faced away from its neighbours, its entrance having a wide gravel drive. A tall red-brick wall gained it further privacy.

But there was life all around: cars, pedestrians, students on their way home from college, and now the sound of police officers, both uniformed and plain-clothes, as they searched the property. They hadn't needed the code to the key-box next to the door – not when officers had been able to swiftly take it apart. It had taken just seconds to gain entry, and the tactical officers had cleared every room. But it was the basement they were interested in, and they had wasted no time in heading down there. Plans of the property had been obtained online by the intelligence team. If their suspect was hiding out, this was where he would be.

Dressed in her forensic suit, Elea hovered, ready to go in. Her heart was a steady drumbeat as she waited for updates. The material of her baggy white oversuit rustled as she moved, the face-mask claustrophobic against her skin. If she were to see her daughter again, she didn't want it to be like this. But Swann had been strict in implementing the rules. She went in on his terms or not at all.

'You all right?' Mitch asked, as they both watched for movement. He had most likely been tasked with accompanying her while Swann and the team went inside.

Elea felt a rocket trip to the moon away from all right, but she offered him an 'Mmm' and a nod of the head. He would not be entering the property; it wasn't a free-for-all. 'Locard's Exchange Principle' had been rammed down their throat during their training – both in the UK and in Finland. Every contact gives and takes away something from a crime scene. Each cough, each touch, each fingerprint or footprint could have a devastating forensic effect. The weight of a step could crush fibres. A touch on a door could smudge or destroy fingerprints. The movement of objects could destroy theories. The opening of windows could mean releasing insects that might have been of forensic value later on. Even flies had their part to play. But Elea had waited ten years for this moment.

They listened as each room was cleared, until finally an update came through on the police airwaves. 'We've found something . . .'

Elea's heart jumped into her throat. Why had they stopped talking? She imagined Swann stemming their words, because this was not good. A separate airways channel had been designated for the operation, but their commanding officers would be listening in. She went to move forward, but Mitch placed a hand on her forearm.

'Wait. Just one more minute.'

But this was killing her. 'I can't . . .' she began to say. She took in Swann's face as he emerged from the building.

His eyes were haunted as he joined her. He dropped his mask to his chin.

'What is it? Is she in there? What have you found?' The words tumbled from Elea's lips. She wished she could shut the hell up, so that Swann could tell her what she needed to know. But once she started speaking, she couldn't stop.

Swann exchanged a glance with Mitch. A get-her-back-to-the-station-before-she-loses-it look.

Elea closed her eyes. Unclenched her fists. Took a soothing breath and started again. 'I'm OK.' She spoke with as much calmness as she could muster. Today she had to be a police officer first, and a mother second. Because Liisa's mother would be racing through that building right now, screaming her daughter's name. She tilted her chin upwards. Brought her shoulders back a touch. Kept her voice steady and devoid of the emotions running riot inside her. 'There's a body inside, isn't there?'

Swann nodded.

Another breath. Elea detached herself from the situation. Yes, she was a police officer simply doing her job. This was any other case. 'Very well. Blonde, female, I take it?'

'It appears so.' Already CSI were entering the building, being careful not to walk over the tyre tracks left in the gravel driveway by the last occupant of the home. Stepping plates were being put down. The property was already cordoned off. People were being suited up, but numbers would be limited. The property owners were being spoken to. Updates were coming in on the radio. This was a crime scene now. 'You don't have to go in.'

'Is it Liisa? What age is she? Have you identified her?'

'It's . . . doubtful that it's Liisa.'

'Christ, Swann! It's either Liisa or it's not? The twelve-year-old body of Chelsea Hobbs or the remains of a young woman – can't you tell the damned difference?' Heads swivelled as Elea's voice rose. She took another breath, her chest rising and falling as frustration took hold. So much for remaining calm.

Swann remained steadfast. 'She's a child, but she's in a freezer, Elea. Caked in ice. That's why we don't know for sure. It's unlikely to be Liisa, after all this time.' Then he talked about the logistics of a perp transporting Liisa to the UK when she was twelve years old, but Elea couldn't take it in. She had waited, as instructed. She'd held herself back. But not any more. Her name should be on the log. Her heart was pounding so fast she couldn't stand still.

She marched up to a young uniformed officer holding a clipboard. 'Give me that,' she said, snatching it off him. Swann nodded as Elea took it from his hands and scribbled down her name. Her shaky writing looked as if a spider had limped across the page. She thrust the log of names back to the officer before turning towards the building. One by one, she took each stepping plate, Swann close behind. She would identify the girl in the ice, and then they would take it from there.

# Chapter Forty-Three

### Liisa

### *2016*

It has been three whole days. I've worked out day from night by the sliver of light over my head and the noises of Johanna's routine. The shuffle of her heavy feet. The cabin door slamming as Mikael leaves for the forest. Every second feels like for ever as I sit wrapped in blankets, rocking on the spot. I talk to myself about home. I talk about my family, about how I will decorate my room. Anything to take myself away from here. I think about my friends and my teachers at school. I can feel myself falling behind. I think about survival and what I need to do to stay alive.

My first night in this pit I dug a hole for a toilet and covered it up. The smell makes me so queasy that I force myself to suck on the liquorice that I found in Mikael's bag of supplies. They make my teeth all furry. I hate the smell of them because they remind me of his breath. But they're better than the stink of my home-made toilet in this cold underground cave. The roof creaks above me.

Today Johanna's footsteps are heavy and specks of dirt

rain down. It's in my eyes, my face, my hair. It stops, as does Johanna. I keep my breath low as I listen out for her. My fingernails are thick with soil from when I tried to tunnel my way out. But to where? I've already tried escaping. There was nothing but trees and ice. Mikael hasn't spoken to me again. I relive the last minutes when I disappeared. Could I have done more? Mama would have taken the gun. She would have shot Mikael first, then pulled the trigger on Johanna. Then she would have taken the keys of her yellow car and driven for help. But would she have done it when she was twelve years old? Then I remember that the gun wasn't loaded in the first place.

My stomach growls from hunger and I am thirsty all the time. Not a regular thirst. There is an itch at the back of my throat that I can't reach by swallowing as my mouth is so dry. I sip from my bottle of water, but it makes a hollow sound. There's nothing left but air. I get thrown one bottle a day, and leftovers that always smell funny. I hate fish with a passion. The walls feel like they are getting closer. There's life in the dirt. Living creatures that crawl on my arms and face when I lie down to sleep. I'm so tired all the time. This morning – at least I think it was this morning – I burned my hand on the heater because I jumped away from a spider. But nobody came when I cried.

She is moving again. My stomach churns as I hear her right above me. She's pulling at the hatch. That gorilla of a woman is coming for me. Every thought involving her is unkind. I cannot help myself. A plan flashes in my mind, and I don't have time to work out whether or not it's a good idea. I lie on my side, eyes shut, playing dead. I feel the light of the hatch behind my closed eyes. Seconds pass as I hold my breath. But

223

I can hear Johanna's, thick and whistling as it passes through her congested nose.

The edges of the hatch creak and I imagine her leaning on it, her big wide head blotting the light out. If she thinks I have fainted, maybe she'll set me free. But there are no steps down to this place. I don't think she can make it here right away, even if she wants to. She grunts as she moves. Can I keep this up? But then I hear a slosh swirling in a bottle of water. I flinch as it hits me in the leg. Johanna barks what I think is a laugh. 'Well, well, little mole. I was going to let you out,' she sneers, her words hard and cold. 'Playing dead earns you another night in the hole.'

Then the hatch slams above me and the white light goes out. I sit up and let the tears flow. I'm crying, not because I am sad, but out of relief. She's letting me out soon. I'm not going to die down here. I clasp my small wooden doll to my chest, taking comfort in its pointy edges. I'm getting out.

I awake to raspy voices from above. How long have I been asleep for? The sliver of light is still there. Johanna and Mikael are arguing. But it isn't the usual shouting match. This is harsh but quiet whispers. I stand as the radio is turned on, my heart fluttering and jumping in my chest. Something is up. What was that? Did I just hear a knock on the cabin door?

Three loud raps. I'm shaking. Help – help is coming. Because nobody comes out this far. There's somebody out there. Voices. More than one. I listen as the door opens. Then I scream.

# Chapter Forty-Four

Elea always knew that she could be called to identify her daughter's body. It's why she never travelled too far. Australia was out for sure, as was any long-haul holiday. She had travelled to Bangkok once and spent every night checking her phone. She didn't want to believe that Liisa was dead. She'd never allowed the flame of hope to extinguish. But the small, practical side of her nature had a voice, too. Nobody but her should be granted the task of identifying her daughter's body when it came down to it.

She saw the pitiful looks from the police officers as she approached the scene. Their quiet reverence was almost too much to bear. She wasn't having any of it. She delivered a nod of acknowledgement, her face stony. She pulled the forensic mask over her mouth, glancing upwards at the house. What had happened within these walls? He'd been under their noses, but for how long? Could she have made it here sooner? *In, out* . . . She reminded herself to breathe as the stepping plates shifted on the gravel beneath her feet. She was shadowed inside the building. The ground was solid, so why did the world feel like it was still moving beneath her weight? Her footsteps echoed down the long, narrow corridor, the cold air stifling as it wrapped itself around her.

Elea took in her surroundings. Yellow walls. A white dado

rail. Pictures of the Lincolnshire wolds. A mop sticking out of a metal bucket near the door. The building was old but clean, the faint smell of bleach hanging in the air. A hush fell as she followed Swann to the end of the corridor.

'Down here,' he said, rustling ahead of her.

Elea kept walking, pausing when Swann stopped.

'Are you . . .'

'Yes, I'm ready.' Elea gave him a stern look. The one that said it was time to get on with it. They were all on a countdown. Every second mattered. But each step down to the basement felt as if they were a million miles apart. She glanced at the cobwebs lining the old wooden beams. At the stained brown lino on the floor. A dusty wine shelf took up a whole wall, empty apart from cobwebs. Boxes lined the other side, as well as some rusted garden furniture that had been stored away for the winter. The air smelt of damp.

She looked at the CSI officers as they cleared a path for her. There, against the wall, was an industrial-sized chest freezer. There was a dent on the front. Smudges of dirt on the lid. The insectile buzz of its motor as it preserved what was inside. Her throat clicked as she swallowed, her tongue feeling like it was stuck to the roof of her mouth. She couldn't speak now, even if she wanted to. Swann gestured to guide her forwards, a world of emotion behind his eyes.

The smell of the mask on her face was making Elea feel sick. She was too confined in this place. The soft creak of the freezer lid focused her thoughts as an officer opened it. She stepped forward. Stared at the sight inside. *'Jumalauta,'* she whispered beneath her breath. But it was too late for God to help her now. 'Can I brush away the ice?' She spoke to the crime-scene officer, looking deep into her grey-blue eyes. She was female, from what Elea could tell beneath the confines of her forensic bunny suit.

'Yes,' she said simply, handing Elea a soft brush. 'Just the face, if that's OK.' They needed to preserve forensics for more in-depth examination, but equally an identification was of the essence now.

Elea took in the young girl's form, forcing her lungs to breathe. The child was lying in a foetal position, head bowed into her knees, elbows by her side. Her feet were splayed upwards in unnatural angles, most likely broken to fit inside the compact space. Her long blonde hair covered her features. Her dress . . . Elea leaned forward. A light was switched on, making everything glisten. The open door was causing the freezer to ice up and she didn't have long.

Swann kept a respectful distance as Elea took everything in. White lace and netting, like a communion dress. Like the one Jenny Flynn had been wearing when she was found. It couldn't be her Liisa . . . could it? This child, frozen in time. With a shaking gloved hand, Elea gently pulled the frozen strands of blonde hair back from the girl's face. Another thought jostled for attention. Logistically, it *could* be Liisa. He could have taken her to the UK when she was alive. He could have found a way to—

Elea exhaled the breath that had been burning her lungs as the girl's frozen face came into view.

# Chapter Forty-Five

It had been agonising watching Elea move ghost-like into the room. Swann had seen his wife at her best and her worst and he was in awe of her strength. He wasn't so sure he could do the same, had it been one of his boys. The room had fallen silent as she leaned in for a better look. Gently she pushed strands of frozen blonde hair away, before sweeping a soft brush over the young girl's face. He barely dared to breathe as every solemn moment passed. He wished it didn't have to be this way, but at least if it was Liisa, some closure would be had.

'It's not her.' As much as she tried to conceal her emotions, Elea's voice was trembling. 'It's not Liisa.'

'Are you sure?' Swann leaned forward, taking in the child's preserved face. It was as if she'd been dipped in marble while she was sleeping. Her eyes were closed, her blonde lashes frosted. Her lips blue and thin. Liisa had inherited her mother's full, plump lips. This child wasn't her. Even he could see that now.

'It's Chelsea. Chelsea Hobbs.' Elea's tone was heavy with sadness. 'She's got a mole, here, near her left eye. It's like a birthmark. See?' Elea tilted her head to one side, slipping into detective mode. 'Her nails – they've been bitten. Chelsea used to bite her nails.'

Swann didn't remember reading that in a report, but it was the sort of thing Elea would have asked her mother about. She had spoken to Karen Hobbs a few times now, picking up details and storing them in a memory that was superior to his.

Elea looked up at Swann, her blue eyes glistening with raw emotion. There was a battle going on behind those eyes, but she was holding it together. 'I'm ninety-nine per cent sure this is Chelsea Hobbs.' She stepped aside as the freezer door was closed, a small woosh of cold air escaping the child's resting place. She had to be protected from minute degradation that every passing second would bring.

This freezer would not be unplugged. They would use a generator and transport her remains, for the coroner to gain forensic samples. Swann already knew every step of each process they would need to take. The house would be swept for trace evidence: fibres, hair, blood and fingerprints. Ultraviolet light would be used to detect what wasn't visible to the naked eye. Careful handling would be needed when transporting the freezer to ensure the temperature was kept consistent throughout. Controlled thawing would be part of the process, as the body was preserved in a way that achieved the best evidence for the police. The coroner would look for patterns such as bruising or tissue damage to ascertain a potential cause of death. Once the body was fully thawed, a complete autopsy would be performed to determine the actual cause of death. Blood, tissue, DNA and fluid samples would be taken for toxicology tests. Then a full DNA analysis would be completed, checking hair and skin cells as well as testing cavities and beneath the girl's bitten fingernails. But while Swann

229

was working out their next steps, Elea's thoughts were firmly with the victim.

'Poor Karen.' She exhaled a sad breath. 'She's going to have to identify her.' Elea looked around the room. 'Any chance that he'll come back?'

Swann shook his head. 'The house has been cleared. He left in a hurry. He's long gone.'

'He?'

'It would seem so. The property was rented out long-term to a man. A Mr John Smith.' He raised an eyebrow. 'I know.' Very original.' Sarcasm bled through his words 'But we've got lots to go on here.' He gestured at Elea to follow him out. 'It won't be long now.'

Elea didn't disagree.

# Chapter Forty-Six

Elea sat in her car, enjoying the precious time alone. She was parked on the street, outside the home of Chelsea Hobbs. Bruised clouds loomed over the horizon like a threat, and all her senses told her that this wasn't the end. Today had been emotionally draining. It felt like every minute of her working day was spent being observed. Had she such a reputation as a hothead that she had to be permanently watched? Then she thought back to her last year in Finland, and how her frustrations with her daughter's case had led her down some dark paths. She had been reckless. She could have killed someone.

Her stomach grumbled. At least soon she would be able to cook for herself. In the meantime she would have to make do with supermarket food. She nibbled at her tuna-and-sweetcorn sandwich, pausing to sip her water. As she sat in an easy silence, her thoughts drifted to the past. The case of Tuomas Lehtonen had almost cost Elea her job. He was a supply teacher, a single man in his fifties who travelled over Helsinki and beyond. He'd been arrested after he'd stopped on Peltokyläntie to offer twelve-year-old Frida Laine a ride home. Her school was located on Sammontie and she had finished for the day. The area was residential, with fields on either side, dotted with pretty silver-birch trees. It was an active neighbourhood, but on that day in January the roads were thick with snow. Frida had sensibly declined the offer, but Tuomas had been insistent to the point where he had followed her in his car. It was only when Frida's mother turned up that he'd driven off. She'd been concerned enough to report the incident to the police. Elea had not been assigned the case, but it had not stopped her trying to beat a confession out of Lehtonen on his way home from the pub one night. Had her boss, Heikkinen, not been driving past searching for her, that night could have ended very differently. She cringed as she recalled the memory. How she had bruised her knuckles. How she'd wished that she'd had her gun. Heikkinen had loaded Lehtonen into his truck and brought him home. Her boss never told her what had been said, but he bought Lehtonen's silence that night. The teacher hadn't taken her daughter, but the similarities had been there, and it had been so satisfying to knee him in the groin. Tuomas Lehtonen was now on their radar, and he would think twice before offering any child a lift home again.

Elea drained the last of her water. That was enough reminiscing for now. Her belly full and her feet rested, she got out of the car. She couldn't put this off any longer. It was time to break the news. Mitch had offered to task a uniformed officer – it was protocol, after all. But Elea couldn't allow that to happen. She had made Karen Hobbs a promise. She would not renege on it now. She took confident steps up to the doorway. The cathedral bells sounded in the distance. How things had changed since her last visit here. Phil Hobbs had been bailed, pending further investigation, and was living in Grimsby now. Karen was working with social services to get her children back. All except one.

Each time Elea saw her, she looked a little healthier than before. Her sweatshirt fitted a little better and her jeans were clean. Her hair was tied up from a face that was make-up-free. But today she would be taking long strides backwards in her progress.

'Ella,' Karen said, allowing her inside, 'I wasn't expecting to see you today.'

Elea allowed the name mistake to pass. Karen had enough to contend with. She followed her through the hall. It still smelled strongly of chip fat and cigarettes, but was cleaner than before. The threadbare carpet had been hoovered, and the school pictures on the walls were free of dust. Elea recognised Chelsea in one of the images; she was standing next to the Alton Towers sign. She wished she was coming with better news.

'Can I make you a cuppa?' Karen asked, watching her intently. She clasped her hands together, taking in Elea's expression.

'Why don't you sit down?' Elea guided her towards the old leather sofa.

'No,' Karen said quietly, her legs giving way as she fell back onto the couch. 'Whatever you're going to say, I don't want to hear it.' Tears misted her eyes. 'I've got the place all shipshape now.' Her chin trembled. 'My girls are coming home. All of them.'

*Dammit*, Elea thought, *I shouldn't have hesitated*. Passing on news of a death was a plaster that needed to be ripped off. 'We've found a body,' she said, sitting next to Karen. 'There's a chance it might be Chelsea.' Elea dipped her head as she waited for her words to sink in. 'I'm so sorry . . .'

'No!' Karen covered her mouth with her hand. 'I told ya, I don't want to hear it. It's not her! It's not my Chelsea! I'm gonna . . .' She wiped her nose on the sleeve of her jumper. 'I'm gonna put things right.'

'We can't say for sure yet, Karen. She'll need to be identified.'

'But you've seen her, yes? Otherwise you wouldn't be here.'

Elea nodded.

'You said you'd find her, and you did. Now you're here, like the fucking Grim Reaper, telling me my little girl is dead. All because of that vile piece of shit!' Her words were engulfed by a howl. Karen buried her head into her hands.

Elea's heart hardened towards the man who had made this happen. She would kill the bastard when she found him. He deserved nothing less.

# Chapter Forty-Seven

'I'm sorry, love, it's going to be another late one, I'm afraid.'
Swann listened as Alice sighed on the other end of the line.
'We've had a breakthrough,' he continued. 'It's a big one.'

'Have they found her? Liisa, I mean.'

'Not Liisa, no.' Head lowered, he stood in his office, the
aroma of takeaway food wafting in through the door. His
team had ordered pizza. Elea had paid, as a thank-you for
the hours they'd put in.

They had worked non-stop since Sophie Miller had identified the house much earlier in the day. The owners of the
rental property were none too happy, given that it was now
a crime scene. Officers had got to work, seizing anything that
appeared to be of interest. The suspect had left in a hurry,
with little time to clean up after himself. He'd taken time to
mop the floor, but fingerprints had been found on the mop
handle. Such mistakes were going to trip him up. But now
it was gone midnight and their officers needed sleep. They
were meant to have eleven hours between each shift, but
Swann knew he'd see them all first thing. Such a rule was
discarded when working on cases like this; they would rest
when the suspect was found. He listened as Alice told him
all about her day, focusing on every word as she spoke about
their boys.

'Night, boss!' his sergeant spoke on the cusp of a yawn, before turning off his desk lamp. Most of the time Ray was sloth-like, counting the days to retirement and doing what was needed to get by. But even he had perked up as they closed in on the suspect.

Swann bade him goodnight. Sighing, he undid the top button on his shirt, watching the last of his officers filter out of the door. Jamal finished tidying his desk, then pulled his coat and scarf on before leaving. He lived on the outskirts of Lincoln, his flat a twenty-minute drive away. Ollie and Kelly left together, laughing at some in-joke. Ness turned back, gave Swann a flamboyant final wave. He acknowledged her with a nod and a smile, keen to end his phone call.

'What are you doing up so late?' Swann asked Alice. 'I thought you'd be in bed by now.' That wasn't entirely true. He'd *hoped* she'd be in bed. He didn't enjoy lying to the mother of his boys.

'I couldn't sleep. You know I worry when you don't come home.'

But Alice seemed to sleep less when Elea was around. 'Go to bed, love. I'll speak to Mum tomorrow, see if she can look after the twins for a few hours, so you can have a break. Go into town. Do some shopping . . .'

'And be on my feet all day? No, ta.'

'Go for a bit of pampering, then. Please. Let Mum come over. You know how much she misses them.'

'We'll see,' Alice said dismissively. 'We'll talk whenever you get in.'

Swann muttered a few choice expletives as the line went dead. Alice had stopped trusting his mum to help out with the kids when one of them fell from the sofa and ended up with a bump protruding from his skull. It could have happened to anyone, but now his mum was in the doghouse. Alice was not quick to forgive. She complained about being tired, but refused to accept help. She would burn out one of these days. It didn't help that he was lying. He could easily be making his way home by now.

The reason for his lateness entered his office, a wry grin on her face. She was carrying a pizza box. Elea was usually pretty health-conscious, but cold pizza was a guilty pleasure of theirs. The nights they had both stayed up, eating pizza and drinking red wine, as they discussed the Ice Angels case. It had consumed them, until the case turned cold. While Elea kept up the momentum over the years, Swann had wanted to move on. That's when the arguments began.

'Trouble in paradise?' Elea's voice rescued him from the past.

Swann shrugged. He didn't want to talk about Alice any more. 'How are you doing?' He put the onus on Elea.

'Good.' She looked at him with sincerity in her eyes. 'It's coming to an end. I can feel it. I'm ready.' She opened up the box and presented him with a slice of Hawaiian stuffed crust.

Swann raised an eyebrow. 'It'll play havoc with my indigestion.'

'Mind over matter,' Elea smiled.

They sat at his desk, enjoying the peace. It was almost like old times.

# Chapter Forty-Eight

The man in Elea's shower was singing out of tune, some old eighties number that Elea couldn't put her finger on. She sat back on the double bed, sipping her glass of Merlot. This was wrong. Very wrong. But after the day she'd had . . . She'd spent the last decade cocooned in guilt, couldn't she just have one night off? Perhaps a little selfishness was needed tonight. It wasn't as if anyone was going to find out.

Her skin still tingled from the sex they'd had. It was good to feel alive. Sometimes she'd felt like she was calcifying, becoming cold, hard and fossilised. But not tonight. Her eyes roamed over the messy bed. The sheets were new. Egyptian cotton. She had bought them from Marks & Spencer that day. But the flat came fully furnished and the mattress belonged to Swann. This was where he had slept with Alice, where his twins had most likely crept in between them both. Elea took another sip of wine as the image played out. She shouldn't be here. She should have rented a place of her own.

A smile crept over her face as the song changed to a Bon Jovi number. He was definitely an eighties fan. She thought of the sauna. Of the view over the Brayford and how beautiful it looked at night, with the twinkling lights from the restaurants and pubs reflecting on the still water. She had her own parking space. A swimming pool. A gym. Lincoln was a small, usually safe city, which suited her fine. The students who attended the university here brought life to the place. She would stay, at least until this panned out.

She thought of her passport, which had recently been renewed. She'd stored it away safely in her bedside cupboard. She was ready to return to Finland should a lead come up, but for now her heart was in Lincoln. Because she'd never felt closer to finding Liisa anywhere else. She thought of the girl in the freezer. Karen had decided to wait until later to identify her. Later, when she wasn't bent out of shape. Later, when she was thawed and lying beneath a sheet. Elea didn't blame her. At least there were no obvious injuries. Elea hoped that death had been granted while she was asleep. That poor girl, with her shitty home life and mother who didn't know how to care for her, most likely because she'd been dragged up herself. She hoped that guilt wouldn't eat away at Karen. What was done was done. If only she was as good at taking her own advice.

She pushed the thought away as the singing came to an end and the shower was turned off. *Have a night off, for God's sake*, she told herself. But she knew it would not be long before her thoughts returned to Chelsea and the man who took her. The man she wanted to kill.

The en-suite door opened and she was met with a smile. He stood in the thick white towelling dressing gown, towel-drying his hair.

'I didn't know you were an eighties fan.' Elea smiled, licking the wine stains from her lips.

'There's lots of things you don't know about me.' He picked up his watch from the other side of the bed and checked the time. 'I suppose you're kicking me out now, to do your milk rounds.'

But Elea did not want to be left alone with her thoughts. Not tonight. 'Stay.'

'Your wish is my command.' Mitch's smile warmed her inside. She was not an island, much as she tried to be. She had sent Swann home to Alice. As much as she disliked the woman, she couldn't break up their relationship. Those boys needed their father, and Swann had made his choice years ago.

Then Mitch had texted her when she was home, asking if she was awake. Their late-night conversation had been a welcome one. When he turned up at her flat with a moving-in present of a bottle of wine, she could not resist. She watched him slip off his robe and get into the bed beside her, the scent of her almond shower gel rising from his toned body. A shiver ran down her back as he planted a butterfly kiss on her neck.

A missed-call notification buzzed on her phone. It was Maria, Anu's mother. But it was late, and Elea needed a break from her despair. She would call Maria first thing in the morning. She turned off her phone before returning her attention to Mitch. She didn't want her 'trauma buddy' to think she was moving on. Most of all she needed a reset, to help her cope with what lay ahead. She entwined her limbs around the man in her bed. For tonight, she would forget.

# Chapter Forty-Nine

'How long will you be?' Elea asked Mitch as he pulled his jeans on. 'Maybe I should go in first.'

'Not on your nelly,' Mitch replied, doing up his button fly. 'I'm not having you making me look bad, getting there before me.' It wasn't yet 6 a.m.

'Yes, but you've got to change and—'

'I've got a spare suit at the nick. I'll go straight there.'

Elea stopped fussing. She wasn't his wife, after all. 'Fine.' She ran a brush through her hair. 'I'll give you a head-start.'

Mitch slipped on his shoes, suddenly awkward. He was smiling, but a little unsure. 'Maybe we could do this again sometime?'

'I'll let you know.' Elea was non-committal. 'But this can't go any further. The last thing I need is Swann chewing me off.'

Mitch blurted out a laugh.

'What?'

'The term is "chewing your ear off".'

'Whatever.' Elea smiled at his obvious amusement. 'Just . . . take this for what it is, yeah? Two consenting adults enjoying a good fuck from time to time.'

Mitch exhaled a soft chuckle, shaking his head. 'I've never met anyone like you before.'

'Then count yourself lucky.' She applied a coat of lipstick. 'See you at work.'

Elea watched him leave. At least she had her own car now, which meant that Swann wouldn't turn up to give her a lift. Alice wouldn't let him out of the house this early, and coming from Nettleham to Lincoln in the morning traffic would be a real pain. She grabbed her phone from the dresser, along with her keys. She stared at the screen as it buzzed a notification in her hand. It was Maria. Elea groaned. She'd forgotten all about her call. Finland was two hours ahead, so it was almost 8 a.m. there. But, still, that was early, even for her. One, two, three, four, five . . . she counted the missed calls. There were voicemails, too. Maria's name flashed up large as her phone rang once more. Elea took a deep breath and answered.

'*Haloo*,' Maria said, proceeding to speak in Finnish. Her English was broken at best.

'*Haloo*.' Elea responded in her mother tongue. 'Sorry, I was asleep when you rang last night. I've only just seen your calls. Everything OK?'

'Oh yes.' Maria seemed breathless. She was whispering down the phone. 'It's more than OK.' She squeaked in excitement, barely able to contain herself. 'It's happened – it's really finally happened.'

Elea's brows pinched together as the woman's voice descended into gibberish. Was Maria finally losing her mind? 'What is it? What's happened? You're not making sense.'

'I promised I wouldn't tell, at least not yet. But you've been so kind and . . . we made a pact.' Maria ruffled the phone line with a shaky breath. 'It's Anu. My baby has come home.'

'Oh my God,' Elea gasped. It couldn't be true. People didn't simply turn up out of the blue. This wasn't like Sophie Miller. Twenty years had passed. Anu wasn't a child any more. The thought of an adult entering Maria's home caused Elea to tense in concern. 'What if this person is lying, Maria? Are you telling me that Anu knocked on your door and—'

'I know it's hard for you to believe, Elea, after all this time. But I know my child. My baby is here, quiet but unharmed.' Maria exhaled a sob. 'But you can't tell another living soul. Not the police. Not anyone. We need some time. One night. That's all I ask.'

'I don't think that's a good idea,' Elea replied, beginning to pace the floor. Her mind was racing ahead. Was she still asleep, dreaming? She would wake up any minute now and—

'We have a pact,' Maria reminded her once more. 'And . . . there's something else. I asked about Liisa.'

Elea's bottom lip delivered a jolt of pain as she bit down hard. Then Maria's voice came smoothly down the line.

'I don't want to push, but I have a feeling Anu knows where Liisa is.'

'Then for God's sake, call Heikkinen. Every second counts!'

But Maria staunchly guarded her offspring. 'I won't answer the door to anyone but you. I'm sorry, Elea, but I mean it. Anu's barely spoken two words. God knows what hell they've been through.'

'OK. I'll book a flight today. But if Anu tells you anything, please call me back.'

'Mamma?' A voice rose in the background.

'Coming, dear,' Maria said, before the call ended abruptly. There was a sweet, happy note to her response that almost made Elea cry. She took steady breaths in an effort to calm down. If Swann rang her now, he'd know something was up, but her emotions were like a runaway train. Anu was home. One of the Ice Angels was alive. Elea clasped her hand to her mouth as she tried to contain a sudden, gasping sob. After all these years. Dare she believe it was real? Her passport. Her movements were mechanical as she tried to formulate a plan. Anu hadn't actually divulged Liisa's whereabouts, but still . . . Maria had good intuition. Elea trusted her friend's judgement. But how could she leave Lincoln, when her leads were here?

She wrestled with her thoughts. What about the case? Should she go or should she stay? But her mind was already in Porvoo. She could be back in England tomorrow. She had to speak to Anu. She searched her bedroom for a holdall. She didn't need much. Toothbrush, toothpaste, toiletries. With trembling hands she picked up what she needed. She quickly pulled the quilt over the bed, plumping both pillows. She would need to wash the glasses and hide any sign of Mitch. She wouldn't put it past Swann to call in to check up on her. She stopped, her head too busy to form coherent thoughts. What next? She'd need a change of clothes. Socks, underwear, pyjamas. But then again, she had spares at home. She paused. Took three long breaths. That was better. All she needed was her passport, then to book a train to the airport and catch a flight. But she wasn't telling Swann. She'd made a promise to Maria. She would arrive alone.

# Chapter Fifty

The atmosphere had changed in the station since finding Chelsea's body. There was no more banter, or the usual black humour that helped keep their spirits afloat. Officers moved quietly around the station, delivering a solemn nod of acknowledgement as they passed each other in the hall. Swann felt their muted sorrow, intermingled with a sense of urgency to bring the killer in. There was guilt, too. Guilt for not protecting Chelsea, a vulnerable young girl who dreamed of playing for England one day.

Swann straightened his tie before entering the press briefing room, which was just down the corridor of police HQ. Being the main police hub in Lincoln, the secure building was ideal for such gatherings. As the senior investigator, this was part of Swann's job role. Delivering a press conference live on TV set his nerves on edge, but at least he was on his home turf. Superintendent Jess Collins was already there, along with the police-and-crime commissioner, sitting at either end of the table, which was laid out with microphones and glasses of water. A navy-blue tablecloth brought a sense of ceremony and the Lincolnshire Police emblem, along with its motto 'Policing with Pride', was positioned at the back. Swann glanced across the room, breathing in the luke-warm air. The heat had been pumped out by radiators overnight as a cold snap hit.

It was a good turnout, with rows of reporters and three TV cameras at the back of the room. 'Before we begin . . .' The chatter came to a halt as he spoke. 'This is a fast-changing situation. I'll take questions at the end, but please speak with sensitivity, keeping the families of the victims in mind.'

He sipped from his glass of water. Waited for the seconds to count down as he prepared to begin. Sensitivity went out of the window for those keen to get the best possible story. Chelsea's initial disappearance had been overshadowed by events in the news, but now word of the girl found in the freezer had captured their interest. The discovery of a body was making headline news. Swann hated the inevitable leaks that came from working with so many people. He knew of journalists who dated police officers specifically to further their career. Checking that everyone was ready, he took a deep breath, leaning slightly into the microphone. The red tally light atop the TV cameras illuminated, signalling they were recording live.

'As you know, twelve-year-old Chelsea Hobbs disappeared on her way home from school in January 2023.' Swann glanced around the room, the click and whirr of cameras punctuating his words. 'We can now confirm that a body has been discovered in a freezer in the basement of a property here in Lincoln, which has been identified as that of Chelsea Hobbs. While I can't go into specific details right now, I can confirm that we are treating her death as suspicious and as part of an ongoing criminal investigation.' He paused, watching the journalists hurriedly tapping into their laptops and making notes. 'We also believe that Chelsea's case may be connected to the death of twelve-year-old Jenny Flynn, whose body was discovered on West Common in 2021; and to the abduction of Sophie Miller, who recently escaped after being reported missing in January of this year. The investigation into these cases is ongoing and we are actively pursuing new leads. For operational reasons, I cannot go into detail about these at this time. But I would like to reassure the public that our team is working tirelessly to bring those responsible to justice.'

Swann gesticulated with his hands to bring his point home.

'Lincolnshire Police is committed to ensuring the safety of our community. We would like to extend our sympathies to the families of the victims involved, and we ask for your patience and cooperation as we continue this complex investigation.' He sat back in his chair, waiting for the inevitable barrage of questions that would follow. He only hoped the announcement wouldn't send their suspects underground.

Several hands shot up, with a local journalist getting his question in first.

'David Fitzpatrick, *Lincoln Tribune*.' A bearded man in a crumpled suit introduced himself as he half sat, half stood. 'Is it true that this investigation is linked to the Ice Angels case in Finland?'

A ripple of murmurs spread throughout the room.

Swann stalled, very aware that he was on national TV. He kept his expression neutral, choosing his words carefully. 'At this stage we are following multiple active lines of enquiry, and the investigation is making significant progress.'

'But . . .' Fitzpatrick followed up, 'Elea Baker, the mother of one of the missing Finnish children, is consulting on this case, isn't she?'

Swann glanced about the room, aware that speculation

would run wild, regardless of what he said. Leaks were sometimes inevitable in such high-profile cases, and he chose each word with care. 'As soon as we're in a position to update you on any developments, we will do so. But at this time I cannot comment further on operational matters.' He turned to another journalist before Fitzpatrick could push for more. 'Next question.'

Swann checked his emails as he sat in his office for the first time that day. He hadn't stopped since the press briefing, which was now being aired worldwide. There were no follow-up questions with regards to Elea's involvement, but Fitzpatrick had earned himself a black mark in Swann's copybook. Speculation on Elea's involvement was already gaining traction online. But there was something more pressing on his mind – keeping up his end of the bargain. He'd promised the public a quick conclusion to the case. His team was closing in, but where was Elea?

It wasn't like her to be so late, not with so much going on. Was she upset by the press appeal? But Elea wasn't shy when it came to the press. There had to be more to her absence than that. He couldn't stop caring, no matter how hard he tried. He frowned to himself as he recalled how they had parted in the early hours. How at ease he had been in her company. How he hadn't wanted the night to end. He hadn't made a pass. He wasn't some letch; he was her husband. It wasn't about sex, it was just about being in Elea's orbit. He thought their marriage still meant something, but now she was willing to give him a divorce. He'd been a fool. He was far too late. Regret rested heavily on his shoulders.

She'd stood at the office door and he'd lingered in her presence, inhaling the sweetness of her perfume. She'd heard him on the phone, telling Alice he would be home late. But Swann wouldn't betray the mother of his children, and as long as he was with Alice, Elea would not get involved. Family meant everything to them both. Finding her daughter – dead or alive – was the most important thing he could do for her right now. But where the hell was Elea? The briefing was starting soon and she wasn't answering her phone. He glanced up at Mitch as he poked his head into the office. Technically it was *his* office; Swann simply hadn't been able to bring himself to move out yet.

'We're heading out for briefing, boss.' Mitch was wearing his usual smile. Swann had never met anyone so amicable. He didn't know a single person who disliked the bloke.

'Have you seen Elea?' Swann looked beyond him, out at the team. At Ness, who was handing out cups of tea and coffee. At Sergeant Davies, who was frowning from behind his computer screen. At Ollie and Kelly, who were deep in conversation with Jamal Jones, who seemed to be making notes. Everyone was there except Elea. Something felt off. He looked back at Mitch, who had yet to answer his question. He seemed twitchy today. 'Mitch?'

The DI blinked twice in quick succession. 'Sorry, what was that?'

'Elea. Is she in yet?'

'Um . . .' Mitch followed his gaze into the main office. 'I don't think so.'

'You've not seen her?'

'I've not seen her this morning, no.' He checked his watch.

'Is that the time? We'd better get a move on. Lots to work through. I'll let you know when she comes in.'

Then he was gone, out into the office, taking a mug from Ness's tray. Elea wouldn't be happy if she found Ness making tea yet again. Swann rang Elea's number once more, this time leaving a message. 'Where are you? Everything all right? We're about to start the briefing. Just,' he exhaled, 'give me a ring.'

He thought about the last time he saw Elea. She'd been putting on her usual brave front. But he could see past the mask. Seeing Chelsea's body in the freezer had hit her hard. Then having to break the news to Chelsea's mother. He knew that was a bad idea, but would Elea listen? Once she made up her mind, there was no changing it. What if it had all been too much? What if she'd given up hope and decided to end it all? What if she couldn't face finding Liisa like that?' Swann's frown deepened. Surely not. The outer office began to clear as each member of his team left for the main briefing room.

Elea's text came promptly. *I'm fine. Slept in. See you later.*

Exhaling a relieved breath, Swann secreted his phone in his suit pocket and joined his team.

They were all ready, sitting in the front rows of plastic bucket chairs. The functional space was big enough to accommodate around fifty officers. He waited for everyone to filter in until it was standing room only. Swann walked to the head of the room and stood before the wall-mounted digital screen that dominated the room. It displayed everything from CCTV footage to suspect profiles, but the two large whiteboards that they'd used in their office had also been wheeled in. Swann appreciated technology, but would not allow it to take over. His brain processed physical evidence better than the digital information that flashed up on the screen. One whiteboard covered timelines, the other focused on the victims and their locations to date.

A low murmur served as a backdrop, but there was an air of focus. Superintendent Jessica Collins sidled in. Officers parted to give her space. Swann scanned the room. Almost everyone was here. The forensic team would provide guidance on the evidence being processed, and CSI officers would update them on their finds. The family liaison officer's job was to support the families involved and liaise with the child-protection unit. They would update on any contact they'd had so far. Then there were the uniformed officers who provided boots on the ground, knocking on doors and giving local reassurance. Eileen was also there: the press officer was a godsend when it came to handling high-profile cases and he was grateful for her help earlier in the day. And Sean, their criminal profiler, would advise on behavioural assessment and patterns.

Deep in Swann's gut, his intuition nagged. Elea didn't sleep in. She wouldn't have missed this for the world. But he was the senior investigating officer and he was exactly where he was meant to be. He cleared his throat and the room fell quiet.

# Chapter Fifty-One

Time. Elea needed to buy time. Because as soon as Swann found out where she was going, he would be on her back. The jolt and rumble of the LNER train carriage eased her thoughts as she stared at the Lincolnshire countryside. *Anu is alive. Anu is alive.* The steady rhythm of the train spoke the words in her mind. Was it really true? If Anu was alive, then where was Liisa? And what about Venla? Elea hadn't forgotten about her. But she didn't have a mother, like Anu did. A mother who never gave up hope. Her conversation with Maria had been so short, and attempts to call her back had failed. The most she'd got was a text, saying that she'd see Elea when she got there. It came with a smiley face. The woman must be thrilled. But it was all so odd. Should Elea have rang Heikkinen? He'd be furious when he found out that she knew ahead of him. But she'd made a pact. In her early conversations with Maria, she had told her: friends first, police second. Tragedy buddies. Elea had assured Maria that no matter what happened, she would put Maria's family first. They had been through enough, after all. But so much time had passed. Had Anu escaped after being held captive in Finland all this time? But what about their suspect? Surely he wouldn't have just left Anu there. Unless that's exactly what he did. Perhaps Anu realised that he wasn't coming back and made a run for it.

There were plenty of stories about victims who had been held for decades and came out of it alive. There was Natascha Kampusch, who had been abducted at the age of ten in Austria. She'd escaped after eight years in captivity. Jaycee Lee Dugard was kidnapped aged eleven in California and escaped after eighteen long years. Then there was Colleen Stan, who had been kept in a box underneath a bed and escaped after seven years. These were the stories that gave Elea hope – a candle in the darkest of days. But could Anu really have simply turned up at Maria's front door? Sophie Miller had got away, proving that their suspect could be careless, but . . .

Elea sighed as the train came to a slow halt at its first station. Twenty years had passed since Anu had disappeared. It was easier to imagine that Maria was losing her mind. But she'd heard someone call out. *Someone* was in Maria's home. She'd also heard the joy in Maria's voice. The absolute conviction that her child was back. Because they never stopped being your child, no matter how old they were.

Her phone buzzed with a missed-call notification as the train pulled away from the station. The three-hour journey had never felt so long. She could have driven, but she didn't trust herself to focus on the roads. She had a four-hour flight ahead of her. *This time tomorrow, everything will be out in the open*, she thought. The case had gone from utter stagnation to galloping along so fast that she could barely catch her breath. What if Swann found Liisa in Lincoln? Then she wouldn't be there to— Elea stopped the thought. *Identify her*. That's what she was about to think. She clutched at the hope that was still there. *The Ice Angels have a connection. Liisa is still alive*. The call had been from Swann. Another voicemail. She pressed the phone to her ear: 'We need to talk. Call me.' Elea nibbled her lip. She knew Swann. This could be a ploy. She searched her contacts and brought up Mitch's number, her fingers pecking her phone screen as she tapped out a text.

*Any news?* She waited for a reply.

*Swann is looking for you. Asked if I saw you.*

*What did you say?*

*I said no.*

Elea exhaled a relieved breath. Good. *Any leads?*

*Lots. But nothing firm. Where are you?*

*OK. Keep me updated.* She ignored his question, but knew it wouldn't end there.

*Where are you? Everything OK?*

Elea stared at the screen. She should have come up with a better cover story than she was sleeping late. Her head was so full of Maria and Anu that she didn't think. She tapped her chin with her fingers.

*Emergency dentist appointment.* She groaned as she pressed send. It sounded so lame. But if she said 'doctor', Swann would be on her back, asking what was wrong. If she said she was chasing up leads, he'd definitely be hunting her down.

*Stay out of trouble. ;-)*

Elea smiled at the response. She waited for more, but that was it. He was leaving her alone. This was why she liked him

254

so much. He might have been younger, but Mitch felt like a kindred soul. Now to deal with Swann. She couldn't ring, because he'd hear the sound of the train in the background. She had no choice but to text.

*I won't be in today. Emergency dentist appointment.*

She had barely pressed send when the phone rang. Elea set her phone to silent, watching it buzz angrily in her hand. She just needed a head-start. Because as soon as Swann found out about Anu, he'd be on the phone to Heikkinen, who would send his units round. Would that be such a bad thing? But Elea knew Maria. If she had knew where Liisa was, she would have told her by now. Anu was most likely traumatised. Any victim in such circumstances was more likely to speak to family than the police. Elea reminded herself of her pact; she wouldn't break it now. She slipped her phone into her pocket, ignoring Swann's texts and calls. In a few hours Anu would speak to her, and her alone. She stowed her phone in her backpack, the lulling movement of the train soothing her thoughts. Every instinct told her that she was doing the right thing.

# Chapter Fifty-Two

## Liisa

### *2016*

My screams went unheard. The police hadn't tried very hard. There were two more visits after they first came to Johanna's home. The second time they came in and searched the cabin. Johanna must have been expecting it. She seemed to know the woman who came, bringing another officer to help her with the search. But they didn't find the trapdoor. I wasn't able to scream that time. Mikael had dragged me into the hole seconds before they arrived, pushing me down ahead of him, where I landed on the mattress with a thud. I couldn't call out if I wanted to, as the fall had winded me. I couldn't breathe. Mikael was fitter than me and jumped down, landing on his feet. The hatch was closed, the rug pulled over from above. I drew a breath to cry for help, but Mikael clamped a hand over my face.

'I'll cut your throat if you bite,' he hissed in my ear, his breath laced with a hateful liquorice stench. The coolness of the blade against my skin was enough to make me stop. 'You're not the first, you know that, don't you?' he whispered.

'I don't want to kill you, but I will, if you make a sound.'

I had no choice. So we listened, me tasting the dirt on his hand as footsteps rose above. There was laughter. Such a thing was in short supply and it sounded alien in this space. Doors closed. Briefly I heard a woman – older, perhaps? She spoke in a warm voice and told Johanna to 'take care'.

'Listen to me,' Mikael whispered, knowing that Johanna would be back soon. 'Listen, if you want to live.'

Then he told me a secret. One that made everything fall away. The cabin door closed. He dropped his hand and we took each other in. That was the day that everything changed.

# Chapter Fifty-Three

Swann didn't have time to think about Elea until 11 a.m., when he bumped into Mitch in the hall. He had just come from an internal media briefing and had a short lull before his next strategy meeting with the forensics team. He was pretty sure they'd picked up the suspect's fingerprints, but without any previous arrests, these were of little use until he was caught. Swann was liaising with his former boss in Finland, but they'd had no updates at their end.

Mitch appeared to be deep in thought, head down as he listened to his mobile phone. He wasn't wearing a tie, as Swann had asked him to do numerous times, and his shirt sleeves were too tight around his biceps for Swann's liking. How was Mitch meant to gain respect when he looked as if he'd walked out of the pages of *Men's Fitness* magazine? Swann watched Mitch's troubled expression as he ended his call.

'What is it?' Swann asked. 'What's wrong?' Because it didn't occur to him that it could be a personal call. Mitch lived and breathed the job. He didn't have any family to speak of and, apart from his fling with Elea, no relationships that Swann knew of. He'd often listened to the banter in the team. It was why he liked his office where it was. Swann rarely went out for work drinks because he was always needed at home.

Mitch shuffled his feet, a hand reaching to the back of his neck. His body language was a map of discomfort as he failed to meet Swann's eye. 'Nothing, boss. All good here.' But he paused. And it was in that pause that Swann read an expression of concern.

'You've not heard from Elea yet, I take it? She fed me some rubbish about a dentist's appointment hours ago. Do you know where she is?'

'Are you worried?' Mitch bypassed the question. 'I mean, I'm sure she'll be back soon.'

'I don't think she will.' Swann replied. 'I should never have let her see Chelsea. I think it pushed her over the edge.'

'You don't think she'd do anything stupid?' Mitch's face clouded over. The reason he had no family to speak of was because his mother had died by suicide when he was young. Swann made it his business to know about the people he worked with. Mitch's home life had not been easy, but it granted him a wider understanding of the world. Now he was standing before Swann and, judging by the look on his face, he was holding something back.

'Elea's unpredictable,' Swann said. 'So, what do you know?'

Mitch exhaled a regretful breath. 'I spoke to her this morning around six. She said she was coming straight to work.' He stared at his hands. Looked at the anti-crime posters on the walls, finally fixing his gaze past Swann as he waited for him to consume his words.

'Right. When you say you spoke to her . . .'

'I'm not being funny, boss, but the finer details are none of your business.'

Swann's eyes narrowed at the challenge in Mitch's voice. He folded his arms.

Mitch sighed. 'She texted me, saying she was going to the dentist. But I've just spoken to her now and . . .'

'You've spoken to her?' Swann raised his voice. So this was what it had come to. Elea would rather speak to Mitch than to him. After everything he'd said to them both. He grounded himself; Mitch was right. Their relationship – or whatever it was – had nothing to do with him. But he was concerned for Elea's safety and her current state of mind. 'Where is she?' he asked.

'She butt-dialled me by mistake. I think she's at the airport. There was a tannoy in the background. It sounded like she was boarding a flight.'

'The airport?' Swann's annoyance fell away. At least Elea was all right. But she was going home for a reason. He needed to know why.

'Call her.'

'I've tried. Her phone is turned off. If she's boarding, it'll be in aeroplane mode.'

'Right,' Swann said. 'Get back to work. I'll deal with this.'

'Yes, boss.' Mitch replied, seemingly relieved that Swann wasn't tearing a strip off him.

Swann turned in the corridor and headed towards the stairs. He needed to speak to Jess. He ground his back molars in frustration. Eight hours. It would take him at least eight hours to reach Elea.

His superintendent was not thrilled about Swann asking for time off. The case was gaining momentum and he was the

SIO. He couldn't imagine how Alice would react when she found out. But he had let Elea down once already, leaving when she most needed him. He would not do it again. He stood in Jess's office, sweating despite the cold temperature, uneasy in his skin. Elea would be the death of him.

Jess arched an eyebrow as she shuffled in behind her desk. She had just come in, fresh from a meeting with the powers-that-be. The press conference had added mounting pressure for a quick arrest. But their budget spend needed justifying and Jess worked hard to keep things on an even keel. 'Really? Now? All the times I've told you to take leave, and you want to do so in the middle of a high-profile fucking case that you're on the brink of solving?'

'I wouldn't ask unless it was an emergency.' But being in the police was a lifestyle, not a job. Part of a bigger family. A very intrusive one at that. Things got personal. Jess had questions: about his home life; about his kids. Because what affected him at home could compromise his job. A ton of debt could leave officers open to being bribed. Divorce could put your mental health under strain. Then there were the domestic incidents to keep an eye on. Whether officers were perpetrators or victims, they would not look away. Swann was just as intrusive when it came to his team's reviews. He wasn't afraid to ask questions, no matter how personal they were. But it hadn't taken Jess long to work out that the 'family emergency' didn't lie with Alice and the boys in Nettleham. 'It's Elea, isn't it? What's going on?'

Swann told her about Chelsea. About the hope leaving Elea's eyes. About the fact that his wife could be going home to die. 'She took off. No explanation. I'm worried that seeing

Chelsea liked that flicked a switch in her head. All these years she's been in denial. But now . . .' He stared into the distance, unable to finish the words.

Jess silenced her desk phone as it rang out. Her hair was coming loose from her clips, and she appeared harried as her brow creased in a frown. 'Can't you call ahead? She must have friends. People who can check on her.'

'She has a good relationship with Heikkinen, her boss. I'll call and let him know. But I'd never forgive myself if I wasn't there for her.' He gave Jess an imploring look. 'Please. It's a four-hour flight. I'll only be gone for a day, two at the most.'

'Alice will have your guts for garters.'

'Let me take care of her.' He paused. Tried to read the room. 'Is that a yes?'

'That's an "Off you fuck",' Jess sighed. 'But get your arse back here as soon as you can. I'll oversee the investigation, although God knows I've got enough on my plate. Mitch can step up and head the team – he might finally get to use his own office. He can move in while you're gone.'

Swann opened his mouth and closed it again. He hadn't a leg to stand on. At least the case would be in good hands, with Jess as SIO in his absence. She was a stellar officer, with some great results under her belt. She might be small in stature, but she took shit from no one. Swann didn't feel guilty for abusing their friendship because he wouldn't be gone long. A feeling of foreboding closed around him. He only hoped he would reach Elea in time.

# Chapter Fifty-Four

Elea inhaled the crisp, fresh Finnish air as she emerged from the airport. It felt good to be home. The memory of Liisa was stronger in her home town. Despite everything they'd found in Lincoln, her little girl would always be in Porvoo, waiting to be rescued. Coping with the loss of her child had been one of her biggest challenges, because even if Liisa was alive, she would be an adult now and Elea would have to get to know her all over again. A traumatised young woman, most likely wondering why her mother saved so many people, but not her.

She pulled her bag over her shoulder. She had left in a hurry, only needing a few basic items, as everything else would be at home. A mobile-phone power bank, a wash-cloth and a change of clothes. She'd dressed for the cold, her boots comfortable but waterproof over her jeans. Her house lay empty in her absence, her neighbour watering her plants and keeping an eye on things. At least she'd managed to get some sleep during the flight.

Elea wouldn't be going home just yet. Her journey would take her straight to Maria. Straight to Anu. She had it all planned. She would ask to be alone with Anu, because some things couldn't be said in front of a parent. There were all sorts of reasons why children wanted to protect their loved ones from the truth. No, Elea corrected herself, Anu was an adult now. She had always thought of Anu as a sad little blonde child, lost and far away. But the monster who took the girls in Lincoln hadn't ventured far from their homes. Had it been the same with her own daughter? There were plenty of lonely cabins in Finland. Places miles away from any neighbour, but still close to Porvoo. Had Liisa been within walking distance all along?

Elea sat in the back of the cab, remembering all the miles she had crossed trying to find her daughter. The search had been thorough. Sniffer dogs, helicopters and an army of officers on the ground. She had driven along every road. Walked the tracks that could not be reached by car. She had got herself into trouble on more than one occasion when night had closed in, saved only by the tracker that Swann had insisted she put on her phone. The nights that she had soaked her numb toes, willing life to come back into them. The countless saunas she had taken, trying to restore her aching body. After six long months the area had seemed so vast, her search so hopeless. That was when she became obsessed with work. Because it would have taken something extraordinary for Liisa to go with a stranger, after everything Elea had taught her about crime. She'd scrutinised each suspect brought into police custody, sure that she'd see that difference – their ability to gain a young girl's trust. They wouldn't have had long to act on that stretch of road at that time of the day. It would have taken more than brute force alone. Elea recalled her conversation with Sophie Miller, and how her captor had used a dog to gain her trust. But did he use human traffickers to steal Chelsea first? It didn't make any sense. Elea suppressed a shudder. Mitch was right. They could have been chasing the wrong lead.

Her brows knitted together as her surroundings passed in a blur. Liisa would have known not to stop for a dog. So unless he was riding a horse . . . Now there was a creature capable of making Liisa dismiss every sensible thought. *No, don't be stupid*, Elea told herself. It just wasn't feasible. There were plenty of car tracks on the road that day, but no sign of bloody horse hooves. As if Liisa would jump aboard and ride into the sunset with a stranger.

She stared, mesmerised by the flecks of snow touching the windscreen. Soon she would have answers. They would come in the quiet darkness, without fanfare. They would come tonight. She could wait.

She thanked the cab driver, giving a hefty tip as she always did. He hadn't been vocal during the journey, and she was grateful for it. Maria's cottage was isolated from its neighbours, down an icy track. Her outside light came on automatically as Elea trudged through the snow. Maria opened the door, her face bright, despite the late hour. Years of grief and loss had sunk her eyes deep into her sockets and sharpened her cheekbones. She was what Elea's father used to call a 'handsome woman', but had aged terribly over the years. Her once-long blonde hair was now chopped into a bob, which hung harshly along her jawline. But tonight there was a sparkle of happiness in her features that Elea had never seen before. The cabin was warm and cosy, the lights soft.

'It's good to see you,' Elea whispered. That was the understatement of the century. They had been on a shared journey that was almost at its end. Maybe Elea was wrong.

The answers would not come quietly. Now that she was here, she felt like she was hurtling towards a cliff edge. She wasn't ready and felt suddenly scared. She'd always thought that Liisa would surface before Anu. She couldn't help the bitterness that bloomed in her chest. Where was Anu?

The question must have been on her face as Maria led her in. 'Come. Anu's in bed.'

Elea nodded, steeling herself as she followed Maria down the hall.

# Chapter Fifty-Five

## Liisa

### 2017

I lie on my bed, staring at the ceiling, gripping my small wooden doll. A whole year has passed. I am still here. Still alive. Mikael seems different to me, now that I know his secret, but I'm no less scared of him.

I was thrown into the hole three more times. Every time I came out, I left a piece of my old self behind. The second time I tried to escape I was left down there for a week. At least it was summer and the earth wasn't quite so icy to the touch, but the smell rising from the ground was unbearable; something was rotting down there. I was stupid to try to escape when I was so unprepared. I'd barely made it through the cabin door when Mikael dragged me back. Johanna roared like a wild animal and came at me with a knife. Mikael grabbed it from her as she gasped for breath, his fingers wrapped around the blade. I'll never forget the look that passed between them when he overpowered her. She stepped back, suddenly afraid. Blood dripped from his hands as he took control that day. But it was Mikael who jabbed me with the home-made stun gun and pushed me down into the hole. If Johanna had been in full health, I wouldn't be here today. Sometimes, during those long hours when spiders crawled over my skin, I wished that she *had* ended my life in this rotten, unfeeling world. The hole broke my spirit. Sitting there in the dirt and the blackness made me feel like nothing at all.

Then my late-night chats in the living room with Mikael changed the way I thought. I was allowed to sit next to the fire, while Johanna dozed on the sofa. She was losing weight, and her gaunt face had taken on a yellowish tinge. As she grew weaker, Mikael told me about my home in Porvoo and explained why I needed to leave it behind. Night after night, over the year, I had no choice but to listen. I was so hungry for company, so grateful for any scrap of kindness, and I wanted to hear about Porvoo, even if it wasn't good.

'Your mama has moved on,' he told me. 'Forget about her, because she's forgotten all about you.' I didn't believe him at first. I didn't need to say it, he could see it in my eyes. Then he showed me the newspaper, and the announcement that made my spirits fall. Mother had married an English man. His name was Richard Swann. 'They're moving to England,' Mikael told me, although he seemed to take no pleasure from it. 'Your house has been put up for sale.' Then he showed me the listing, which he'd printed off on his computer. I believed every word. He comforted me as I cried. 'This is why we chose you,' he whispered, one cold stormy night. The wind whistled through the windowpanes and Johanna had fallen asleep again in the living room. 'We knew that you would not be missed.'

'Mama loves me,' I cried, staring miserably into the fire that danced and swayed.

'Only because she had to,' he replied with a shrug. 'Now

she's free.' Then he looked at Johanna. 'Mothers are meant to protect their children. But they don't.' The scar on his face said as much.

Mikael didn't speak many words, but on nights like that, each one was a knife to my heart. He has so many layers. I don't know him at all. I don't think he knows himself. But now, as the year has passed, Johanna has got sicker, and Mikael has become more in control.

On the days when she is well, Johanna sits at her sewing machine, making dresses for me. I'm not allowed to wear regular clothes because, according to her, in this 'modern day and age', women 'dress like sluts'. But I'm not a woman. Not yet. When she is sick, Johanna lies on the sofa with her knitting, her needles clacking as she watches us both. Her breath is so rancid these days that it fills the room. Mikael says it's a side-effect of her medication. Nice-smelling things are a distant memory now. I miss the scent of sweet-grass in the meadow near our home. The warm cinnamon buns that Grandmother would bake in our small kitchen, and the smell of the sweet cloudberry jam that she would have bubbling on the stove. On those days Mother would come home from work, inhaling all of its goodness, and smile.

Johanna speaks to Mikael about me often. She is waiting for me to be ready. For our so-called wedding day. When she can, she walks to my bedroom, her movements stiff and slow. She rips the blankets from my bed and closely checks the sheets. I have never been scared of nature until now.

If I'm good, Mikael shares his newspaper. I read it from cover to cover. Sometimes pages are missing. There is nothing about me. Some days he brings me chocolate, other times he calls me a brat and tells me to shut up. I've seen him watch Johanna as she sleeps. The emptiness in his eyes makes me feel scared. He tells me about the bad things that happen to children in foster care. 'You'd better hope the police don't find you,' he says as night draws in. 'Terrible things happen to children in those places.' And I wonder: how could foster care be worse than here? Then he reaches out and squeezes my hand, and I try very hard not to pull away. He's told me about the girl who came before me. She was exactly my age, with long blonde hair and blue eyes. 'She wouldn't stop screaming,' Mikael told me once, after drinking too much beer. 'Johanna lost her temper and then we had to get rid of her.' I think about her often. I wish she didn't have to die.

I still can't believe that Mama has left the country. That someone else is living in my home. On my birthday I sat, miserably, in my chair. Mikael brought a cake out. He'd bought it in town because he's useless at baking, and Johanna wasn't up to it any more. He lost his temper when I wouldn't blow my candles out. Then he dragged me to the front door by the scruff of my neck and told me to run. It was a test. I stared into the snow, my feet glued to the ground. Johanna was asleep in her room. I looked up at Mikael, imagining all the different ways in which things could turn out. Soft flakes of snow touched my skin as a blizzard rolled in. He offered his hand. I took it and allowed him to lead me back inside. 'I am yours and you are mine,' he said. 'We don't need Johanna any more.' It felt like a test. One that I had passed.

That night I heard muffled sounds coming from Johanna's room. I heard the creak of her door as Mikael left. The next morning, when I got up, Mikael told me that she was dead.

# Chapter Fifty-Six

Elea stood in the hall of Maria's home, a small, unassuming abode cluttered with artwork leaning against the walls. It was clean but somewhat neglected, its carpets and furniture well worn. Maria sighed. 'I hope I've done the right thing.' Her face was bright with emotion. 'It all feels like a dream.'

The corners of Elea's eyes wrinkled as she smiled. 'I'm happy for you, my friend.' She meant it. But it didn't lessen her pain as she approached the truth. According to Maria, Anu knew that she was coming. Elea only hoped the time away from the investigation in Lincoln was worth it. She took her friend's hand – an uncharacteristically tactile gesture. 'Don't worry. I won't push things.'

'It's Liisa's turn next.' Maria spoke in a gleeful whisper. 'We'll bring her home.'

Anu's bedroom door made no sound as she pushed it open. The room was just as it had been, decades ago. Popstar posters on the walls. A wardrobe filled with clothes that wouldn't fit any more. A museum to the child that Maria had lost. And now there was an adult, sleeping in the wooden-framed single bed.

As Elea took in the scene, her world moved on its axis once again. Yes, Maria had kept everything of Anu's – including pair upon pair of Velcro-strap shoes. They peeped out from under the bed beneath Anu's sleeping form.

'Are they . . .' Elea's throat constricted, 'Anu's?' She already knew the answer, but she had to hear it from his mum.

'Yes,' Maria whispered. 'Anu couldn't tie his laces, no matter how hard he tried.'

Elea nodded, unable to reply. Anu returned home at the same time their suspect was on the run. Anu, the troubled young blonde-haired boy who had become a man. The air was sucked out of Elea's lungs as the revelation hit her with force. Anu wasn't cared for like Liisa when he was young. He had been referred to social services because of neglect at home. Maria had spent her life paying for her mistakes, but what if it was too late for Anu? Had he run away, the day he disappeared? Had he—

'Sweetheart, wake up.' Maria approached his bed, unaware of the awful jigsaw puzzle being put together in Elea's head. There was no movement from beneath the covers, only the shape of Anu's sleeping form. 'It's OK. You're safe now.' Maria waited, hesitant. Scared to touch, for fear her son would simply fade into the ether. Elea knew those feelings. She'd dreamed about Liisa's return countless times. It must have felt surreal for Maria, too.

No response.

'Anu?' Maria touched the blanket. 'Are you OK?' She gasped as she moved the bedding. Cried as she pulled it back to reveal nothing but pillows beneath.

*No, no, no,* Elea wanted to scream. *He can't be gone. Not now.*

'Anu!' Maria cried out. 'Where are you?' She looked at Elea before checking the room, under the bed, in the wardrobe.

There was nowhere else to hide. Elea followed, trying to keep it together as she ran through the house, searching for Maria's grown-up child.

'Anu, I'm sorry. Anu!' Maria's tortured cries rebounded against the walls. Finally she turned to Elea, her breath ragged. 'I should never have brought you here! Why didn't I let him have just one night?'

'Maria, take a breath. It's OK,' Elea said. 'I'll find him.' But her focus had shifted away from her friend. If Anu *was* her suspect, then she was about to tear Maria's life apart. She fell into detective mode, asking Maria the usual questions to ascertain Anu's whereabouts. But Maria was trembling, barely able to string a sentence together in her grief. A small part of Elea wondered if Anu had been there at all. But she'd heard a man in the background, calling out for his mum.

'He . . . he said he was—' Maria looked around the room again, checking behind the door.

'Maria,' Elea stood before her, 'focus. He said he was . . .'

'Tired. He was tired. We had a hot chocolate. I made him lohikeitto. We hugged. We cried. I said there was no rush. That we'd talk things through in the morning. He wanted one night together before the world got involved.' Her body jerked in a sob. 'Why didn't I listen?'

'Stop beating yourself up.' Elea couldn't afford to delay. 'What does he look like? Describe him for me.' She also needed to know if Anu fitted Sophie Miller's description of the man who took her.

Maria clasped her shaking hands. 'His blonde hair is more of a brown now – it's cut short, like a buzz cut. Soldier-style. He's dressed all in black.' She exhaled a shaky breath.

'What build is he?'

'Um . . .' Maria wiped away a tear. 'Slim, yes, he's slim, but sturdy. Strong. He has a . . .' Elea's heart faltered as Maria traced a line from her mouth up to her cheek. 'A scar. Here. It broke my heart to see it, but he wasn't ready to talk about it yet.' She sniffed. Her eyes locked onto Elea's. 'What's wrong? What do you know? Is it the scar? Who hurt them? Do you know?'

'I don't know anything!' Elea shouted, sharper than she'd meant to be. She was trying to stay calm, but her thoughts were spiralling out of control. Anu fitted the description of Sophie Miller's abductor. There was little doubt now. 'You've no idea where he's gone?' she had to ask. He wasn't getting away from her this time.

Maria shook her head. How would she know, after all these years? It was hours since he'd gone to bed. Anu could be anywhere. Elea tried to work out her options. She'd go to the police station. Update them with the details. Get a team together. She relayed this to Maria. She had no time to spare.

'Wait!' Maria called, as if hit by a sudden thought. 'His phone . . .' She raised her hand to her forehead, as if forcing her panicked thoughts to clear. 'I put a tracker on it when he was in the bath. One of those apps.' She took a breath to speak. 'I was scared this might happen.'

Elea followed her into the kitchen, her pulse rapidly picking up speed. *Please let the tracker be turned on.* As Maria examined her phone, the look on her face said it was. Maria flicked off the app screen and brought up her contacts.

'What are you doing?' Elea fought the urge to snatch the phone from her grip.

'Ringing him, of course.' Maria took a breath and rested a hand on her chest. She was on the verge of a panic attack.

'Wait.' Elea touched her arm. 'What if you spook him? He might turn off his phone.' She forced a reassuring tone. The smiling assassin came to mind. She felt sick inside. 'I'll find him. Bring him back. He's not far. He might even lead me to Liisa.'

'Should I go with you?' Maria blinked, her eyes filled with trust that Elea didn't deserve.

'No. Stay here, in case he comes back.' Elea's emotions were at war. It was unthinkable. Monstrous. But it *was* possible. Nobody talked about Anu's childhood and the concerns of social services regarding his mental health. In the press he was portrayed as a blue-eyed angel. But what if they were wrong? Elea stared at the tracker location on Maria's phone. It was remote, but he hadn't gone far. Less than an hour's head-start. 'Leave it with me. I'll update you as soon as I can.' Elea groaned, 'I should have hired a car.'

'Take mine.' Maria turned to the hook on the wall and grabbed a set of keys before thrusting them into Elea's hand. Elea couldn't look her into her eyes. If Maria knew what was going on in her mind, she would never hand her those keys.

Maria called after Elea as she left, her words fractured with worry. They rang in Elea's ears as she watched the tracker on the mobile phone. 'Find him,' she cried. 'Bring my boy back home.'

Elea had no choice but to divert to the police station. She had made the decision to go alone, but she certainly wasn't going unarmed. Anu's location was static. He had no knowledge of the tracker, and it didn't look as if he was going anywhere. Anu had run for a reason. He had something to hide. Elea prayed that she was wrong. She hated the ugly thoughts rising in her mind. The other Ice Angel might not be so angelic after all.

# Chapter Fifty-Seven

## Liisa

### 2017

Johanna's body was removed from the cabin. She was sick, so I guessed no questions had been asked by the authorities. Mikael sorted everything out. I spent a lot of time in my room. Mikael had cooked me a meal, but I was so woozy afterwards that I slept for a whole day. When I woke up there was dirt in my hair. I think he drugged my food and put me in the hole. I was glad I didn't remember it. Glad that Johanna was gone. I didn't think of home, because it wasn't there any more. Mikael never missed a chance to remind me that Mother had moved on. But I still yearned to be free. Free to study. Free to go to the shops. Free to choose my own clothes. Because there was nothing here for me. Nothing until, one day, Mikael told me that he had a surprise. He must have felt my uneasiness, now that Johanna was gone. 'Tomorrow,' he said. 'Sleep well. Because tomorrow will be a happy day.'

But I couldn't sleep that night. Because Mikael's idea of a 'happy day' was not the same as mine. I thought through my options. Mikael was quietly cheerful now that Johanna was gone, but I didn't know how he would react if I tried to run. Where would I go? It wasn't as if anyone was looking for me. I ached to see my mother, wherever she was. I hadn't given up on her yet.

Now it's morning and I wish Mama was here to tell me what to do. I get dressed early so that Mikael won't get to watch. I feel even less safe, now Johanna isn't here to set down the rules. The cabin feels so weird without her. I expect her heavy footsteps to come thumping down the hall. To hear the drilling sound of her sewing machine at night. Mikael will need to leave me alone at some point, to get supplies from the shops. Milk, bread, butter, toilet rolls – we are low on everything. Maybe he will take me with him. Maybe that is my surprise. The thought of seeing other people lifts my spirits.

Mikael is smiling as he opens the door. 'Come,' he gestures. He is dressed for outside.

'Are we going shopping?' I follow him out and pull on my boots.

'Better than that.' He hands me Johanna's old gloves and thick knitted scarf. The smell of fish rises from the woolly material, bringing Johanna back into the room. I shudder as her memory wraps itself around me. Mikael stops at the cabin door. 'Don't run. You'll be sorry if you do.' He stares, his blue eyes boring into me. 'Really sorry.'

But I can't see his stun gun. There is nothing but hope on his face. Hope that I'll see this out with him, whatever *this* is. I wonder if he misses Johanna or if he's glad she is gone. I nod and take his hand. It doesn't creep me out so much these days because I'm used to it now. He takes something from his pocket. It is a small brown pouch. His lips creep up in a smile as we trudge through the snow. The cold air feels like a blessing on my skin. And the sun is weak but wonderful. I blink, inhaling every precious second of the outdoors. In the distance a bird calls.

We turn a corner to the back of the house. There's a building that I've never seen before. I hear movement in the snow. I see the hay first and almost lose my breath as a horse comes into view. I blink again. It's still there. It whickers at the sight of us. This beautiful creature with a thick chestnut coat and gold mane. Mikael lets go of my hand and gives me the bag. 'Sugar lumps,' he simply says, the smile on his face wide. 'For Kukka.' The name means 'flower', but she is much more than that. It's as if she stepped straight out of the pictures I used to draw. She is everything in this moment, and tears rush to my eyes.

'Kukka.' I breathe the name, too scared to ask the question, *Who owns her? Is she mine?*

'Go on, say hello to your horse.' Mikael nudges me forward as Kukka approaches the fence. Not a sharp punch to the back, like Johanna. She would never have allowed this.

I slip off one of my gloves and place a sugar lump in my palm. Kukka blows out from her nose, wanting to say hello, too. I blow towards her nostrils. Feel the blissful sense of her muzzle against my palm. Laugh at the tickle of her whiskers on my skin. 'They're called vibrissae,' I say, demonstrating my knowledge of my most favourite creature in the world. 'Their whiskers help their senses. You must never trim them.' I've forgotten what it's like to be this happy. It's a warm, comforting feeling as a little part of my old self returns.

Kukka is impatient and hungry for more. I look at the water trough, hooked up to electricity so that it will never

279

freeze. Then I notice that the stable has two sections. One for shelter, one for straw.

I have to ask, because I can't bear it any more. 'Is she . . . is she really mine?' I swallow. Wait the agonising moments for his response. She is so beautiful; I can hardly bear it.

Mikael leans towards me, the familiar smell of liquorice on his breath. 'She's yours if you behave.' His voice drops to a menacing calm. 'But if you don't . . .' His face hardens, shadows darkening his expression, 'I'll put a bullet in her head.' He points a finger at her temple, mimicking the pull of a trigger with a sharp clicking sound. He blows out his cheeks, the sound of imaginary gunshot cutting through the air. 'Ride her in the paddock, but not a step beyond.'

Then I understand. Johanna isn't here to watch me any more. But Kukka is enough to make sure that I never put a foot wrong. I know he is capable of doing it. Because when Mikael gets angry, he is not in control. Johanna did not die on her own.

'Thank you,' I say, before wrapping my hands around the base of Kukka's neck and burying my head in her mane. I breathe in the scent of her and bask in the heavy weight of her chin on my shoulder. The moment is bittersweet. I know that I will never leave. At least not without my horse. She might be my only chance of escape.

# Chapter Fifty-Eight

Swann pushed his phone against his ear, side-eyeing the toddler who was making a fuss. He gave her mother an empathetic nod, but hoped that the child who was kicking her would not be seated next to him on the flight. He knew he was micromanaging Mitch, but he couldn't afford to take his foot off the pedal when it came to the case. He asked Mitch about timelines and the coroner's early reports. They stated that Chelsea's cause of death appeared to be an overdose of sedatives – the same way in which Jenny Flynn had died. Mitch talked about the fingerprints that had been recovered, but not yet identified. About the images of a man obtained from nearby CCTV, which matched the description of the male that Sophie, their only living witness, had described. He talked about the landlord who said the man spoke with a 'foreign' accent, but had never met him in the flesh. Then Mitch told him about the breakthrough involving the human-trafficking ring, which would be hitting the news soon. And then he said exactly what Swann had been waiting to hear. 'Sienna Thompson is talking. Your plan worked.'

Swann hadn't forgotten about Sienna Thompson. He'd been dealing with her in the background. Just because he wouldn't allow her to sell them her precious information didn't mean that he had given up. Sienna had wanted to get away – at any cost. Which is why he and his superintendent had worked something out. Witness protection gave Sienna the new start she was desperate for. Her parting gift was her selling out the gang that had terrorised her and Ant. Ant wasn't the angel she professed him to be, but he had lost his future wife and child. For Swann, that was punishment in itself. Sienna wasn't stupid. She'd kept enough evidence to send the gang down. Ring-camera footage, photos, plans, iPhone recordings. All insurance in case one day the police came knocking for her. But nothing bad involving Ant. Nothing at all, apart from documented threats to his life.

'She's given them all up.' The relief carried on Mitch's voice. 'You'll get a commendation for this.'

'What about Chelsea? And Liisa? Or Sophie, for that matter? Have the gang anything to do with any of our girls?' The girls mattered more to Swann than any commendation. He rose from his seat, keeping an eye on his boarding time, wishing that Elea hadn't taken off.

'Phil Hobbs lied through his teeth. It was his idea to sell Chelsea to pay off his drug debt.'

'Fuck!' Swann said, receiving a dirty look from the woman with the child. He delivered an apologetic smile before sidling away from them both.

'Sienna has a recording of one of his phone calls with Ant. We've got him banged to rights,' Mitch continued.

'So Ant and his cronies took Chelsea?' Swann frowned.

'No, according to Sienna, they weren't interested. Chelsea's disappearance had nothing to do with them.'

Swann shook his head in disgust as he imagined Hobbs trying to sell Chelsea to the highest bidder. Had their suspect overheard Phil's conversation in the pub, or was Chelsea a walking target as she walked home alone? Sienna had little reason to lie, now that she was in witness protection and had cut all ties with her other half.

'What about Liisa? I don't suppose Sienna gave you anything—'

'She said she was bluffing,' Mitch interrupted. 'The gang *is* involved in human trafficking, but it deals in blokes for slave labour, not young girls – not that we know of anyway. Sienna just wanted a way out.'

Swann should have been happy with the result, but when it came to the Ice Angels case, another door was slamming in his face. 'Any luck with CCTV?' He'd instructed house-to-house enquiries for Ring-doorbell and dashcam footage in the vicinity of their suspect's rental home.

'I've been saving that until last. We've got a clear image of what looks like our suspect leaving the rental house. Dashboard footage from a taxi firm tallies with Ring-doorbell images from neighbouring houses at different times.'

Swann frowned as boarding was announced. What a time to be away from work.

'But that's not all. Jamal targeted his movements on CCTV and tracked him down in town. We've got a clear image of him walking into a Tesco Metro.' Mitch's voice carried a current of excitement. 'I've sent it over. It's clear, boss. The super's putting out an appeal.'

Swann's phone dinged in his hand. 'Hang on.' Swann enlarged the image with his fingers on his phone screen.

'Boss?' Mitch's voice filtered through.

Swann stared at the image, trying to process the picture

before him, while getting in the queue to board. Those haunting, hollow eyes. The thin worried lips, the high cheekbones. The unmistakeable scar on his cheek.

'He's got some balls, walking around Lincoln like that,' Mitch muttered down the line. But desperate people did stupid things, especially those on the run.

Swann checked the supermarket time-stamp. It was taken two weeks ago. He cradled his phone to his ear and fiddled with his passport. 'Send it to Elea. Tell her we've got our man.'

'But . . . we haven't got him. Not yet.'

'Send it anyway.' The image could be enough to pull Elea back from the brink of whatever cliff she was ready to hurl herself off.

Swann presented his passport to Finnair staff before returning his attention to the face of the man that had devastated so many lives. Was this Liisa's kidnapper? Chelsea and Jenny's murderer? And countless others perhaps? He followed the line of fellow travellers, but his mind was with Elea and how she would react. He barked some more orders at Mitch, detailing instructions for the team's next moves. 'I'm boarding the plane. Keep in touch. Leave a message if I can't pick up.'

They ended the call. Swann would plan a new strategy during the flight. His phone rang as he approached the plane. Alice. The last time they spoke she'd called him a piece of shit for chasing after Elea. He'd have this inevitable conversation later on, but right now he couldn't afford any more distractions. He silenced his phone.

Swann showed airline staff his boarding pass as he got on the plane. His pulse was drumming in his chest as he secured his hand luggage beneath the seat in front of his own. He hated flying more than anything. It was only when he'd pulled his seatbelt securely across his waist that he allowed himself to look at his phone. Something was niggling him. He flicked through other images that he had saved previously. For a moment his fear of flying was sent to the back of his mind. Back and forth he flicked the images, as his suspicions played out. Was he imagining the resemblance to Anu, the original Ice Angel? Was this case more complex than they'd ever imagined? Phil Hobbs and his cohorts had been a huge distraction. Swann stared out of the window as the plane prepared for take-off. Maybe he wasn't just following Elea. He could be chasing their suspect, too.

# Chapter Fifty-Nine

Elea parked Maria's car outside Porvoo police station. The squat, utilitarian building stood solemnly in the quiet night. It was set just off the main road, its brick exterior weathered by relentless Finnish winters. The air was crisp from a recent snowfall, the roads sparkling from newly formed ice. Tense with trepidation, Elea pushed through the door into the warmth of the station lobby. It was eerily quiet. She nodded at the front-desk officer.

'Evening,' he said in response. The broad-shouldered man was called Markku, and he spoke with little emotion as he keyed something into his computer from behind his security glass. He recognised her sufficiently not to question her movements as she let herself inside. She kept her expression neutral, despite the stomach-churning events taking place. Fluorescent lights lit her way as she walked down the dim corridor, the outside cold still biting through the material of her jeans. A faint smell of stale coffee hung in the air and Elea's fingers brushed the walls as she passed, grounding herself in the rough texture as she planned her next move.

The armoury was at the far end of the hall, past the large open-plan office where local detectives worked during the day. Porvoo wasn't as busy as Helsinki and tonight the room was faintly lit by the glow of computer monitors in sleep mode. The unpaid hours she had spent in that office, working between there and Helsinki, chasing dead-end leads. Hours wasted in the search for her child. But now it was bearing fruit. Her heart felt like a metronome: strong, steady and relentless in her search. Her earlier earworm still played on a loop: *Anu is alive. Anu is alive.* She reached the armoury door, touching the cold metal of the security keypad. The beep of each number echoed in the silent corridor as she punched in the code. Something about this felt so familiar that she almost expected Heikkinen to sidle up behind her, smelling of coffee and cigarettes as he asked what the smoking hell she was up to. The lock clicked as the door was released and she pulled it open.

The smell of metal and gun oil offered comfort as she assessed the rows of locked cabinets lining the walls. Each one was marked with the name and badge number of the officer assigned to them. Elea found hers quickly. She had no time to waste.

She gripped the familiar weight of the Glock 17 in her hand. The pistol was standard-issue, a light and reliable model. Its polymer frame and steel slide were built for durability. Elea knew every facet of this weapon. It had served her well. She always felt more powerful when it was strapped to her side. It held seventeen rounds of 9mm ammo, enough to face whatever lay ahead. She wrapped her fingers around the textured grip. There was no manual safety clip to fiddle with. All she had to do was pull the trigger, if it came to it. She recalled Maria's face and hoped that it wouldn't. Her mind swirled with conflicting thoughts, her emotions in turmoil. She inhaled deeply to steady herself, but her thoughts still raced ahead. The tracker on the mobile phone displayed an address. She knew exactly where she needed to go and it wasn't that far from here.

She clipped the holster to her belt, the leather cold as it touched her bare hip. She shoved the extra magazine into her pocket. Her grip lingered on her gun. It felt heavier tonight, the weight of responsibility pressing down on her. She prayed she was wrong about Anu. It couldn't be him. He was the first to be taken. How could he turn round and do the same thing? Yet it felt as if a long-missing piece of the puzzle had clicked into place. Either way, Anu was involved, and Elea would get the truth out of him. She recalled the sight of his room, left just as it had been when he disappeared. The clothes in his wardrobe – the row of Velcro-strap shoes. How could she tell Maria the real reason why her son was on the run?

She turned to leave, catching her reflection in the glass door of one of the nearby offices. Her face was serious, but streaked with worry. All the hours she'd spent analysing paperwork, retracing steps, linking each case. All the people she'd looked into, both here and in the UK. Broken mothers. Criminals who put a price on human life. She had seen the worst of humanity and she wasn't done yet.

She walked towards her car, her skin prickling from the sudden return to the cold. She fixed the phone in place and turned over the engine. A sudden beam of headlights made her blink. She exhaled in relief as it passed. She would take things steady. Snow-chains had been fitted to the tyres of Maria's car. She'd need them where she was going: to the cabin, deep in the woods.

# Chapter Sixty

## Liisa

### 2018

'Have you got everything?'

Shoulder-to-shoulder, Mikael and I walk through the lonely supermarket aisles. He is embarrassed because I'm here to buy what he calls 'female things'. He walks awkwardly by my side as I pick up tampons and sanitary towels – items Johanna had told me about, two whole years ago, before she died. It seems like an eternity ago now. Until recently I've been so embarrassed that I'd been making do with balled-up socks and wads of toilet paper. I kept my secret for as long as I could. It is hard when you don't have a mother or sister to turn to for advice. I don't know what size to get.

Mikael scratches his whiskery beard as I stare at the shelves. 'Get one of everything,' he says, keen to be out of here.

I eye the bars of Tupla chocolate near the checkout. He pauses to fumble with his wallet and, as the checkout lady turns away, I grab two bars and shove them in the pocket of my coat. When she turns, all she sees is a red-faced idiot girl, embarrassed by her big brother's presence as she scans the sanitary items. Living in the wilderness has aged Mikael, and his beard covers most of his face. As for me, in my plaits and this stupid smock I'm the picture of innocence.

'Don't worry,' she whispers and gives me a maternal wink. 'It will get easier.'

I wish with all my heart that she could see who I am. I open my mouth to speak, but already she is handing Mikael his change. His fingers bite into my shoulder as he guides me outside. I am a quiet soul, unused to human interaction. My only love is Kukka, the horse that I fight to protect. The horse with a scar running down her beautiful neck. That was my last escape attempt, when I jumped the confines of the paddock fence and tried to leave with her. It's healed over the course of the year. I have a similar scar on my stomach, as Mikael didn't want to mark my face. The sound of my beautiful Kukka in pain hurt far more. His cruelties were enough to break the last threads of my spirit. But still there are times like these, when we are out in the open, when I hope. Hope that someone recognises me. Hope that someone takes Mikael away. Hope that Kukka and I can live the rest of our lives in peace.

The journey home is made in silence, and I gaze in wonder at the falling snow. We pass children playing and a giant black dog running off his leash. The children are dressed in different-coloured coats, red, blue and yellow. I watch them laughing, chasing, falling over and getting up again.

We return to what is now my home. I carry my purchases from the car. Mikael has been to the hardware store. He is a regular there, always making things that you can't buy in the shops. A ball of dread knots my stomach as we enter our cabin. I'm allowed a once-monthly trip to the supermarket as long as I behave. But my breathing has become out of sync. It feels strange to be out of my room.

I used to stare at the CCTV cameras in the hope that somebody would recognise me, but Mikael knew what I was up to. He gave me such a beating when we got back. Now I walk with my head hung low. Besides, there are no 'Missing' posters. If people *are* still looking, someone would have recognised me by now. Mother lives in England. Mikael said she has started a new family without me. 'Out of sight, out of mind,' as they say in the UK.

At least I've been able to study. After Johanna died, Mikael bought me every book I asked for and more. Some days he could be kind. He has many different faces and I've not yet seen them all. I've learned about law. I know everything about horses, my first love. I escape through my books every day. I'm still here, still alive, and nobody except Mikael cares.

# Chapter Sixty-One

Elea stared out into the dizzying snow, her windscreen wipers working hard to clear her view. The flurry was ending as quickly as it started, but more would come soon. She had turned off the main road and was now being bumped in her seat as she negotiated the track to the cabin where Anu was holed up. It would not be long before her colleagues caught up with her. She didn't realise that she'd accidentally called Mitch until it was too late. He would have heard the background sounds of the airport. Swann would have dropped everything to hunt her down. She didn't blame him. He was more afraid for her than for the person she was chasing. Afraid of what Elea might do and of the career she would put at risk. Because he must know that she was chasing someone. Why else would she have come home in such a rush? At least she'd got a decent head-start.

She inhaled a sudden breath as the cabin came into view in the clearing. One window boarded, a light behind another. A small rusted yellow car. The broken-down outside porch. She had a blurry memory of her initial door-to-door enquiry, one of many they had made in the hunt for her daughter. Elea had insisted on a return visit, with a proper search to be carried out. She had planned to return herself, but the local neighbourhood officer, a woman on the cusp of retirement, had attended the location and brought a probationer to tag along. The woman who lived here was a recluse, with a sister in Helsinki, if Elea's memory served her right. Nobody suspected the quietly spoken woman who lived in a rundown wooden structure near the woods. There was still no evidence to say that she'd had anything to do with it, but Elea felt like she was close.

She turned off her headlights and slowed the car as it approached the address. Gently she pressed the brakes, biting her bottom lip as she pulled up a short distance away. Her feet sank into the snow as she stepped outside and, quietly, closed the car door. She was near. The sky sparkled above her. She glanced around the yawning abyss. At the dilapidated wooden cabin planted like a mushroom in the snow. At the backdrop of woodlands that seemed to stretch on for ever without a neighbour in sight. She breathed in the silent isolation. Had her daughter been brought here, all those years ago? Yanked from that yellow car? Dragged through the snow? But she had visited; she would have known if Liisa was there . . . wouldn't she?

Elea forced herself to keep moving. She stilled as the steps of the cottage creaked, barely daring to breathe as she listened for signs of life. Slowly she tugged on the door handle, surprised to find it open. She supposed you could do such a thing when you lived in the middle of nowhere. She pushed through the screen door. There wasn't a sound in this place. Nothing except the strong, pulsing rhythm of her heart. Her gun was nestled securely in its holster, ready if she needed it.

She walked through the cabin, adjusting to the darkness and seeking out the hiding places from which someone could ambush her. She entered a large open-plan room, a soft lamp in the corner guiding her way. A thick, cloying dampness caught the back of her throat as she was hit with layers of festering smells. Damp books. Smoke. Rotten food. Mouldy furniture. She quickly stifled a cough. This place had not been lived in for years. A wooden crucifix hung crookedly over a dirty fireplace. Loose strings of cobwebs danced from the rafters, and the bookcase housed an array of . . . She peered through the dim light, her heart tugging at the sight of an old law manual next to a horse encyclopaedia. Their pages were mottled with mould, curling at the edges. Elea pushed her rising emotions down. *Tough times don't last*, her father's voice spoke in her mind. *Tough people do*. This was about survival now.

Her senses on high alert, she explored the old cabin, every muscle in her body tense. She glanced at the tracker one more time on Maria's phone. At the small blue dot, which lay outside this space. Satellites didn't always get it right, but Anu could be in an outbuilding. She shoved her phone back into her pocket and gripped her Glock. Should she call out for Liisa? Reassure Anu that everything was OK? As she walked through the silent space, Elea listened to her gut. Anu didn't know she was coming. He had run for a reason. She couldn't risk making him act it out.

She stopped as the repetitive creak of a door flapping on its hinges cut through the silence. Adrenaline flooded her veins, keeping her senses sharp as she reached the rear of the cabin. The kitchen was a haven of mouldy food wrappers and rusted soup tins. An old fish carcass stared out of a nearby bucket. A dreamcatcher hung from the ceiling. And still Elea did not call out. She rubbed her sleeve against her runny nose, maintaining her grip on her gun with the other hand. She was not dressed for these temperatures. She glanced at the clothing hanging on the back door. Male and female coats. A long pink knitted scarf. A pair of flowery boots. A bridle. A hat. She could not dwell on them now. The door creaked open, revealing a single set of footprints denting the snowy track. It led into the woodlands. To Anu, and to God only knew what else.

Elea followed, each step breaking the fragile stillness as snow crunched beneath her feet. The noise had an oddly rhythmic quality, and she regretted not taking the scarf on the door as shards of cold air stabbed her throat. There weren't just layers of snow in Finland, there were blankets, with sheets of hardened ice beneath. The swish of blood in her ears was relentless as the cold chilled her bones. Where was Anu? Were these the footprints of a man who couldn't tie his laces, but was capable of murder?

A flash of white. A sudden screech tore through the air. Elea's grip tightened around her gun as an owl flew, fast and low. 'Jesus!' she whispered on an inhale. She had to get into cover. She was a moving target out here. She walked past the outdoor paddock and the rickety stable within. Her eyes were streaming with the cold, her cheeks and nose slapped red. Everything about this place was hostile. She carried on until she reached the shelter of the woods and kicked snow off her boots against a thick tree trunk. The trees seemed to go on for ever. They offered no guidance in her journey, just more of the same. She felt the heat of dozens of eyes boring down on her. There was wildlife in these woodlands, but it was keeping its distance for now. Her ears pricked to the sound of lone sobs. There, in the moonlight, was a figure kneeling in the snow.

'I'm sorry,' he cried. 'I'm so sorry. We weren't the right fit, were we? No matter how hard we tried.' The man seemed oblivious to the cold, his gloved hands clasped together, his head bowed in misery.

Elea cursed the broken branch that cracked under her foot. He spun round and took in the sight of her. It was Anu. Not the blonde haired twelve-year-old boy who had disappeared, but a grown man. He was exactly as Maria had described, but was wearing his dead father's hat and navy coat. Anu hadn't been there for his funeral. He had missed so much.

Elea raised her gun. 'Hands over your head!' she commanded, her words echoing through the watchful forest.

But the man before her didn't move.

'Where is my daughter?' Elea shouted, taking a few more steps. 'What have you done with Liisa?'

'You look like her,' Anu said, his head tilting to the side. Fresh tears glistened on his cheeks. Everything about him was off-kilter as he delivered a mechanical smile. 'Have you figured it out yet? Do you know who I am?'

'I know exactly who you are, Anu. You're the bastard who took my daughter. What have you done with her?'

'Stay where you are!' Anu shouted, as Elea took another step. He was sitting on a mound of snow beneath a tall pine tree. He stared, exhaling a bitter laugh. 'So you care about your daughter . . . Nobody gave a shit about me.'

'What?' Elea's frown deepened, her eyes never leaving Anu's.

'Mama said you investigated my case.' His eyes flicked to

the cabin beyond the woodlands. 'I stopped to help her. She took me home. Then she never let me go.'

Elea took a breath as the pain played out on his face. She needed to change tack. Anu would only lead her to Liisa if she empathised with him. But, inside, her fury burned. She pushed her personal feelings down and slowly lowered her gun.

'Then tell me. Who took you, Anu? What happened?'

'Johanna. That's what happened. That crazy fucking bitch. She made me do things. Fucking repulsive. She was handy with a knife back then.' He emitted a deep wail of frustration, his voice echoing around the forest. There was a flurry of wings above him as birds left their nests. 'But she made me love her, too—'

'What about the others?' Elea interrupted, unable to stomach his self-pity. 'Venla. Liisa. Jenny. Chelsea. Sophie.' Each word was spoken with the force of a bullet splitting the frostbitten air. 'Why did you do it, Anu?'

'Because she fucked me up!' Anu screamed. 'Said I had to find my perfect partner! But they weren't the right fit. None of them were.' His shoulders hunched over as his words descended into whines.

'Where is Liisa?' Elea repeated. 'What have you done with my daughter?'

The cruel edge of Mikael's laughter pushed her to the brink. This was Liisa she was talking about. Beautiful, sweet Liisa, and this man – this murderer – was laughing at her.

'Tell me!' Elea demanded, raising her gun. 'Before I blow your brains—' The words became lodged in her throat as she followed his gaze. Only then did she notice that the mound of earth covered in snow was human-sized. Her eyes flicked to the small wooden home-made cross.

*No.*

As Elea's gun quivered, Anu reached for the rifle behind the mound.

The sudden crack of gunfire sent wildlife fleeing from the forest.

# Chapter Sixty-Two

## Liisa

### *2018*

Kukka didn't solely belong to me. Mikael used her, too. He rode her into town and used her to carry logs. She could even pull a sleigh. But he was cruel when he was moody. His love of animals was forgotten when the black cloud came down. I hated the way he'd slap Kukka. I loved that horse so much that it pained me. I didn't love Mikael, but I *was* reliant on him. Sometimes, when he spoke about Johanna, I felt sorry for what had happened to him.

That night, when I was in the hole, he told me the truth about her and how she had taken him. He was walking home from school one day, just like me. Maria, his real mother, had forgotten to pick him up. Maria was an alcoholic. Some days she was blackout drunk. Anu told me about the times he would go home, clean up her vomit and try to get her to bed. There was barely any food in the house. His father came and went because he couldn't stand her moods.

Johanna drove up beside Anu when he was walking home alone. She offered him some liquorice and asked if he would like a lift. I imagined Anu climbing into her warm car. She said that he was too thin. That he needed a good meal first. She brought him to her cabin and made him a feast. Then she said it was too late to drive home and let him sleep in the spare room. The next day she bought him new clothes to wear. Told him how handsome he was. When Anu asked to go home, she said that she was sorry, but his mother had been found dead. She'd gone into detail about it, saying that she'd choked on her own vomit. Then she told him horror stories about foster care. I imagined all of this taking place and I believed every word. Mikael didn't talk about the things that Johanna made him do, but I knew that none of it was good. She had taken him for her own. Not as a son, but as a companion. Everything else was a front. Their relationship was so messed up as he came to depend on her. I think it made him mentally ill.

I thought of when Johanna said that my presence was hard on her, too. Now I realise that she was jealous of my life with him. It was only when she was dying that she wanted to find him a wife. Mikael won't talk about the girl who came before me. He said that it makes him feel bad. He told me that he and Johanna had sent a white feather to her foster home. They wanted people to know that she was an angel, free of misery. Free from pain. There's something broken in him.

I will never be a wife to Mikael. I have outgrown the stupid white dresses that were made for me. But he still wants to keep me around. I cook, I clean. I do all the things that Johanna did for him. But now that I am older, I sense that he wants more, and I can't. I just cannot bear the thought of it. Sometimes I hear him mumbling to himself at night, talking about finding the 'right fit'. But any escape attempt from me will put

300

my precious Kukka at risk. As much as it breaks my heart, I have to let her go. She knows her way into the village. I don't have long. She can run faster without me on her back, and I don't have time to saddle her up. Mikael will be here soon.

'I love you,' I whisper to my most beloved possession, tears blurring my vision as I run my bare fingers through her thick coat. I can't stand to let her go, but neither can I allow Mikael to hurt her again. I attach the note to her head-collar and open the paddock door. She whickers in my presence, looking for a sugar lump. I only hope that she runs. That Mikael doesn't see the note. That I can stop him from taking after her. She has galloped into town many times. I whisper a silent prayer that she will do so again. 'Go!' I shout, hating to hit her on her rump with my spare piece of rope. Powdery snow sprays out behind her as she gallops into the distance and, as much as I will miss her, she is free. A hard lump forms in my throat. My beautiful Kukka is free.

I turn to see Mikael watching me, eyes filled with rage. He does not chase my horse. He comes after me. There is a hatred in his eyes that terrifies me. He grabs me by the hair and drags me towards the woodlands, his gun beneath his other arm. I scream at the top of my lungs. There is no going back, because he has seen everything. He knows Kukka didn't simply escape. If he had sense, he'd take after her and bring her back. But there is no room for sense to be had when you give yourself to madness. I cling to the hope that Kukka is free. That someone will find my note, and the story of what happened here will be known to all.

But as Mikael forces me to my knees in the freezing-cold woodlands, I know it is too late for me. I bury my head in my hands, unable to look at him. No amount of pleading or begging will get through to him now. I shut my eyes tightly as the cold barrel of the gun presses against my temple. I think of Mama. Of being in her arms. I have never wanted her so badly until now. All I hear is Mikael's heavy breathing in this cold, isolated woodland. Then the trigger is pulled.

# Chapter Sixty-Three

Swann turned the rental-car heater up a few degrees. He'd been wrong about Elea. She hadn't left abruptly because she'd had a death-wish. She was chasing their suspect, going it alone. And now he was following her trail. He'd forgotten how crisp the air was here and how dark the landscape was in the absence of street lights. Sometimes the night could be even more beautiful than the day. Swann wasn't prone to romanticising things, but Finland had captured his heart. Tonight the darkness was animated as stars twinkled, the moon reflecting off the snow in a bluish hue. Forest pine trees loomed large, their heavy crystalline branches reminding Swann of the Bradford collectable ornaments that his mother loved to buy. But the landscape all seemed so similar, and his journey to the cabin had felt like a never-ending trail. At one point Swann was convinced that he'd been driving in circles. Heikkinen had given him detailed directions, but everywhere looked the same.

But now Heikkinen was standing before him, looking every inch the Finnish detective, with his solid build and stubbled beard. His once-blonde hair was cropped silver, cut in a young style that he managed to get away with. His POLIISI reflective jacket acted as a barrier against all weathers, along with his gloves and boots. His insulated tactical pants came with large cargo-pockets. Police-issue, designed to prevent hypothermia. Swann had left so quickly that he hadn't dressed for the Finnish weather. His English winter coat was beginning to feel paper-thin. Heikkinen delivered a strong handshake, his expression grim as he looked Swann up and down. 'Come. There's a spare jacket in my truck.'

Swann dutifully followed. Heikkinen's first call had come as Swann disembarked from the plane. The news that Elea had shot their suspect had come from left field. The man was believed to be Anu Korhonen, otherwise known as their first 'Ice Angel'. The fact that Anu had been involved was a complete mind-fuck, but the description and the timings added up. Anu had returned to Finland just before Swann and his team started hunting him down.

'She's in there,' Heikkinen jabbed a thumb back at the cabin as Swann pulled the spare jacket on. 'She's shaken, but physically unhurt.'

'And Anu?' Swann walked shoulder-to-shoulder with his former boss as he approached the cabin.

Heikkinen shook his head.

'Shit!' Swann muttered.

'Self-defence,' Heikkinen replied. 'Elea had no choice.'

'And you can make that stick?'

Heikkinen sighed, each footstep pressing into the snow. 'She's in a whole world of trouble, but nothing that will incarcerate her.'

That had always been the bar for Elea. To stay out of jail.

'Try not to touch anything . . . And keep her inside. At least until we know what's going on.'

Heikkinen told him about the mound of earth with the

small wooden cross. Swann's heart sank at the news. But at least now they would be able to bring Liisa home. He glanced up at the rickety wooden cabin as Heikkinen left him to return to the crime scene. It was large, but far from homely, with rotting, creaking timbers and a roof thick with snow.

*Jesus*, he thought, taking in his surroundings as he pushed open the screen door. Rusted hinges, splintered floorboards – everything moved and groaned. Swann's muscles contracted and tensed as a damp, smoky smell enveloped him. He found Elea in the living room, after he'd pulled on a forensic suit over his clothes. A pitiful sight, she warmed her hands before a two-bar electric fire that Swann recognised as Heikkinen's own. He kept it in his truck, there for officers in need. Tonight was such a night.

The officer with Elea stood up at their arrival and, reading the room, left them alone. Elea looked at Swann, her crumpled expression reflecting her pain. She was swamped in her bunny suit, the zip pulled down slightly to reveal a police-issue grey tracksuit beneath. No doubt a trade-off for what she'd been wearing before. There was dried blood under her fingernails. Specks in her blonde hair, from when she'd dragged it off her face. The cabin was dim and cold. The furniture was falling apart. The fireplace was blackened, thick with damp soot.

'*Hei*,' Swann said, lightly touching her back.

'*Hei*.'

'You OK?' He took the spot next to Elea on the sofa, which groaned beneath his weight. Was there a part of this cabin that didn't have a life of its own? Soon they'd be asked to vacate it and wait in a heated vehicle or portable tent. In weather like this, heated temporary accommodation would need to be set up. But in the meantime, as temperatures nosedived, compromises had to be made. 'Sorry, stupid question.' Swann said flatly, as Elea failed to respond.

'I didn't mean to kill him.' Elea sniffed. 'I aimed for the bastard's shoulder, but he moved and . . .' She looked at Swann, her words laced with sincerity. 'He was my last link to Liisa. There's so much I need to know.' She swallowed. 'And Maria . . . oh God.' She wiped her tears, unable to continue.

She went to stand, but Swann gently pulled her back down into her seat.

'I should be out there.'

'Heikkinen will get us as soon as there's news,' Swann told her.

Elea eased back into her seat, nodding. 'He will. Yes.' But her voice was strangely detached, as if her mind couldn't take any more grief tonight. Her body trembled beside him.

'You're freezing.' Swann unzipped his forensic suit and took off his jacket. He draped it over her shoulders. She didn't move. She hadn't noticed that it was there. He sensed her emotions: a mixture of shock and trepidation. She was preparing herself for what was to come. Building high walls. He might never be able to reach her again. He hated to witness her pain.

'Bit of a shithole, eh?' Elea said, dovetailing her fingers together.

Swann followed her gaze. 'It's not going to win any Tripadvisor awards.'

'There are law books on the bookshelf. Horse manuals, too.'

306

Swann nodded, aware of Liisa's love of horses and youthful aspirations to become a judge when she 'grew up'. But those days were gone.

'Are you sure you're OK? We can wait at your house, get food, thaw out. You don't need to be here if you're not up to it.'

Elea looked at him as if he'd asked her to run naked in the snow. 'Do you know me at all?'

Swann shrugged. 'It seems not. I thought you'd left England to top yourself.'

Elea snorted in response.

Time passed. They waited in silence. They were kept updated on proceedings. Anu's remains had been removed from the scene, and now they were searching for the body buried beneath the snow. The mound of earth was a grave. Elea and Swann sat in silence. There was nothing more for either of them to say.

The creak of a door hinge broke through their vigil. It was Heikkinen. Elea stood. Swann's coat fell to the ground. She didn't notice as she followed Heikkinen outside. Swann picked it up and pulled it on, pausing only to turn off the heater before he left. He knew without asking. A body had been found.

# Chapter Sixty-Four

Elea didn't wait for Heikkinen to update her any further. Nor did she allow Swann to guide her to the grave. She had been in this position with Chelsea. She wouldn't believe it was her daughter until she saw for herself whatever remained. There were times when she had faltered, allowed doubt to creep in. But tonight the tears she cried were out of frustration. She had told Swann the truth. She'd been aiming for Anu's shoulder. He had moved, right in the line of fire, and she'd hit him in the temple instead. There was no saving a man whose brains were blown a foot behind him. She couldn't accept that her hope of finding Liisa – and uncovering everything that had happened to her – had died with him. Elea had wanted to know everything, no matter how bad it had been. And now she'd blown it all away. She'd had no choice. It was an instinctive reaction as he drew his gun to shoot her.

She stood over the grave and took in another facet of the devastation he had caused. She buried her head like a tortoise into the thick scarf that Heikkinen had wound around her neck. The man had a virtual wardrobe in the back of his van. She couldn't feel her toes, and the tips of her ears were going numb, but she didn't notice any of it. Because the corpse in the grave *wasn't* Liisa. She had gained yet another reprieve. The hunt to find her daughter went on.

Heikkinen hadn't needed to inform her. The strands of long, greying hair that clung to the decaying skull were enough. She took in the old-fashioned clothes. The items that had been buried alongside her. Ornaments. Books. Cards. Elea hunkered down for a closer look. The bones appeared intact. No obvious signs of injury. But the coroner would shed more light on that. All Elea needed to know was that the corpse buried in the ground was not her little girl.

'It's not Liisa.' Elea voiced her thoughts aloud as she stood. 'And I've killed the one person who could tell me where she is. Dammit!' She shouted into the darkness, unable to contain her frustration a moment longer. Heikkinen reached out a hand to guide her away from the scene, but she shrugged it off. She wasn't some fragile little woman. She wasn't hysterical. She wasn't 'losing it', as he'd led others to believe. She turned to look for Swann, his presence oddly absent. Where was he?

'Elea,' Heikkinen was still talking, 'you look beat. Why don't you go home? We'll take it from here.'

'No.' She pointed to the cabin. 'Not until every inch of that place has been searched.' She looked into his eyes. Saw the worry and concern that were there. Heikkinen had known her for a lifetime. Dearest Heikkinen, the man she'd always admired. The person who lived for his job, but was never happier than when he was on his own. He was more than a work colleague. Much more. 'Honestly, I'm fine.' She managed an apologetic smile. 'And thank you. For everything.'

They walked away from the crime scene, retracing their footprints in the snow.

'It's not as if I don't know her . . .' He was talking about Liisa. 'I care about her, too.'

'I know.' Her words were little more than a whisper as she kept her emotions in check. At least he was still talking about her daughter in the present tense.

Heikkinen checked over his shoulder before closing the gap between them. 'It wasn't my decision, Elea. You didn't have to go it alone.'

'No regrets,' Elea replied, eyes shining. 'Not now.'

'Of course.' He cleared his throat. Took a step back. This was the socially inept man that she knew and loved. Her time with Heikkinen had been fleeting, all those years ago. Her decision to carry on with the pregnancy had been monumental. Heikkinen had offered more, but his heart wasn't in it, and Elea was satisfied with the trust fund that he contributed to every month. He watched over them both from a comfortable distance. Elea had made it clear from the start: nobody could ever know. She had no time for the judgements that would follow. For the whispers behind her back. For the career opportunities that she would have missed. Heikkinen had never wanted children and that was entirely fine by her. Her subsequent failed marriage to Swann was proof enough that Elea was better off as a single mum. *Only* . . . She walked towards the cabin where Swann was on the phone. No. She couldn't think that now. But the thought came anyway. *Only, when was the last time I was a mum?*

She watched Swann fumble with his forensic suit, unzipping it to shove his phone into his pocket. Watched him scan the forest where Heikkinen was working, relaxing as he turned to his right and found Elea by his side.

'Want to help me search this shithole?' Elea said on a frosted breath. Officers had already checked each room, but there were notebooks, books, old electrical devices – something would surely provide them with more clues.

'I've got to get back.'

'Fine. I'll do it myself.'

'You're coming, too.'

Elea frowned. 'No, I'm not. There could be anything in there.'

'We've got a lead. A good one this time.'

Elea didn't dare to believe it. She'd been down this road before. Swann saw her mistrust. He fumbled once more, then handed Elea his phone.

'What's this?'

'CCTV captured in Lincoln just an hour ago.'

Elea stared at him, then back to the high-res black-and-white image on the screen. It looked like her, twenty years ago. Why was he showing her this? She blinked, peered closer. Her plump lips, open in surprise. Her arched eyebrows. Her strong cheekbones. Her long blonde hair. A ghost of her former self, trapped in time. But it wasn't her. It was someone who carried the same genes. Slowly Elea's hand cupped her open mouth.

'Where did you get this?' She couldn't tear her eyes away from the image.

'Mitch picked it up,' Swann said. 'She checked into the Castle Hotel, along with a man fitting Anu's description, the same day he left the rental house.'

Elea's voice would not come. She was locked in that moment, staring at the image of a beautiful young woman.

A woman who looked so much like her little girl, all grown up. False hope was a dangerous thing, but she was ready to jump in, feet first, yet again. 'How . . .' she managed to say.

'Digital breadcrumbs. We found burner phones in a bin in the alleyway at the back of the rental house. Mitch worked with the tech team to analyse them and that's when they discovered the hotel booking.'

But this wasn't enough for Elea. 'More – I need more.' Swann was a dinosaur when it came to technology. 'I need to speak to Mitch.'

'Bloody hell, all right then, if my word isn't good enough for you,' Swann grumbled. 'But inside. My toes are going to fall off if I stand here any longer.' He gestured towards the van that had pulled up to the busy scene. Hot drinks were being handed out, and it didn't take a lot of persuading for Elea to follow Swann.

He handed her the phone as soon as they were safely inside the warm vehicle. He'd attached his mobile to a battery pack. The cold weather was zapping his battery fast. With a paper cup of coffee in one hand and Swann's mobile phone in the other, Elea settled down to make the call. Mitch seemed happy to relay the news that Elea was desperate to hear.

'OK, talk me through it,' she said, relishing each word.

Mitch explained how the cyber-crime team had accessed the suspect's metadata and call-logs that had been wiped. 'He was using a VPN to cover up his tracks. But it must have dropped out and connected to the rental home's Wi-Fi when he made the hotel booking. It pinged back to the house's IP address.'

'Good,' Elea said, pleased with the strong chain of evidence.

But there would be no case to answer. In that moment she'd forgotten that her main suspect was dead. She brought herself back to the present moment. She was running on adrenaline. 'So what now? You think the woman captured on CCTV is returning to the hotel?'

She didn't dare to call her Liisa. Not yet.

'She checked out. Dropped her key in the box,' Mitch replied. 'We've got eyeballs on both the rental house and the hotel, just in case.'

But Elea didn't understand. If the woman in the hotel *was* her daughter, why didn't she hand herself in to the police? She knocked back the last of her coffee, the warm liquid hitting the back of her throat. Swann was right. There was nothing here for her any more. It was time to return to the UK.

# Chapter Sixty-Five

Elea barely remembered the flight back to England. It was mercifully quiet, with plenty of empty seats. She had fallen asleep not long after her seatbelt clicked into place. Exhaustion – emotional and physical – had caught up with her. She and Swann had eaten in the airport before departing. They had both been ravenous and the food in Nordic Kitchen had never tasted so good.

Swann smiled as she woke from her slumber. 'I don't know how you slept through all that turbulence.'

'It was soothing.' Elea stretched lazily in her seat like a cat. 'It felt like I was being rocked to sleep.' She stifled a yawn. 'Any updates?'

Swann shook his head. 'It's the middle of the night, love. We'll get a result in the morning. I'm sure of it.'

*Love.* He'd used that term of endearment in the old days. A silent exchange passed between them. An acknowledgement of what they once had. Elea cleared her throat and pulled back her jacket sleeve to check her watch. She'd been home for a change of clothes. Her house was just as she had left it, Liisa's room still as it always had been. She had lingered in the doorway, knowing in her gut that things would be different the next time she was home. After so many false starts, she was ready for it.

Swann was right about his team. They would be tucked up in bed now, ready for a fresh start in the morning. But it didn't mean that the search had been called off. A night shift of officers was patrolling Lincoln, both on foot and in their cars. There weren't as many officers as they would have liked. According to Swann, the numbers had been cut and many experienced officers pensioned off. But their younger counterparts would do the best they could.

'Manage to get any sleep?' Elea relaxed as the plane descended, knowing she'd done all she could for now.

He shook his head. 'I'll have a quick nap when I get home. I've got to sort things out with Alice.'

'Oh dear.'

'Oh dear indeed,' Swann grumbled. 'I've really pissed her off this time. She's sent me hundreds of texts.' He showed Elea his phone.

Elea blinked as she tried to make out the words on the screen. They had descended into profanities well into the early hours.

'I don't know what to do.' Swann thumbed past each text message.

'If you're looking for sympathy, then I'm in short supply.' Elea watched Swann put away his phone. 'Sorry. But you've got to see it from Alice's perspective. You flew over to Finland to chase me around while she's at home minding the twins.'

'But I wasn't gone long.'

'I know you weren't. But has it occurred to you that she might have been scared that you weren't coming back?' Elea kept her voice low enough for only Swann to hear.

Swann looked at Elea blankly. 'Well . . . no.'

'Of course it didn't.' She looked at him in earnest. An unwelcome thought made itself known. 'Is that what the flat is about? Are you feathering your nest with me before you make the jump to leave?'

'No!' Swann said, a little too loudly. 'God, no.' He lowered his voice. 'Not at all. I've booked counselling. I'm trying to give our relationship a chance. For the boys. I know what Alice is like. If I leave, she'll never let me see them again. She barely lets my mum in through the door.'

Elea shook her head in disbelief. Helen was the nicest, sweetest woman. How on earth could Alice take exception to her? She pushed the thought aside. She had to stay firm. 'You chose to be with Alice. She gave you what I couldn't: stability. Focus on your relationship and forget about me. I can take care of myself.' But the words felt sour on Elea's tongue as Swann stared at her. She would always love him and she would never like Alice, but those little boys – their soft wavy hair, their small sleeping forms – were so precious, especially at that age. She wouldn't destroy a family. 'But thank you,' she said softly. 'For being there.' She knew she was contradicting herself, but couldn't let it go unsaid. She was grateful to this big, intelligent man who had kept her together over the last twenty-four hours.

'You'll always be a big part of my life.' Swann gripped the armrests more tightly as the plane jolted, the blood draining from his face.

'I can't believe you're still afraid of flying.' Elea chuckled as the plane approached the runway.

'Not afraid,' he managed to say, his knuckles whitening. 'I just don't like it very much.'

Elea smiled as they touched down. She never imagined that she'd be back in the UK so soon, with a heart filled with hope.

It was bright by the time they returned to Lincoln. While Swann went home to Nettleham, Elea went to see Mitch, who had taken over Swann's old office. It felt strange to see the desk devoid of his things.

'You're back,' Mitch stated the obvious. 'How are you feeling? You must be running on fumes.' His words came in quick succession, his pleasure at seeing her again evident.

'I'm fine. Slept on the plane.' Elea relayed her thoughts to Mitch. She had spent the journey from the airport analysing every new piece of information they had gained in the last twenty-four hours. *If* the girl pictured was her daughter, then where would she most likely go? The rental house was still under observation, with a police officer posted outside. Sonar equipment was being used to search for bodies in the garden. Officers would finish up at the house by the end of the day. But if Liisa *had* been in the rental house, it wasn't for very long. She might not have been emotionally invested enough to return. Would she go to Finland? Did she even have a passport?' She looked to Mitch for answers. He'd done a good job in Swann's absence, and the superintendent had never been far away.

'Well—' Mitch began speaking, but was interrupted by a knock on the door.

'Sorry, boss.' Kelly glanced between Mitch and Elea. 'I just spoke to two PCSOs in the hall. There have been complaints about a homeless woman hanging around the horses on West

Common.' She hesitated, directing her question at Elea. 'Liisa liked horses, didn't she? It might lead to nothing, but . . .'

'No, that's great. Thanks, Kelly. Good work.' Elea's voice was steady, but her pulse wasn't, as she watched Kelly leave.

Mitch was already pulling on his coat.

Elea reached for his arm, gripping his sleeve. 'You don't think . . .' The words stuck in her throat, swallowed by the sudden pressure building in her chest.

Mitch's hand closed over hers, steady, warm. 'Maybe.' He paused. 'You OK?'

Elea swallowed hard and gave a small, sharp nod. Her hand tightened on his for a second before she let go. 'If it's Liisa—' She exhaled shakily, forcing composure. 'I need to be the one to talk to her first.'

Mitch held her gaze for a beat, then nodded. 'Let's go.'

# Chapter Sixty-Six

Elea tugged her coat against the biting wind as they surveyed the vast expanse of open land. Mitch understood her need to keep things low-key, but had insisted on tagging along. An endless canvas of dreary winter stretched out before them. The brown, damp grass thawed beneath the late-morning sun, which cast streaks of orange on the landscape in the promise of a new day. Scattered across the common the shapes of grazing horses moved slowly, their warm breaths rising in soft puffs. Their thick, muddy coats provided protection from the cold, their heavy hooves leaving imprints in the damp grass. Liisa would be most at home with the horses. But why hadn't she reached out to the police? Deep in thought, Elea continued walking next to Mitch, her gaze falling between the underbrush and clumps of tall, dormant grass.

Heads down, they passed dog walkers along the paths. 'This place is huge.' Mitch's words came on a frosted breath. 'We could get the drone up – it would save time.' They had been walking for thirty minutes and were getting nowhere.

'Go. I'll get a taxi back,' she suggested. Because if Liisa was here somewhere, Elea needed this reunion to be just the two of them.

'We'll give it another ten minutes,' Mitch replied. 'Then I'm calling for backup.'

Elea ground her back teeth as she tried to gather some semblance of patience. She'd fantasised so many scenarios in which she'd find her daughter. The last thing she wanted was an audience. She trudged through the grass. Ten minutes. Then she'd tell Mitch to leave.

'Look. Over there.' Mitch said, pointing at a lone figure in the misty air.

Elea's breath caught in her throat. There was movement between two horses. A flash of long blonde hair. Elea exchanged a glance with Mitch. The moment she had fought for, longed for, suddenly felt overwhelming and she became rooted to the ground.

'Go,' he said. 'Call if you need me.'

It couldn't be, could it? Yet every fibre of her being told her it was. She made a beeline towards a lean-to where a group of horses was congregating. Quietly she approached the small wooden structure, her heart punching her ribs as she got closer to the woman, who was speaking the sweetest of Finnish words.

'*Hyvää huomenta, rakas. Miten voit tänään*?' The young woman stood, her back to Elea. She was talking to the horses, asking them how they were. Elea wanted to stay in this moment. In this beautiful bubble of hope, relief and love. She took precious seconds to breathe as her emotions came in waves. It was Liisa. She was alive. A sense of unreality washed over her. That was the voice of her little girl. Swallowing the tightness in her throat, she called out.

'Liisa?'

The young woman was standing beside a piebald horse, feeding it Polo mints. Her sleeping bag lay crumpled in the straw. Her mouth dropped open, the packet of mints falling to the ground. She moved aside as the horse greedily nuzzled the spilled mints at her feet.

'Wait!' Elea said, speaking in Finnish as Liisa backed away. She looked like a frightened animal searching for escape. 'Please. Liisa. It's me. It's . . . Mum.'

The young woman stared, eyes wide, nostrils flaring as she looked Elea up and down.

Had Elea got it wrong? Was this really her daughter? After all this time was there a chance she was seeing through the lens of a desperate mother?

'M-Mama?' The girl's hopeful blue eyes grew wet with tears.

'Yes.' It came in a whisper.

It was Liisa. Liisa was alive. Arms open, heart aching, Elea moved towards her daughter.

Liisa took two steps back. 'No. No, no, no . . .' Tears trickled down her face as, hand raised, she instructed Elea to stay where she was.

'It's OK.' Elea sniffed. 'You're safe now. It's me.' But Liisa was in shock. Elea shoved her hand in her pocket and brought out a crumpled photograph. 'Remember this?' She blinked away her tears, for clarity of vision. 'I took it at the riding school.' She exhaled a laugh at the memory. 'That pony was so fat, you called him—'

'*Lihapulla* – my meatball,' Liisa finished her sentence, transitioning to English as she approached.

Elea closed the space between them. She was aware of Mitch moving in.

Then Liisa was falling into her arms, burying her head in

Elea's shoulder and gripping her tight. 'Mama,' she cried. 'It's really you.'

'Yes,' Elea laughed, tears reaching her eyes. 'I'm here.'

Liisa was trembling now. 'Why didn't you find me?'

'I tried,' Elea spoke into her daughter's blonde hair. 'I really tried.' She wanted to offer comfort, but Liisa's body turned tense.

'Not hard enough.' Liisa erupted in a maelstrom of emotions as she pushed her mother back. 'Not hard enough!' she repeated, both fists on Elea's chest.

Elea faltered, then regained her composure, willing to take the blows as her heart broke more than she knew was possible.

'Hey,' Mitch stepped between them, halting Liisa's movements. 'I'm Mitch. I work with your mum.' He smiled, taking Liisa in. He glanced pointedly at the sleeping bag. 'You must be freezing. Let's get you somewhere warm.'

Liisa stared at him as if she'd been dropped into another reality.

*It's too much for her*, Elea thought, grateful as Mitch intervened. Their unease was unsettling the horses, which had moved away.

'Where's Anu?' Liisa slapped away her tears, her face pink from the cold.

Mitch picked up her sleeping bag and a nearby rucksack. 'My car isn't far from here. Let me just . . . gather up your things.'

'Take me to him.' Liisa's voice sharpened. 'I need to see Anu. Now.'

'OK,' Elea said, because she needed to get her away from

322

here. A police station would provide safety. People to talk to. She couldn't tell her about Anu yet. 'Mitch will bring us to the station. Yes?' She still couldn't quite believe her daughter was standing in front of her.

Liisa eyed her cautiously. Looked around the space with dazed eyes. Elea was hit by the surreality of it all, too, as her daughter gazed wistfully at the horses as they plodded through the frosted grass. 'I used to have a horse. Her name was Kukka. Anu bought her for me.'

Elea nodded, feeling sick as she listened to Liisa describing the man and his affinity with animals. 'You've always loved horses.'

Liisa nodded sadly. She took her rucksack from Mitch's grip. 'Let's go. Before her owner comes.'

This was not the reunion Elea had dreamed about, but inside she was elated. She wanted to sing, to dance, to cry. Liisa was alive. But she was looking at Elea with the eyes of a stranger. Her daughter was fragile and broken. She needed handling with care.

Elea dialled Swann's number. He picked up after two rings. Finally she uttered the words she had longed to say for countless years. She took a deep breath as Swann asked if everything was OK.

'We've found her. Liisa's alive.'

# Chapter Sixty-Seven

## Liisa

## 2026

After all these years, I am free. But I don't feel free. Fear has wrapped itself around me, squeezing so tightly that it's hard to breathe. It feels like I've been living underwater and have come up for air in a world I don't recognise. The city air feels sharp and dirty, foreign to my lungs. I had to get away to an open space, to the quiet, where the horses are.

Lincoln is a small city, but it feels loud and chaotic to me. The drone of aeroplanes flying to the nearby military base. The music rising from buskers on the city streets. The soft chatter from people who ask you to give to charity. Then there's the restaurants. Students eating junk food in the open air. Laughing. Shouting. Litter. Traffic building up, halting at the sound of the pedestrian crossing as it beeps that it's safe to walk. Everything tears at my insides. I can't cope with the smells and sounds. It's all too full of chaos. There are so many people. I went looking for the nearest police station after I left the hotel. But then I remembered Anu talking about the horses on West Common. I started calling him by his real name sometime after Johanna died, long after he'd shared his secret with me.

I follow my mother to the car, feet tripping over each other as if I've forgotten how to walk freely on my own. I flinch as the man standing at the door raises a hand to guide me inside. He smiles an apology. I ask if I can sit in the front. He agrees. My mother gets into the back. The scent of her perfume takes me to a life long ago, but I can't bear to look at her. The woman who forgot about me. How can a mother do that to her child? I stare at my feet, head down, as I always did when in the car with Anu. Hands clasped on my lap. No sudden moves. My hair hanging over my face like a curtain.

'Are you OK?' My mother's voice is strained.

I won't—I can't talk to her any more. The palms of my hands are clammy and I can't stop the tremble in my limbs. I clasp my hands tighter together. I need to sit in peace. She sits back. We drive in silence. I am grateful.

I lower my window as the countryside comes into view and inhale a breath of fresh air. We reach a wide car park. I glance upwards at the building before me. The man – I think his name is Mitch – speaks with a kindly voice. 'We're at the police station, Liisa. You're safe here. We can get you some food, a drink . . .' He pauses as the sound of my mother crying softly rises from the back seat. I sense these are happy tears. Why? She never came for me.

I am taken to a quiet room, with blue sofas and window blinds. There are cameras in the corners of the ceiling. My body aches with exhaustion. I haven't slept properly in weeks. I recognise the man who comes to greet us. He whispers something to Mum. Whatever it is, it makes her smile. I sense a closeness between them, and jealousy harpoons my chest. He is tall and broad and blocks the light from the window as he stands before me.

'You're her husband,' I say, narrowing my eyes. 'You took her away from me.'

His eyebrows rise at the accusation. He seems taken aback. 'What? I . . . no—'

'You're not her husband? Your name isn't Richard Swann?'

'I am, but . . .'

'You have children?'

Swann appears confused. 'Well, yes, but—'

I interrupt him for the second time because I don't want to hear about their happy family life. 'I don't want to talk to you, and I don't want to talk to her.' I'm too hurt. Too sad. Too overwhelmed. Every sound of her sobbing is like a splinter pushing into my skin. 'Take me to Anu.'

They bring me tea and toast. Mother dabs away her tears. I sense she is desperate to talk, but knows that I need space. The other man, Mitch, is younger. Less intrusive. He tells me that he's a police detective inspector. I agree to talk to him. There is another lady, there for my welfare. My mother is dry-washing her hands. She looks like she's found the last piece of a puzzle, but can't quite make it fit.

We are left alone, just Mitch and me, and he explains that our interview is being monitored. I don't think I have a choice, so I let it pass. I'm used to being told what to do. He asks me questions, but I have one, too.

'Where's Anu?'

He takes his time answering. His eyes are sincere. 'There was an incident. Anu died.'

I stare at him as my world moves around me yet again. 'He . . . he's dead?'

He nods. 'Yes.'

Heat rises from my chest up to my neck. 'How . . . where?'

'In Finland. I can't go into details about the investigation, I'm afraid.'

I feel dizzy and sick. He asks if I would like a drink of water and hands me the glass. I sip slowly, buying time. There's a ringing in my ears. Anu can't be gone. Not yet. I look to the man before me, my eyes puffy from crying as I speak my thoughts aloud.

'What do I do now?'

Mitch leans forward in his seat. 'Tell me everything.'

My old self died the day Anu pulled the trigger in the woods. I lay there, crouched in the snow, believing I'd never see Mama again. I've felt real fear. But I've never before experienced loneliness as intense as that day. I'd always put Mama on a pedestal. She was a superhero in my childish eyes. That part of me – the part that still believed in her – dissolved in the snow that day. Anu's gun wasn't loaded. He hadn't had time to do that. Nor had he pulled the trigger to frighten me. I saw the surprise register in his eyes when the gun didn't go off. It gave him enough time to cool down. To emerge from the rage that controlled his movements and warped his thoughts. He dragged me inside, my horse nothing but a speck on the horizon. He asked me why I did it and, through a haze of snot and tears, I blurted out everything. I confessed that I'd written the note and told him I'd wanted to escape. I don't know why

I blurted it all out when I should have been thinking about my precious horse. But I was in shock, and everything fell away.

The strangest thing happened that day. Anu looked around the cabin as if seeing it with new eyes. He gazed at the shoddy furniture that was falling apart. At the smoke-stained walls and the cracks in the floors. He said if I wanted to leave, then we'd leave. I think he feared what he might do if we stayed there any longer. He said there was nothing holding us there. Then he promised to bring me to England and reunite me with my mother. After everything he'd told me about her, his words didn't feel real. All he asked for was my loyalty, because people wouldn't understand. That night we stayed up for hours discussing our escape plan. He told me Johanna had a sister named Katariina. The thought of someone else knowing about us shocked me to the core. Anu didn't like being asked questions, but he said they weren't close. Johanna went to see Katariina a few months before she died and told her everything. 'And she didn't call the police?' was all I could think of to say. Anu had shaken his head. 'What would be the point?' he'd replied. 'It was too late by then.'

He said that Katariina had contacts. That she'd promised to help us move away. It would take time, but it would be the best thing all round. I cried with relief. I sobbed for my beautiful horse, which I would never see again. My bedroom door was unlocked. I had no reason to run. But I should have known that Anu was only doing it for himself. The next day we were on the road. He was only running because he was scared someone would find the note. We rented a room in Helsinki while Anu sorted everything out. Johanna had left him money. He told me not to worry about things. It took him twelve weeks to sort out my passport. I never left the flat during that time. I used to hear him on the phone, talking to Katariina. I tried asking about Johanna's home life; I itched with curiosity and a need to understand what drove her. But Anu said that Johanna was just like everyone else. That sometimes people took what they wanted because it felt good. I didn't like the way he looked at me when he said that and it brought my questions to an end.

After all my years in captivity, the airport terrified me. Being surrounded by so many people left me unable to speak. Anu bought me headphones and told airline staff I was autistic. We rented a flat in Lincoln. Two weeks later he sat me down and said that Mama had moved away. He made me hope that I'd see her, bought my compliance with a promise to keep trying to find her. But it was lies, all of it. Because that's what Mitch is telling me. He said Mama never gave up. Mitch asks if Anu hurt me. I can't bear to talk about the time he tried to make me his 'wife'. It didn't work out long-term. If I was able to do everything he wanted, maybe he wouldn't have gone out looking for other girls. I cleaned and cooked while Anu worked as a delivery driver for cash in hand. I liked keeping busy. We settled into a routine. I didn't know about the other girls until much later on. By then, it was too late.

Mitch makes notes as he slowly prises all of this from me. I haven't told him everything. I don't know who I can trust, and Anu's hold is still strong.

Hours have passed. He stops to give me a breather. I've asked for some time alone. I still feel distant from myself. I know that Mother is watching. I'm too ashamed to speak any more. Too scared to open my mouth. It's like there are four different people nudging each other for space in my brain. Liisa from Porvoo; she's scared and wants her grandma. Then there's the girl in the rundown cabin whose mother didn't come for her. There's the person who hated Mikael and Johanna. Then there's the woman who felt sorry for Anu, who needed him – the person who is so mixed up in the head that she wants to see him one more time. I am all of these things.

Anu said that he'd come back for me. I waited. Hours passed, then days, living on my nerves. He left me in the hotel, with no money and no food. He didn't have Kukka, my beautiful horse, to manipulate me with; he had something else. Something so strong that I was forced to do anything he asked.

I nibbled on the hotel's Lotus biscuits, every mouthful turning to dust in my mouth. Made tea and coffee until the little plastic cartons of milk ran out. Took some more from the cart in the hall when the maid wasn't looking. Then the time came to check out. I waited until the last possible moment, paralysed by fear. I had no choice but to leave. I knew in my heart that Anu was either arrested or dead. I never imagined that he would abandon me. I can't believe that he's gone. I press my hand to my stomach, willing the nausea to settle. I'm used to rules. Orders. Consequences. But now there's nothing and that terrifies me, because now I don't know what to do. I've got another secret, and it's tearing me apart. I can't keep it in, but who can I trust?

# Chapter Sixty-Eight

Swann had watched Elea as she observed the interview from the monitoring room. She'd sat, unblinking in her swivel chair, her face illuminated by the computer screen. Someone had left a notepad and pen on the desk, but Elea hadn't needed them. Swann knew she was committing every word of the interview to memory. He'd stood silently, watching each emotion play out on her face. Now she was respecting her daughter's request for privacy, even though she didn't know what she was being punished for. Now that Swann understood the bond of parenthood, he admired her even more. She had stayed so strong, steadfastly believing that her daughter was alive, despite evidence to the contrary.

His team had been elated when the news came in. As for Swann, he still could barely believe it. If Liisa didn't look so much like her mother, he'd be asking for a DNA test first. But there was no doubting her parentage, at least on her mother's side. Elea had never disclosed the identity of Liisa's father. Swann presumed she'd had her own reasons for that. He had pushed her for a name after Liisa was first taken, but Elea had refused to budge. She'd made it clear from the start that Liisa's father was not in the frame.

Now she was sitting, mesmerised, watching her daughter onscreen, drinking a cup of coffee and staring into space. Liisa was a traumatised young woman whose view of the world had been skewed. Swann couldn't predict her reactions now that she was physically free, because they had barely touched the surface of what she had been through. Her mental chains would take much longer to escape from. Such things were best left in the hands of the professionals. Swann had made calls. Referrals had been set up. Plans were under way. Both Elea and Liisa needed their help today. But first they had to update the case. Had Liisa been present when Chelsea Hobbs died? What if she'd helped with the disposal of Jenny Flynn's body? He prayed, for Elea's sake, that wasn't the case. Because Liisa hadn't come forward or reported herself missing to the police. Anu had been a victim once, too. Judging from the information they'd gathered, he had turned killer over the years. Was Liisa really held captive all that time? Or had she turned a blind eye? Questions would be asked with regard to her involvement in the crimes. Swann left Elea alone with Mitch as he slipped into the monitoring room.

He met Ness in his office. Their meeting had been prearranged after she'd updated him on her latest findings. Swann had requested full call-logs from Anu's recovered mobile phones.

She handed him the paperwork. 'I've highlighted the most interesting passages, boss.' She kept her voice low. He'd already received the email, but preferred paper copies. When it came to policing, he was a proud dinosaur. Now his team's movements were guarded, as they couldn't afford for Elea to find out. Not until they were sure. Because if the texts found on Anu's phone were correct, Elea's life was going to change yet again.

'Not a word to anyone – not until we've had a chance to check this out,' Swann instructed Ness as he read each word. It was a matter of urgency. If this was true . . . it was another bombshell about to drop.

Ness nodded gravely, understanding the seriousness of the situation. 'How's Elea going to take this, if it comes to fruition?' Her voice was so low that he could barely make out her words.

'I don't know,' Swann replied. 'But be discreet. You've told Control that you're making local enquiries?' Such an update on the system could relate to anything.

'Already done – we're on it. I'll keep you in the loop.' Ness cleaned her glasses with the end of her floral shirt before turning for the door.

Swann watched her go. DC Ollie Evans was waiting in the car park to back her up. He could trust Ness and Ollie. Discretion was key. Because if his hunch was correct, the Ice Angels case was about to take another shocking turn.

# Chapter Sixty-Nine

Elea's elation was overshadowed by her daughter's reluctance to spend time with her. It wasn't Liisa's fault. The more she listened to her, the more Elea realised the depth of Anu's manipulation and lies. Not only did Anu tell her that Elea had got married, but he'd also claimed that she'd moved to the UK and had started a family of her own. He'd kept track of Swann's movements, showing Liisa a picture of him with the twins. Anu had even moved to Lincoln, in the guise of helping Liisa find her family and start again. But then he dashed her daughter's hopes by saying that Elea had mysteriously moved away. By cleverly weaving in truth with lies, he gave Liisa enough evidence to slowly turn her against the person who loved her most in the world.

As for Chelsea and the others, Liisa claimed they must have been kept in separate locations. She said that Anu would disappear for days on end. That they were always moving around. There might have been times when Liisa could have escaped, but she had become bound to her captor in a way Elea couldn't understand. A deep dive had been done on Johanna, who had a sister living in Helsinki. She did not come from an honest family and was far wealthier than her cabin in the woods implied. Johanna's mother had hanged herself when she was forty-two years old. Johanna herself ran away from home as soon as she was able, becoming a recluse from a young age.

Elea wanted to believe Liisa. She sat across from her daughter after the interview had ended, trying to explain it all to her. The air was fresh and clean, sweetened by the occasional puff of a plug-in air freshener. Liisa's jeans needed a wash, and her hands disappeared into the sleeves of her knitted pink jumper. 'I never stopped looking for you,' Elea said. 'I never gave up.' She looked to Swann, who was sitting next to her. 'We're separated now. He lives with his new partner, Alice, and the twins.'

'Your twins?' Liisa finally said.

'I don't have any other children, apart from you,' Elea assured her.

'Who lives in our house now?'

'Our house? In Porvoo?'

Liisa nodded.

'Us. I mean, me. It's just as you left it.' Elea tilted her head to one side. 'Why?'

But Liisa didn't answer. Her pretty face contorted in a frown. She was too young for the worries weighing down upon her.

Swann had left them to it. There were still briefings to be conducted. Post-op conclusions to be made. Remaining enquiries to be followed up.

Liisa yawned, pressing the sleeves of her jumper against her mouth.

'I'm renting an apartment in town. It's on the Brayford, so not too busy. There's swans and ducks, a canoe club.' Elea delivered an awkward exhalation of breath. 'We have a sauna. A swimming pool . . .' But she was losing her audience.

335

Liisa shifted in her seat.

'Liisa? Would you like to stay with me? Is that OK with you?' But there was a force-field of lies between them. Years of conditioning had separated her daughter from the rest of humanity. Elea was happy to give her time. Liisa was alive. She was loved. But right now she was in pain. 'I'll give you as much space as you need.'

Liisa rose from the sofa and moved towards the window blinds. Elea sighed. At times like these, she needed her own mum. Hilma had been elated to hear the news. Elea's thoughts fell away as she heard the door open. Then she watched Liisa's face light up.

Hilma's presence felt like a dream as she entered the room. Elea blinked. The surprise reunion was the last thing she had expected, but she was so grateful for it. She watched with a tinge of envy as Liisa fell into her grandmother's arms. There were no such boundaries there. No recriminations. No blame.

Elea and Swann stood back, observing the happy scene: Elea's mother, in her billowy clothing and Buddhist beaded bracelets, uttering comforting words. 'I have a place to stay, in the countryside. You will come with me, yes?' Hilma said, holding Liisa tightly.

'Yes,' Liisa replied, as Hilma soothed her.

'It's for the best,' Swann said, in a voice meant only for Elea. 'Your mum will talk Liisa round.'

'How did you get her here so quickly?' Elea asked, a little in awe of him.

'I can't take all the credit. My mum has been keeping Hilma updated. That's where she's staying.'

'Does Helen still live in Sudbrooke?'

'She does,' Swann replied. 'Near the woods, with horses in the back field. She'll take good care of them both.'

He was right. Liisa didn't need the city. She needed peace and recuperation. But Elea had waited so long to be with her daughter. She couldn't bear to be separated from her.

Swann dipped his hand into his jacket pocket. He opened his palm to reveal the small wooden doll. 'It's a bit premature, taking it from the property department, but I don't think we'll need it now.'

'Thank you,' Elea whispered. She felt like an outsider as she approached her daughter. But that was OK – time was finally on their side. 'I've got something for you.' Elea delivered a weak smile as she reached out her hand. 'Here. It's yours.'

'How did you . . .' Liisa accepted the small wooden doll, examining it under the light.

'I told you,' Elea said. 'I never gave up.' Now the doll had made it full circle and was back where it belonged.

Things might not be perfect, but it was a start.

# Chapter Seventy

## Liisa

### 2026

I am ready for this meeting. It's only been three weeks, but my head is in a better space. It's still going to take time, but already I feel like I'm over the worst. I'm sitting in Helen's living room, which has an autumnal vibe, despite it being winter. The cottage is filled with the warmth of the old log burner, but it doesn't emit even a puff of smoke. The inglenook fireplace is spotless, with stacks of timber on each side. There are candles on the hearth, and tiny string lights that glow as soon as it gets dark. The sofas are clean, deep and squishy, with plump orange cushions and soft, freshly laundered throws. The carpet is a thick hazelnut pile, and the wooden beams above my head are cobweb-free. There are no cluttered ornaments here; everything in this room has been carefully thought out. Helen used to be an interior designer and has travelled all over the world. She and Grandmother Hilma get on so well that they might as well be sisters. Helen's cottage has four bedrooms, enough space for us all. I think she's been lonely since her husband died. We haven't worn out our welcome yet.

I've enjoyed being in all-female company – they're happy to let me just be. In the evenings I sit quietly and knit as they chat and giggle over glasses of wine. I won't eat fish and I can't stand the smell of liquorice, but some domestic habits are hard to let go. Helen said that I'm too young to be a home-maker, but I have no aspirations to do anything else yet. Sometimes I'll feed the horses in the back fields, my thoughts with Kukka. Mother did some digging into her whereabouts. What she discovered was a gift that she did not need to wrap. Kukka was found loose in town and taken to an animal shelter. They took one look at the scar on her neck and believed that she'd been abused. They didn't search too hard for her owner, and she was later rehomed. A nice lady named Jakki still has her, and she's even sent me photos. Kukka's whiskers are grey, her back slightly sunken, but she has had a happy life. The note I attached to her head-collar must have got lost in the snow.

I was angry with Mama after she admitted to killing Mikael. But part of him was Anu, too. I grieved for the little boy that he once was. For the stupid loss of life. For my Ice Angel twin. If only he hadn't let Johanna influence him. Why didn't he go quietly with my mother when he was found in the woods, crying over Johanna's grave? Why pull his gun? My emotions concerning him are confusing, veering from attachment, to pity, to hate. I still use his names interchangeably. Had it not been for Johanna's sister Katariina, we might not have got away. Mitch has kept me informed about the details of the investigation. Katariina's husband recently died in prison of a heart attack after serving time for forgery. I knew Anu could not have got the passports on his own. Perhaps Katariina wanted rid of us after her sister passed away. Johanna's body was too badly composed for a definitive cause of death, but my gut tells me that Anu helped Johanna on her way.

The girl taken before me was called Venla. Police found her buried in the earth under the hole. To think, all that time, she had been beneath us. I can't dwell on such a thing. The reality of the situation is grotesque. Johanna turned Anu into a monster. Police are still looking for other graves.

Grandmother has taught me meditation. It was difficult to live with my thoughts, but I am slowly finding peace. Silence is often my friend. The police have finished asking questions; they are satisfied with my account. The Ice Angels case is closed. Mother has tried speaking to Maria, but she won't have anything to do with Mama now. I managed one long phone call, told Maria the bits that she'd needed to hear. Maria told me she's struggling to stay sober because she blames herself for everything. I said there's no point in looking back, because, in the end, Anu went home. At least Maria saw him one last time. But the boy she lost wasn't there any more. Johanna changed him. Maria has asked if she can come and visit. I've managed to put her off for now. We are linked, she and I. I've promised to see her when I'm well enough to travel again.

I can't describe how I feel about Mama because my emotions have been hard to figure out. Perhaps our bond was so strong that I thought nothing would break it. Maybe deep down I'm scared of getting that close to her again. I straighten on the sofa at the sound of a car pulling up on Helen's drive. Grandmother's eyes are alight, full of love and hope. Helen glances my way as she stands to go to the door. She is anxious but happy, after orchestrating this meeting. She and Hilma look so alike. She feels like family, even though she's not. 'Are you ready?'

'We're ready,' I say, because I am not alone. I look down at my daughter, sitting next to me on the couch. My Bekka. My rock. My reason for doing everything that Anu asked. He didn't need Kukka – not when he had our child. She is five, so bright and inquisitive. Every day she asks me questions. After every explanation I give, she responds with a 'Why?' She is a happy soul, despite her background. If it wasn't for Bekka, I don't think I'd be alive today. Anu would have disposed of me just like the others, when it didn't 'work out' or when I wasn't the 'right fit'. He would never have abandoned his search for his child bride. Johanna had carved her strange obsessions into him, shaping his warped desires. Superstition drove Anu's actions as he repeated her same patterns, taking children of the same age at the same time, trying to replicate what Johanna had described as the happiest time of her life. But deep down, Anu must have known that it was wrong. I was nothing more than a cook and a cleaner, the mother of his child. It was agony each time he took Bekka away from me. If it wasn't for the texts found on his phone, I wouldn't have had her back in my arms so quickly. Anu had made things very clear: call the police and I'd never see my daughter again. When he died, he took her whereabouts with him.

Mr and Mrs Marshall were an elderly couple from Langworth, who asked no questions when my daughter was left in their care. They were well paid for their discretion, and Anu used Bekka as a bargaining tool. He was capable of

341

anything. I had to put Bekka first. But still I'd been making plans. Teaching myself how to use the computer. Trying to work out how I could get us both away. My earlier email to the women's refuge absolved my involvement in the crimes. I told them I was a victim of abuse. Asked if they could take Bekka and me in. Wrote that she'd been removed from me time and time again. That small, simple email told a story of its own.

Now she's here by my side and I can't quite believe it. We're safe. We're free. The front door is opened and I fix Bekka's hair. Her plaits are like the ones Mummu used to braid for me. She's wearing blue dungarees and a pretty pink top underneath. No ill-fitting home-made clothes for her, apart from the occasional knitted scarf.

Mama's wearing a soft wool coat, her arms laden with gift bags: dolls, books, clothes; she rests the bags on the floor as she takes us both in. She doesn't push forward, respecting my space. God, I've been so mean. I open my arms for a hug. It's quick and functionary, a baby-step towards where we need to be. She is breathless with happiness as she breaks away.

'And who is this?' she asks, despite knowing of Bekka's existence weeks ago.

Swann wanted me to be the one to tell her, but I let him break the news. I was scared that Mama would feel disgusted, seeing a reminder of my captor. I need not have worried. She couldn't wait to meet my little girl. I've punished her by making her stay away, and lingering guilt blooms inside me. My therapist said it's natural to direct my feelings of anger and frustration towards the person closest to me.

I force feeling into a smile, because Mama deserves more. 'This is Bekka.'

I watch as Elea kneels. 'Well, you are so beautiful.' Her eyes are moist with tears and she sniffs, trying to force them away.

'Mummy?' Bekka whispers, suddenly shy as she points to the bags. 'Are they for me?'

'They are.' I touch her shoulder reassuringly. 'But say thank you first, like I taught you.'

Bekka smiles at my mother, filled with delight and innocence that I wish she could keep for ever. '*Kiitos*, Mummo.' Her thumb reaches her mouth, and I allow it. She's had a lot to deal with, too. It won't be easy when she learns of her family history, but for now Bekka brings joy to everyone she encounters. Anu insisted that she spoke only English, because he didn't want her to stand out. Now she's picking up the language quickly and we're arranging for her to attend a primary school in Nettleham.

'You speak Finnish, too? How clever!' Mother's eyes widen in amazement. 'Can I have a hug?'

Bekka checks with me first. I smile and nod. She walks shyly into Mother's open arms. Mama closes her eyes at the joy of finally meeting her granddaughter in the flesh. Grandmother clasps her hands together, while Helen wipes away a happy tear. I slip my hand into my pocket and clasp my small wooden doll. We're here, we're together, and that's the best I can hope for today.

# Chapter Seventy-One

The air nipped at Elea's cheeks as she walked to the post office on the High Street. The grey sky pressed low over the streets of Lincoln, but Elea's heart was filled with light. Her breath came in visible puffs as she clutched the small parcel in her hand. Her gloved fingers gripped it tightly as if it might evaporate, along with the promise that she had made.

The small city moved around her in its usual rhythm, a steady stream of cars snaking their way through the streets. She inhaled the sharp tang of petrol fumes as she waited for the beep of the pedestrian crossing. Such pauses in her day used to frustrate her. She was always rushing, her nerves raw as she hunted down her daughter's kidnapper. Now the world felt entirely new, her body and mind fully relaxed for the first time in years. The strain she'd carried for a decade had been replaced by pure, unadulterated joy. Her feet carried her to the post office, where she pushed open the heavy door. She welcomed the sudden warm air, which tingled her skin and brought the tips of her fingers back to life. The sturdy woman behind the counter wore large, round glasses that magnified deep-brown eyes.

'I'd like to post this to Helsinki, please, first-class,' Elea said, placing the precious parcel on the scales.

The woman smiled, taking it from beneath the Perspex.

'What does it contain?'

'A tubed cigar,' Elea replied, her words catching in her throat. This was just another package to the postal worker. She had no idea of the meaning behind this small, seemingly insignificant parcel. Elea's heart fluttered as she watched the woman print a label and affix it with care. She thought of her colleague Niall opening it, and of his pleasure at joining in the celebration of her daughter's return. He would handle Liisa's story with care.

'Anything else?

Elea blinked. 'Sorry . . . yes, I have this to post: recorded delivery, please.' She pulled the envelope from her shoulder bag. This hadn't warranted being carried in her hands. It did not bring any spark of joy, but it *did* bring closure. She slipped it beneath the glass. She could have dropped it straight into Swann's solicitor or even given it to Swann himself, but it felt better to distance herself in this way. 'That's it, thanks.' The signed divorce papers were finally on their way.

She felt lighter as she left the post office and wrapped her scarf in a loop around her neck. The world hadn't changed. Lincoln was still bustling, the sky still heavy above her, the wind still sharp. But, for Elea, everything was different. She pushed her hands into her pockets and allowed herself a smile.

# Acknowledgements

Writing and publishing *The Ice Angels* has been such a great journey. It started with a seed of an idea as I chatted with my brother, Robbie, about where each of us lived. He spoke of the Finnish woodlands, its pristine beaches and expansive lakes. I talked about Lincoln and its breathtaking cathedral, of the cobbled streets and characterful pubs. Later that day, Lincoln and Finland blended in my mind as the idea for *The Ice Angels* took hold. Now, I can't quite believe that it's out there, and I'm so grateful for all the people who made it happen.

First and foremost, to my family – your endless patience, love and understanding have been my foundation. Love to my sisters in Ireland, and my brother too. To my husband, Neil, for putting up with my late-night writing sessions and even helping me to fix a plot hole or two. To my children, Paul, Aoife, Jessica and Ben, who have grown up listening to some strange conversations as I work out murderous plot lines and character traits.

A heartfelt thank you to my wonderful literary agent, Madeleine Milburn, to whom I dedicated this book. Thank you for your steadfast belief in my writing and for patiently guiding me through the traditional publishing world. We've been together for ten years now and words cannot cover how much I love working with you and your amazing team.

To my editor at Penguin, Claire Simmonds. Not only are you a thoroughly lovely person, but a dream to work with too. Your keen eye and thoughtful feedback have turned this book into something I am truly proud of. Thanks also to your fantastic team, who have shaped, edited, designed and marketed this book. To Camila Ilardia Jimenez in Editorial, Jade Stratton in Production, Olivia Thomas in Publicity, Rosie Grant in Marketing: I'm hugely fortunate to work with you all.

To the lovely book bloggers who have given up their time to read and share my books. As always, I'm forever grateful. Book bloggers have been at the heart of my writing career since day one. Thank you for being part of my author story over the last ten years.

To my ex-police colleagues who continue to read my work – know that, all these years later, I still think about you! Being in the police brought its share of challenges but I treasure the memories that have added richness to my writing. Kudos to those still fighting the good fight. To my author friends, knowing I'm not alone in this journey has made all the difference. A special shout-out to the hugely talented Mel Sherratt and Angela Marsons, who have been there from the start.

To Amy Musgrave, your stunning cover design captured the essence of *The Ice Angels* perfectly. I'm in awe of your talent.

Finally, but most importantly, to you, the reader – thank you for picking up this book. If you have enjoyed the story, you can find me on social media. I love it when readers across the world get in touch.

Can't wait to dive into
Detective Elea Baker's
next case?

Turn the page for an exclusive sneak
peek at the first two chapters of
Caroline Mitchell's brand new novel,

# The Night Watcher

# Chapter One

*January 1997*

Nine-year-old Belinda Hollis crept from her bed. She had begged Mum and Dad to let her have the kitten in her room instead of keeping her basket in a cage downstairs. It was her birthday, after all, the one day of the year when she pretty much got everything she wanted. But her parents had drawn the line at her having a kitten in bed. She tiptoed out of her room. It was gone midnight and Mum would not be happy if she caught her. Mum was funny about things like that. Most of her friends got to stay up late, but not her. Belinda's family got up early and they went to bed early. That was the rule. But Belinda needed to see Tinkerbell one more time. To touch her fluffy grey fur and kiss her tiny pink nose. And those little marshmallow toe beans . . .

The smile fell from her face as a figure emerged on the landing, closing the door of her parent's room. Dressed in black. Holding a knife. Belinda's heart flip-flopped at the sight of him, her open mouth unable to release the scream lodged in her throat. Terror had stolen Belinda's breath. He moved like a shadow in the blackness . . . except for the blood sliding off the blade.

The intruder's face was wrapped up in a balaclava, and as

351

he smiled, all Belinda could see was the chilling flash of eyes and teeth. Seconds passed. His breathing was ragged, chest rising and falling, as he stood at the far end of the landing. Belinda was next to the stairs. She wanted to call out for her daddy. But the blood . . .

As if a starting pistol had fired, Belinda ran. Her little legs pistoned down the narrow stairs. She would run next door, to Mrs Healy. Her husband was in the RAF. He would know what to do. The warm kitchen air enveloped her, still smelling of pizza and extinguished birthday candles. A limp 'Happy Birthday' balloon floated in mid-air. Cake crumbs littered the kitchen counter. Her kitten moved in the corner of the room. But Belinda could only hear the slow, heavy footsteps hitting each stair. No rush. Just one after the other, *thump . . . thump . . . thump*. Her heart beat like a trapped bird in her chest. That strip of white teeth. Those cold, narrow eyes. Why were they out of breath? What had they been doing? And where were Mummy and Daddy? She had to get out. Belinda pulled on the locked kitchen door, hands shaking, breathing in quick short spurts. But the door wouldn't open. The key that usually sat in the lock was gone. She screamed for her father who had given her piggyback rides and her favourite ice cream that day.

Her scream became a squeak as her mouth was cupped by a cold leather glove. The heavy footsteps had turned to silence. The man had sped through the kitchen like a ghost and now he was all over her. Nostrils flaring, she struggled for breath. It felt like she was kicking a wall. In the corner of the kitchen, her kitten mewed. The clock on the wall ticked. But there was nothing of Belinda's parents in any of this. Just the stink of the man's sweat, garlic breath and the ugly tang of blood. She fought against the body pressed tightly against her own, his leather glove grazing her face as she tried to bite down. A voice came, his breath cold against her ear: 'Shut up if you want to see your mum and dad again.'

*They're alive?* Tears brimmed in Belinda's eyes.

'Do you want to see them again?' The glove loosened.

Belinda nodded fervently.

'Then hush. I'll take you for a drive. Then I'll let you go, alright? I just need time to get away. It'll take you half an hour to walk back. But you don't want to know what happens if you scream. Understand?' His voice was strong and commanding as she nodded. His knife was gone, but he wore a black backpack. It terrified her to think what could be in there, and what he had been doing in her parents' room.

She was ushered into the night, past her dad's Wellington boots and the bicycle parked up against the side of the house, past the silly garden gnomes that her mum had bought at the market for a laugh. The sudden biting cold shocked her skin as the air crept under her nightdress. Her eyes widened as he opened the boot of the car and a blanket was pulled across.

'Lie down. Cover up. Don't move. Not a sound.'

He lifted her into the boot of the car, her body convulsing with fearful sobs.

The lid was shut with a frightening sense of finality. She huddled her knees beneath the scratchy blanket, her cheek pressed to the stale carpet of the boot. The darkness closed in around her, burying her in the smell of dog and air freshener.

A tune filtered from the car. The whispery vocals of 'I'm Not in Love' masked Belinda's whimpers. She jolted as the car bumped the kerb. Warm tears trickled down her face as the journey continued. But they weren't moving for long, as the car came to a juddering halt. Perhaps the man was going to let her out now. Or maybe he was going to do something bad.

A jumble of voices rose outside. She pushed the blanket to see a chink of light through the backseats. She remembered Daddy letting the seats of their car down once when Mummy bought that big plant from B&Q. If the man was talking to people, it meant he wasn't letting her out. She needed to see more. She pressed against the seats, her heart fluttering as they moved just enough to give her hope. Shuffling in the small space, she positioned herself with both feet against the seats, held her breath and kicked hard. Then she was out, tumbling into the backseat of the car, pulling at the door. Her heart plummeted as it failed to open, but as she glanced out the window, she realised that she wasn't alone. 'Help!' She screamed, hammering both fists on the glass.

The man driving the car wasn't wearing his balaclava now. He glared out the window at the faces of two police officers in uniform staring in at her. Then she was jerked forwards, leaving the officers running back for their car.

Belinda gripped the seats as she waited for the threats and recrimination. They never came. His shoulders hunched, her kidnapper was staring ahead as they sped down the dark and winding road. 'They'll try to box me in ahead,' he muttered, eyes fixed on his mirrors. 'Standard tactic. It won't work.'

Belinda took in his short brown hair, his thin, worried face glancing over his shoulder as blue lights started flashing from behind. 'Get down!' he shouted as she blocked his rear view.

She pulled at a door that wouldn't open, tumbling over onto her side as the car bumped hard over a grass verge. He was driving faster into the night. Too fast. Fast enough to kill.

'Strap yourself in, love.' Belinda heard her father's voice above the sirens that were getting closer by the second. Soft, kind, so unlike the man driving. Four words. That's all it was. The last time she would hear the sound of the man she loved most in the world. She reached for the seatbelt, swallowed back her tears and pushed it firmly into place. It gave a final 'click' and they seemed to move in slow motion as the car came off the road. Spinning, tumbling, in a never-ending sequence of weightlessness, as air bags activated, pressing against her fragile body as they spun, round and round, in the night.

# Chapter Two

## *January 2027*

*Happiness is a place between too little and too much.* Elea mused on the Finnish saying as she cradled her cup. She leaned back in her seat next to the coffee shop window, steam curling up from the surface of her coffee. As usual, she sat alone, her leather handbag on the surface of the blond wood table. Once, her thoughts had been so busy that she'd left without her bag. Now it sat in plain sight as she stared beyond it through the large windows that offered a welcome view. Inside the bag was a snow globe. A purchase for Bekka, her granddaughter in England. She'd given her so many presents at Christmas, but couldn't resist one more. Bekka – huge blue eyes, blonde hair and an insatiable curiosity towards the world. The corners of Elea's mouth turned upwards at the thought of the little girl.

Aleksanterinkatu stretched before her, bustling, even in the bitter cold of January. The snow was building in icy layers and, with little sun, there was nothing to induce a thaw. The tramlines cut a trail through the street, their metal rails slick with a sheen of ice. Elea sipped her coffee, watching the yellow glow of tram lights break up the bluish-white light of dusk. Soon, the coffee shop would be closed and Elea would be going home alone. Her day at work had been long and satisfying, but policing had been hit with budget cuts and now there was talk of redundancies. Maybe it was for the best if she gave in her notice and returned permanently to the UK. She hadn't seen her daughter in a month. Each night on the phone, it felt like she was talking to a stranger. No. Not a stranger. Someone with a grudge. Liisa's feelings towards the man who took her as a child were complex and would never go away. Elea had hoped that, by moving back home to Finland, Liisa would follow. But she couldn't force the issue. She was still the bad guy in the story taking residence in Liisa's head. Elea wanted to be a mother and play an active part in her granddaughter's life. So what was she doing here? She mulled each thought over. Six months, Elea had been here, making regular visits to the UK. Liisa was finding her way around in this new world of hers, and she would never be alone again.

Elea drained the last of her coffee, watching the pedestrians move briskly outside. They were wrapped in thick coats, gloved hands buried deep in pockets. Across the road, the last few shoppers weaved outside the entrance to Kluuvi Shopping Centre. Elea watched, cocooned in her favourite coffee shop, a place to rest her weary bones after a long day. But outside . . . she peered down the street. She sat her cup down. Something was off. It was the hooded figure standing on the corner that caught Elea's eye. The gaunt man had come onto her radar in the past, and her eyes narrowed as she watched him scanning the crowds. The tug in her gut told her to keep watching. She followed his gaze as he crossed the road.

Elea left a tip before picking her bag up from the table.

She exited the coffee shop, almost barging into a stout elderly Finnish woman wearing a thick furry hat. She held a wrapped leg of reindeer meat like a weapon, grumbling about its weight as she passed. '*Katsos tees, hölmö!*' Her handbag flapped loosely from her shoulder, bumping against her hip. Elea swiftly apologised, despite being called a fool.

Several seconds later, she dipped her head as hoodie man passed. He was too laser focused on the woman to notice her now. Reindeer woman's fur coat wouldn't have been cheap, and sent a signal to the man on the hunt. Elea told herself that she was being paranoid. That the people she dealt with tainted her view of the world. But, still, she followed his steady, lumbering gait, trying to recall the last time she came into contact with him.

Reindeer woman turned left into Kluuvikatu, oblivious to the fact that she was being followed. The narrow street was tucked between aging buildings, which stood high over smooth paving stones. Her breath rose in puffs as she walked with a wobble, brisk but off balance. *Arthritis in her joints, perhaps?* Elea wondered, as she took stock of the unfolding scene. The woman didn't see the man dip his hand into his pocket, but Elea did. Elea also heard the faint click of a flick knife. Hoodie man was closing in on his prey.

'*Hei!*' Elea shouted. 'I wouldn't do that if I were you!' She spoke in Finnish, her words a sharp slap in the frozen night. Hoodie man spun around, turning the knife on Elea. It was only when she saw his distinctive green eyes that she remembered him. That rare shade that was possessed by less than two percent of the population. Reindeer woman stopped, gasping as her leg of meat hit the ground with a dull thud.

'Put it down, Aleksi. It doesn't suit you.' The man was a petty criminal, who usually shoplifted to feed his drug habit. The introduction of a knife was new. She saw the shake in his hand, the growing menace in his eyes. He was desperate, and Elea had just called him out. But she stood her ground, eyes flicking between Aleksi and the woman behind him. Elea took a step forward. Half a second passed before Aleksi turned on his heel. But he wasn't leaving with nothing. Elea watched as he approached Reindeer woman; watched as he reached for her bag and pulled it from her shoulder with a sharp yank.

Elea slipped her hand into her bag, then sent the snow globe she'd bought for her granddaughter hurtling through the air. It reached its target, hitting Aleksi on the temple with a sharp clonk. It was enough to bring him down as he lost his footing in the snow. Elea grabbed the knife first, following it as it went skittering down the alley. She was quick in her movements as she turned towards Aleksi, just in time to see Reindeer woman deliver a sharp kick to his stomach.

'*Perkeleen nulikka!*' She swore, then calmly picked up her leg of meat from the ground. A groan drizzled from Aleksi's mouth, his face planted in the icy snow.

'Still intact.' Elea regained custody of her snow globe. 'Impressive.' The young man moaned beneath her as she placed a knee into his back. He would have one hell of a headache. 'Excuse me!' She called after the woman. 'Would you like to give me your details?' But she was gone, giving Elea a deaf ear as she went upon her way. Elea sighed as she pulled her phone from her bag. *Shitting paperwork.* She'd have to call this in.

She raised an eyebrow as her phone rang, and DCI Swann's name glowed on the display.

'Free to talk?'

'Make it fast,' Elea replied, slightly out of breath.

'We need you on a case. Now.'